ALSO BY RACHEL KOLLER CROFT

Stone Cold Fox

"A fresh take on vampire lore and frenemies galore! . . . Prepare to be mesmerized."

—Liv Constantine, bestselling author of
The Last Mrs. Parrish

"While fashion and music trends may change, Rachel Koller Croft proves that vampires never go out of style. Especially when those vampires are disco-loving 'it' girls prowling the streets of London. A sultry and sparkling tale of female friendship gone wrong, I felt about this book the way I feel about any great night out on the town—I never wanted it to end."

—Chandler Baker, *New York Times* bestselling author of
Cutting Teeth

"Cinematic, immersive, heart-pumping, and so freaking cool."

—Andrea Bartz, *New York Times* bestselling author of
We Were Never Here

"Perfect skin. Eternal youth. Wicked hearts. Rachel Koller Croft reclaims the vampire story for disco queens who want to dance forever with their friends or die trying."

—Nina Simon, *New York Times* bestselling author of
Mother-Daughter Murder Night

"SO. MUCH. FUN. Walking the line between effervescent and unsettling. . . . Let's toast a glass of the finest red to Croft's slick and sexy tale."

—Julia Bartz, *New York Times* bestselling author of
The Writing Retreat

"An ode to disco and toxic friendships, this book is a truly wild ride."

—Ella Berman, author of *Before We Were Innocent*

"These dueling perspectives, coupled with memorable side characters and a beautifully paced plot, make *We Love the Nightlife* an engrossing, darkly funny, twisted breakup story that's perfect for vampire fiction lovers and fans of relationship drama alike."

—*BookPage*

"Croft's books are the ultimate good time not only because of her clever twists or bitingly honest depictions of women's social lives, but because, like the best girl's girl, they radiate a genuine love of women in all their fangs, finery, and fierceness. What a breath of fresh air."

—Ashley Winstead, author of *Midnight Is the Darkest Hour*

"Put on your dancing shoes, this is the book equivalent of a wild night out. A glamorous, thrilling page-turner as effervescent as a French 75, that sinks its fangs into the complex power dynamic between two friends who both want to be the life of the party. Clever, inventive, and wickedly fun."

—Rachel Harrison, national bestselling author of *Black Sheep*

"A biting work of paranormal fiction with the intensity of a thriller, this book is a party I didn't want to leave."

—Clémence Michallon, author of *The Quiet Tenant*

"With vivid imagery and masterful prose, Rachel Koller Croft has penned a thoroughly enchanting and inventive novel that is simply irresistible!"

—Wendy Walker, bestselling author of *What Remains*

"This sexy new vampire novel brings the suspense, but it also tackles mature themes like toxic female friendship."

—Katie Couric Media

"Croft is at her sly, sardonic best in this suspenseful tale of friendships gone sour." —CrimeReads

"We love the nightlife . . . and we love a book about female friendships and vampires." —Book Riot

"*We Love the Nightlife* promises a gripping and entertaining vampire story for readers." —ScreenRant

"A pounding disco beat is the backdrop to this tightly plotted, inventive vampire tale. Grab your fangs and join the party!"
  —Books, Bones & Buffy

WE
LOVE
THE
NIGHTLIFE

RACHEL KOLLER CROFT

BERKLEY

NEW YORK

BERKLEY
An imprint of Penguin Random House LLC
1745 Broadway, New York, NY 10019
penguinrandomhouse.com

Book design by Kristin del Rosario
Title page art: Disco ball © Lukasz Ptaszynski / Shutterstock

ISBN: 9780593547540

The Library of Congress has cataloged the Berkley hardcover edition of this book as follows:

Names: Croft, Rachel Koller, author.
Title: We love the nightlife / Rachel Koller Croft.
Description: New York: Berkley, 2024.
Identifiers: LCCN 2023048240 (print) | LCCN 2023048241 (ebook) |
ISBN 9780593547533 (hardcover) | ISBN 9780593547557 (ebook)
Subjects: LCSH: Vampires—Fiction. | Female friendship—Fiction. |
Nightclubs—Fiction. | LCGFT: Vampire fiction. | Novels.
Classification: LCC PS3603.R63556 W4 2024 (print) |
LCC PS3603.R63556 (ebook) | DDC 813/.6—dc23/eng/20240202
LC record available at https://lccn.loc.gov/2023048240
LC ebook record available at https://lccn.loc.gov/2023048241

Berkley hardcover edition / August 2024
Berkley trade paperback edition / July 2025

Printed in the United States of America
1st Printing

The authorized representative in the EU for product safety and compliance is
Penguin Random House Ireland, Morrison Chambers, 32 Nassau Street,
Dublin D02 YH68, Ireland, https://eu-contact.penguin.ie.

For my disco-loving mom.
And for my dad, who,
according to her,
"hated that whole thing."
Except for one song.

WE
LOVE
THE
NIGHTLIFE

PROLOGUE

should have known the party was over when she casually suggested killing my husband back in 1981. I shut her down immediately, but I never forgot the way she said it. With a quick shrug of the shoulder. Up and down, like a spasm. Her dark eyes rolling up to the ceiling. Painted lips pushed together with a small *hmm?* as if she was innocently putting the ball in my court. Like we were just deciding what to do with the rest of our night. Acting as though she wasn't making a literal threat on his life while she let the needle drop on a Donna Summer album, her voice warbling around us about bad girls and sad girls.

Message received.

Yes, I left my husband, but I *never* wished death on him.

So I did what she asked me to do and she promised we wouldn't hurt him.

But since he was still looking for me in London, we had to stay home.

Well, *I* did.

Nicola was always free to do as she pleased.

How could I not see that it was only going to get worse?

So much worse.

Maybe because I couldn't even imagine the betrayal that was coming my way.

I didn't know yet. That she did this to everyone she cared about. Past and present.

How could any of us have known at the beginning? Nobody anticipates the hit from behind, especially when you're supposed to be on the same goddamn team. It didn't even cross my mind to try to leave Nicola back then. I mean, where was I gonna go? I didn't have anyone else. She was my brand-new best friend in a brand-new city. Why wouldn't I trust her when I was a total amateur and she was an old pro?

Emphasis on the *old*.

There was just something about Nicola that was so irresistible to me when we met. Yes, she was funny and vivacious and beautiful. The two of us together grabbed the attention of everyone in the room, even when we weren't trying.

But it was the way Nicola answered to no one but herself, taking anything she wanted, whenever she wanted, that really got my attention. She had her own money, she had her own home, she was self-possessed, wise and whip-smart; she suffered no fools and had zero issue with burning any bridge she saw fit to set on fire.

Did I really think I'd avoid getting singed myself one day?

More than that.

Scorched.

On the night we first met at Tramp, I instantly recognized Nicola, even though rationally I knew I'd never seen her before in my life. But we were two sides of the same record. I can cop to being the A-side. The hits, the crowd-pleasers, the lead single that pulls you in. But that's why I liked Nicola so much. She was the B-side. The dark, the weird, the experimental, but with the potential to break through with the right crowd, the right person, to appreciate her for what she was: *extraordinary*.

I think that was part of her strategy all along.

Not just with me, but with all of us.

Every single so-called treasured friend that she deceived. She told us we'd live forever with her. Eternal youth. And that she would take care of everything for us. Nothing to worry about ever again. When you're a good-time girl in a bad situation, with seemingly no other way out, how are you going to turn down an offer like that?

Nicola made it seem like we had a choice, but I'm not sure we ever did.

Once you were in her sights, she wouldn't let you out.

Nicola knew what she was doing. What she was taking. From me. From the others.

From her sister, too, even though she won't admit it to herself.

It was her past that dictated all our futures.

We just couldn't see it.

But I see it now.

Still, I never thought our friendship would come to this, a place so dark that I don't even recognize myself anymore.

But it's the only way out.

It makes sense. In a sick sort of way. All things considered.

We're vampires.

The darkness is all we know.

It's all we have.

ONE

AMBER

Sometimes, when I was alone, I'd follow my husband and his third wife around Central London at night. Not like a complete psycho, but I'd see what they were up to in Mayfair or Marylebone. It was hard to believe he'd be out after sunset since he never wanted to bebop around town with me when we were together.

No, Malcolm Wells liked to curl up with a dusty old book about World War II to wind down on a weekend, sipping on a hot toddy or a cup of tea until it ran cold. Even way back then when he was still only in his thirties. He'd always been an old fogey in a young guy's body.

But soon enough, and much faster than I'd like to admit, he *was* old, and so was his current wife, Geraldine. Still, there he was, regularly taking her out on dates in the city, enjoying their retirement together. Dinner. Drinks. The theater.

I guess the third wife was the charm.

Malcolm was probably mortified when I started going out alone without him, not long after we got married in the summer of '79, but what was I supposed to do? Sit around and listen to him spout off facts about Winston Churchill? I mean, respectfully, *who cares*? I was twenty-three years old and, come on, we're only young once.

Or so I thought at the time.

When we met earlier that year, Malcolm said he was attracted to my joie de vivre and I swooned. Just imagine some sophisticated British man speaking French to you when you're a small-town Wisconsin girl who came to Chicago for the day, only to get rejected at the Rockettes audition you've been waiting for your whole life.

I was devastated when they didn't call my name.

It was supposed to be my ticket to a whole new life. I really didn't want to go back home to my miserable family, who wanted to control my every move. So as I was drowning my sorrows at some fancy businessman bar in River North before getting the late train to Milwaukee, Malcolm swooped in with his accent and handsomeness and money, offering to fly me back to London with him instead.

Listen, it was the '70s and we were delightfully tipsy and how could I reject such a juicy invitation? I'd never been out of the country before. What was meant to be a one-week jaunt on some richierich fella's dime quickly turned into something serious, and before I knew it, we were engaged.

I fell in love with London the second I got here. And yes, I probably got that mixed up with true love for Malcolm, which now seems a little nuts. It would be a few months before I admitted it to myself, but we were a god-awful match. Unless it was for business reasons, he wasn't much for being social, and all I ever wanted to do was flit around town. Go dancing, see live music and shows, alongside other young people. But Malcolm? It was books, tea, the BBC and repeat. *Nightmare.*

Not that I knew what real nightmares were just yet.

I didn't tell anyone back home in Wisconsin about my potential screwup. It was a different time and I'd never confided much in my parents. Everyone was always hanging on by a thread as it was. Emotionally. Financially. And I knew my dad would have just said something about getting what I deserved after being so impulsive. My mother didn't have too much to say about it, but she didn't protest either. Money talks, obviously, and Malcolm had it. We never did. So Godspeed to her eldest daughter. One less thing to worry about.

And she still had the little one.

I feel bad about leaving my sister behind to this day.

But I try not to think about it.

The first time I revisited Malcolm, after I left him and after I turned, it was the early '90s. He was still in his second marriage with Cheryl, the show pony with no personality, who was also the mother of all three of his small children, so I figured he'd be up for a cheap thrill. Enough time had passed by then, over ten years, and I didn't see how a quick cameo would cause much of a fuss.

The two of them were having a nightcap at the American Bar in the Stafford Hotel. Not the Savoy. Way too much of a scene over there for Malcolm, with the chatty pianist and the tourists and the hustle-bustle of the Strand. The Stafford was understated and classic, tucked away on a quiet street not far from St. James's Park. Honestly, I had always liked it, too.

For kicks, I asked for my usual at the bar to get his attention. A French 75. Malcolm told me once he thought it was a charming order. I agreed. When I was sixteen and on vacation in the Dells with my family, using the term *vacation* lightly, a much older man ordered one for me at the Ishnala Supper Club. My parents made me send it back, but when I could finally order drinks of my own, that cocktail was always my go-to because I never forgot the sweet smell from its quick stop at our table.

The second Malcolm heard my voice at the bar that night, we made eye contact. I smiled, but he did a double take. *Eeeep!*

He could *see* me.

Someone from before.

The *only* one from before.

I started to feel warm in my body, but it had to be in my head only, since the blood in my veins was downright frosty. Oh, it was just nostalgia, which always feels great until it doesn't anymore, taking a quick turn before you know what's what, the kind that feels like a good friend stabbing you in the back, hurt by someone you thought you knew so well.

"Amber?" Malcolm whispered softly. I think only I could hear him. I raised an eyebrow, pretending to be confused. *"Amber,"* he said again, louder this time, with more conviction. So much so that Cheryl looked over Malcolm's shoulder, visibly annoyed, with pursed lips, showing more emotion than she had all evening.

"Hello," she snarled, trying to intimidate me.

Good luck, babe.

I bite.

"Hi there!" I said, laying my American accent on extra thick.

"Do you know her?" she asked Malcolm, but he couldn't stop staring at me. His big brown eyes blinked rapidly, highlighting his crow's-feet. The kind I'd never have.

"Sorry, darling." Malcolm brought his attention back to Cheryl. "Thought she was someone else. Have a good night, miss."

He didn't even turn back around.

The bartender handed me the fresh cocktail and God *damn* it, she smelled so good. I missed the fancy buzz of a French 75. Its tall flute, the fragrance of the gin shamelessly flirting out of the glass, complete with a sweet lemon twist on the rim. The preferred drink of a party girl with pizzazz. That's me. Always was.

"Cheers," I cooed at the couple, hoping for one last lingering look with Malcolm, perfectly timed to the dreamy Cranberries song playing softly in the background.

But he didn't look my way again.

I didn't make a habit out of showing myself to Malcolm over the years. Especially as he got older. But something came over me one night as I was following him alongside wife number three.

The night I saw him for the very last time.

He was standing outside Annabel's—just for dinner, of course. Malcolm never did like to party and he wasn't going to start as a senior citizen. He looked about ready to go home and crack into the book he probably had waiting on his nightstand. A thousand pages minimum on the Normans or Oliver Cromwell or whatever. His hands were in his pockets, eyes staring off into space, as he waited dutifully for his wife to wrap it up inside. I had to give the guy credit. Sure, he'd gotten old and tweedy, but he was still handsome despite the cranky resting face. His mustache looked great on him now. A little salt, a little pepper.

I rushed over to him, through Berkeley Square, as if I were just another busy bee off to enjoy the nearby nightlife. And then I gently bumped right into Mr. Malcolm Wells.

"Oh! Excuse me," I gasped, wondering what he was going to do, just as that mysterious warmth flooded my body again. This time, though, there was no confusion from him at all. He smiled at me. It was sweet and sincere. Almost amused. Reminiscent of when we first met.

"Ah," he sighed, as if it all made sense to him now. "You're a ghost, aren't you, love?"

I lightly touched his shoulder and laughed, hoping something genius would fly out of my mouth, maybe even something poetic, but we were interrupted by someone behind me, clearing their throat.

I knew who it was before I even turned around.

She was watching us.

God knows for how long.

Her dark hair was swept up elegantly in a loose French twist, a few pieces falling at the front of her face. That hourglass figure of hers was draped in a silky crimson dress that accentuated her waist, long and flowy at the bottom, with an asymmetric hem. And those dark blue eyes, so deep they looked violet, grew smaller as she squinted at me in disbelief, before opening wide again alongside her signature twisted smile.

Nicola Claughton.

My best friend.

The vampire who made me.

Nicola always said my past was off-limits. It was too dangerous, too complicated. No one would ever understand my decision to turn. It was the fair price you had to pay to live forever. Vampires and humans could not knowingly coexist. At least not for very long. But these days? What was the harm? Malcolm was an elder states-man now, for God's sake. What trouble could he have caused us at this point, *really*?

But that wasn't the issue anymore at all, was it?

Nicola knew he was still important to me, in his own way. Because no matter what had happened between us in our whirlwind romance, Malcolm Wells was my last living link in London to the woman I used to be.

Before Nicola.

A time she never wanted me to think about, much less openly acknowledge.

Nic had promised me she wouldn't touch Malcolm, and even though I believed her, I still kept my sporadic visits a secret. I knew she wouldn't like it. I knew she'd hate it. But now that she knew the truth, so many years later, I wasn't sure what she would do about it, if anything.

Yes, Nicola could be ruthless.

Of course. We're vampires.

But with *me*? Her companion? No way; she always had my back.

Still, I couldn't shake the thought.

What if?

In the moment, Nicola acted like everything was fine as she shuffled between Malcolm and me in front of Annabel's. She smiled again before ascending the steps into the club, passing Geraldine on her way out. The entrance was completely decked out with a display of roses. Hundreds of them in white and pink and yellow.

Nicola plucked a single white one before she went in.

I scurried away without another word to anyone, but I followed Malcolm and his wife at a safe distance, back to their town house in Belgravia. Watching and waiting. I stayed there as long as I could, but I had to get home before sunrise.

I told myself that Nicola would let it go. Yes, she was probably mad, but I'd assure her that I wouldn't show myself to him again and I'd mean it. It would all be fine.

She hurt a lot of people.

But she would never hurt me.

A few days later, Malcolm's death was all over the news. Murdered in his own home. Found in the bathroom. He was brushing his teeth. His wife was already in bed asleep. No suspect identified yet. Nor any motive. My hands shook as I held my phone in bed, scrolling through story after story, reading the words over and over and *over* again, visceral descriptions like *grisly* and *bloody* and *vicious* cementing the truth.

Malcolm was gone.

The last one left who knew me before.

And his death was my fault.

I felt this hollowness inside me growing bigger by the second, like nothing would fill it up again or round me out or nourish me or bring me back to some semblance of a moral center. It felt like there was no trace of the woman I was born to be, stuck now and forever with the monster she made.

Was this it?

I mean, was this really *it* for me?

Just Nicola and me and the night?

She'd sealed Malcolm's fate, just like she thought she'd sealed mine back in 1979. That was always the message, no matter how big or small the vessel. Her way or nothing at all. I can admit that I've always known that about Nicola, but most of the time our interests aligned.

Didn't they? I wasn't so sure anymore.

Malcolm's death was a punch to the gut that made me rethink everything about Nicola. About us. About our friendship. Because if she could break a promise like this, a serious promise she made to me, all those years ago, at such a vulnerable time, what else was she capable of?

What else had she done?

What else would she do?

I think Nic was always jealous I still had someone out there who knew the real me, someone who cared for me once and maybe, on some level, still did. It wasn't about romance with Malcolm anymore, but it was about a connection, no matter how thin the thread had gotten.

Who did Nicola have, except for me?

All the others were gone. I had no idea where they went. She never talked about them, except for her sister, and even then she didn't say too much, muttering about legacy and loyalty and the Laurels, our home.

But maybe Nicola didn't really care about me at all.

Maybe she only cared about *keeping* me.

My mind raced, like a movie playing backward, sped up and slowed down, retracing the course of our years together, pausing at moments I might have mistaken for friendship but might actually have been a show of control or manipulation or untruths to keep me close and afraid of the world around me, even though I knew we were both predators in our own right.

But with Nicola, I'd always be younger, the baby, the progeny.

She thought that I belonged to her.

But I didn't want that anymore.

Had I ever?

I made a promise to myself right then and there.

It was time to leave Nicola behind.

For good.

Others had left, hadn't they?

I could figure out how they did it.

And then I would do it, too.

Nicola never wants to talk about her previous companions. Whenever I tried, she said it was too painful. Like bringing up an ex-boyfriend, but even worse because the relationship between maker and companion is the kind that can't be fully defined or explained. Female friendship on another planet, from a different world, a darker and deeper place where language doesn't apply, unable to fully hold the weight.

So I know leaving Nicola won't be so simple. I don't have any real friends. I don't have any money of my own. I don't have a safe place to go. Yet.

And I don't know what she'll do about it once she finds out.

I have to tread carefully, but I can't play small either.

Big swings only.

No risk, no reward.

Sure, I've clicked around on the internet in hopes of finding other vampires, but there's no way to know, 100 percent, if anyone's telling the truth online. Besides, vampires are slippery little suckers as it is, not to mention the whole strange human spectrum of pretending to be vamps on Reddit and the like.

And Nicola aside, I already know it's not an easy thing to just pick up and go as a vampire. We're at the mercy of the sun. Seriously. It's the *only* thing that can kill us. So, there's time zones to consider. Any travel delays or issues with documentation could be deadly. And let's say you miraculously arrive safe and sound in your chosen location. What if the welcome wagon isn't so welcoming? By and large, vampires are with their makers or respective companions. Being a loner? Better watch your back. Property, land, territory, money, possessions. All of it is very fraught, to say the least, with our kind. You can be captured and you can be kept or you can be shown the daylight for the very last time.

Nicola has told me all about that.

Threats from humans who could never understand, but also threats from vampires who know all the rules, trusting no one outside their circle.

Part of me understands the harsh nature. When you can't roam fully free out in the world, living the nightlife forever, a vampire's home is like a fortress, their territory is a sanctuary, and any trespassers need to be vetted very, *very* carefully.

I'm keeping that in mind.

I snooped around this week in Nicola's bedroom, looking for anything about previous companions. Specifically, I rifled through her jewelry box. I never went into Nicola's jewelry box. She's funny about *stuff*. Look, I like nice things, but she is a *material girl*, if you know what I mean. Whenever Nicola lent me a piece, noting that a particular bangle would look good with my dress, or pointing out a specific ring that would make my manicure pop, it came directly from her hand. Her jewelry box was never open for casual browsing.

But I know that a jewelry box often holds many baubles of sentimental value over the course of a woman's life.

I was right.

There it was.

My *own* wedding ring from Malcolm, tucked alongside others in the ring roll, the diamond even bigger than I remembered. I had no idea she kept it for herself or when she took it, and obviously I was tempted to snatch it back, but that's not what the mission was about, and she'd notice if it was gone.

She notices *a lot*.

I picked up each ring and bracelet, of which there were so many, looking for engravings or anything personalized, replacing them carefully when I came up short. Earrings were anyone's guess. A solid-gold pocket watch was in the back of one of the little drawers, with no discernable markings, aside from being pretty masculine, and I had a hard time believing Nicola would ever take a male companion, her opinion on men pretty grim, to say the least, human or otherwise.

But when I ran my finger through the hangers of necklaces, I stopped at a locket. Silver and tarnished, in the shape of a heart, not really in style anymore, and something I'd never seen Nic wear before.

Because it didn't belong to her.

There was a photo of a happy couple inside.

And I *recognized* one of them.

Why would Nicola have this in her possession?

Unless . . .

We've had some brief run-ins with the other vampires in London since I joined Nicola. There's not many in this city, much less worldwide, and all the interactions I've witnessed have been chilly and removed. We generally keep to our own territories. Nicola won't have it any other way and the others don't seem to have a problem with it. No one crosses into an area where they don't belong. According to her, it's just better to stick to your own.

And maybe she's right.

But what if she doesn't want me talking to them because she's afraid of what they'll tell me?

Nic says that the only vampire you can trust is your maker.

We're supposed to live and die by that rule.

But then why does it seem like one of Nicola's former companions, the woman pictured in the locket, is *still* in London—and she's living with another vampire?

So I'm not playing by Nicola's rules anymore. I'm off to Chelsea tonight to confirm my suspicions and get the real story, or at least some version of it. Chelsea is not our territory, but really, what are those girls going to do if I ask them a few quick questions?

Kill me?

TWO

NICOLA

1979

never felt more human than when I was in the middle of a dance floor. Tramp was always a favorite of mine. It was a nightclub that attracted a crowd in their prime, but age had nothing to do with it. It was about presence. Well-heeled and well-dressed, everyone out to have a phenomenal time, no matter the cost.

Hedonism *always* prevailed.

Sublime fashion, too, of course, but that's London for you. Polyester was practically prohibited, as one could imagine. Silky jewel-toned gowns on the women, leaving little to the imagination. Sparkles twinkled on the sky-high stilettos. Ears, wrists and necks were awash in flashes of gold or silver, sometimes both. Long and shiny hair slicked with sweat by the time the wee hours crept in. Hips stayed strong all night, side to side, as they ran manicured fingers up glistening napes, giving those strands a little tug, for a lift, some relief from the body heat. Sharp elbows remained at attention, swaying in the air along with the music.

The men at Tramp? Just as divine. Very Savile Row after-hours. Sharp dressers only. Smart jackets eventually tossed aside in the banquette. Shirts unbuttoned, revealing that delightful patch of masculinity I always loved to run a finger through, plucking just one hair to get a rise out of him, followed by a quick and nervous laugh. Trousers tailored in a way that made a man's bum practically beg for a wayward graze or wanton grope. And plenty did with pleasure. Because if you were at Tramp, you were a proper dish, served up to all who wanted to have a cheeky bite.

Which could make it difficult to stand out in a place like this.

But somehow *she* did.

I always gained admittance to Tramp, even though I wasn't on the revered members-only list. Like anything in life, it's all who you know, and doormen typically made for worthwhile acquaintances in the city. As a result, there was never any problem when I'd add a guest to *my* unofficial list.

See, I preferred to have a meal at the ready come closing time.

Solo male travelers were simple enough to meet, especially just after sundown. Leisure or business, London attracted plenty of men having a wander about the city all alone, looking for a bit of a frolic. I'd pop into any given pub to find an unsuspecting gentleman who likely had no other prospects for the night. The type of bloke probably nobody would miss. I'd tell him to meet me at Tramp or Annabel's or Regine's or some other smashing locale that they'd just die to get into, an irresistible invitation.

Not to worry, darling.

You'll be on the list.

Just tell the doorman you're with me.

Nicola Claughton.

The DJs at Tramp were incomparable. Classic. Spinning the hits only. They knew our desires. Kept us all in motion, kept us all in good spirits. We became a visual feast for the eyes. All of us, possessing a single body amidst a swarm of others, always considerate of the collective movement, but purely in charge of our own contribution.

Disco was a bloody *rush*.

I knew it would be fleeting, like every passing music craze, but I wanted that one to last as long as possible. I wholeheartedly appreciated the melancholy understanding that time was ephemeral—for *most*—and we better have a sodding good time while we still could.

The night I met her, I finally spied Jeremy from down the pub earlier emerge just after one in the *fucking* morning. Took him long enough, but at least he heeded my pointed wardrobe recommendation. He had changed into a collared shirt, unbuttoned of course, as the trend dictated showing off a thick neck and some furry pecs.

Fantastic.

Here we go.

I waited for him to approach me first, like a gentleman should, striking an alluring pose with my pins on full display. But he was whisked away to the dance floor by some willowy woman in white I'd never seen before in my life.

Her teeth shone bright in an enormous smile, straight and large and even, hardly diminishing that pillowy pout of hers. She was lips upon lips upon lips. Her wide-set glacier-blue eyes gave her an almost feline appearance, and her nose was in a near-permanent crinkle as she grinned earnestly at everyone she passed by, delighting them all with her stunning beauty and obvious congeniality.

An ivory jumpsuit clung to her lithe little frame, the plunge of the neckline both tasteful and a tease. Her massive blonde hair was luminous, wavy and wild. In a room where everyone was a ten, she was about a fucking hundred. She had that vim about her. The kind that made everyone want to be near her. Completely enchanting without even trying to cast a spell.

I never had that.

Most don't.

My sister did.

This mystery woman who compromised my midnight snack was "Born to Be Alive" indeed as the song bellowed through the club. Jeremy gave her a confident twirl in the center of the floor and she responded with incredible enthusiasm, glossy pink lips agape, her tongue on the roof of her mouth in appreciation. To her supreme delight, she'd bagged a bloke who could actually dance, an absolute shock by the look of him.

As they hit it even harder, beads of sweat formed on her forehead in a flattering glow and she started to laugh aloud. I knew the feeling well. With the right partner, dancing looked and felt blissfully effortless. These two were *so* good, in fact, that people started to *gawk*, a circle forming around them in a proper audience, and I was left wondering just who the fuck was this guy? He said he was from Leeds, for God's sake. Since when did Yorkshiremen dance like that?

But more importantly, who the fuck was *she*? Olivia Newton-John?

He finally dipped her dramatically near the song's end, the part with the heavy synth, and she extended her arms out over her head before slowly curling back up, a hand fluffing up her hair, the other wrapping around his neck, finger by finger, to the beat. They were finished, and it was as if we'd all been through something together; like a climax.

The two of them breathed heavily, still holding that final pose to soak up the resounding applause in the room. They smiled at one another, but then the woman looked around at all of us, making eye contact with every person she could, getting off on the attention while sweaty Jeremy skulked away to get a refreshment.

What a little tart.

I adored her instantly.

Wild game I wanted to capture, not necessarily hunt.

After all, I was *technically* in the market. I'd been without a companion for nearly a year; other recent prospects had not panned out. It couldn't hurt to see what this girl's story was and if there might be a window of opportunity. I assumed she had everything— just look at her—but a challenge was never a deterrent for me. In fact, it had become something of an appeal.

I relished bringing a light like her over to the dark side.

The shimmering mirrors from the disco ball above lit up her cherubic face and then the giant rock on her ring finger. Oh, marvelous! A little conversation starter.

I sauntered towards her, in perfect time with the change of song, at the first shift of the beat. Eight bars of guitars and drums only, but everyone recognized it before the horns and whistles chimed in. It was a crowd-pleaser. Like all of Donna Summer's catalog.

I parted the sea of the swarm effortlessly, everyone around me accepting my *gentle* suggestion to remove themselves from my path once they met my eye.

A perk of the vampiric job, as it were, the epitome of the saying "works like a charm."

Right on cue, the belle of the ball glanced at me. I managed a broad smile in return, though it took everything I had to conceal my fangs, due to exhilaration. At the very first *toot-toot*, I playfully tugged on her hand with the hardware, choreographing our first interaction to perfection.

"Now, what does your husband think about his wife sharing a dance with a strange man?" I asked, running my thumb over the top of her diamond. She threw her head back, bursting into a peal of laughter.

"How do you know that guy's not my husband?" she asked me, her shoulders alternating up and down to the beat. An American accent. Perhaps on holiday? Hmm. Ideal for snacking, but not necessarily for the taking. More time was necessary for the seduction.

I whispered into her ear, dangerously close to her long and lovely neck.

"Because I invited *that guy* here tonight."

It was the first time she'd stopped beaming since I laid eyes on her. The girl's lips closed in on each other; mortified. "Oh, shit. I'm sorry. You're not mad, are you? It was just a dance. He's not even my type. Not that he's some kind of ogre or anything. I'm sure he's great. I mean, *you're* dating him and—"

I put her out of her misery swiftly since she had been readily imbibing all evening. "Darling, I'm obviously *joking*."

"Well, there's plenty of foxy women around with all kinds of men for all kinds of reasons." She shrugged casually, like she knew everything about the ways of the world.

"What about you?" I asked her, pointing to her ring.

"Oh God," she muttered. "Why *did* I marry Malcolm?" She laughed aloud again as if this was a perfectly normal thing to say to a stranger and not the beginning of what was likely an existential crisis. Excellent. "It sounded like a big adventure at the time, and I was in need of one."

"Marriage is an adventure?" I sneered.

Really?

Was she that provincial?

"No!" She shook her head, ramping up her volume as the music swelled. "Moving to London was an adventure! I've only been in town since the spring! You might have picked up on the fact that I'm not from around here!"

"Yeah, no shit, darling!" I laughed heartily and she joined in right away. Instant friends. Always the sign of potential. I never wanted to work *too* hard at it. Could throw off the power balance in the future, and I always wanted the upper hand, especially when they didn't realize I had it.

"I love this song!" she shouted.

Who didn't?

I took her by the hand, back to the center of the dance floor, feeling a current of energy pulsing through my wrist all the way up to the back of my neck.

I wondered if she felt it, too.

Beep-beep.

The two of us could not stop chatting as we danced to Donna, booming bass be damned. "Malcolm's pretty good-looking, I can tell you that much," she explained, taking my hands and lifting them up over our heads before releasing them. Then she wiggled her fingers down alongside her face to the sides of her breasts, shimmying forward and then back up again. "There's nothing *wrong* with him, really. I guess I just feel kinda—"

"Bored to fucking tears?" I guessed, hoping that I was correct because it could make everything so much easier. I spun around and knocked my hip against hers, but she had stopped moving.

"How'd you know that?" she asked. I detected a slight annoyance in her voice that I had her pegged. Everyone prefers to believe they're mysterious, don't they?

"You came to a nightclub without your husband, darling," I gently reminded her.

"Oh! Do people not do that?" She widened her eyes in jest, showing that she was up for a bit of banter. Ideal. No one wants to spend eternity with an easily offended clod.

"More people should." I winked.

"It's just, like, it's almost *1980*, and I think there could be so much more coming, but I flew into this thing with him and I'm worried I might be stuck now."

Oh my God, she was perfect.

"What's your name?" I asked.

"Amber Wells," she said, her name floating off her tongue, obviously enjoying the sound of it.

"Wells? Is that his name or yours?"

"His. I used to be saddled with Borkenhagen, if you can believe that!" She laughed with a little snort that would sound dreadful on anybody else, but it was captivating on her.

"A proper mouthful." I smiled. "I'm Nicola Claughton."

She shook my hand, which made me laugh, and then Jeremy interrupted, sidling up in between us when I thought he had buggered off for the night. He should have been grateful he was still alive!

"Nicola, I see you've met Miss America," he said suggestively, the twat, as if the two of us would ever consider doing anything remotely scandalous with a man like him.

"I have," I said.

Amber yawned with a big stretch, really putting it on. "Guys, I'm thinking about calling it a night. I'm exhausted."

Jeremy and I both jerked our heads back, completely aghast.

"Surely you want another go on the disco round with ol' Jez?" he exclaimed. "What's your favorite song? I'll get the DJ on it."

"Sorry. I'm beat. Fun dancing, though!"

Amber started to sashay away, but there was no chance I was going to lose her now, so I locked into Jeremy, holding his gaze with purpose. Within seconds, he was off and out the door, zipping in front of Amber without another word.

Her mouth fell open, both startled and delighted by his sudden departure.

"*Thank God* he got the hint," she said. "I didn't really want to leave yet, but I also didn't want him following us around all night either. Why do guys like that think they can get fresh with girls like us?"

"The sensual dancing probably didn't help."

"Hey, a lady should be allowed to dance with someone without the expectation of fucking them."

"Spoken like a true lady!" I cackled.

"Come on. I'm dying of thirstation. Let's get another drink," she said, grabbing my hand, not noticing at all that I never had a cocktail of my own.

Before we got to the bar, she stopped in the center of the dance floor once again and placed a hand softly on her heart. Soused and sweet in the perfect amount.

"Nicola. Can I just say that it is *so* nice to make a fun new gal pal? I mean, honest to God, is there anything better?"

She *had* to be the new one.

Maybe the one who would stay forever.

Loyal.

Like a best friend should be.

Or a sister, for that matter.

"What did your parents think about your move here?" I asked

Amber as she waited for our drinks, knees popping back and forth to the rhythm. I had to get a larger sense of the people in her life and, more importantly, their proximity to her.

"It's kinda like they were surprised," Amber began, "but also not surprised at all. I lived in a very strict house, so they had to know I'd run wild eventually. But I took care of a lot for them, and my little sister. I doubt they thought I'd go so far away, but it was only a matter of time before I got the hell out of there."

"Why?" I asked as the bartender returned with two French 75s. Amber took a big swig of her drink. I just held the other in my hand, listening closely to her story, intrigued she had a sister as well.

We might understand each other more than I'd hoped.

"Oh, my dad is a rotten cheat and awful to my mother. Very controlling. Of all of us. And they're always fighting about money. I feel sorry for her, but I wish she would just stand up for herself. She should have left him years ago, but she won't. Mom's not really at the forefront of women's lib. She's staying married and miserable. *For sure.*"

"But you're married and . . . ?"

"Well, I don't think I'm *miserable*." She chuckled, but I wasn't wholly convinced about that. "Malcolm's nothing like my dad. He's a good guy. When we met, I just had a dream of mine that was crushed to shit, and he was like . . . a life raft?"

"You know, *my* dad was a dickhead, too," I said, clinking my glass to hers as if challenging her to a duel. I also wanted to get her mind off Malcolm's alleged kind demeanor as some sort of savior. "In fact, I bet he's *more* of a dickhead than your dad."

"Oh?"

"My dad was *also* a cheat, but he had a child with one of his mistresses. She came to live with us after her mother died giving birth, not long after I was born. So we grew up together, though the staff was charged with her care since *my* mother was not pleased by her arrival, but my father insisted it was the right thing to do. We were treated differently, of course, but we were very close. Sometimes it felt like we only had each other. But as soon as she turned sixteen, my father dismissed her from our home."

Amber hung on my every word, taking small sips of her cocktail. Tears started to form in her eyes. She felt sorry for my sister.

Sometimes I did as well.

"*Dismissed*?" she gasped. "What does that mean? Where is she now? Are you in touch?"

I shook my head. No need to go into details. Less would be more.

"Jesus, your dad *is* a dickhead." Amber looked up at the ceiling again, thinking out loud. "Malcolm's definitely not a dickhead. But he is dull. And he doesn't pay any attention to me."

Poor dear.

I would pay attention to her.

"Dickhead or dullard?" Amber mused. "Are those really our only options?"

"No." I grinned at her, showing off only the slightest flicker of my fangs since it was just dark enough to play a bit and she was just drunk enough not to question it.

THREE

AMBER

It's pretty easy for me to get into Raffles, or any private club in London, even though I'm not *technically* a member at any of them. All I have to do is stare deeply into the doorman's eyes—being hot helps, too, obviously—and soon enough after his jaw drops and his mind becomes, well, more *moldable*, down goes the velvet rope and I'm invited right in.

I've always heard that Raffles is one of the best clubs in this neighborhood, and since the Chelsea vampires weren't at Embargo, my first stop, this must be where they are tonight. But I'll keep going down the list if I must. The duty of a lifelong party girl.

The bass is pounding, the drinks are flowing, the decor is all purple and red and velvety and pretty nouveau riche, to be honest, despite the club being one of the oldest in the city. Nicola would hate it, but I know how to embrace an environment and enjoy it for what it is.

Probably one of the many reasons she loves having me around.

Someone needs to be a good time.

Plus, the music is on point tonight, so I just get right down to it, sniffing around as I step in time to the beat, keeping my eyes peeled for the other supernatural beauties who hopefully have the As to my Qs, when a smokin'-hot guy with BDE takes my hand.

Hel-LO, handsome!

He has long, shaggy dirty-blonde hair, the kind that he probably doesn't even have to style because it looks good every which way, if you know what I mean. And his light-gray eyes really pop next to his sun-kissed complexion, flecks of green adding extra contrast. And, oh gosh, he has these gorgeous full lips in a boyish grin, showing off just the teensiest little gap between his front two teeth that is so cute, not to mention the dimple that pops in one cheek only.

God, I almost want to dip my finger in it; he is *so* scrumptious.

Completely my type, when I used to have one, but I don't screw around trying to fall in love anymore.

Why bother?

It won't work out.

But you don't have to be in love with someone to dance with them.

This guy and I are in total sync as the beat changes to the sexy, poppy Giorgio Moroder number he did with Sia a while back. Lots of tempo changes. Lots of modulation. And we're both playful dancers with great musicality, hitting every note with a worthy move. God, this is too much fun. To be good-looking *and* a good dancer? It's the holy grail.

Our bodies connect like one until he whips me out by the hand before pulling me back in, hoisting me up on his hips like a regular Johnny Castle, hand wrapping around my waist, as I lift my legs to take a sexy S shape, toes pointed through my heels, never sacrificing any lines for comfort because we! are! *performing!*

I know all eyes are on us now. We're both loving the attention.

It's rare to see anyone dance like this anymore, certainly not any of the clubs' regulars, like the cast of *Made in Chelsea*.

The song drops in tempo, in the middle, right before she really belts it out again, so the DJ changes the spotlight from bright white to soft pink, and my arms hang around his neck, fingertips remaining in varied extension for the visual.

I know my angles.

We sway with the music ever so slightly, but as it starts to pick up again, back to the chorus, we wordlessly decide to keep it low and slow because I know he's about to lay a big fat one on me and I don't want to miss it for anything, because making out with a cute guy in the middle of a goddamn dance floor has always been my personal highest good. I mean, we don't even know each other's *names*! Is there anything hotter?

I pull away from him as the song ends, even though I'm tempted to dry hump him in front of all the London glitterati, but sorry, bud. I've got bigger fish to fry tonight. Though to his credit, I could feel he's *pretty* big. I give him one last sultry look over my shoulder with a little double clap to the music. His lips are still apart, craving more from me, but I just mouth, "Good night."

Mission accomplished.

I knew something like that would get their attention, drawing them out of the shadows where they like to sulk.

They're watching me over by the bar. Two of them. Both stunners.

The type of women that can only be one thing.

Tamsin has the permanent snarl of a serial killer's mugshot, which is kind of hilarious because she looks like an actual angel with natural white-blonde hair and the type of skin an old novel would call *alabaster*. Pale as hell, even for a vampire. She must have been walking around looking like a demonic doll since childhood.

I recognized her right away in that locket I found in Nicola's jewelry box, pictured right next to a hunky guy with his arms wrapped around her. It was jarring because both of them looked so happy, but I've never seen that bitch crack a smile.

And then there's Margaux, who looks like a gorgeous yet goth French exchange student sporting a chic little bob and an orange-red lip with an exclusively black wardrobe, smiling politely enough in passing, but never with her teeth. Even though she appears friendly, at least to me, she has the air of someone who's seen it all and is no longer impressed by anything or anyone. I think it comes from age, but I'm not sure if she's as old as Nicola. Still, I can feel the power buzzing from her, as if the strobe lights bouncing off her glowy skin could be wielded to burn me or bless me, depending on her mood.

They look absolutely stunned to see me in the flesh, eyes fixed on me, barely blinking, so I need to make it clear that I'm not interested in starting any sort of turf war with them. Far from it.

"Hi! I was looking for you guys!" I shout over the music at Margaux, who towers above me in black heeled boots. She squints at me, suspicious, so I make a joke, saying "I come in peace," with this alien affectation in my voice that makes me feel like a true-blue moron, but it should more than establish I mean them no harm.

"Are you alone?" Tamsin asks, looking around the club, eyes like laser beams. I know she's wondering where Nicola is. I'm sure they both are.

"Yep." I smirk. "She doesn't know I'm here . . . I'd prefer to keep it that way."

Margaux sizes me up with her piercing green eyes before exchanging a look with Tamsin, who taps her fingers at her cheek, her shimmery black manicure starting to chip on the thumbs.

"What do you want?" Margaux asks.

"Some free advice." I grin, trying to be charming again.

"No such thing." Margaux smiles with her teeth now, despite herself.

Maybe it's working.

There is a part of me that acknowledges the danger of trusting them with confidential information, of course, but I need to start pushing my own boundaries if I'm ever going to leave Nicola behind. I used to be such an adventurous girl. I moved across the world and married a man I didn't even really know, for God's sake.

I want to get back to being more like her again.

Maybe a little crazy, but ballsy as hell.

"I'm thinking about leaving Nicola," I say, keeping to myself that I've already decided. I lock eyes with Tamsin, aiming for bravery. "So I wanted to ask how *you* went about doing that."

Margaux looks over at Tamsin, who is shaking her head like she'd rather do anything else than get involved in my mess. *"Aaaaab-solutely* not!" Tamsin says with a quick flash of her fangs, but after a stiff stare from Margaux, she backs down right away.

Well, I've seen *that* particular dynamic before.

"Where did you hear about that?" Margaux asks, taking charge of the situation. I have my phone at the ready with a picture of the open locket. I turn up the brightness so Tamsin can see it, too. She stares at it for a moment, one side of her mouth twitching, as if daring the other side to join in for a full smile, but then she looks right at me with her typical glower.

"Put it away," she commands.

I do as she asks, thrilled to know my instincts were correct.

Now, how can I get to the good stuff?

"Why don't you come to ours for a chat?" Margaux suggests, completely ignoring Tamsin's wishes. "We have plenty of time before dawn. A little nightcap. It would be our pleasure to host you."

She can sense my hesitation. Right now we're in public. Relatively safe.

"This is a sensitive topic, as I'm sure you can tell. If you want *us* to trust that your motives here are sincere, we have to trust you, too," Margaux says. "We know all about the animosity from Nicola, but you? Who's to say?"

"Margaux, I don't want her in our—" Tamsin begins, but Margaux hisses at her to hush.

"Don't you mean *my*?" she whispers.

I take a deep breath, unsettled. But I really want to know more, I *need* to know more, and they're the only game in town because there's no way in hell I'm going to the other vampires in London. Those guys are really wild.

"Fine," I agree, my curiosity getting the best of me, considering the mission at hand.

Besides, I think I could take these two if it came down to it.

I'm scrappy.

From the outside, Margaux and Tamsin's flat looks like any other in SW1, which is to say, pretty darn fancy. Small bricks of soft brown and taupe up top lead down to the large white ones, all surrounding a blue door, the color of a robin's egg, cheery and inviting if you don't know who lives inside. But the interior is on a whole other level.

Margaux has the taste of Marie Antoinette or, like, Liberace, which is a total shock because I half expected some kind of tasteful Queen of the Damned dungeon paradise with onyx lampshades and dark damask curtains. Instead I'm greeted with fresh-cut purple and pink hydrangeas on the credenza, absolutely spotless white marble floors and long mint-green draperies that really make the toile wallpaper and gilded ceilings stand out.

"On the settee." Margaux points straight ahead to the drawing room, the double doors ajar.

When I open them, I see a young man in a sharp navy jacket and shiny brown shoes, hooked up to an IV of sorts. He's completely petrified, with his lips sewn shut and his body chained to a tufted ivory chair. He must have been plucked from Southwark earlier that night, part of their territory where business bros, both local and international, roam free.

The display is a little gross, even for me. Quick and dirty has always been my hunting style. Painless as possible, even if the guy's an ass. Why make it so drawn out when we all know what's coming? We need to eat, but do we need to be evil?

We're all God's creatures—*sort of.*

"Care for a drink?" Margaux asks me, gently squeezing my shoulders as she passes behind me. She's certainly warmed up in my presence without Nicola around. Strange. Margaux picks up a gold-rimmed coupe glass from the gleaming bar cart and fills it with blood via the small spout connected to the man's vein.

I watch as a giant lone tear falls down his cheek. He makes eye contact with me, but I look away. I don't like a slow death. He can't even scream. The seam on his mouth is super tight, the stitches so close together that it looks like he was born with some kind of deformity. It's a scene from a horror movie.

I know we're the monsters.

"Here," Margaux says, handing me the glass. It feels rude to drink right in front of him, while he's still living and breathing, but I'm the Chelsea vampires' guest and decide it would be ruder not to, Midwest manners taking over. I put my lips to the glass and take a swig of his balmy blood. God damn it, he's delicious. That shit is *fresh*. The perfect temp with a smooth, slightly creamy consistency. Men like him always taste expensive *and* nutritious.

"Cheers!" Margaux holds up a glass of her own and Tamsin reluctantly joins in as we clink all three together. The man winces in his seat and stays that way.

Good call, buddy. Keep your eyes shut. The end's gotta be near.

I get the conversation started as a sort of power play. "So, Tamsin . . . what brought you here to Margaux's?" I lean back into the sofa, crossing one leg over the other. The two of them look at each other before staring at me blankly again.

"I think you need to answer that question first." Tamsin laughs, trotting over to refill her glass, but then she decides to suckle the spout instead like a baby on a bottle. She stops smacking to speak again. "I mean, I *know*, but what was it specifically that Nicola did to set you off on such a dangerous path?"

I'm not sure how much I should tell them, but I can see that it's going to be a very tit-for-tat situation around here, like anything with vampires. I try to ignore Tamsin's blatant mention of a dangerous path, but my ears are pricked accordingly.

"She did something that I asked her not to do," I say plainly, sitting up straighter, projecting confidence. "Something terrible."

The spout of blood runs out, that man finally tapped. Tamsin wraps her hands around his neck anyway, snapping it quickly with a small laugh, doing it for fun since he's already dead.

"That sounds about right when it comes to Nicola," Tamsin scoffs. "So who did she kill, exactly? Your friend? Your lover? Someone else?"

"Who was the man with you in the locket?" I ask Tamsin, bolder than I mean to sound. She doesn't say anything, waiting for me to answer her question first. I suppose it's not some big secret. "My husband. From a long time ago."

"I'm sorry, Amber," Margaux says, her tone surprisingly sincere. "Tamsin was also very upset when Jacob was kill—"

"Don't say his name," Tamsin mutters softly, as if she can't openly scold Margaux in mixed company. "Please."

I could put two and two together.

Nicola killed someone Tamsin loved, too.

"So what is your grand plan, *ma chérie?*" Margaux asks me, changing the subject as she rises from her chair. She opens a square metal door positioned in the middle of the back wall. It looks like it could be a dumbwaiter, with a small window in the center, but it's not.

"I'm not sure yet. That's why I thought I'd talk to Tamsin about how she went about . . ." I trail off, watching as Margaux pulls out a large slab of metal from the door, nodding at Tamsin, who grabs the dead man's body, drags it over and flops it onto the slab, like she's taking out a big bag of trash for her boss.

And then it strikes me that Tamsin probably doesn't want to be *here* either.

"*I* took Tamsin in to protect her from Nicola. And bolster my own status, quite frankly," Margaux continues, pushing the slab back inside. "No vampire would dare come after two all on their own, hmm?" She winks at me knowingly, slamming the door shut. Tamsin flips the nearby switch, setting the flames flying behind the window. "I tried to get close to Nicola when I arrived in London after the war. I think we'd all be better off sticking together, but she is not interested in the company of a vampire like me. The two of us? We're equals. Quite similar in many respects. But she prefers to be the only one in control, as I'm sure you well know."

"She knows." Tamsin laughs, a sinister sound, the light from the fire flashing against her face, fangs out. I don't appreciate her dismissal of me, but I feel like I got the information I needed, more or less. Tamsin failed where her freedom was concerned. Sure, she technically got away from Nicola, but *this* doesn't look too different from my own situation.

"She'll hunt you down, Amber," Tamsin warns me, almost excited by the prospect. "And then she'll trap you, maybe starve you and leave you for dead. That's what happened to the rest of them, which I'm sure you were wondering about. With very rare exceptions, just three by my count, myself included."

"Thanks to me," Margaux says harshly. "If I hadn't opened my *maison* to you, you'd have been dead or ended up in Wapping with—"

"Who else?" I interrupt, all manners going out the window, blown away by the thought of Nicola going full Liam Neeson on my ass. I was largely thinking about the logistics of leaving safely, along with the emotional ramifications and maybe a vicious yet empty threat of violence from Nic—but I never really thought she'd try to *murder* me.

She *made* me.

"I wouldn't pop round the other one still in town if I were you. That's a whole different situation, and her rules don't seem to apply to him." Excuse me? *Him?* Who?! "He knows a lot, but it won't come for free. And then I have my suspicions about that long-lost sister of hers. She must have gotten away, the way Nicola goes on about it, but I doubt she's still in London at all," Tamsin says, throwing me a couple of juicy crumbs. "I didn't get the full story there. But you never get a full story from Nicola, and yet she always seems to know everyone else's. Something to keep in mind if you decide to go through with it."

"You'd have to get ahead of her somehow," Margaux muses, two fingers hovering at her lips, as if she yearns for the drag of a cigarette. "But even then, you'd always have to look over your shoulder.

Vampires have nothing but time to exact their revenge, and if I know Nicola, which I do, she'll go to the ends of the earth as long as you're not spoken for."

"What if I left London? Like to Paris or Barcelona?"

I've considered both places. I wouldn't have to worry about the sun cramping my travel style, plus I know the languages and still want to be somewhere with a solid social scene, but it crosses my mind that I'm sharing too much with them too soon.

Tamsin starts in again with that shrill laugh of hers. "As if either of those places are remotely far enough to keep her from punishing you!"

"Punishing me? She's not my mother—"

"Have you considered going back to America?" Margaux asks, which is something I've never thought about before. What if I could? "I wonder if Nicola would make the effort to go overseas. Oh, honestly? She probably would. Amber, the truth is that it's very dangerous to travel at all. You don't know the people. You don't know the other vampires, and there are at least a couple in every major city, as far as I know. You don't know the housing situation until you get there. And it's just that there's no room for error at all. Do you even have a human lined up to assist you? Personally, I don't trust them, but it's imperative for any long-haul travel these days. Lots of paperwork, unless you engage with those outside the law, but I wouldn't want them holding my life in their hands either. But when your back's against the wall, I suppose you'd try anything."

"I don't think I necessarily want to go back to—" I start to say, but she won't let me get a word in edgewise. I had no idea she was so goddamn chatty. It feels like the beginning of a pitch, but I don't think I'm buying what she's selling.

"I haven't traveled at all since I arrived in London," Margaux interrupts, leaning in closer to me, a little false intimacy for show.

"That was in the '40s and there was *a lot* going on, obviously, but I got here through sheer will and probably a bit of luck. Now, though? Everybody knows everything. Even a Luddite like Nicola. She'd find you, Amber, but don't feel bad. Most vampires can't make it alone. You're either with your maker or you can be taken by someone else, or join them, rather?"

There it is.

Margaux wants me, too.

Nicola would absolutely lose her mind.

"Those are the options?" I scoff, irritated by my present circumstances. How can we be so stuck when we're meant to be these immortal and all-powerful beings with literal fangs and endless bloodthirst? For God's sake, they just slowly drained a man dry in the comfort of their own home and fried up his remains with a houseguest present like it's nothing. But we can't *relocate*?!

"Or you could kill her and stay in London," Tamsin snarls with a deranged singsong tone in her voice. "But you don't strike me as the type."

I don't know whether that's a compliment or an insult. Probably the latter coming from her, but who cares? It's not like *she* killed Nicola. And that's not even something I want to entertain. I don't want to be around Nicola anymore, much less live with her, but I don't want her dead.

I just want to slip away.

Undetected, unscathed and unbothered.

Friends grow apart all the time.

Margaux swirls what blood remains in her glass as if it was a big Cab Franc that needs to fully open up so she can taste all the notes on her tongue. "Killing your maker is not as easy as Tamsin makes it sound." She sighs, suggesting firsthand experience. "They know you better than anyone else. Not easily falling into any traps where you can starve and sun them. And there's the emotional impact, which no one ever wants to address, but something like that, Amber. Well, it changes you. Why do you want to be alone anyway?"

It's not that I want to be alone.

I just want to be in charge of my own life for once.

I went from my parents' house to Malcolm's house to Nicola's house.

And I'm realizing I shouldn't have trusted either of them in the end . . .

But Margaux and Tamsin make a fresh start seem increasingly impossible.

Maybe Nicola and I used to bring out the best in each other, back when we first met, but that isn't true anymore. Was it ever? Did I always have blinders on about Nicola? I never thought she would kill Malcolm, but was that naïve of me? She loves to go for the jugular.

Will she go for mine even harder?

I know the two faces of Nicola Claughton. I've seen her show the dark side to everyone else, and with Malcolm's death, it finally came for me. I was surprised, but was she surprised, too? If this happened with her previous companions, why did she think it would be different with me? Maybe she thought I'd always be the girl I was in December 1979. A little lost. A little wild. In need of guidance. A friend. A big-sister type.

But I don't owe these girls an explanation of my innermost feelings on Nicola. At the end of the day, Tamsin isn't any better off than me, and I have no interest in poking around the male vampires' turf. But now I can't stop thinking about Nicola's sister.

Is *she* still alive?

I smile at Margaux, who continues to gaze at me like a piece of meat, ready to wrap this visit up. "You've given me a lot to think about," I say.

"Good. That's good. We're just trying to help you," Margaux says, putting a finger under my chin so sweetly that I almost believe her.

"Why?" I ask. "You don't know anything about me."

"No, not really," Margaux agrees. "But we do know Nicola Claughton. And she's simply not one to be underestimated. I wish we could all be peaceful with one another, but as the saying goes, misery loves company."

"She's a ruthless bitch, Amber, and you know it." Tamsin cocks her head to the side, scowl intact. They're not wrong, but it's still pretty rich coming from two women with an in-home incinerator.

"But if a change is what you seek," Margaux continues, a slight lift in her voice. "You *could* return and talk to us about it anytime. Never a bad idea to get your numbers up if the trust is there, not that it's easily built, but I see the potential in you."

She raises her glass to me and takes another sip, but I don't see myself returning to their little *maison du* gore anytime soon. There's a clear hierarchy between them and I'm already second in Nicola's mind. Who wants to willingly sign up to be third place? Someone who wouldn't know any better.

But I do.

FOUR

NICOLA

1979

observed Amber closely the rest of that week after we met, especially when she was at home with her husband in the evenings. I
kept an eye open for any quandaries or clues in her world, little
tender spots I could push to my advantage when we were together
again so I could seal the deal as soon as possible.

She was correct about Malcolm. He appeared to be a nice
enough bloke and he did care for her, but it was a rare man who
could keep up with a woman of Amber's caliber. And it didn't look
like he was putting in much effort. What a pillock.

He should have stood up straighter when she walked into the
room, more eager to receive her sterling company. He should have
smiled more, with his teeth, but he wouldn't. Very English, but
come on, man, you married an American girl. And a lively one at
that—throw her a bloody bone! And if he did find something amusing with Amber, he'd only allow for a small *hmm* to escape his lips,
still clamped together, upturned ever so slightly.

Amber liked to put on a record after dinner and have a little dance around the room, hoping in vain that he'd join her. She held out her hands and he'd just shake his head with that nearly imperceptible smile of his. It was a miracle that Malcolm could resist her. She was completely adorable, singing along to the music, her hair bouncing on her shoulders like she was in a shampoo advert.

Was he really that stiff? Why did he care if he looked like a fool? He was in his own home. Hold your wife in your arms, sir. No wonder the marriage was quickly losing its luster for Amber. They weren't a suitable match, like she said, despite her best intentions and his middling ones.

Amber offered him entertainment. Something beautiful to admire. Someone to be proud of in mixed company. So of course, Amber was *his* dream girl, but what he offered her was already done. He took her far away from home, the last place she wanted to be, but I knew that wasn't going to be enough, hence Amber's trawling about London nightclubs on her own past midnight.

Well, not any longer.

We did that together.

proposed meeting Amber at Annabel's on Saturday night, but the happy couple were having Malcolm's colleague and his wife over instead. She had told me on the phone, positively thrilled to hear from me and flattered I looked up her number, but she declined, citing the wifely hosting duties set upon her.

Amber wasn't officially cooking the meal—they had help and she was a self-proclaimed terrible cook—but she was doing the flowers and the table decor and baking an apple pie for dessert. *Good God.* Malcolm, despite not being an outright dickhead, was indeed trying to turn her into a housewife. The exact thing she didn't want to become.

"Do you host these gatherings often?" I asked.

"Once in a while, and it's the only time Malcolm wants to be social, so I go with it."

"Do you enjoy the guests' company?"

"It doesn't matter. I'm more of a prop than a person at these things," she said ruefully. "I'm learning that Malcolm is kind of a careerist. I think it's the most important thing to him."

"More important than you?" I scoffed.

"He asks me to tone it down in front of his coworkers. And the wives just want to talk about recipes or their children. They're sweet enough, but who cares?"

"Amber," I said, trying not to laugh, because that *was* what most people cared about in those circles. But she was not most people. "I'm certain they're just trying to be amiable and engage with you. Probably wise to befriend them, no? For Malcolm's sake?"

"I guess. But I don't want to," she whined.

"How else are you going to create a social life in London?"

"I found you, didn't I?"

She certainly did.

"Well, we'll go out another time," I reassured her. "I really can't wait."

"Me neither."

I could hear her smiling through the phone.

decided to attend this dinner obligation myself. Discreetly, of course, from just outside their dining room window, using nightfall to my advantage. I was eager to see how Malcolm treated Amber in mixed company since I'd only perceived their dynamic thus far alone.

Careerist was right. The man switched on an actual personality the moment this couple waltzed through the doors, with Amber linked delicately to his arm. He cracked jokes. Nothing knee-slapping, but enough to garner the appropriate chuckles. He made intense eye contact with them, waxing on about his worldwide travels for business or hunting with his father in his youth and even the story of how he met Amber in Chicago earlier that year.

Malcolm included her at the dinner, just as she said he would, like a prop. He'd place an arm around his wife on occasion, or he'd lob her a simple question that required a one- or two-word answer, usually in the affirmative of whatever he was saying. Or he'd ask her sweetly, "Would you please get them a top-up, love?"

If I was Amber, I'd be irritated, too. This behavior would only worsen over time.

She had said Malcolm was like a life raft.

I would offer her the equivalent of a luxury ocean liner.

But still, things weren't *so* dire between the two of them just yet.

She might require a little push onto the gangway.

Amber and I had planned to meet outside Regine's on a Tuesday evening. Our gallivanting around town together had become much more frequent and delightfully louche over the past few weeks. We chatted on the phone almost nightly when we didn't see each other in person, and we went out to different nightclubs at least twice a week, sometimes three.

It was perfect. I could feel that we were on the express route to our final destination.

But when she arrived at Regine's that night, she was decidedly not dressed for the occasion. She'd clearly been crying but had tried to hide it with makeup. *A lot* of it. Her cheeks were still flushed, but she went thick on the eyeliner in an ill-begotten attempt to mask her distress. In fact, she went heavy with everything in her ensemble, as if in period costume. The flamboyance of it all and, honestly, a lack of taste—unusual for her. She'd donned a big skirt with a corset, her blonde hair assembled at the top of her head in some sort of makeshift updo, symmetry obviously the least of her concerns.

Disco it was *not*.

"I want to do something wild tonight!" she declared, raising both her hands above her head, meeting my eye with a feral stare.

"Are you all right, darling?" I asked. "This is a . . . new look. I'm not sure it's up to the dress code. We could—"

"We're not going to Regine's tonight," she barked. *Easy*, girl. "We're going somewhere new and exciting!"

"All right . . . What brought this on?" I asked, picking up one of the giant ruffles on her skirt and letting it loose again. She looked ridiculous.

"Cool, right? I overheard these art students today when I was walking by St. Martin's. They were dressed like this, like they were from another planet, or, like, from the future already."

God help us if *this* was the future.

"They were kids, I guess, but not that much younger than us," Amber continued. "And the way they were talking about this club, it was like it's going to be the greatest night of their lives. If they actually get in. And you and I always get in everywhere, so I thought we could try."

I placed my hands on the sides of her shoulders in an attempt to settle her, squeezing them tighter and tighter, until finally she yelped in pain. "Oh! Sorry, love," I said, but I wanted her to focus on me, not art students at St. Martin's.

This wasn't about *them*.

This was meant to be the night I set everything in motion.

"Amber, what's happened?" I inquired, even though I already knew the answer.

She took a deep breath and then launched into a full tirade, barely coming up for air.

"Malcolm and I got into a huge fight and he must think I'm a real idiot because he is flat-out denying it, but I *know* he slept with somebody else! Can you believe that? I never expected it from someone like him. *How* did I still end up with a cheater? Oh, I yelled at him, Nicola. And *he* even yelled back at me! And it was crazy because he has a booming yell, I would never have guessed. But I *also* wouldn't have guessed that he'd sleep with someone else either, and I guess that's what I get for marrying someone I barely know. I feel like such a dumbass. Do we all just turn into our parents? Is it inevitable? I've been trying so hard to avoid it, and apparently I'm in the same exact situation, just in a foreign country with nowhere to go but back home, and I'm not doing that! I'm just not!"

She was coming undone.

Excellent.

"Perhaps Malcolm grew weary of your solo exploits in the night and this *affair* was some sort of retaliation?" I asked, knowing it would stir up even more negativity towards Malcolm. Amber's nostrils flared with disgust at the thought. Good.

"I don't know." She sighed. "I need to sit down and figure out my fucking life, but not tonight. I just wanna have fun and dance our asses off."

Well, I wanted us to curl up in a VIP booth together at Regine's. Let her rip on Malcolm while our favorite music pulsed around us. Plant the tempting seeds about a potential eternity together, doing what we love, watching them all grow wild in her eyes.

But Amber couldn't go into Regine's dressed like *that.*

"So where are we off to?" I asked.

"Have you heard of the New Romantics?" She grinned, raising her hand for a taxi.

O f course I had heard of the New Romantics, but that didn't mean I wanted to engage with them. I saw it all as more of a working-class thing. You know, being edgy for edgy's sake, to make a mark, considering the political climate as of late. The New Romantics' idea of glamour, if you could call it that, was gauche on purpose, to call attention to the youth and what they wanted, instead of the mainstream. It was put-upon and almost mocking sophistication and the upper class, which of course I valued, as was my birthright. So I had no interest in slumming it with "the Blitz kids" that night, but with Amber coming across a bevy of burgeoning artists that day, of *all* days, it was what I was up against.

Blitz was a wine bar in Covent Garden, not a favored area of mine. Rubbish everywhere. People grousing all the time. Struggle on the streets. The '70s had been unkind to the country at large, and though the latest election promised a new dawn, it would be at the cost of the Labour Party, so no wonder the youths were rebelling, as they are wont to do worldwide when such threats of conservatism come about. I understood, of course, but I was far too old to care any longer. I'd already lived through so much. Life is a pendulum. You win some, you lose some. So I looked out for myself.

That club, if you could even call it that, was a grimy little thing, still in its infancy as a once-weekly destination only. Tuesday nights were *the* night. It was "new and exciting" for a certain crowd that distinctly wasn't ours. Though looking at Amber that night, you wouldn't know it. And here I thought she was as devoted to disco as me. I mean, what on earth *was* this place?

There was a menagerie of youths congregating at the entrance, each one's style more outlandish and distasteful than the next. Women in oversize suiting that flattered not a single curve. Men in little vests and loud patterned trousers. Scarves and hats and other accessories weren't minor flourishes, but main events for everyone. It was akin to fancy dress, in my opinion, likened to pirate garb or the costumes of circus performers. Their makeup was overly colorful. Heavy. Tasteless. Crass. Nothing I would ever have used to describe Amber, but against all odds, she fit right in, delighted by the handiwork she'd put into her outfit for the occasion. She heard whatever rubbish those students were talking about and ran with it, right into a funhouse mirror.

It was unclear who was making the decisions for entry at the doors, more of a mass than a proper queue, but I couldn't fathom a world where we weren't immediately escorted to the front. And despite the wild appearance of everyone in one giant ball of energy, someone in charge quickly zeroed in on Amber almost instantly. Because of course they did.

They *always* did.

A happy little chappy in red lippy waved us closer, the music growing louder as we approached. A bizarre combo of electronic clicks and robotic voices, set to a compelling beat, but almost sinister in style, particularly when I clocked the lyric "burning bodies in the sun."

"Come in, love! *Look at your hair!*" he squealed, clapping at the sight of Amber. She smiled back at me and grabbed my hand in a show of unity. But the smile quickly fell from this fellow's face upon seeing me in my long-sleeved Pucci gown, covered up from the cold with a chic black Burberry overcoat. "I'm sorry, but I can't let your friend in," he said to Amber without looking in my direction again.

"What are you talking about?" Amber asked, genuinely outraged on my behalf.

"You can come in, like I said. But *she* can't. Too posh. Too *Mayfair*."

He said *Mayfair* as if he was saying the name of a venereal disease, and I knew I wasn't among my people, and I'm sorry, but since when was being posh a *bad* thing? This was utterly humiliating. Neither Amber nor I knew what to say. He was quite serious about denying my entry into the club, the wanker.

"Are you comin' or not, love? You're gorgeous, but we are busy." His red lips smacked together obnoxiously, making a popping sound.

Of course, it occurred to me that I could easily *make* him admit me, with the power of my influence, but I wasn't sure that would be in my best interest where Miss Amber was concerned. I was no fool. I already knew disco was on its way out. Even punk was about to be put to rest. The New Romantics was the future with the '80s upon us. Who knew what else was about to change? Amber might get a taste of this futuristic bacchanal and absolutely adore it, leaving me behind entirely.

God, it felt like anything could happen that night.

Particularly if she decided to go in there without me.

I could see it all.

She'd say she'd tell me about it later. Another evening at Tramp. We'd catch up. Whenever. She'd offer to help me with an outfit for a future Blitz Club outing.

Perhaps.

Perhaps not.

Or perhaps we'd never go out together again.

She could very well make new friends. Maybe she'd end up properly leaving Malcolm and go to *art school* of all things, or worse, she could meet another man after leaving her husband and fall in serious love with him; they'd grow older together and she would have a real human life like just about everyone else in the world.

Except for us vampires.

I couldn't stand the thought of any of it.

Truth be told, I seriously considered killing her instead.

But as luck would have it, it wouldn't come to that.

Because Amber waved her hand dismissively at the odd little sprite without a second thought. "No, I'm not going in without my girlfriend," she scoffed at him, defending my honor.

They were turning people away left and right that night, but they were going to let her in.

And she chose me instead.

Loyal.

"Then I guess you're not going in at all," the doorman replied definitively, not giving Amber a second thought as he waved on in a trio dolled up like nineteenth-century harlots.

Amber just shrugged and turned back around to me. "Whatever, Nic. Who cares? Do you think I can still go to Regine's dressed like this?"

I laughed at the thought, relieved by the whole outcome of the night, and she joined in.

"Absolutely not, but I know a place we can go instead," I said.

"Great!" Amber clapped her hands together. I had her by the lead once again.

"Amber?" I said, with the requisite gratitude. "Thank you."

She wrapped her arms around me in front of the whole sideshow behind us, holding me close. "Oh my God. *Stop.* Of course! What kind of girl would I be if I ditched my best friend?!"

She chose me and I chose her.

It was time.

She wanted change. She wanted an adventure. She wanted a new home.

That's exactly what I could give her.

After that show of allegiance, I could not wait any longer.

I would tell her everything that night.

Well, not *everything*.

Not about how simple it had been to compel her husband to let me inside their home.

Not about popping my lipstick on his collar.

Not about spritzing my perfume to linger on his jacket.

And definitely not a word about those little satin knickers that she found poking out from under her marital bed.

FIVE

AMBER

No one, and I mean no one, loves a chaise lounge more than Nicola Claughton.

That's always where she is, waiting for me to come home, on the few nights we go out alone. I usually stay out later than she does. Meanwhile, she'll be at the Laurels, her favorite place on earth. Curled up, spread out, draped over, back arched, belly down or full-on straddled across that violet and velvet antique that juts out from one of the corners in the study, right next to that old baby grand that neither one of us ever plays. Instead, we play albums on the turntable, or I share Spotify lists with the hits, both past and present.

But she only ever wants to listen to the old stuff.

The Laurels is a full-fledged Victorian home from top to bottom. Never really my vibe, but I can still appreciate it. Nic loves a pattern, loves a tchotchke—though she calls them *trinkets*—and there are tapestries galore on the walls and far too many plants around for two undead women. Basically, there's *a lot* going on in every single room, but she likes it that way.

For obvious reasons, we're rarely in the kitchen. Our bedrooms are primarily for safely resting during the day. The other bedrooms are never occupied, but the staff changes the bed linens every two weeks like clockwork anyway. Sometimes Nic and I will lounge outside in the garden together on a warm summer night, but not often these days. The parlor is beautiful but kind of a no-touch room, for entertaining only, which we never do.

So we hang out in the study a lot, underneath its giant glass-domed ceiling, the only window to the outside, the walls covered with built-in bookshelves. It's especially festive on nights with a full moon, when we're playing cards or watching reality TV or having a dance party, but it has this insanely heavy door with a finicky latch outside, so we have to keep that baby propped open with a clunker of a doorstop so we don't get locked in and have to call Jonathan the houseman, pushing eighty years old now, to come and get us out, which *has* happened once or twice.

Ah, the charming quirks of living in an old-ass house, or as Nicola likes to call it, her *ancestral* home.

Nic told me that the Laurels is even a stop on one of those London walking tours, Hampstead edition. It's not like gawkers are able to see much beyond the huge hedges. Still, the history is shared about the owner, descended from generations of the Claughton family, rarely seen or heard from in the community. Not that the neighbors give a shit, as long as the property remains meticulously maintained, which it is.

Nicola will always take care of the Laurels.

Like she said she'd always take care of me.

But it's time to take care of myself now.

mber?" Nicola calls out for me when I come in the door, fresh
from Chelsea. It never matters how quiet I am. She always
knows when I'm close by. And a full report is part of our agreement
whenever we go out solo, which I never used to mind. I like hearing
about her exploits, both sexual and predatorial, as much as I enjoyed telling her about mine.

But not anymore.

I don't want her to suspect anything's up, so I roll my shoulders
back and smack a smile on my face to greet her, ambling into the
parlor like my mind isn't reeling about how to get out of here ASAP,
maybe back to the US, and where the heck her sister might be—
hopefully thriving somewhere out there, far away from her.

"Hey," I say. "How was your night?"

Nicola's partially propped up by a tasseled brocade pillow
behind her shoulders, one leg slung over the top curve of the chaise,
the other hanging off the end, her big toe grazing the rug below,
swinging back and forth. She has a record going as usual. Fleet-
wood Mac, one of her favorites to read by. She's already in her gold
pajamas, silk of course, the glow of a nearby scented candle flickering back on her severe yet sexy face.

You know, with all her self-importance and social pedigree,
you'd half expect Nicola to be flipping through *War and Peace* or
whatever, but mostly she reads *Tatler* and the *Daily Mail* plus an oc-
casional Jackie Collins novel.

"Uneventful," she replies, her voice slow and sultry as usual. "I
just grabbed a quick snack in Soho before going home. The guy I
met earlier didn't show up at Dean Street, so beggars can't be choosers. You, on the other hand, look *very* well fed!"

Yeah, thanks to noshing on Margaux and Tamsin's company, I

do have an extra-radiant glow on my skin. The guy's tie was Hermès, for God's sake, so his diet must have been just as lush.

Nicola stands up to face me, with her dark eyes and bright red lips turning into little lines, all gathering toward the center of her face. She starts flicking her pinky against her thumb, the long nails clicking together, like a tic. I've never seen her do that before.

"Where *did* you go tonight?" she asks.

"I found a bachelor party at some pub." I came up with a juicy enough lie on the way home. "The groom was all about ready to fuck me, so he deserved it. And then I helped myself to one of his friends who I saw slipping something in a drink he was buying for a girl."

"My little vigilante," she says, tilting her head to the side. I hate when she patronizes me. I'm fussy with my kills, trying to make sure they mean something the best I can, which she thinks is so silly. Fine by me. I need her to keep thinking I'm not as strong as her, and maybe I'm not, but I *am* going to be smarter. "Well, you made it home just in time."

She's not kidding. It'll be daybreak soon. We can always feel it in the air, without even looking at a clock, as if the dread seeps in through our skin like some kind of biological warning.

Nicola's expression turns softer. Well, as much as possible with those sharp angles and a jawline that could slit throats. She drifts back over to the chaise and sits down again, tucking her legs into a crisscross. "You seem underwhelmed by the evening."

I shrug at her. "I guess. But a girl's gotta eat."

"Come, darling." She pats the spot next to her. "Sit."

I do so, like a little trained Pomeranian, and I hate myself for it. I'm so, *so* sick of this.

But she can't know that.

I don't know what will happen if she knows I want to leave.

"I'm feeling similarly these days." Nicola sighs, staring above at the stars instead of looking at me. She reaches for my hand, her long and lean fingers outstretched before wrapping around mine. Her thumbnail goes back and forth, scratching the top of my hand gently, but hard enough to leave a little white mark before it disappears. "It's all getting a little tired, isn't it? A bit dull?"

I slow-blink at her, not knowing what to say.

Is she feeling the same way I am?

"And sometimes you just have to take matters into your own hands." Nicola lets go of mine before getting back up again to loom over me, looking down into my eyes with a vacant smile I can't read. I haven't seen this expression on her before. Like a ventriloquist's dummy meets Mary Tyler Moore.

Unsettling.

"You know what I'm talking about, Amber. Don't you?" she asks.

"No, not really . . ." I shake my head, thinking it's best to play dumb until she says whatever the hell she means. What is she up to? Is this a trap to get me to admit something? Is she playing a game with me?

"We need to mix it up!" she exclaims, arms flailing around like a wild woman. "We need a change!"

"I completely agree," I say, nodding effusively even though I have no idea what she's talking about, letting her take the lead. She reaches for me again, pulling me off the chaise, and then dashes over to the turntable in the study to put on a record.

Alicia Bridges.

Oh God.

We used to *loooooove* this song.

I can't help myself.

I smile as I think of the past, when it was good between us, *so* good, when everything still felt possible.

Nicola's hips start to go back and forth before she fully rolls her neck with a matching turnabout to face me. She sings, "AC-SHUN!" with gusto and grabs my hands again, lifting them up above our heads, putting mine around her neck.

Of course I dance with her.

It's my favorite thing we ever did together.

When Nicola and I have fun, we *really* have fun.

"Wasn't this the start of the best year of our lives?" she asks, nodding to the beat, saying out loud what I was already thinking.

"It really was." I smile, remembering the immediate heinous transition, but also the buzzy excitement of being a brand-new vampire. Something fresh to learn every night. Each experience felt like a different and better sensation than before. Dancing felt better. Eating felt better. We were having a great time, all the time. She taught me how to be the best little vampire I could be, and I was her willing student, who only wanted to impress her.

But that was a long time ago.

We can't go back.

Not after what she's done.

"So, let's do it!" Nicola cries out.

"Do what?" I laugh because she looks so unhinged, but also happy for once, like the vivacious woman I met at Tramp all those years ago who told me she could change my life.

"None of these people now were around back then!" Nicola waves a hand over her face with a puff of air. She's about to get on a soapbox. "1979? 1980? Not the way *we* were. You and I were *the* moment, Amber. And the ones that *are* still around are too old to care about doing it right. All these old men and their portfolios. It's so different. Annabel's isn't the same as it used to be, right? Not even close. Tramp? Please. I know it's the changing times, but *where* is that level of glamour we once had? That spark? Now it's just a bunch of men in the booths with too much money and a bunch of women with too much bloody contour and everyone looks identical and has a phone that they can't stop looking at and it's all so fucking boring, Amber! Isn't it all so positively fucking boring?"

Nicola says all this as she spins around like a lunatic in the study, arms bent at the elbows, in time to the part when the saxophone really slaps in the song, and of course I agree with her, but none of that is going to change.

Which really gets me thinking . . .

"Let's open our *own* nightclub!" Nicola announces triumphantly—shocking, since she's never worked a day in her life as far as I know. Is she losing it, too? Relatable, but I hear what she's really saying, even if that's not what she's trying to tell me.

I want to leave and cut my losses.

But she wants to recapture the *feeling*.

Not only of 1979, but of how we used to be the stars of each other's shows. She was obsessed with me; I was obsessed with her. And we lived for the nightlife. For disco. For the sweetness of my fresh youth that she stole from me, when I didn't yet understand the entirety of what she'd taken.

"Tell me more." I smile, listening to her rattle off her wild plans, knowing that all this is going to take some time.

And a little time is exactly what I need.

The Chelsea vampires said I can't escape her.

But what if I could get Nicola to *let me go*?

Opening a nightclub will be a huge undertaking, a big distraction for her, and will give me plenty of wiggle room to find the ideal man to help me relocate farther away. Of course it's going to be a man; that'll be the easy part. I mean, look at how long Nicola has had Jonathan under her thumb. I'm sure she hasn't touched him in decades, but he still does anything she needs him to do. So how hard can it be to scope out a well-to-do businessman in London with close ties to America? I mean, really, what the hell else is LinkedIn for these days other than identifying rich guys attending networking events to then scam into relationships of all kinds?

But also, this would give me enough time to find the perfect *woman*.

Someone as young and bright and shiny as a spinning disco ball above a dance floor.

A total star, even though it's a tall order.

But she's gotta be *the one*.

The one to replace *me*.

SIX

NICOLA

1835

When I let Georgie play with my dolls, Mama gets very cross about it. She huffs and puffs around the Laurels. She slams the doors as she moves from room to room. She sighs so loud. I watch her chest go up and up and up and then melt back down again. She does all of this because she wants Papa to hear her, but he pretends that he doesn't. It's some sort of game they play together, but I don't quite understand the rules.

And then Mama waits for Georgie to do something naughty because she believes that Georgie is a very naughty girl.

Georgie and I are playing with my dolls in the study this morning. We come up with mad adventures for them. The sort we hope to go on together one day. Georgie holds a porcelain one tightly in her hands. It's the doll in the dark blue dress with white flowers on the skirt. She is new and my favorite. Georgie knows the doll is very special because she's being so careful with her. She's always careful with my dolls, but especially with this one.

I don't think she's going to be naughty today.

If Mama leaves us alone, Georgie won't be naughty.

She cradles the doll, back and forth, just a few times before handing her back to me.

"Her name should be Nicola." Georgie smiles at me. "She's as pretty as you are."

"You can play with her today," I say, but Georgie shakes her head at me, picking up one of the rag dolls instead. She doesn't have a name.

Mama storms into the study unannounced, startling us both.

"It's time for piano, Nicola."

The porcelain doll falls out of my hands before Mama can finish telling me to practice. She shatters into pieces all over the floor. Georgie and I do not move. I start to cry.

"Georgiana!" Mama shouts at her when she sees the broken bits of the doll all over the floor. "That's *Nicola's* doll!"

Mama takes me by the hand and rushes me out the door, leaving Georgie alone in the study. She slams the door so my sister can't get out. The latch is strong and heavy and often gets stuck.

Mama is punishing Georgie for my mistake.

Did she not see that I was the one who let the doll fall?

"By the time I return I expect that every shard of glass will be off this floor!" Mama yells through the door at Georgie.

Georgie does not respond, but I can hear her breath on the other side.

It is very fast.

In and out and in and out.

She's frightened.

But this is not the first time Mama has locked Georgie in the study.

"How will I practice piano now?" I ask Mama as she pulls me into the dining room.

"Practice your scales there." She smacks a hand hard on the edge of the table and leaves me to tap away at the wood. It's not at all the same. I stop and listen closely, knowing Mama will be with Papa now. He can no longer pretend. She went upstairs in such a fury.

I hear her muffled voice, noisy and high and endless. Papa's voice is low and unmistakable. He hardly says anything in return to her at all, but he's listening. Mama is making sure of that.

I want to hear more, so I tiptoe to the foot of the stairs in the foyer, just around the corner, holding the banister as I tilt my head to the side.

"She cannot stay at the Laurels any longer," Mama commands. She always says horrible things like this about Georgie, but she never uses her name outright, unless she is scolding her. "It will be best for Nicola if that girl goes to an orphanage. Think of your daughter, I *beg* you."

There is a long pause this time.

I hold my breath.

No, Papa.

Please, no.

"They are different girls, my darling," Papa finally says, "but they are both mine."

Mama is silent. She has tried in vain to have Papa send Georgie away so many times. I hope she gives up this request soon. Papa paused for so long this time, but I don't ever want Georgie to leave us.

Besides, I was the one who broke the doll.

I want to tell the truth, but I don't want Papa to be cross with me either.

I think Mama already knows the truth.

I scurry back over to the study and open the latch for Georgie because Mama will act as though she forgot to release her. I watch Georgie pick up the pieces of the doll, one by one, then I notice the tip of her right index finger is bleeding.

"Oh, Georgie! You're hurt." I rush over to help her, nearly tripping over my dress, but she bats my hand away gently.

"Don't! I'm all right," she reassures me. "It has to hurt, Nicola. If it doesn't, she will only punish me harder."

I think she may be right about that.

"I'm sorry," I say, taking Georgie's hand. I put her finger in my mouth to clean it up. She allows me to pay her some kindness. The bitter taste rests on my tongue for a moment before disappearing.

"Will she send me away?" Georgie whispers.

"Papa will not let her." I pray that's a promise.

I know my father. He loves both of us.

Even if we're different.

Papa replaces the porcelain doll in two days' time with a warning.

"But this one is just for *you*, Nicola."

The flowers on her skirt look different, but I don't complain.

And I don't allow Georgie to play with any of my porcelain dolls anymore.

I think she understands why.

I hope so.

SEVEN

AMBER

Nicola excitedly flashes her fangs at me before yanking on a brass handle on an unmarked door, right smack-dab in the middle of Soho. It's painted black and we must have walked by it a million times, but I've never been inside. I don't even know what this place is, but she has that cuckoo smile on her face again, like a longtime locked-away maniac finally on the loose.

"You're going to be *so* surprised, darling." She grins at me. I follow her inside, and a petite, bubbly hostess with a giant ponytail greets us at the end of a dark, narrow hallway.

"Welcome to Blacks," she says, and after Nicola utters her last name, we're led around the corner. "Right this way."

I immediately notice this club has more of an alternative feel to it than our usual spots. All the walls are dark gray and the rooms smell of leather, each chair and sofa cloaked in it, resting on top of the aged wooden floors. The music is eclectic and loud; the crowd is hot and edgy—a blend of bodies where conversation probably ranges from Britpop to Bach. A place that's brainy *and* bumpin'.

"Are we doing some kinda nightclub recon?" I ask Nic, looking closer at the women in the club. I wonder if there are any keepers in here tonight. Any falling stars to catch in my net.

"Something like that," she trills cryptically.

We're taken to a private dining room, fully set for no reason at all, in the back area of the ground floor. Taper candles are lit on the center of a long table, the fireplace is crackling with robust flames and a giant window faces an overgrown courtyard garden, intentional for the aesthetic. Honestly, it's all very Anne Rice, which feels extra on the nose considering Margaux and Tamsin are waiting for us, sitting next to each other at one end of the table.

Oh God.

I could be sick.

It appears we're having some kind of vampiress summit tonight and I have no idea what the hell it's about. Does Nicola know I was with them at Raffles the other night? Did they snitch on me? Seriously, am I screwed right now? Is this a trap?

Nicola and I sit down at the opposite end. We're all obnoxiously quiet as the flames from the candles flicker between us. I'm shocked Nic hasn't taken the lead yet. What is she waiting for?

I inadvertently start to bounce my knee under the table, not even noticing until Nicola places her hand on me with a gentle squeeze on my leg.

I stop right away, but she keeps it there, digging her fingers into my skin.

"Well, this is new," Margaux says, breaking the silence, and Nicola releases me. I don't know if Margaux means being in our territory at Blacks or the fact that the four of us are about to break bread together after aggressively avoiding each other for almost half a century.

She leans in toward Nicola, eager to see what may happen next, but Tamsin is avoiding making any eye contact with our maker. Can't say I blame her. The energy in the room feels mercurial, like anything could happen. When I start to bite my thumbnail, Nicola clears her throat. She knows I'm having trouble playing it cool.

"Thank you for coming," Nic begins, signaling this was her doing. "I know you must have been a bit rattled to hear from me personally, but Amber and I are embarking on a rather large project together. Huge, really, and while we likely *could* do it alone, I wonder if there's an opportunity to mend some wounds between us *and* sweeten our respective pots of pounds. For the good of the project in question."

Some relief.

This is about the club.

But why would Nicola want to get them involved anyway? Does she know I went to see them? No. It's impossible. We would have sensed her, especially between Tamsin and me.

Tamsin keeps her eye on the exit, tapping her toe in time to a souped-up version of Depeche Mode blaring in the other room. Who knew she had any rhythm? But also, we both need to chill out. I get it, babe. You don't wanna be here. *Me neither.*

"Amber and I are opening a nightclub," Nicola declares, cutting to the chase. Margaux tries not to react, pressing her lips together, but Tamsin sits up straighter, alarm bells going off as she tries to make eye contact with Margaux. "And we want you to buy in. Forty-nine to our fifty-one. *Silent* partners, to be clear, but if you were interested in participating on a larger scale, it's something we could discuss. Over time. As we build some trust."

"Silent partners?" Margaux raises an eyebrow. "Nicola Claughton. Lady of the manor. Are *you* asking *me* for money?"

"It's an *investment*, Margaux," Nicola says with a cluck of her tongue. "Not a loan. But this isn't just about money. I've been considering that perhaps the alliance you once suggested could be wise at this time."

A silence falls between them.

Nicola's officially extending an olive branch back to Margaux after all these years.

But why would she do that when Margaux took Tamsin away from her?

"*Fantastique!* Then let's hear the pitch," Margaux responds, eyes shifting to me. I look away instantly, scared to blow my cover from the other night. Would Margaux say anything about my visit to their flat? Not if she offered me an escape hatch, too.

This behavior feels so uncharacteristic of Nicola that it makes me wonder if her intentions could possibly be . . . good? The nightclub. New "friends"? Is she doing this for my benefit?

Does she know I want to leave?

As Nicola waxes on to Margaux about opportunity and skin in the game and power in numbers and a funnel of cash and corpses for as long as the business flourishes, I keep my eyes on Tamsin. Margaux nods along, actively listening and clearly intrigued at the perceived clean slate presented, but Tamsin's attention remains on the floor. Like she'd rather be anywhere else, but it's not up to her. She traded one tyrant for another, just with a French accent.

Whatever happens tonight, no matter Nicola's intentions, I'm not going to end up like Tamsin.

The fireplace cracks loudly, but none of us jump. It's hard to startle a vampire.

"Have you spoken to Pierce about this business endeavor, at least where territory agreements are concerned?" Margaux asks Nicola, knocking my startle theory right out the window. My cheeks fill with air and I let it hiss out quietly, waiting for what Nicola will say about that freak show. A very handsome freak show, but a freak show nonetheless—and one of us. Nicola looks down at her lap for a moment, almost submissively.

Even Tamsin is eager to see what Nicola has to say about this notorious vampire, her eyes showing their first sign of life all night.

When she raises her brows at me, smug and satisfied, I get it now.

Oh, sure, of course . . .

Pierce is the other one that got away.

Tamsin. Pierce. Nicola's sister.

And soon enough?

Me.

"No," Nicola says sternly, looking back up at them again. "This is only for us. It's none of his concern. Territory agreements are irrelevant as we won't be opening anywhere that's been claimed by them."

"He's added three more to his growing brethren recently," Margaux says. "Does that have anything to do with your proposition?"

Pierce already had four companions that I knew of, each more terrifyingly hot than the next. Those dudes roll deep and hunt widely, with a much larger territory in the city. Supposedly they keep a bunch of young women at their compound in Wapping. Like groupies who don't want to leave, not that they would be allowed to, but then again, that's hearsay.

None of us have ever been to their place.

At least I don't think so.

"Yes," Nicola answers Margaux. "I do believe banding together would decrease our vulnerability in some ways, not that we can ever completely let our guard down, hmm?"

Tamsin leans over to whisper in Margaux's ear, but we can all hear her.

"Never trust Nicola Claughton."

It lands like a goddamn brick through the window. Margaux bristles at Tamsin's behaving downright insubordinate, in front of others no less. And it's quite a loaded burn from a former companion, so much so that I can't even believe we're not storming out of the room together after hearing the barb.

Instead Nic audibly smirks, putting a hand on *my* shoulder.

"Amber, why don't you give us a minute?"

I beg your pardon? She's asking *me* to leave? Just when things are getting extra juicy around here? And I don't want to leave them alone. What will they talk about? What if they talk about me?

If Nicola finds out I even *thought* about leaving, much less talked to *them* about it, would she actually kill me like Tamsin said?

Nicola can feel my hesitation and starts to use her gentle tone of voice, reminding me of when we just started out together. "Not to worry, darling," she whispers with a small smile. "I only want to address some outstanding business from the past. It all predates you, and a resolution could come quicker with some privacy. That's all."

I'm not totally convinced, but before I can make my case for staying, Nicola flashes her fangs at me. And *there* she is.

"Bad blood takes time to heal," she hisses. "If at all."

Yeah, no shit.

I'm sure it's a power move—but also, I'm positive Nicola doesn't want me to know Tamsin was her companion.

We all have our secrets.

Are they going to come out?

I can't be sure, but I swear I see Margaux offer a small, moderately reassuring wink.

So I nod and get up from the table, not wanting to let on that I know anything about their history together. Feels like the safest move for now. What else can I do without looking suspicious?

Time to take a lap.

She has her plans.

I have mine.

Wandering around Blacks, I keep my eyes open for any inter-esting replacement prospects, looking into the tucked-away alcoves and sneaky hollows on each floor for getting into trouble. I notice a gaggle of girls making their way to the ladies' room, and one of them, a blonde with a black-netted fascinator on her head, looks over her shoulder at me. She waves, clearly mistaking me for someone else, but I'll take it as an invitation. Maybe Nicola has a thing for blondes. I mean, who doesn't? I gotta start somewhere.

Then I hear someone shout from across the room.

"Hey, it's you!"

When I turn around, I see the hot dancer guy from Raffles, this time with a giant camera in his hand. Did he have that before? He strides over to meet me, putting out his hand to shake like he didn't just suck face with me in public a few nights ago.

"I'm Roddy Bow," he says, finally leaning in to give me a kiss on each cheek, revealing what I'm pretty sure is a Geordie accent—the sexiest one in the UK, in my opinion.

"Roddy Bow? What kind of name is that?" I ask. He bursts out laughing, almost dropping his camera. "What?"

"Sounds a bit rank when *you* say it. *Rah-ty!*" He mocks me, so I push him playfully but keep my hand on his chest because it feels so good. Geordie boy works out.

"Excuse me, but my vowels are adorable. Don't be an ass."

"Apologies," he says, still laughing, now putting his hand over mine. He's so warm. "I do quite like your vowels. And you are?"

"Amber Wells."

"To answer your question, Amber, my legal first name is Roderick, but that's a bit ridiculous, isn't it?"

"That's Rod Stewart's real name," I inform him, a superfan since I was a young girl with a paper route, a wagon and a radio with a long antenna.

"I know." He winks at me. "This is embarrassing, but he's my namesake. Middle name and all. My nan's favorite."

"Rod's everybody's favorite," I assure him. "He's universally adored."

"Something to aspire to." He grins.

"What's with the camera?"

"I'm a photographer. Nightlife mostly. Fashion and music, too. Really anything interesting . . . or that pays well enough. It can be rough out here when you're still on the come-up."

He flips through a few photos on the camera screen to show me his stuff. He has a really good eye. These aren't just snapshots. They're art.

But sorry, cutie.

That's my cue to bounce.

Listen, if I was a regular woman with a regular life, I'd be on him like a bun on a brat. But I need to find a man ready to make some money moves, not indulge in an all-night fuckfest with some wayward artist, no matter how hot he is.

"Have a good night then." I start to walk away from him, focusing on the task at hand.

"Probably for the best!" he shouts. "Couldn't ask you out anyway."

I roll my head back around and he looks pretty pleased with himself to have my attention again.

"Why not?" I ask.

Roddy gets close to my face, but our lips don't touch. "I suspect

you're the kind of girl that can derail a guy from his best-laid plans.
I mean, look at you."

I scoff happily, taking the win. Who doesn't love a compliment
like that?

"What kind of plans are you making?"

"I'm moving to New York after the holidays. Ticketed and everything. New Year's Day. No one wants to fly with a hangover, but I
shall persevere for the cheaper fare and promise of fame and
fortune."

"In New York?" I ask, my interest fully piqued. I've never been
there, but it's a whole ocean away from London.

"Yeah. I want to be, like, the next Richard Avedon," he explains,
holding up his camera again. "Does that sound crazy?"

"I don't know who that is," I say honestly, giving Roddy another
once-over, not just taking in his attractiveness, but sizing up his
whole situation.

What do we have here?

A relatively broke artist.

A big dream.

And what appears to be a good heart, at least from my gut instinct, which, sure, could still be proven wrong.

But still, there's potential.

Maybe I've been thinking about this human accomplice piece of
the puzzle all wrong? Especially considering the human accomplice
at the Laurels I'm already acquainted with.

"You're going to have to show me his stuff sometime," I say.
"Then I'll tell you if you sound crazy or not."

You know, I've crossed paths with enough rich businessmen in
London. They always want a hot young thing. Check and check. But
the relationship isn't the goal at all for me, nor is a good feed. That's
not what I'm after now.

I'm in need of *service*.

Some loyalty.

A person I can trust to tend to the precious cargo when we make a run for it together, life and death on the line. The type of trust I can earn under the guise of love, playing the damsel in distress. It makes me think about sweet Jonathan at home and what Nicola always said about him along with the other housemen she's "hired" for the Laurels in her time. She looked for a decent man who was down on his luck to some extent, because all they wanted was to feel needed and necessary and loved.

Then they'll do anything you say.

So I guess I didn't really need a guy with money.

Come on, I could get my hands on some cash, right? I'm resourceful enough to figure that out. So maybe this *would* be worth exploring with Roddy.

I mean, he already had a plane ticket to New York.

Jesus, did *this* sound crazy?!

"But I'm not asking you out." Roddy shakes his head, looking down and laughing, knowing full well he's going to ask me out as I grab his phone from his pocket, putting my number in it. To really seal the deal, I delicately place a hand behind his head and give him a soft, slow kiss with a little bite on his lower lip to finish it off.

"So you say." I smile. "I'll let you get back to work."

Flawless execution.

A solid lead.

I wonder if I'd like New York as much as I love London.

When I go into the ladies' room, the girl with the fascinator is still in there with her friends. It's obvious they've been snorting coke, talking fast with dilated pupils, giggling about God knows what, but they're having fun. In *very* good spirits. And Blondie is the ringleader.

"Omigod," she says to me. "I totally thought you were my friend Alannah, but you're not. She got married, so we barely see her anymore, the *slag*. But doesn't she look *just like* Alannah?" Her friends all nod, making varied sounds of agreement, except for one.

"I dunno, babe. She kinda looks like *you*."

Does she? Maybe that's why I noticed her before? Yeah, I'm a vain little b, okay, fine, but that's what this is all about where Nic is concerned. Now, did I have anything else in common with this girl? We're about the same height. Same coloring. She smiles a lot. But get real, that can't be the *only* reason Nicola wanted me for a companion. Can this girl dance? Nicola loves a stellar dance partner.

But when I think of Tamsin, or Pierce, for that matter, the whole companion comparison theory throws me off, because what did *we* all have in common that attracted Nicola in the first place?

"You guys having a good time?" I ask the girl.

"Oh yeah!" She winks, patting the side of her nose. "Did you want—?"

"No, thanks." I shake my head, noting her friendliness and willingness to share illegal drugs with a stranger. Also probably something I would do, in theory. She shrugs off my rejection with a happy little giggle and the four of them stumble out of the room.

"Have a good night!" she calls out to me.

But I follow them.

They all head back upstairs, clomping in their heels to the main floor, the same one as the dining room. They perch in the common space, on an open love seat, bobbing their heads to the music. Roddy even takes their photo, which they happily pose for, in various mental states. Blondie's starting to look worse for wear, like she's really overdone it, flopping her head on the shoulder of one of her girl-friends, who immediately rolls her eyes.

She's a mess, but she's cute, isn't she? I mean, would Nicola find her interesting? I try to think back to when we met. I was the life of the party. Cocktail in hand. Making sure everyone was having fun, too. Yeah, I was a catch—young and hung and ready for action!

Also, easily taken for a ride . . .

In the corner of my eye, I see the dining room door swing open again. I freeze, as if caught in something, but Nicola nods at me with a big smile. What does she know? Did it go well? I *need* things to keep going well with her nightclub plans. Keep her distracted. I look back to the blonde girl before rejoining Nicola and the others, wondering what her name is.

I don't ask any questions when I sit back down next to Nicola, waiting for her to bite first. Tamsin looks to be on the verge of tears, not that she'd let them fall in front of us. I think it's a good sign.

"They're in!" Nicola announces proudly. "We're going to make a marvelous team. There's so much to do before opening night, but for now, let's celebrate our unprecedented partnership!"

The melodic tone of her voice suggests she doesn't know any-thing about my night in Chelsea. I don't think Margaux told her, but how can I get her to confirm it so I can calm down? Tamsin proba-bly didn't speak at all.

"When do you want to open?" I lock eyes with Nicola.

I need the timeline.

I need the pressure.

I can't let myself down.

"Do you really have to ask?" she laughs. "New Year's Eve, dar-ling. Always a special night for us."

Is Nicola actually doing something sweet for me?

She knows I love New Year's Eve, despite everything.

I can't resist a good party.

"Wonderful idea," Margaux says, but she's looking at me. "The past is the past. We begin anew, *oui*?"

I nod, a mutual understanding between us. Looks like my secret is safe for now. Tamsin gazes at the fireplace, forlorn and resigned to her fate. But when Nicola slaps her hands on the table as hard as she can, she demands all our attention.

"Well, I could eat!"

The four of us slink around a tucked-away alley near Blacks, seeking out someone who not only smells good but also has the bad luck of being alone tonight while we're on the prowl. Nicola and Margaux take the lead, walking in lockstep together, staying in front of Tamsin and me, when we happen upon Blondie from the bathroom. She's sitting on the ground with her legs straight out and her back leaned up against a brick wall, ditched by the rest of her friends.

"Hey," I say to her, wondering if Nicola will notice any resemblance between us, if she'll find anything intriguing about her at all. A little test. "Are you okay?" The girl's fascinator is in her hand now, along with her purse. She's been crying. Where the hell were her friends? Why was she all alone, drunk and on drugs, in a dark London alley?

"No." She shakes her head. "I'm *not* okay!"

Nicola looks at me, perplexed and almost disgusted, with one side of her nose curling up, not at all curious to get to know more about this train wreck. Fair enough, probably not the perfect fit. But now that I've made contact again, I don't want to leave her here without *any* help at all.

Something terrible could happen.

"Do you want me to grab you a taxi?" I ask her, looking through to the end of the alley. There's plenty. It would only take a second and we'd be back to our hunt. But the others surround us now as I help her up off the ground. I get a whiff of her as I pull her close, and she's *very* young. Maybe twenty-five or so, she smells incredible, like a guilty pleasure, Britney Spears's Fantasy mixed with Reddi-wip.

Nicola catches it, too.

She wraps an arm around the girl and moves her hair away from her neck, breathing her in. "Where's home, love?"

Wait. I've *never* seen Nicola do this to a woman before. Maybe there *is* something there. She does love to take someone under her wing. Someone in trouble. Wasn't this how she was with me the night we met? Minus the coke. Okay, but half a quaalude. Still, I wasn't being picked up off the floor. I had my wits about me. I can't say the same for this one.

"Dalston," the girl says.

"We're headed that way ourselves," Nic replies, lying through her teeth. We never step foot anywhere in East London. "Shall we all taxi together? I reckon we'll all fit!"

Nicola grins at Margaux and Tamsin.

Oh shit.

They want to eat her.

"What's your name?" Nic asks.

"Nicola!" I practically scold her, because why is she getting so personal with this girl if she just wants to kill her? It's sadistic. Nicola and I never hunt like this together. We don't do this to women. A bond we share. Our only moral code. But maybe this is some kind of show for Margaux and Tamsin, now that we're working together.

For me, too.

A warning of some kind.

Does she know I want to leave?

"Wait," the girl screeches. "*My* name is Nicola, too!"

"It is *not!*" Nicola launches into hysterics and everyone else joins in, except for me.

"It is! It is!" The other Nicola clumsily pulls out her ID from her bag. "See! Look!"

She holds it up to Nicola's face for her to examine. "That is mental!" Nicola exclaims, looking back at me. I wonder if she's changing her mind about killing the girl. "*My* name and she *resembles* you?"

"Maybe it's a sign," I say with a shrug, not knowing what Nicola will do next—the theme of the night. I can usually read her like a book, but that's because we're always alone. In the company of other women, vampire or otherwise?

Well, I'm learning that Nicola is a goddamn live wire.

"What a fun little find," Nicola says to me as she unhinges her jaw, releasing her fangs, and unceremoniously dives right into the girl's neck. Tamsin and Margaux quickly join in, ravenous. The girl screams, but music pulsates through the bustling streets of Soho at night.

No one can hear a thing.

No one looks out a window.

No one is down that particular alley at this late hour except for us.

And once I get involved, taking straight from the girl's thigh, ripping flesh apart right through her dress to find a vein, she's dead within seconds.

Four mouths to feed will do it.

Jonathan picks us up in the Rolls to return to the Laurels, and the Chelsea vampires head back to Sloane Square. I'm nauseous with guilt, the girl's blood sitting in my stomach, a bleak reminder of what we just did. Jonathan can tell something's up with me, his eyes sympathetic through the rearview mirror, glasses slightly crooked, resting on his nose.

We understand each other in some ways that no one else can.

I've never killed a girl before, but I couldn't stand there like some loser, pretending I wasn't a vicious beast like the rest of them. Though Nicola, Tamsin, and Margaux appeared turned on by her pain, it almost made me feel sick, like eating dessert when you're already too full.

But I did what I had to do.

Nicola would know something was off if I didn't follow her lead.

Does she know something's off?

"Why did you want to know her name first?" I ask Nicola. It seemed dark, even for her.

"I always ask when it's a lady." She smiles.

I look back out the window. So she's killed women before, just never in front of me, until tonight. I try to keep my conscience in check, as Nicola taught me to do. We *are* vampires; this is *what* we do. But I thought we had an unspoken agreement about it. Now that I know we don't, it'll be even more complicated finding someone to replace me.

I have to figure out what the difference is.

Between random conquest and potential companion.

Is there a difference?

I start to wonder if she ever thought about killing me before she convinced me to turn.

"We don't take any prisoners, do we?" Nicola grins.

Jonathan turns up the radio, just a touch, like he can't bear to listen to her anymore.

No prisoners?

Just Jonathan and me, I guess.

For now.

EIGHT

NICOLA

1979

The front gate of the Laurels creaked open as Amber and I exited the taxi idling in front. The intricate wrought iron at the entrance was both impressive and intimidating, massive in size. I watched Amber closely as we entered on foot, clocking the appropriate level of awe emanating from her. My ancestral home had long been a tool in closing the deal with a new companion. I rarely had the front gate opened at all, opting for the side door instead, allowing for more furtive comings and goings, but theatrics were key in this sort of proposal.

Jonathan was always on the clock whenever I needed him. As the houseman for the past ten years, he had earned my full trust and then some. I knew better than to fall in love, but it never hurt to have a bit of eye candy around either, if just temporarily until his body no longer called to me. More than that, I prioritized longevity in a houseman. I'd keep Jonathan until he ran himself into the ground and then, well, I'd make it quick.

But he knew his way around the Laurels, and how I expected things to be run, so once he recognized that I was at the front of the manor that night, he knew to *really* turn it up where greetings and salutations were concerned. Any guest of mine was a guest of honor at the Laurels, since I rarely had one at all, so Jonathan embraced the formalities, awaiting our presence at the double doors at the first sound of the gate.

"Welcome home, madam." He nodded at me, gloves on, tie affixed, always professional.

"Good evening, Jonathan. This is Mrs. Wells," I said. He offered her a gentle smile as he removed her coat. Amber scoffed at the introduction, but I could tell she secretly loved it.

"Jonathan, *please*, you can call me Amber."

Of course, Jonathan wouldn't dream of it, but he nodded in acknowledgment all the same. "Can I bring you anything, Mrs. Wells? Tea? Coffee? Biscuits?"

"Jesus, I am starving. Any little snickie-snackies you have around the house would be great."

"Right away, Mrs. Wells." Jonathan scurried away with a chuckle at her peculiar vernacular and we progressed further into the Laurels together.

"Am I crazy, or is your butler kind of a hunk?" Amber giggled. She should have seen him ten years ago! A bit drug addled and very broke, but still easy on the eyes, especially when I got him cleaned up and offered him the post of a lifetime.

Amber could not believe her eyes at the size and grandeur of the Laurels, the foyer extra inviting with a crystal chandelier the size of a Saint Bernard, candles flickering in the gold sconces and flowers in a grand vase on the round table in the center. Dahlias. Peonies. Ranunculus. All the showstoppers.

Just like her.

"Listen, I'm trying to play it cool here, but this house is outrageous!" Amber exclaimed, tracing a finger along the carved wood banister at the foot of the stairs. "Who else lives here?"

"Just me. And Jonathan, who keeps the manor in order. There are a few other staff during the day, gardeners, housekeepers, but that's under his discretion. I trust him implicitly. We know each other *intimately*." I was merely stating the facts, but Amber was so captivated by the upstairs/downstairs of it all that I added a little fuel to the fire to keep up her interest. "Anything you need, he can bring it to you here or find someone who can."

"Wow," Amber whispered. She was agog and I was completely chuffed by her reverence for the Laurels; it was always a thrill to show her off to someone new—my most prized possession.

"I cannot believe you live here all by yourself!" Amber's voice went up a full octave, still not over the manor, taking herself on a tour, cavorting about from room to room. A bit rude, actually, but I allowed it, tailing her around. "You know I heard you give the taxi driver the name for the address and he basically blew a gasket. I think he thought we were high-end call girls! How do you have all of this, Nicola? If you don't mind my asking."

She was so blunt, but pretty girls get away with far worse.

"It's the family home," I said, keeping it brief. She couldn't know *everything*. Nobody else would understand that. Not even Amber.

"And what kinda business was your family in?" Amber skipped through the hallway, enjoying herself thoroughly, examining the portraits on the wall.

"Oh, the Claughtons have long been lords of the land in this country. But this is boring, Amber, it's just money." I didn't like to talk about my family, or my finances, for that matter. It was private. And once we hit the 1930s, I couldn't really dole out the sole-survivor cholera story any longer. Since then, I'd explained that I was a "descendant"—I changed up my hair color often enough—and I'd inherited the home of my ancestors. End of story.

"Did it involve something illegal?" she asked, completely serious.

"No!" I exclaimed. "Amber, some people are—"

"But how does *one* woman live like this? I don't get it. Where is everybody?"

"I was born to it," I said with a crackle in my throat so she could pick up that I wanted to change the subject. She looked down at her feet, embarrassed by her impudence.

"Must be nice," she said, finally looking back at me.

"Yes. It is," I said, smiling warmly at her to ease the tension.

After all, I was willing to share it with her.

Amber continued to delight in the house, selecting the record of her choosing from my vast collection, stuffing her face with chocolate biscuits. "Will you see your family for Christmas?" she asked.

"No. It's a bit of a sore subject," I began strategically. "My family is no longer intact, so it's not a time of year that I necessarily revel in like most Brits."

Amber nodded in complete understanding. "I'm sorry. I shouldn't have said anything. If it makes you feel any better, this is my first Christmas away from home and I feel pretty weird about it, and this fight with Malcolm isn't helping. But being here with you is, of course!"

"What are you and Malcolm doing for the hols?"

"We're supposed to have his family over and I'm sure he'll want me to pretend like everything is just fine. They still don't seem that thrilled about me, so I planned on making a Bakewell tart. Apparently, it's my mother-in-law's favorite. Watch. She won't even touch it."

Even more reason for her to leave Malcolm. She didn't really have him. She didn't have his family. Or her own, for that matter. She would only have me.

"*Your* family isn't coming over?" I prodded, wanting to dig deeper into the holiday traditions, pressing into any wounds that might be extra sensitive around the festive season.

"Too expensive." She sighed. "Malcolm offered to pay for their flights, but my dad said no. Not surprising. And my mom would never come by herself. I'm not sure she'd want to, but my dad wouldn't let her, even if she did."

Even more excellent fodder for stoking the exit-strategy flames that night.

"I'm sorry to hear that."

"Oh, it's fine. It's not like I'm super close with them, but they're still, you know, like *Christmas* to me. We talked about going to Wisconsin next year. Malcolm and me. If I stay with him. I still don't know if I'm coming or going. Maybe this is all a sign that I need to rethink some stuff . . ." She trailed off, a lost soul that needed claiming.

"We'll figure it out together, babe," I said, giving her a full-body squeeze. It was remarkable how Amber could eat practically a whole tin of biscuits, drink two full pints and still look miraculously beautiful, even in that wild New Romantics getup of hers.

"Shit, Nicola! Have you had any?" Amber laughed, finally noticing the dwindling supply. "We've been gabbing away and I just keep piling it in. Trying to enjoy my youth because once thirty comes, the party is *over*. That's what my mom always says anyway. She doesn't eat. Kinda like you."

"Oh, I eat. Don't you worry about that." I laughed, bracing

myself for the proposition. Amber and I had properly bonded over the past month. I was confident. But this conversation always required careful deliberation before beginning in earnest. "I just don't care for chocolate."

"Why didn't you say anything to Jonathan?" Amber asked. "He can get you some plain ones."

My, my! How quickly she adapted to the finer things at the Laurels!

"Because I'm the hostess and you're my guest and I don't want any biscuits," I said.

"Just have the last one," she insisted.

"I said that I don't want it."

"But they're so good. You really don't want it?"

"Take the last biscuit, Amber," I commanded.

It was now or never.

I had to show her.

I *compelled* her to take the biscuit.

A point of no return.

I watched Amber attempt to work out what was happening, her eyes shifting madly, blinking rapidly. She wanted to fight it, but she could not, confounded by her body's disobeying her. Her posture stiffened. Her eyes grew larger; she was baffled by her own fingers' grasping the sweet treat. Even more bewildered when she took a bite. She chewed, slowly but surely. And when she began to swallow, it looked almost painful, anguish all over her face, the sound labored and loud.

I stopped.

That was enough.

Whatever bits were left in her mouth, Amber spat them out. She was hyperventilating, hands clasped over her chest. I had frightened her, but this part was always unavoidable. The trick was turning the fear into fascination and ultimately a fixation. An offer impossible to resist.

It was enticing for most, at least on the surface. There's often even some relief that there's still a bit of magic in the world. After being crushed about the nonexistence of Santa and the Easter Bunny and their ilk, a universe where vampires existed sounded rather enchanting.

Eternal youth? Eternal beauty? Eternal life?

What's not to like?

I knew that Amber was the type of woman who would be drawn to that magic, seeking a way out of a humdrum existence. She could be thrilled by the unexplained. She'd see it as an adventure. That's what she wanted, and I could give it to her.

"What. The hell. Just happened?" Amber trembled with fear, but I had to keep going. I didn't want to lose her forever. She would say yes. She *had* to say yes.

"Amber, I'm going to share a secret with you."

I compelled her to be still, in the event she tried to dash away before hearing my explanation, but I couldn't feel any resistance coming from her. She was too mesmerized by the sight of my mouth, fangs having just emerged for their first full appearance.

"You don't have to be frightened," I said. "I promise I'm not going to hurt you."

"I'm not scared," she lied, lips quivering. "What do I have to be scared about? This goofy Halloween costume of yours?"

Do it, Nicola.

Do it.

Now!

"Amber, I'm a vampire."

Our eyes connected. She couldn't look away. The record stopped.

ELO. *Face the Music.* It needed flipping.

"Why don't you go turn that over," I said to her. "And then I'll tell you everything. It may be a lifestyle you desire for yourself. Something I could give to you. Something very special."

H istorically, after I've revealed myself to be a vampire to a potential companion, the reaction went one of two ways. Endless screaming or hysterical laughter. Not surprisingly, Amber's reaction was the latter, which of course I preferred. Even in its higher pitch and unnatural staccato, it was still melodic to me. Her fear was exhilarating. The laughter matched that frenetic energy of the first track on the second side of the album playing. All of it was literal music to my ears. This was going to happen for us. The intrigue would be too much to bear. The unknown had to be explored. She couldn't say no.

"You've lost your goddamn mind." Amber kept on laughing, avoiding eye contact with me. "You've been living alone for too long, Nicola. This is absolutely insane!"

"I'm telling you the truth, darling. I know it's quite a thing to wrap your head around, but—"

"I think I should get going," she said. Of course that was her instinct. Still, she didn't move. And she could have if she wanted to . . . at least for the moment.

"Oh, don't leave," I pleaded, even though I knew she wasn't going anywhere. I'd make sure of that.

"You know what, Nicola?" Amber let out a full-on cackle this time, tinged with darkness. I adored seeing that side of her. She could become more like me if she wanted to be. Then we'd really get up to some mischief together. "*Prove it.*"

Her voice deepened. She was cross, losing her patience with me, so even though I didn't want to frighten her any further, it was the only way.

I did what she asked.

Within seconds I had Amber pinned to the ground, illustrating my point with enhanced strength and speed. It was slight—we're not superheroes, but there was a competitive advantage that could not go unnoticed.

Amber turned her face away from mine, my sharp ivories at attention, hovering just above her neck. Not now, I admonished myself. Not *yet*. Because I needed *her* to make the decision. I didn't want a prisoner for a companion. Never again. No. I craved loyalty. I wanted her to choose me, but still, the pure ecstasy of having her in my clutches was beyond temptation.

God, I really was a saint sometimes.

Amber was rendered speechless but turned her head back to face me, our mouths so close we could feel each other's breath, one beat off from one another, our cumulative sounds quick and urgent.

"Are you going to kill me?" she asked.

"Never," I replied, hoping I could keep such a promise.

Track two began and I remembered how that record skipped right at those fanciful familiar notes. Not at the opening orchestral part that most people forget about. But after. At the perceived beginning. Those eight counts. Over and over. The notes where everyone finally recognizes the song.

"Strange Magic" in a strange loop.

"I love this song," Amber whispered.

"Me, too," I whispered back, releasing her, helping her up off the ground.

We stared at each other while the song kept skipping and skipping.

Until finally it found its groove.

Amber found her footing as well, running as fast as she could, back to the foyer and straight out the double front door.

At least she didn't go darting and screaming down the street, waking the neighbors.

I didn't worry.

She'd find her way home.

Jonathan watched her flee. "Do you reckon she'll return, madam?"

I nodded at him confidently. Of course, I could sense she was going to run, but I decided to let her go. I had learned a lot in my very long life. Sometimes a woman just needs a little time.

I focused productively on my rage, instead of indulging in it. My instincts were to chase after Amber, to harm her, but I imagined the scene dissipating before my eyes, like rose petals falling off the bud, floating slowly down from side to side.

Calm yourself, Nicola.

Amber would be worth the wait.

I'd give her until New Year's Eve.

She had to choose me.

And if she didn't, what of it?

I'd still have her anyway, an appealing alternative.

Bon appétit.

NINE

AMBER

Roddy invited me to an opening at one of the Gagosian galleries tonight, which seems promising when I think about his potential to help me. I don't want to get carried away too soon, but I have a good feeling about it. I can get everything lined up in the next, oh, eight weeks or so, right? The pressure cooker is *on*.

I even invite Nicola along for the ride tonight, knowing she'll have no interest whatsoever, and when I bring it up to her, as a place to get a little nightclub decor inspiration and to respectfully keep her in the loop, she turns up her nose at me as predicted.

That's my girl.

Nic's not a fan of modern art, which is obvious when you see what's hanging around the Laurels. Creepy portraits from another time. Dark, sweeping landscapes. Lots of dogs and horses, too. She *is* British. All of them, though, are as old as the hills. She doesn't seem to care about any kind of public art appreciation at all. I can't even get her to go to the West End with me, and who gets so offended by, like, *Les Mis*, or a bit of Bob Fosse? Like, okay, you're too good for jazz hands? Fine.

"Pass," she puffs at me. "But don't be long. We have a lot of work to do."

"I'll be a couple hours max."

Just enough time to get my hooks a little deeper into Roddy and see if he's man enough to be my knight in vintage oxfords.

Roddy waits for me outside the venue looking like a total rock star plus art aficionado plus generous lover. I'm *sure* of it—and hope to find out firsthand soon enough. A perk of the job . . . if I'm able to hire him. His five-o'clock shadow really flatters him, I don't mind a little scratch, and he wears shiny black shoes and a tastefully rumpled collared shirt with enough buttons undone to show off some of that hubba-hubba hair on his chest. But the real cherry on top is his square eyeglasses. A pleasant surprise, maybe just for fashion's sake, but he really looks the part and I appreciate the effort for our first date.

"There she is." He grins, taking my hand and kissing it. I laugh out loud. "Too cheesy?"

Not from him! By all means, babe, put your mouth anywhere you damn well please. I'm available.

"So, what are we seeing tonight?" I ask.

"One of the very best." Roddy's eyes widen as he takes my hand, leading me into the packed gallery of people equal parts cool and pretentious. I love an eclectic scene, especially one with a little soft Jefferson Starship in the background. Will Roddy make me believe in miracles? Time will tell.

We're at a Richard Avedon retrospective, the guy he mentioned at Blacks. One of his idols and his inspiration for moving to New York. I might have heard of him in passing, but I'm more familiar with his celebrity subjects, not that I'm paying much attention to that.

I'm paying attention to Roddy.

He's *really* into this whole thing. He cares about his work, about others' work, very enthusiastic about all of it, pointing out his favorites to me, making sure I don't miss anything.

This here is a grown man who gives a shit.

A very promising trait.

Time to turn it up a notch.

"So are your glasses for real or for show?" I tease him, taking them off his face and putting them on mine.

"Cute." He chuckles, because duh, I am. "A little of both, I'd say. Normally I wear contacts, but the frames felt appropriate for the occasion. I think I look rather chic, but really I'm just trying to impress you, Amber. I do hope it's working."

"It certainly is," I say, moving the glasses up and down from the temple tip, matching his cheesy yet sweet flirting style. I pop them back on his gorgeous face. "So what do you like about this guy?"

Let's hear more about what makes Roddy tick . . .

"Just about everything. Even though much of his work is posed instead of candid, he captures this vulnerability that's so authentic and fully realized and *feels* candid. And that counts for everyone. Not just the real people, but the models and celebrities, too. I admire it."

We stop at a photograph of a woman holding a cigarette, wrapped up in a sheet. Richard Avedon's wife Evelyn, Roddy tells me.

"Avedon puts himself in the work, even the ones when he's not the subject. It's not some simple thing, but I think most people think photography's easy. Everyone with an iPhone thinks they can do it. But tell me your dad could snap a photo like that of your mum on a family vacation. It's just not possible, is it?"

Evelyn is obviously not staring at the lens in the photo, but at her husband. It's intimate and sexy. I see what Roddy means. It's not just her. It's both of them.

"I can't imagine my dad taking a picture of my mom, period," I say, testing his empathy for family strife. Roddy takes my hand and squeezes it, carrying on through the crowd. "And I don't think photography is simple, for what it's worth. Almost nothing is, though, especially these days."

I'll stroke his ego to get what I need, but also, I think he's probably right.

"I know what you mean," Roddy says. "I'm nostalgic for the past all the time, especially London in, like, the '60s and '70s, which I know I wasn't alive for, but come on, it was so cool. You can see it in all the photography. And there's something about all this *shit* today—social media, going digital, constantly being sold a product—that really turns me off. Everyone and everything looks exactly the same. Sometimes it feels pointless trying to make it, as an artist I mean, if that's what everyone wants. But I promised myself I'd make a go of it in New York, at least once. I could always come home if it doesn't work out. That's what my nan said when I left Newcastle and came to London. I think it applies across the board."

That's one of the sweetest things I've ever heard.

I wish one of my parents said something like that to me.

It's also adorable to hear him nostalgic for a time he didn't experience. I bet a lot of people his age feel the same. The before and after so stark, especially once the internet came around.

Maybe I can use this . . .

"That's why I like my job in nightlife, taking photos, trying to capture the eccentric or left of center. Anything retro feeling or with character or some semblance of a soul," Roddy says, pointing at another photograph, this one of a man with unsettling eyes and a penetrating stare.

"He might not be the best example then." I smile, noting the caption.

Dick Hickock, Murderer, Garden City, Kansas.

But Roddy shrugs. "Souls can be good or bad. Usually both. I'm not all that interested in capturing only the purest of hearts. It's a photograph. Not necessarily an endorsement."

"Do you think good people can do bad things?" I ask him.

"All the time, darling. All the time."

As we finish up in the gallery, after having long conversations about art and music and life that I've never really had with anyone before, I know how to really kick the plan into motion.

Roddy has a general unease about his finances, so he could use a break.

He wants to make his mark as an artist, a romantic notion if I ever heard one.

And I know he would love nothing more than to fall in love with a soulful girl.

Not that he outright said it, but with men, love is always about action. His hand was at the small of my back all night, ensuring no one ever bumped into me. He asked if I needed a refreshment not once, not twice, but three times—spread out appropriately so as not to be annoying. And he hung on my every word and responded specifically to everything I said to illustrate he had been listening carefully.

Of course I could tell he wanted to sleep with me, too, but you can't fake chemistry.

Well, I can, but from him?

It's genuine.

He even *said* we're both old souls, and hey, he's not wrong, but I know what he means. He recognizes a part of me in him. Not altogether surprising. It appears we both have adventurous spirits and an appreciation for the good stuff in life. Great work, Amber. I know what I need to do next to keep him close, but I have to be *very* careful since it requires some unexpected double-dipping.

But the plot twist will be too juicy for him to pass up.

It certainly is for me.

I'll make sure it is for Nicola, too.

As Roddy and I walk toward Hyde Park for a leisurely nighttime stroll, I ease into the conversation. "Where are your favorite clubs to work?" I ask.

"Raffles when I need a bigger paycheck, even if the crowd is a little much. Blacks is great for some of the bolder images," he says. "Shoreditch House, too. The beautiful people are often there. And then there's this great one with just the best dancing and DJs, in my opinion. It's in an old town house. 25 Paul Street. But yeah, I prefer the vibe of East generally. I live over there. In Shoreditch."

East. Where the young people are. The real young people.

Someone Nicola could take an interest in . . .

"Ever spend any time over there?" he asks.

"Not really, but that's why I was asking about your faves. My cousin and I are opening a nightclub," I say. "Like how they used to be. No phones. Very disco. Everyone has to dress up. A judgy doorman. All that good stuff."

"Really?" Roddy jerks his head back a little bit, impressed. "How are you managing that?"

"It's something we've always wanted to do, so we're pulling the trigger. And I know you're on your way to New York and I don't want to derail your plans, but I thought maybe we could hire you to take photos of the process, at least until you left? We could really use someone with your eye. Plus, I think it could make for a good art book or exhibition down the line. Two young women starting a business in the male-driven world of London nightlife? It's a win-win. Also, my cousin and I are obsessed with each other, so a few personal shots would also be appreciated. I'm sure you can deliver." I wink at him, seeing him light up as I compliment his skills.

"Interesting . . . What were you two doing before?" he asks. Fair question, and I love lying about jobs when I meet a guy. I just filter through all the things I thought about becoming when I was a little girl. Dolphin trainer. Fashion designer. Radio City Rockette. It never mattered because it's not like they were going to fact-check anything after I ate them.

But with Roddy, I need to tell him something he wants to hear so he'll stay on the line.

"This might be too direct," I say, getting closer to his ear, "but we have some family money. Since school finished up, we've been thinking about what kind of business we'd like to start. A nightclub was the obvious choice for us. We love to dance, as you know."

But when Roddy almost looks disappointed in me, I worry I've made a mistake.

He's a man of the people. He works for a living. He's a starving artist.

And yes, I *get* it, my dude, but this is how you get the bag. Money talks! Get involved!

But now to appeal to his artistic side, his ache to be seen, to be needed.

"So yeah, my cousin and I have the money, but we're still obviously, you know, *amateurs*, and since you're so tuned in to the scene, professionally, it would be a huge help to have you involved because we really need to make it a stunning success. There's a lot riding on this for us. Image is everything, not that I need to tell you that. And after tonight, getting to know you better and what's important to you, artistically, well, I'm not lying when I say that we need your help. We'd be stupid not to have you on board."

"When does it open?" he asks, a smile sweeping across his face.

Yes! We have a live one!

"It's ambitious," I say, "but we're aiming for New Year's Eve."

"Will Daddy kill you if it flops?" he teases me, but it's not that far from the truth, since Nicola is basically my "Daddy" now. *Jesus.* I need to get my story straight if everyone's going to be mingling for the next couple of months. And I can't just compel Roddy when I'm playing the long game with him. That's only for a quick solution for a little snack or stealthy escape, depending on the situation.

That type of influence wears off over time with the same person.

It could chase someone away once they remember.

So how to best explain Nicola without losing him . . .

"Not exactly. My mom's been on the outs from the family for a long time. I'm the black-sheep cousin, if it makes you feel any better," I say, weaving my tall tale, though Nicola and I have used the cousin schtick before in mixed company. "Our mothers went their separate ways, hence my vowels from my father and growing up in America. I came here for high school. They wanted to get me in line; I was kind of a handful. Then I took up with Nicola when I got here and, well, turns out we're both trouble." I grin, sticking the landing.

"So you're a rebel!" He grins. "Do you miss home?"

"Sometimes," I whisper, planting the seed in his mind now.

Take me back, baby. USA! USA! USA!

"All right, let me think about it." He smiles, pretending to play it cool. "Why are you offering this to me?"

"Because you're good and we need you, Roddy. Honestly." I squeeze his hand. "*And* I'm starting to really like you."

God, I kind of was really starting to like him, but that's not the point.

It's never going to be the point.

Roddy blushes, right on cue. "Did you always want to be a night-club proprietress when you were growing up?"

"Not exactly. Don't laugh," I say, twirling in front of him, taking both of his hands so he'll stare into my eyes.

"I would *never* laugh at someone's dream," he declares most seriously.

I believe him.

We're in front of the fountain called the *Joy of Life*, near the east entrance to Hyde Park. Two bronze figures dance in the center, all lit up, and Roddy mimics the pose, expecting me to join, so I do, raising my arm above my head and popping up my leg against his. His timing is impeccable.

"Believe it or not, I wanted to be a professional dancer," I say, thinking it sounds so insane now, but it felt within reach way back when.

"Amber! What are you on about? There's still time!"

"I don't think I was good enough to make it."

But did I even give myself enough of a chance to try? One failed audition and I went running off with Malcolm. But I don't like to think about those forks in the road of my previous life. What for?

"I find that very hard to believe based on your performance at Raffles the other night. I reckon you need to get back on the audition circuit tout suite, madam."

I can't help it, but I tear up at the thought, letting them fall because men can't resist trying to help a crying woman. Of course I should have kept going back then, but now? It feels ridiculous to think about. Auditions and rehearsals. Often *daytime* activities.

Roddy instantly apologizes for making me cry, for making it sound so simple, which makes me feel even worse. If I was who he thinks I am, it could be that simple. Open calls. Taking classes. Commitment to my craft. In another life, it's what I might have been doing. I'm sure I would have found my way back, with or without Malcolm.

I just happened to meet Nicola first.

Maybe in New York, I could dip my toe back in somehow.

Something to dream about when I finally get to the other side with Roddy's help.

"And where did *you* learn to dance like that?" I ask, turning the conversation back to him, lightening it back up. Crying in front of a guy is tricky business. You want him to comfort you but not get so upset that he thinks you want to be alone.

Roddy sweetly wipes the tears from my face. "My nan made sure of it. I was a handful, too, as you say. So to keep me out of trouble up in Newcastle, she had me take ballroom and salsa and disco with Miss Julie," he explains with a laugh, lifting his arm up, gently pushing me through in a twirl, and then back to a firm hold. "And I always pretended like it was a punishment, but I fucking loved it. Still do. Not that I told the lads back then. Joke's on them, though. You can *always* get a pretty girl on your arm when you're a good dancer." He dips me with some major drama, confirming his thesis.

And at that, we say good night with our tongues for a good twenty minutes or so, getting hot and heavy in the park before I break it off to go home. Leaving a man with blue balls is always a power move this early on in the game, but I think sleeping with him soon will only help my case.

He knows I need him.

He knows I like him.

And he needs a job. A hit. A big break.

We're gonna get to New York together.

I can *feel* it.

B ack at the Laurels, I take a closer look at the art hanging down my hallway before going to my bedroom. What can I say? I left the night feeling inspired, not to mention sneakier than ever. With the Roddy piece of the plan coming together, I still need to uncover more about Nicola's previous companions, especially her sister, so I can find my replacement and get the hell out of here.

What haven't I noticed before that could have been right in front of my face this whole time?

I stop at a familiar portrait of a couple. Nicola's never admitted to me that they're her parents, nor have I asked, but she resembles the man pictured, so I'm certain it's them. Neither is smiling. Stiff, with hard faces. The man's hand rests on top of the woman's. Mild affection. Probably instructed by the artist. I can't imagine this couple ever touched genitals for recreational purposes. Procreation only. The "close your eyes and think of England" types.

"Toot-toot!" Nicola shouts from down the hall, surprising me, flicking the light switch on and off. "Are you getting excited, darling? I've got a great location for us to look at tomorrow night. I think it could be the one!"

"Beep-beep!" I shout back at her with a nod. "Where is it?"

"You'll see."

She grins at me and turns the light off, leaving me alone in the dark.

In bed for rest, I take a few minutes to scroll through the Instagram and TikTok mentions for the clubs Roddy talked about in East—Shoreditch House and 25 Paul Street—scoping out all the girlies. It's a far cry from the crowds at Tramp and Annabel's, even Blacks. A little grittier, but very trendy. They don't scream cash; they scream cool.

I see some of these gals on repeat. Fixtures. Regulars. The party girls of today, typically pictured in a group. They all make me smile, like we'd be great friends; I check their profiles if they're tagged. They post photos of families, friends from work or childhood, pets, all showing off their full lives in addition to their night lives. A lens into the world of a young Londoner, just doing their best to make their way in the city while still having a good time.

But one of them who keeps showing up is always by herself.

Just dancing to the music solo.

She's *fantastic.*

She's never in a photo with others, not even a group selfie. Someone else is always taking a video or a picture of her. Probably photographers like Roddy. The camera loves her. But she's never tagged on social media. Never mentioned by name. She's a confident dancer, but possibly not confident about anything else.

I'd know that look in her eyes anywhere.

The kind that screams she's hoping she'll be saved before she's gotta buckle down and figure it all out for herself.

I cross-check the dates on the posts.

She loves a late Saturday night at 25 Paul Street.

Might be time for a little market research.

TEN

NICOLA

1979

The phone rang on the evening of Christmas Day. I knew it was Amber. There was no one else who'd be concerned with my whereabouts on such a remarkable day. Or any day. As predicted, she came crawling back after spending what was likely a dreary holiday with her husband. I let it ring just long enough to make her panic a bit.

"Hello?" I answered brightly.

"Merry Christmas, Nicola." Amber's voice sounded tinny, slightly pained.

"Happy Christmas, darling. Are you okay?"

"Not really." She sniffed. "My family didn't send me anything for Christmas. My own mother. Not even a card? When I called her today, they were on their way out to go to church in the morning and she said she'd call me back, but she never did. I barely got to say hi to my sister."

Splendid. The less contact she had with them, especially the little sister, would be best. Oh, the holidays. A magical time of year when everyone is super sensitive about absolutely everything. Anything could be perceived as a slight. This was always an ideal season to take in someone new.

"I'm sure your mum didn't mean anything negative by it," I said. "She knows you're married now, her little girl's all grown up, and you know it can be expensive to send gifts in the post. What did you get from Malcolm? Something sparkly, I imagine, after his gruesome behavior."

"Did you hear me, Nicola? I said not even a card! From my *mother!*"

I let the silence take over for a few seconds so she would get to the real point of her call. I knew she missed me. It had been days since we'd seen each other last and we hadn't spoken on the phone at all. I didn't want her to be frightened of me, so I had to proceed with caution, waiting for her to return to me. A Christmas greeting was a fantastic place to resume negotiations.

"I've been thinking about you," Amber finally said, sighing. "And I'm sorry I ran out of the house the other night after you told me such a big secret, but I was really caught off guard. I'm not sure how to say this. I know what I saw and I know what you told me, but it's unbelievable, isn't it?"

"You're *very* fast." I chuckled. "It's all right. I really did not want to frighten you, Amber, but there's no perfect way to say it. I so rarely share it with anyone at all. Very few can understand, but I'm confident that you can."

Make her feel special. Make her feel wanted.

"Would you like to go for a bit of shopping tomorrow evening?" I suggested. "We can purchase our own presents. All the Boxing Day sales will be on."

Amber let a few seconds pass before answering, but I knew she'd come around.

"That sounds nice," Amber said. "Very nice, actually."

"Fabulous. Let's meet in fragrance at Liberty tomorrow evening at half five."

L iberty had long been a favorite of mine for purchasing the latest and greatest fashions from up-and-coming designers or when I wanted to add to my ever-growing makeup collection or indulge in yet another bottle of intoxicating perfume. The massive Tudor Revival building was constructed in the '20s, though its history went back even further, to Regent Street. Now it was the marvel on Great Marlborough, luring in the stylish sort who sought something unique and different from the rest of the department stores and high-street shops. I could spend hours in Liberty, roaming from floor to floor, particularly in the winter, when the nights were much longer.

In fragrance, my personal favorite, I spritzed a bit of the new Guerlain on my wrist and gave it a whiff, as if to test it with my body chemistry. But perfume smelled exactly like it did in its vessel as it did on my body, nothing human to interact with anymore.

Rose, peach, bergamot.

A little bright for my taste.

"Let me try."

I looked up to see a trepidatious Amber just behind me. She was dressed in a matching baby-blue skirt set with white tights and block heels. Pretty as a picture. She'd even donned a little hat, her hair hanging down past her shoulders, wild waves briefly tamed for the festive occasion.

She rolled up a sleeve, just an inch, and I took her little wrist in my hand, giving it a spray. I held her up to my nose and noticed how different the concoction smelled now. The rose sprang forward while the peach faded away, Amber's natural musk clinging to the bergamot, fighting the rose for center stage, but not quite succeeding. The complexity of the perfume had been given its due. She pulled away from me to see for herself but immediately turned up her nose.

"Not for me," she said, pivoting to Penhaligon's, using the sample papers instead of her skin. She waved one in my face. "Does this smell like an old lady?"

"Let's go to cosmetics," I said, linking my arm through hers, which she allowed. Neither one of us had addressed the real issue at hand yet, but shopping was such neutral ground for two women. She was at ease, generally, in a place she found so comfortable.

I picked up a dark red YSL lipstick and touched the tip with my finger, applying it softly to my lips in the counter mirror.

"You can see yourself?" she asked, watching my reflection.

"Yes." I popped my lips together. "What do you think?"

She nodded in approval. "It looks great on you. Too dark for me. What about garlic? And crosses?"

I laughed. "You go to church?" I raised an eyebrow, handing her a softer pink sample to try.

"Not really," she admitted, giving the color I selected a whirl. Of course it looked sensational.

"Well, you'd still have the option should a pious mood strike. Don't believe the rumors," I said. "That looks good. You should buy it."

She shrugged and put the lipstick back. "What about stakes to the heart?" she inquired further, looking for excuses to say no.

"Untrue," I said. "Nothing can really kill a vampire, except for the sun, and in some respects, starvation—leading to massive vulnerability in the wrong hands—but you'd never have to worry about the latter in a city like this. Even so, a starving vampire *can* be revived. The sun, though . . . well, come now, you won't even miss it. You hardly see it in London as it is. And the nightlife is where all the fun is anyhow."

I needed to provide excuses for her to say yes.

"Now, let's go upstairs," I said. "Where the real goodies are."

The women's wear floor at Liberty was immaculate. Everything chic and modern. New trends expertly displayed alongside the enduring classics. It's a fashion-forward woman's dream scenario, except for the price tags. No sales to be had here, but that was part of the fun, especially as a vampire.

Most of us had money.

All of us had powers of persuasion.

Amber made a beeline for a pink-sequined dress on a featured mannequin across from us on the other side of the banisters. It looked as if it had been created specifically for her. I followed, delighting in the sounds of her enthusiasm, the spectacle of a happy girl oohing and aahing over a luxurious piece to covet.

"This is *gorgeous*, isn't it?" She grinned at me, pulling out one of the sleeves, caressing it all the way down with her fingertips. What all women do when we love a garment and just want to see how it feels in our hands, price irrelevant, a purely sensual delight.

But of course, she stops at the tag, flipping it over just in case.

"Well, shit!" She laughed. "Some Boxing Day sale."

"It's perfect for New Year's Eve," I encouraged her. "Go on. You have the means."

"I have Malcolm's *means*," she clarified.

"What's his is yours, no?"

She nodded with pursed lips, still tugging at the sequined sleeve longingly. "It's just a hard number for me to wrap my head around. I don't know. I know he has it, *we* have it, but I grew up pulling from the sales racks and thrift shops, Nic. I'm not the kind of woman who just ups and *buys* this kinda thing!"

"Not yet," I said with a wink, motioning for the shopgirl coming our way. When she was close enough, I locked into her quickly, watching as a tranquil sort of stare washed across her face. "Actually, this gown *is* discounted, isn't it?"

The shopgirl slowly began to nod at me without saying another word.

"Nicola," Amber said, almost as if she was scolding me, but I shrugged with a cheeky smile. Let's have a bit of fun, my girl. This is how it could be all the time.

"Fifty percent off?" I gasped at the shopgirl, still lingering at my doing. "Is that true?"

She nodded again.

"We'll take it," I said. We watched as she disrobed the mannequin and followed her to the cash wrap to ring us up. Amber was mystified. "Nicola, I didn't even try it on. I don't think that's—"

"Nonsense," I said, removing a stack of cash from my pocketbook, making sure she saw how thick it was. "My treat then. It's going to look stunning on you, we both know that."

She gazed at the money in my hand and then again at me.

"Thank you, Nicola," Amber said.

We decided to walk back to Belgravia together, equipped with multiple shopping bags each. A very successful night; we had stayed out until closing time. A completely quotidian activity that any pair of girlfriends would do—it was important to present what wouldn't change as well. It was a lovely evening outside, not too cold, with all the festive lights still ablaze around the city. London always twinkled for all of December and into January.

I told Amber everything she needed to hear. I knew what she desired. To get out of her marriage and into the world again, but with even more promise of the extraordinary. She craved a life of adventure and spontaneity and limitless possibilities. She wanted to be beautiful forever. Who wouldn't? The world was ours if she'd take it with me.

"What about the blood?" she finally inquired. I had felt it bubbling inside her all night. Of course this was going to come up. The process of turning. The fuel we needed to live. And the reality of the night. The endless night in the life of a vampire.

How could I position all of it in a way that would appeal to her? She had a light spirit, so different from mine, but the light always needed the dark. They've always needed each other. And we would bring out the best in one another. Of that I was certain.

"Let's put it this way. How often do you think about food on any given day?" I asked.

"All of the time," she said begrudgingly. "I try not to, especially around the holidays, but what woman doesn't? And it'll only get worse. Something to look forward to."

"But that all goes away," I explained, dangling the proverbial carrot. "The stress, the dieting, the gain or loss. Aging of the face. Sore knees. Thinning hair. You never have to worry about any of it. You'd remain just as you are right now. Twenty-three years of age. Forever. A small price to pay for a bit of blood, no?"

"Does it taste good?" Amber bit her lip. What to say? I did not want to sound too macabre, as that would be off-putting to a girl like her. Of course it's delicious and I craved it when the time came to hunt, at least every two days, but it *was* more biological than anything else.

"It's satisfying," I said, "but hardly the main event of eternal life. Think about it, Amber. We could go out dancing every single night, young and beautiful and free forever, in the most fabulous city in the world. What would you be leaving behind? *Really?*"

I didn't say it aloud, but I knew that Amber, deep down, still simply wanted someone to take care of her. That's why she married Malcolm after being unappreciated at home for her efforts with her real family. That's why she'd set her sights on another man of means one day, if she got the courage to leave Malcolm of her own accord, which felt unlikely. Her fate seemed inevitable if she carried on as is. She didn't know how to be anyone else yet. She was a young woman of her time, like we all were once.

Maybe she would learn how to be stronger one day, in theory and *if* I let her go, which I wasn't planning on, but I really thought I'd be rescuing her, too. Not only from the monotony of the life of a human woman, but also from all the pain and suffering that came along with it. Vampires didn't have to play by any societal rules or adhere to gender norms, no matter the year, never beholden to the glacial pace of progress.

She didn't need a man. She only needed me. She didn't yet know that all of them would be dull like Malcolm, or, far worse, like our fathers, or the type to string a woman along for years, ultimately reaping no benefit at all when they decided to leave and break your heart. That was the reality of the world we lived in—and really, it wasn't *just* men, was it? It was everyone. Women could be just as dreadful, but I believed Amber to be a kindred spirit.

She would never betray me.

So yes, she'd be much better off in my careful hands. It would be so easy to take care of her. We'd have a life of absolute leisure and laughter together. Just us two. Bashing and dashing around London for all time. I mean, really, how could she deny it? How could she deny me?

"Do I have to decide right now?" she asked me as we approached Malcolm's front door. Number 114. Amber briefly looked left, then right. All the town houses on the row had identical exteriors, connected to one another, with black iron terraces that overlooked the private garden in the center of the road, marked for resident key holders only. The bone-white columns were painted perfectly, with the individual house numbers in black, flanking the steps to the entrances. It was grand, but it was nothing like the Laurels.

"No." I shook my head. "Take all the time you need, darling. Would you like to see anything . . . again?" I started to ascend the steps behind her. "If you invite me, I could come inside and show you how if Malcolm is home—"

"No!" she cut me off, turning around to face me, eyes fearful. "I don't want to involve him. At all. Ever. Please."

"As you wish." I smiled, albeit perturbed she still had shreds of loyalty for this man.

"Do you need to be invited?" She raised an eyebrow at me.

"Yes," I admitted. That part of the lore was true. "To enter a place I haven't been before, I need to be invited by someone inside. The owner. A guest. Or the doorman, for example. And the invitation remains unless explicitly withdrawn once you leave, if you leave, but I haven't run into much issue there. Everyone will want us at their party." I smiled. "Anything else?"

She shook her head, deep in thought.

"Actually . . . would you show me your teeth one more time?"

I obliged, keeping my mouth agape for her to observe the whole process. My fangs were initially at rest, but I let her watch as they grew into their full form, extending longer and sharper, out from the gums, shifting into small shivs just below my lips. She held out a finger to touch, and maybe I should have stopped her, but I wanted to indulge in the scent of her blood.

"Ouch!" she cried out upon making contact, the slightest little pool of red forming on her index finger. "Shit, those are sharper than a bowie knife!" It was difficult, but I retracted my fangs and showed her that they were gone before taking her finger in my mouth. It was only for a few seconds, as I gently sealed the wound shut for her. She didn't move until I finished, a new level of trust forming between us.

"Take all the time you need," I reiterated. "But I was thinking that New Year's Eve would be so festive to mark such a momentous occasion. Just imagine. When the clock strikes midnight, it'll be a—"

She said it before I could finish.

"New year. New me."

That irresistible fantasy for every human on the planet, year after year.

A fantasy that rarely became the reality for anyone.

But for Amber, it could.

It would.

ELEVEN

AMBER

'm wearing one of my cutest outfits, a strapless gold mini that makes the girls look great, since Nicola said dress to impress tonight for the potential location tour. So why am I standing in front of a total dump? In *Hackney*?

I know it's the right address because Tamsin and Margaux are here, too, right on schedule, but what the hell is Nicola thinking? How are we going to turn this shithole into a nightclub by New Year's Eve?

We're looking at two floors of abandoned office space next to a KFC and some low-rent lingerie shop with headless mannequins in the window front, little tassels on their huge tits. *Bleak*. I know this neighborhood is technically "cool" now or whatever, but it's still *Hackney*. It doesn't even sound glamorous.

Not that I care, since I'm leaving, but I do care about the ticking clock.

I want this to work with Roddy, and he's leaving New Year's Day.

Nicola slithers out of the front doors, picking up on my disgust right away.

"Use your imagination, darling."

"I'm gonna have to!" I laugh with a snort.

"Come on. Look *around*, Amber," Nic says, taking my face in her hands like I'm her child. "Don't you see it?"

I take stock of the surrounding streets to humor her, and oh, all right, I do know what she means. Everyone's young and cool and a little bit drunk and a whole lot of fun. The fashion is effortless, but a little schlubby if I'm being honest, though that's the style these days. Big jeans. Tiny tops. Sneakers over stilettos. Style and taste *should* swing back around eventually, but here we are for now.

"They'll step it up for our place," Nicola reassures me, reading my mind, something I know she's very good at, so I need to improve my poker face. I refrain from outwardly shivering at the mention of "*our place.*"

"Are you sure?" Margaux chimes in, just as skeptical of the location.

"It's a bit rough, innit?" Tamsin adds with a scoff. Margaux slowly turns her head toward Tamsin, suggesting she spoke out of turn.

"Let's go inside. I'll paint you all a promising picture!" Nicola suddenly possesses the sunny attitude of a kindergarten teacher as she pulls open one of the two heavy doors. She watches each of us step inside, one by one by one.

I'm last.

"Better use a big brush," I say, needling her in that way we like to do, and she laughs and laughs, slamming the door shut behind us.

We really used to have fun.

———————

Walking through the building, Nicola points out all the walls that are going to come down. Most of 'em. It really *is* going to be a ton of work. Not great. Margaux's also having trouble seeing the vision; she hasn't stopped squinting in suspicion, looking extra French and discerning, but before she can voice any alternative opinions, Nicola pipes up with unbridled enthusiasm once again.

"I know, I know, but believe me—the upper floor is where all the good bones are! Come on! You'll love it!"

It's bizarre to see Nic all lit up, genuinely excited. She almost always plays it cool, but not tonight, with this spring in her step, lightly touching the railing as we go upstairs, tracing it with one fingertip like she's waving a magic wand about to turn this rotten old pumpkin into a disco-party princess.

I know this is the spot. She's already decided. We won't even take a vote. Because what Nic wants, Nic gets. I'll echo everything she says tonight. The fewer hiccups between us, the better it'll be for me.

"Here comes the best part!" Nic swings open yet another non-descript office door. I expect to stay mortified by the location, but I'll bite my tongue.

I look up, taking in the enormous glass-domed ceiling, reminiscent of a cathedral, with the London night sky glittering above us with full moon, a few stars and a flash of the future.

Oh my God.

I *see* it now.

Her vision.

"Just like our dance parties at home, darling!" Nic squeals at me, shaking my shoulders from side to side so hard that I can't help but laugh along with her. "What do you think?"

"It still looks like a lot of fucking work," Tamsin mumbles, un-impressed as always. Before Margaux can add her thoughts, I chime in to support Nic.

"This is amazing! You're right, Nic. These *are* great bones!"

"That's the spirit, Amber!" She squeezes me again before glow-ering at Tamsin, for whom the feeling is obviously mutual. "And the office will be a safe room, not to worry, should we cut it close before rest one night or two."

Margaux nods in understanding, with a shrug of appreciation at me.

Nicola's really thought of everything, hasn't she?

"I mean it," I say to Nic again, thinking it wise to keep gassing her up. I pull out my phone to take some photos to up the ante where my enthusiasm is concerned and segue into the next phase of my plan. "I totally see the potential here. And I know you're *on it* with the finance end of things, but I've been thinking a lot about the press and marketing, too."

I turn around to look Nicola in the eye. She stands still, listen-ing attentively, watching me with appreciation. But I have to strike the perfect balance between seeming helpful and intelligent right now and seeming bossy and overbearing.

There's always a line with Nicola, and I can't cross it.

This will be a constant tightrope act until opening night, but luckily, I've always been light on my feet.

"I met this nightlife photographer the other night," I continue. "At Blacks. Really nice guy. And very talented. He knows a lot of the players in the business, so I thought we should consider hiring him."

Nicola *almost* rolls her eyes at me, but she stops herself midway, pretending to be lost in thought as she stares up at the ceiling in-stead of immediately dismissing me.

"Hire him for what, darling?"

Keep going, Amber.

You've got her ear.

"A couple things. For one, I think a chronology in photos would be useful. We can share with news outlets and blogs and influencers et cetera. Maybe we can get a big feature somewhere that will attract our ideal clientele before opening night? We won't be forthcoming about *everything*, obviously, but we know how to handle mixed company with humans by now. And we can keep it mysterious with any of the photos we're in. Pseudonyms. No full-on faces. Just hair. Bodies."

"Mouths, if we're feeling cheeky?" She laughs. "Amber, come on, I'm not sure—"

"But *also* I thought it was something we could have for us. All of us. Some personal photographs to commemorate what we're doing. It's pretty special. We'll have him shoot on film, not digital. Retro vibes only. And we could use some new art in the Laurels, don't you think?" I wink at her, knowing she never wants to change up the Laurels, but how could she not be touched by this sentiment?

I see it wash over her, a wistful look; cue Barbra, "The Way We Were."

It's working . . .

"You said you met him at Blacks?" Nic asks, clearly intrigued by my proposal.

"Yeah." I nod, omitting the truth. I wonder if Margaux noticed. "Of course, *you* all need to meet him before we make any kind of hiring decision, and he'll show you his work to make sure you approve. We could always look at other candidates, too, if you like the idea."

"I trust you," Nicola says, looking up at the ceiling again. "We all do, right? It's a lovely idea. Might even encourage us all to be on our best behavior and operate in good faith with one another. And we could look back on them in a hundred years and see how far we've come."

Oh my God, the thought of a hundred years or more with Nicola makes me feel like my throat is closing up.

"And conversely, if he does anything out of turn, we all know how to handle it, don't we?"

I swallow and nod with a smile.

"Do you really think we can open by New Year's Eve?" I ask.

"I'm sure of it." She smiles at me. "Have I ever broken a promise, darling?"

It pains me to smile at her, shaking my head, but I won't take the bait.

I have too much on the line now.

Has she been waiting for me to say something about Malcolm? I won't.

I just have to make it to New Year's Eve.

"While we're over here, there's a place we should go check out," I say, deftly changing the subject.

"Great. I'd love to be anywhere but here," Tamsin snarls.

As the four of us leave, Margaux pinches Tamsin hard right on the back of the neck.

I get everyone in a taxi over to Shoreditch under the guise of showing them what a nightclub in East can become in the right area with the right alchemy. Nicola's very impressed by my suggestion. Fantastic. I want her to believe I'm obsessed with our nightclub.

But if I'm lucky, her new obsession will be awaiting us tonight on the dance floor.

"I heard about this club from the photographer I mentioned. It leans disco, too. We should take note of what we like and what we don't. I bet a lot of our customer base will cross over from Shoreditch. We need that intel."

Nicola looks out the window, watching the city go by, eyes gleaming, with a big grin on her face, and I wonder how she decided on East at all for our nightclub. We never hang out here, but I'm admittedly impressed by her willingness to branch out for the sake of her vision. And presumably the budget. She's got money but doesn't always like to spend it, having piles of it locked around the house for a rainy day that will never come. You know, like most rich people.

"This *is* where the youth is now," Nic says to me, as if she'd been listening in on my thoughts again. "We'll always love Mayfair, darling, but in that area of Hackney there's room to roam and create and make our mark. Not so crowded. I mean, look how quickly Shoreditch got built up!"

"It's unbelievable," Tamsin says, taking it all in. They must not have come here often either. As far as I know, most of East London hasn't been officially claimed territory, not even by Pierce, but I can see it's going to be a hot commodity soon enough. Especially if Nicola's just decided she's going to take it for herself without any discussion.

Seeing Nicola want the nightclub to work so badly, I *almost* start to feel bad for scheming behind the scenes. I wonder how I would have felt if she'd suggested this project earlier, *years* earlier, but I push the thought out of my mind.

It doesn't matter now.

Nicola's not changing.

Remember what she did to Malcolm.

To you.

But I can change.

She won't control me anymore.

I'm the one in control.

Just a few more weeks to go.

"We're here!" I announce, practically levitating out of the taxi when it comes to a stop in front of a club already teeming with people in sharp outfits and sly smiles. "25 Paul Street."

"This address has been a lot of things over the years," Nicola interrupts, winking at me. So she has been around here before? Noted. Something to keep an eye on. What's her connection to East? She never said a word about it to me. Did she say anything to Tamsin?

"But now it's a nightclub, and a great one at that." I bump my hip into Nic's, keeping the camaraderie up.

"We shall see."

Nicola links her arm through mine like old times, and we head for the entrance, Margaux and Tamsin not far behind. They're a team, but I notice they never seem to touch or share laughs or have a real bond the way Nicola and I once did.

She always said there's nothing like the relationship between maker and companion.

And Margaux didn't make Tamsin.

Nicola did.

2 5 Paul Street is as cool and chic as Roddy said it would be. A *total* vibe. Great dancing, great music, great crowd and it's absolutely packed, everyone moving to a bass-heavy Kylie Minogue song remixed with Sylvester, and the DJ is soaking up the love, feeling like a celebrity himself. The place feels fresh, but with a vintage touch. For free spirits and nostalgic romantics and fun-loving freaks. My people.

I can't help myself when I start to dance as we walk through the club, my bod always getting the best of me with a hot beat. A fog machine fires up as all four of us enter the dance floor, bobbing and weaving through others who are already on another planet. It is very late, so by now the scene is boozebag central, no question nor any judgment, but the moves are more erratic than anything else at this hour. Lots of flailing arms, heads hanging down, no one moving their feet too much for fear of falling over.

Except for *her*.

I clock that girl right away.

The one who was always alone.

In every photo.

In every video.

And she's alone now.

It's impossible not to notice her. You can even hear her coming in that silver chain-link dress that clinks as she walks, accentuating her hips as she does, swinging them from side to side. She glides to the center of the dance floor all by herself because none of the guys there are worthy enough to take her for a spin.

Not that she needs them anyway.

I watch her go.

Her tight brown curls are long and highlighted and voluminous, enveloping her face like a giant rainbow around her head. She's even prettier than social media let on, standing out among the other girls, who've all flat-ironed their hair stick straight. She has a little nose piercing, just a flash of bling, and tons of mixed-metal bangles on her arms. She's in hot pink sneakers, *a choice*, but it really works with her personal sense of style.

And better yet, she can really fucking move in those things.

How she's striking the perfect balance of looking natural yet choreographed is impressive. She knows she's the star of this show, taking the role very seriously. Always on beat, but she finds every little kink in the music with her body. A flick of the wrist when the rhythm shifts in the background. A sway of her hips when the syncopation takes an unexpected turn. She knows the whole song by heart, and I don't mean the words; she hears the soul behind it. The stuff that most people don't notice.

But I do.

I shift my eyes to the left to see if Nicola's watching.

She is.

"Come on," I whisper to Nic. "Let's go show her up." Nicola loves a competition for attention, but she shakes her head, laughing at me.

"You go on ahead. I'll watch."

Challenge accepted.

I approach the girl, who welcomes me with a smile once she notices that I'm on her level, too. As we start to dance closer together, everybody looks, but the only one I'm paying attention to is Nicola, her eyes darting back and forth from the girl to me and to the girl again.

I think something resembling nostalgia has completely taken over Nicola, and she finally makes tracks toward us on the dance floor. Nic twirls me first and then the girl, and I swear I see a flicker of fang, but it's too dark to be sure.

Something's different, though.

No doubt about it.

Nic doesn't play *like this* with her food.

She's not hunting.

She's dancing.

Like she did with me when we met.

I back off slowly, to see if they dance as close together without me, but also to listen in on what other people might be saying around the club. I hear whispers, other regulars wondering who

Nicola and I are, and then I keep hearing the other girl's name thrown around.

Courtenay Cooper.

They say both. First and last. Every time.

I need to find out more about her, but from what I see so far? She's *perfect*.

Will Nicola notice if I leave the dance floor, or has she finally found someone else to keep her occupied? I pace backward to Margaux and Tamsin, who are in their usual stance on the sidelines, observers always, never entertainers. A couple of Good-Time Sallies, those two.

"Do you guys *ever* get out there?" I ask, unable to mask the judgment in my voice.

"Only if it's helpful to the hunt." Margaux grins, looking at Courtenay.

"Not exactly an inconspicuous choice," I say, trying to deter her from going after my potential prize pig for the evening.

"No kidding. That's Courtenay Cooper," Tamsin scoffs. "She's at Raffles a lot, too."

"How do *you* know her?" The thought of Tamsin having the pulse on something I don't is too much for me.

"We don't *know her* know her. Courtenay's just there most Thursday nights. Sometimes Sundays," Margaux says. "She's a party girl. That's all."

You're goddamn right she is.

Me, too.

Nicola and Courtenay haven't stopped dancing once, going from one song right into the next and the one after it. They look good together. *Great* even. Did we look like that, once upon a time, back at Tramp?

Did she ever look like that with Tamsin?

Or with her sister?

Where else does Courtenay go?" I ask Tamsin, Margaux flitting away to flirt with some beefy-armed guy across the room. She must be hungry.

"Raffles is where we've seen her, usually on a Sunday night. Sometimes Maggie's. Embargo. But then I guess she pops over to this side of town, too. We all contain multitudes, hey?"

"It's weird you go to all these nightclubs and don't even dance."

"Where else are we going to go, Amber? And I used to dance with her," Tamsin says, looking at Nicola. "It was a different time, though. The '60s were mental. We ran wild on Carnaby all the time." She starts to laugh but quickly stops herself.

"When did you turn?" I ask, wondering if she'll shut me down or want to talk about her past. Who knows the last time she's had the opportunity?

"1956, but I didn't really get out until 1960 or so. I'm sure you know what I mean," she says with a raised eyebrow. "It was a long time ago, Amber. I don't really remember and I don't want to talk about it. None of it matters anymore."

"It's still your life," I say, trying to get more from her, hearing a parallel to my own story. 1956, but she didn't get out until 1960? Nicola cut Tamsin off from her past right away, too.

"What life?" She laughs, so high-pitched it almost hurts my ears. "I see what you're trying to do, but it won't work," she growls. "Courtenay's a shiny penny and Nicola likes to snuff the light out of anyone, but I don't know how you convince a girl today to even go through with it. They've got more going for them, compared to when we were young."

"I don't know what you're talking about," I scoff, covering my ass just in case. I don't need Tamsin in my business, but I consider what she's saying. I'll have to make a very compelling case, sure, but some girls will always want an easy way out. I certainly did. "How'd she get you?"

"I was a housewife in the 1950s, Amber." She sneers at me like I couldn't possibly understand. "It's like I've been a caged animal my whole life."

"Was that man in the locket your husband?"

"No," she barks at me, so loud it echoes in my ear. "Not that it's your business, but he's the man I *should* have married. Alas, I was led down another path at my family's urging, but once I was . . . this, I thought maybe we could . . . and then Nicola put a stop to that."

Tamsin inhales sharply. She doesn't want to cry.

"I'm sorry, Tamsin."

"Margaux didn't want to listen to me because *she's* in charge, not to mention her interest in *you* should it all go tits up, but none of this so-called alliance feels right. She wants peace with Nicola, as if we can all move on and feel safe around each other in this stupid life we lead, but just you watch. This is going to end in a fucking bloodbath, which is just as well . . ."

I watch Nicola and Courtenay dance together, trying to push what Tamsin just said out of my mind, but there's a small part of me that knows she could be right.

"I'll leave you to it then," I say. Tamsin nods once, watching the world have fun around her, the bitterness inside irreparably taken hold of her.

That won't be me.

Nic and Courtenay start to chat, and my instinct is to leave so they can get to know each other better without me involved. If I appear too eager about their friendship, Nicola could know what's up. I know the girl's name now. Where she likes to go. What nights. I can do some more digging in the coming days.

For now, I have a deal to close.

When I text Roddy u up? I get an answer right away.

Why not?

I mean, he lives right here in Shoreditch.

When Roddy answers the door, I can't seem to stop myself from pawing at him right away. His hair, his chest, down to the front of his jeans. He rewards my enthusiasm by picking me up and throwing me over his shoulder like a goddamn caveman. Hell yeah! This is going to be *good*!

His flat is *very* small, but he takes care of it. Bachelor pad to the max with a sweet view, five floors up in a modern building. We could enjoy it if we'd care to look, but we sure do not. When he tosses me on his bed—complete with a fitted sheet and *two* pillows— he wastes no time running his hands up my little gold dress to artfully remove my frilly pink delicates, swirling his fingers at my hips, placing them underneath the lace and tugging all the way down my legs slowly, his lips lightly grazing my thighs, then my knees, then my shins and finally the tops of my feet after removing them completely.

A kiss on the left.

A kiss on the right.

A sweet lover is another good sign. He'll take extra care of all the special arrangements for me when we get to New York together.

Working on those logistics as we speak.

God, there's so much to do.

I can't miss a single step.

No room for error.

"Am I about to sleep with my boss?" Roddy asks me, resting his head on my ankle.

"You tell me."

He moves his fingers back up through the same route, applying soft pressure with his thumbs on my calves, the inside of my knees, and finally wraps his hands around to hold me from underneath, pulling his mouth to where I really want it. I can barely control myself, my fangs start to emerge, and I need to *get a grip* because I need this guy under my spell, not the other way around. I focus, popping them back in before flipping him over to take charge. When I straddle him, putting a little pointed pressure on his package, he finally says, "When do I start?"

"I'll keep you posted." I laugh, kissing him again.

Perfection.

He's in.

And God, he's *so* cute.

Ah, well.

Amber Wells doesn't fall in love anymore, but she still fucks.

Roddy and I hold each other afterward, and I hate that I have to keep checking the clock, because the postcoital state is always so dreamy. He asks me if I want anything to snack on, and boy, do I ever, but I can wait until tomorrow night to refill that particular tank.

"I'm impressed, you know," he whispers into my hair.

"Did you really think I'd fail you in the sack?" I joke, and he laughs, pushing me playfully back and forth, wrestling a bit, the sheets getting twisted again, and God, it's bittersweet to remember what it's like to have a cute boyfriend.

"No, stupid!" He holds my wrists above my head. I happily surrender. "I'm talking about the nightclub. I didn't mean to sound weird about it when you first told me. It's just a big fucking deal and maybe I was a little jealous at first because I'm not exactly where I want to be just yet. So, I'm sorry."

"Thanks." I smile as he pushes a lock of hair behind my ear. I don't remember anyone telling me they were *impressed* by me before. My parents weren't exactly vocal in that department, preferring to focus on everyone's shortcomings instead. How charming. "You're going to be a part of it, too. And between us, Nicola's the one really leading the charge."

"Don't sell yourself short."

"I mean it. We *have* to keep it professional in front of her. She's more . . . serious than I am. Okay?"

"Whatever you want, sweetheart. But I'm looking forward to meeting this 'serious' cousin of yours. Nicola Wells. Your evil twin."

"Oh, don't let her catch you calling her that."

"I know you're cousins; it was a joke."

"Yes, but Nicola's a *Claughton*. She won't let you forget it."

"Well then, I won't." Roddy grins before delivering the sweetest little peck on my nose.

My eyes practically roll to the back of my head.

His neck smells *amazing*.

TWELVE

NICOLA

1979

I slipped Paul, my favorite doorman at Tramp, a healthy wad of cash to secure the secret room for Amber's turning. It was historically invite only, even more so than the club itself, very hush-hush, down a long tunnel whose entrance couldn't easily be found, typically reserved for the likes of Mick Jagger or Princess Margaret. Not together, but maybe, who could say? I didn't know their business. All I knew was that it was lush and exclusive and to have access that night? On *New Year's Eve*? Let's just say that Amber would be wildly impressed by the gesture.

Especially since I knew the actual turning wouldn't be what she was envisioning at all.

She must have been dreaming about the midnight balloon drop, a final champagne toast underneath the disco ball, all culminating in a dramatic transformation from party princess to an inimitable empress of the night.

That's not quite the reality of the situation, but nobody wants to hear about any difficulty prior to its occurrence.

And if I revealed to her the *whole* truth about turning, she might retreat.

Turning was atrociously painful, felt not just in the immediate wound on the throat, but in the whole body, as if you're inexplicably drowning and choking and burning all at the same time whilst a portal to hell forms inside you, deep in the belly. The infernal heat that only continues to build throughout is dry and coarse and feels inextinguishable.

I *wished* I could forget it myself, but when the subject of turning ever came up, I got a quick flash of the wretched feeling, too. All vampires do. To remember how serious the commitment is, not only for the would-be turner but for the maker as well.

And to know that specific pain is not even the absolute worst imaginable; allegedly that's the *end* of a vampire's life, when the sun engulfs your earthly body in the slowest of burns; well, it was even more motivation to keep going no matter the human cost.

You know how these women waxed on about forgetting the pain of childbirth once they held the actual baby in their arms? Not so with one's turning. You'd remember that exquisite agony for all eternity. Do anything to avoid it in the future. Enough to get your vampiric instincts to activate at full tilt. Any moral high ground one possesses as a mortal goes swiftly out the window. Never again. We stalk and we kill and we feed so we can survive. Full stop.

Fuck me, Amber was fucking *late*. Was it possible she'd reconsidered? But she seemed so certain after our Boxing Day shopping spree. She was resolute when I left her at Malcolm's doorstep—fearful, yes, but positively titillated to move on to redder pastures.

She would meet me at half ten at Tramp on New Year's Eve.

She promised.

Not that I'd heard from her since.

But I had to trust the process, knowing she had to come to her own conclusions and make her own choice. Still! Faced with a lifetime alongside a proper bore like Malcolm Wells—and as far as she knew, a right cheat—it would make anyone want to take a flying leap into the unknown, wouldn't it?

Not to mention the lack of a real family nearby.

Not even a Christmas card from Mum?

Luckily, I'd snatched it from their mailbox a few nights before, tossing it into a dumpster behind Bond Street. Her mother probably had no idea what she was on about, if Amber even brought it up to her at all. It didn't sound like they spoke much.

So where was she?

No second thoughts, I'm sure.

She couldn't have spoken to anyone else about it, hmm?

She was cross with everyone but me.

Especially her husband.

There's always that risk when revealing my ultimate secret, but Amber wouldn't betray me.

I was sure of it.

Yes, I was sure of it.

Quite sure.

She was *twenty* fucking minutes late now. It was nearly eleven, for fuck's sake! Was it really possible she was not coming? She was standing me up? On New Year's Eve? What on earth was going on? Was it all for nothing?

Oh, she *really* thought she was something special, didn't she?

But we'd been having such a good time, hadn't we?

How could she do this to me?

How *dare* she leave me like this, so abruptly and without any fanfare.

How could this be?

Amber was innately a kind person, I could smell it on her, oozing out of every pore, her sweet eyes all but giving it away. The way she looked at me when I navigated the discount on that pink dress, like it was immoral. Even though I was the one paying for it! She allowed it anyway, of course. Because she wanted the damned dress, and when I handed her that Liberty shopping bag she looked just like the cat that got the cream. Like she had gotten away with something.

So yes, Amber might be mischievous, but no, she wasn't malicious.

She wouldn't do this to me.

Not without telling me.

Unless perhaps she was hurt?

What if something happened to her on the way over to Tramp?

Everyone *is* a lunatic on New Year's Eve, people drink-driving, not looking where they're going. Or maybe some brutes secretly followed her and jumped her in the night? It was not out of the realm. I was sure she looked absolutely ravishing.

So what *if* someone ravaged her on the way over?

What if she needed my help?

How would I find her?

We weren't connected yet to sense one another. Only after the turning would that connection activate. I would always have a larger radius as the maker, the upper hand belonging to me, something I declined to share. Conversely, as my companion, Amber would only sense when I was *very* close by.

But really, where was she?

I was making excuses for her.

I *knew* what had gone on here.

She'd changed her mind. She was going to stay with Malcolm. Give him another chance.

They were wearing sad little hats and sipping on punch with the television on in the background.

All was forgiven.

The easy way out.

Betraying me.

Just like everyone did.

No.

Something else.

She *did* leave her husband.

She'd left London, hadn't she?

Missed her sister. Went home. Finished with her European adventure.

No. That wasn't it either.

Perhaps she'd gone somewhere else. Paris or Rome. The Greek islands?

With what money, Nicola?

Well, her husband had money.

But she had been so reluctant to spend it.

A good girl from the wrong side of the tracks.

Yes, she was a lost soul for the taking.

And she wouldn't leave me without saying goodbye.

I knew it.

She must be hurt.

Or dying.

Or dead.

Every single potential horrendous scenario continued to run through my mind.

I felt unwell, sick, yes, *sick*, like an absolute *sicko* over her, and there was only one way I could knock some sense into myself and pull myself back from the brink.

I needed to remember who I was.

What I was.

When Amber finally arrived at Tramp, she looked absolutely gobsmacked at the sight of me, like she'd been put through the wringer, like she couldn't believe she made it, though I'm sure I looked the same upon finally setting eyes on her.

She was a vision in pink sequins, the dress well worth it.

But I had thought for sure she wasn't coming . . .

Still, what a relief! I was already plotting to visit her *and* Malcolm in Belgravia the following night, sweetly enough so she'd let me in, but unwilling to hear any sort of apology.

Thankfully, fate had other plans for us.

"Oh my God, Nic! I'm *so* sorry I'm late! And then when I got here, I couldn't find Paul anywhere!" Amber explained in a huff, pushing her hair out of her face, revealing a dazzling look with the perfect cat-eye liner coming to a sharp point just above her lids.

"It's all right, darling," I reassured her, but she kept on going, her voice rattled.

"I almost didn't get in, but then that other fella recognized me from the other night. I don't remember his name, is it Clint? Or Clive? You know the guy. The one with the cleft in his chin that's so deep it looks like it hurts? And only after I practically begged him he decided to let me in because it's the holidays. But then he wouldn't stop talking about how he could get fired, *sacked*, he said, he kept saying that. '*I could get sacked! I could get sacked!*' and that I owed him a favor, a *big* favor, wink wink, hint hint, and it was all very disgusting and gross."

She shivered at the thought and I didn't blame her.

Clive is vile, which is why I had always preferred sweet Paul.

So *why* didn't I go after Clive in my blind rage?

I wasn't thinking clearly at all.

Oh dear.

Poor Paul.

"I didn't think you were coming," I said to Amber, feeling not guilty exactly when it came to feeding on Paul, but not at all proud of falling prey to my own frustrations when she didn't show up on time.

I took it as a sign that she was the correct companion for me.

After all, the best ones could make you feel a bit out of sorts.

A little crazy.

"I know, I'm sorry to be late, but I had a lot to do," she explained. "I took my time getting ready. It's a lot of pressure to set yourself up in a look for all eternity. And then of course, I wrote—"

"You know you can change your clothes and do your makeup, love," I interrupted her.

We had gone over this already. Why was she stalling? Why was she really late?

"But not my very essence!" she cried out. "I want to capture the moment. I mean, I'm at peak foxiness right now, so why not really double down? It took forever to put these falsies on just right, but aren't they magnificent?"

She did look otherworldly already, batting her lashes. I could not *wait* to see what she'd become when the turning was over. A vampire's beauty was unmatched. I wondered if I would be envious once she was complete.

"And then I had to sit down and write *something* to Malcolm, you know."

Pardon me?

"Write what to whom now?" I sputtered.

"Well, I didn't want him to think I *died*."

"Why not?" I scoffed, annoyed she was already making diversions from our supposedly concrete plans. "You're meant to let him come to his own conclusions. What did you—"

"I just told him that I'm leaving him, Nicola! Moving abroad, I didn't specify where. But he shouldn't be surprised considering what he'd done."

"Amber!"

"What? I didn't want him to worry about my well-being!"

"I'd argue he's going to worry even more now!"

"No. I'm sure he'll just be mad. But that's the point. It's always easier to get over someone when you're pissed off at them. Trust me. This will be easier for everyone, including Malcolm."

Why did she care at all about the man she was leaving? Especially since she believed he was having an affair due to my handiwork. "And what's he going to tell your family then?" I asked her.

"Oh, I sent them a letter, too."

Bloody. Hell. None of this was the end of the world, but a clean break was always preferred for a companion. What if someone came searching for her? She wouldn't want them to wind up dead, would she? Because that was a distinct possibility if we weren't careful.

Some vampires had tried to stay in the lives of their family from before, or so I'd been told. It never worked. Either you're lying and ultimately slip, scaring the living hell out of your loved ones, or you tell the truth and then nobody can handle it, too much for most people to comprehend. It was a mess no matter how it was framed.

Like I said, a clean break, above all else, was always best.

"What did you write to your family?" I pressed.

"That I left Malcolm. That I'd be okay. And that one day they might hear from me again. I suppose that isn't the easiest thing to stomach, but—"

"But they *won't* hear from you again, Amber. We already went over this!"

"But why not? I mean maybe down the line I could talk to my sis—"

"I'm afraid you haven't taken this as seriously as you should have! Maybe we should both reconsider tonight . . ."

I was goading her, but I wanted her to feel ashamed by such reckless actions and establish the order of things around here. I was the maker and the leader and she needed to do what I said for this to work properly. And when she didn't follow my rules, she should feel very remorseful about it indeed.

"Reconsider?" she shouted. "After I've blown up my entire life? No way! I want this, Nicola! I want to do this with you! I'm here, aren't I?"

"Are you afraid?" I asked.

"No! Just a little sentimental I guess, but who cares?"

"Sentimental over what?"

"Malcolm. Never seeing my family again. There's—"

"But you don't even love him—and he stepped out on you! You said you didn't want to end up with someone like your father and look what happened. You don't see your family as it is."

"But you can still miss the familiar. There's gray areas to life, Nicola. God! Don't you miss *anyone*?"

No.

At least that's what I told myself.

But I would never tell Amber anything about Pierce.

Or my sister.

"You won't miss anyone or anything when you're a vampire,

Amber. You will happily lose that silly part of yourself. The one that's overly emotional or spends too much time thinking about what others think of you. It's quite liberating. You'll adore it. Trust me."

"But what if I like that silly part of me?"

Cut it all loose, Amber. Put that energy towards us. Towards me.

"So you *are* changing your mind?" I looked away from her, wanting her to feel horrifically guilty and then immediately contrite.

"I'm not, but aren't I allowed to talk to you about this and my feelings? If this partnership is going to work—"

How amusing. She thought it was going to be a partnership. She didn't yet understand that *I'm* the maker. *Her* maker. And almost no vampire could rid themselves of the one who made them, certainly not Amber.

She wouldn't have it in her . . .

"If you've changed your mind, just come clean about it so we can both move on—"

"I haven't changed my mind!" she yelped at me, catching other partygoers' attention. Not ideal. I took her gently by the arm towards the side of the room by the coat check.

"You had better be sure," I said, keeping my voice neutral the best I could. Any lower could sound like a threat. Amber's bottom lip jutted out as the gravity of the situation landed.

But I wanted her to want it.

For her and for myself.

Yes, I might have steered her, quite deftly, in this direction, but she had to be the one who jumped into the ether.

If not, I might as well just kill her tonight. Not the worst consolation prize.

"I've thought a lot about it, Nicola," Amber began seriously,

shoulders back and chin up, reminding me of a little Girl Guide trying to earn a new merit badge. "I might miss my sister and even my
parents. I might even miss Malcolm for reasons you won't understand. But I'm more concerned about missing out on the opportunity of a lifetime. I need more. I've always known this about myself,
but not the destination. Until I met you. I was supposed to meet
you, Nicola. I'm meant for this. All that time and youth and power?
Who wouldn't want all of that? I'm doing this with you. I'll regret it
if I don't."

Now, that was an unexpected response from my very favorite
life of the party.

There was much to covet with the vampiric lifestyle, but the
thirst for power was treacherous.

It wasn't given in our world.

It was taken.

But again, I didn't think she'd ultimately have it in her to do
anything about it down the line.

I guess we'd find out.

All we had was time.

Amber and I held hands as we headed down the low-lit corridor
together, having entered through a door masquerading as a
utility closet, not far from the entrance to Tramp. Paul had personalized the door code for us, just as he'd said he would, and even lit a
few candles just outside. Bless. The sounds of Sylvester pulsed
through the walls, faint but loud enough to carry us through the
countdown and all that would come afterwards. Amber would appreciate a soundtrack.

"I didn't know this was here," Amber said softly.

I smiled back at her, this time with my fangs out. I couldn't help myself. We were growing so close to the finish line. I noticed Amber feeling her own teeth with her tongue, first the canine on the left, then on the right.

Her eyes widened upon seeing the storied back room. VIPs only. All plush red velvet, gold ceilings, sparkling crystal chandeliers and an inviting Borne settee in the middle, waiting for us to get the real party started.

The countdown began from the main room of the club.

We could hear them all out there.

Having the time of their lives.

Ten! Nine! Eight!

"Are you ready?" I asked, motioning for her to sit. She nodded. "Nervous?" She nodded again, suddenly at a loss for words. They had all poured out of her by then. Nothing left to say.

Except one thing.

Seven! Six! Five!

"Amber. I need to hear you say it."

Four!

"I'm ready."

She stared at me with an intensity in her eyes so fierce that I swear I saw fire behind them, red flickering behind the blue, willing me to believe her.

So I did.

Three!

Amber leaned back into the settee and turned her face up, eyes closed, Sylvester wailing in the background amidst the cry of the crowd counting down, the anticipation building with each note, each number.

Two!

I pushed her wild hair away from her neck and gently tilted her head to the side. Her eyes remained closed, but I could picture every shade of blue they possessed, every little glint that would only shine brighter when this part was all over.

One!

I didn't hesitate. I couldn't stand it any longer. Quick was also kind.

I clamped down and consumed her.

HAPPY NEW YEAR!

I focused on meticulous timing, the precise amount, despite her dreadful screams in my ear. When killing, the silence would come quickly, unless you were in the mood to be dastardly for the sake of it. One had no choice with the slow pace of a turning because you had to keep them alive.

But only just.

No one could hear Amber's awful keening sounds.

It was all audible cheers and clinking glasses and party horns out on the dance floor. I wished I could have reassured Amber that this was the worst part, but that would come later, when we were at home together, back at the Laurels, maker and companion-to-be.

The breakneck convulsions. The seemingly endless nausea. The unbearable cold and scathing heat, alternating all night long, wishing for death, as it would be a relief. Nothing could be worth all that torment, could it? At least not in the moment. I decided not to say anything to Amber during the process. Silence was golden.

There was nothing I could share that would make her feel better regardless.

She'd only feel better when it was complete.

For the next twenty-four hours, it would be absolute torture.

For her, that is.

Not for me.

Amber tasted exactly as I'd hoped she would. Positively delectable. She ran hotter than most, the flavor very sweet with a tinge of bitterness on the back end that sent a spikiness down my throat. Pleasurable in the way of a good Scotch, as I recalled, having had a nip here and there in my former life. Yes, it was as if her body welcomed being savored, her blood too rich to wash down willy-nilly. Top-fucking-shelf.

I was absolutely dismayed when it was time to stop. It had gone so fast from my end.

Next, I crunched into my left wrist, a shallow slash, just enough to accomplish the task at hand. It wouldn't take much to finish the job, a relief for the one turning, as it's difficult to focus on anything when you're in that much pain, much less a routine bodily function like swallowing.

"Amber." I gently tapped her cheek in hopes of gaining her attention, but her face was soaked in tears, her dress now dripping in blood, her mouth unable to form words. "Almost finished. Don't fret."

I pulled her bottom lip down to open her mouth and held my wrist close. Her body continued to writhe in misery, though soon enough, she wouldn't be able to move at all. I watched the drops of blood falling from my vein and landing on her tongue, loose and limp inside her mouth.

"Neck it, darling." I pressed her jaw shut with my thumb and ran my other hand down her throat, encouraging her to swallow.

Poor thing.

It would feel like ages before she felt well again.

She had to die first.

The gorgeous dress I bought for Amber would need a thorough dry-cleaning, but it would be dark enough that no one would notice on our way to the car, Jonathan idling nearby on Jermyn

Street. I wasn't worried. Any outdoor revelers whose path we might cross would be pissed to shit at that hour anyway.

I carried my new companion out of Tramp just before one. Amber's arms were slung over my shoulders, pale and dry. Mine were around her waist so it looked like I was dragging her, just another New Year's Eve gone too far, even though just below the hem of her dress her feet were floating above the ground.

Amber moaned, her eyes barely open, her breath uneven and her skin clammy to the touch. Clive at the door watched, laughing like a fool when he got a better look at her, but he would get his. What an absolute twat. "Fuck me. What did someone put in *her* drink? She looks rough. Make sure you've got hair-of-the-dog at the ready come morning. She's gonna need it."

"Will do, Clive."

"Happy new year," he said, still laughing at my girl. "Welcome to the '80s, ladies!"

Well, for me, yet again.

THIRTEEN

AMBER

'm back at the Laurels around 3:00 a.m. after leaving Roddy spent and satisfied, thank you very much. I've whipped up a whole other hunting story to dish out to Nicola, who will undoubtedly ask what I've been up to all night after ditching her at 25 Paul, but when I'm ready to deliver another award-worthy performance, I realize that she isn't even home yet.

I don't sense her anywhere.

At all.

She's *still* out?

Maybe with Courtenay at the club.

Did they go somewhere else?

Maybe they really hit it off!

But wait.

She wouldn't kill her, would she?

No. Those weren't looks of hunger.

I'm sure of it.

Sometimes it feels like I'm on the right track, but nothing's a sure thing when it comes to Nicola Claughton. My body feels on edge at all times, tight and constricted, like I can't make any sudden movements at all. Every single action requires very careful thought. A new dynamic for me, but a necessary one.

And I want to firm up my case with more intel about Nicola's former companions, dead or alive, and what we have in common so I can play into that with Courtenay if need be. Considering they're still out, maybe this is a good opportunity to poke around again.

I can make it quick.

I'll smell her before she walks in the door.

I go back into Nicola's bedroom and open her nightstand, a woman's most sacred drawer, but it's completely empty. What kind of psycho doesn't keep anything in her nightstand? I have at least a candle, a matchbox and a vibrator in mine at any given time. But no, Nicola's is barren, much like her soul.

I check the nightstand on the other side of the bed. Same thing. I don't know why she even has *two* nightstands. No one ever stays over. Maybe she likes the symmetry or she's sentimental that this was her parents' room, their bed frame, once upon a time. What a perv. But she keeps a lot from the past very close to her, Freudian ick factor aside.

The whole house is a relic.

Wait.

I should be digging around in *my* room. Did all her companions live in there at one time? Did she as a little girl? That doesn't sound right. I doubt she would have let me change anything about it. And I have changed *a lot*.

When I moved in, the room was still *very* Nicola. Dark and moody like the rest of the Laurels, outfitted for a resident vampire, but I didn't even think about her previous companions at the time. After a year of not being able to go outside, I asked her if I could redecorate the room. I knew she was super precious about the house, so I half expected her to say no, but I think she must have felt sorry for me since she didn't put up much of a stink. She just asked that I consider reusing any pieces that I liked since they were antiques and valuable and part of the Claughton *legacy*. But I was welcome to freshen them up with a coat of paint or some new knobs.

Oh, how generous.

But I was grateful. A project would keep me busy as I adjusted to my new reality. I chose everything else from a catalog, placing orders on the phone for bed linens, which is funny to think about now. I did everything by hand; desperate for something to do, I wouldn't let her hire anybody to help me. I painted the walls, taking extra time for the trim. I kept the big antique dresser with a vanity mirror because it was so pretty and had big bulbous drawers for all the clothes I didn't hang in the closet. It was chestnut but I painted the exterior a soft white. I hammered every nail for every picture on the wall, trying to make it feel like home. The bed frame and the nightstands that I didn't want to keep were moved to another room in the house.

The only nonnegotiable was the window dressing, for obvious reasons. Blackout curtains in front, dark shades behind them that click into place, locking at the bottom. Airtight.

I hated it, still do, but it is what it is.

Even so, my bedroom's the only place in the Laurels that feels like it belongs to me.

But it must have belonged to the other companions at some point.

The other guest rooms don't have the window coverings like ours do.

I survey the room from the doorway. Did I get rid of something important, some clues to Nicola's past, when I made it my own?

The only thing I kept was that dresser . . .

I rifle quickly through each drawer, wondering if there's something I missed when taking it over for myself. It had been empty, hadn't it? I take everything out, drawer by drawer, feeling around for anything that could be loose or stuck or tucked away. Then I pull out all the drawers and place them on the floor, looking inside the gaps of the dresser. The back of the piece is still the original dark brown. I didn't bother to paint the interior. Who was going to see it?

I look at all the empty drawers on the floor.

Nothing.

But when I start to put them away, I notice that one of the drawers isn't quite as deep as the others.

What's that about?

Yes, the top drawer *is* a little bit smaller.

I slide my hand into the empty drawer box, where the top one belongs, and push into it at the back. It sounds hollow when I knock at it, different from the other ones, which feel more solid. When I trace my finger from the top and down to the bottom edge, I place my hand flat to see if any part of it moves or slides.

Not left. Nor right. But then I pull my hand forward with a firm grip and it loosens right up, the bottom panel coming out under my palm.

There's a small secret compartment carved out at the back, and it's not empty.

It's filled with old letters that feel delicate, wafer-thin, like they could crumble in my hands if I'm not careful. Eyeballing it, I'd say there're about thirty of them.

And they're all addressed to Nicola.

When I scan to the bottom of one of the letters, I see that it's from her sister. Glancing through a few more, I see they all are. She signed her name. Nicola's never said it aloud.

Georgie.

So this *was* Nicola's room at one point. Did she want me to find these? Is that why she wanted me to keep the dresser? I don't remember her pointing it out specifically. She was more concerned about their being antiques, not about the contents. I wonder if she forgot about these letters, but come on, Nicola doesn't forget about *anything*, especially when it comes to her sister.

She's mentioned her often enough over the years. Never by name. Just "my sister this" or "my sister that." Occasionally, it's a sweet memory about how they played together with one of the little dolls she keeps on the mantel, but most of the time, it has this bitter tinge to it. Not in what she says, but in how she says it, rubbing her tongue across the front of her teeth or exhaling with this big "harrumph" sound. But her sister was the one who got kicked out of the house, so I don't know what she's so angry about.

I don't know the whole story.

Tamsin said she thought the sister was still alive.

Did she turn Nicola? Did Nicola turn her?

That's when a waft of tuberose hits my nostrils, with a hint of copper and spice and blood.

She's coming home.

Very soon.

I shove the letters back inside the little compartment, except for the one in my hand, so I can take a closer look, working as quickly as I can to reassemble the dresser. The top drawer gets stuck, I can't push it all the way closed, and before I can fiddle around with it anymore, I know she's behind me.

"Where'd you run off to tonight?" she asks. "We were having fun."

I turn around to face her and bump the drawer with my butt as hard as I can, the letter I'm holding still crumpled up in my fist. "I got hungry," I said, leaning back on the dresser again. "How was the rest of the night? You stayed out later than me for once. End up with anything good?"

"Something like that." Nicola chuckles. "Fantastic idea to pop round to that spot. Good fun, wasn't it?"

"Yeah, we'll have to go back now that we're exploring the East more."

"Do you like it?"

"It's a little gritty, but I don't mind the—"

"That's not what I meant." She smiles. "I mean the exploring. The branching out a bit. Making new friends."

I nod at her, just once, and she returns the gesture.

"Well, we better get some rest," I say, but Nicola lingers in the doorway, tracing her fingers up the frame like a little spider.

"I'd quite like to go out with her again," she says. "Courtenay Cooper. I think she could use some women like us in her life—I suspect she's in a bit of a bad way. And there's just something about her that reminds me of you . . ."

It takes everything I have to stop myself from shimmying—the sweet smell of success!

"That's sweet, Nic," I say. "She seems cool."

"Yes, well, good night, darling."

When Nicola closes the door, I open my fist back up and pull out the letter again, noticing deep divots in my palm from squeezing my fist so tight, the nails digging into the skin.

December 15, 1843

Dearest Nicola,

I do not want you to worry for me. Know I will return once I get on my feet, no matter how long it takes to do so. I will

learn to become my own woman, just as I said, and teach you
as well. We are friends and sisters and we will always have
each other.

We are always family.

Have a wonderful Christmas and happy new year.

Ever yours,
Georgie

When did Georgie come back? What happened between the two of them?

Always a family.

That's what Nicola thinks we are. That's what she wanted from me. What she wanted from all her companions.

If Georgie was kicked out of the house by their father, she must have felt so alone, but look at her letter—she still believed there was more *out there* for her, and she wanted to share it with Nicola. Georgie doesn't sound bitter at all. She sounds loyal to her sister. She also sounds scrappy.

Like me.

Maybe like Courtenay Cooper?

I wonder if Courtenay is in a relationship, because I believe that's part of the appeal for Nicola, too. She likes to win someone over, make them a prize.

I poke my head out of my bedroom and call out to Nicola before she goes to rest.

"Tamsin and Margaux said Courtenay likes to go to Raffles, too!"

The hallway is empty and dark, lit only by one of the warm sconces, until I see Nicola's hair falling in a cascade, her head tilting back into view.

Her teeth shine bright back at me.

"Maybe she'll be there tomorrow," I say. "We could all go. If the Chelsea vampires are cool with us being in their territory."

"You *are* enjoying this." Nicola laughs before disappearing into the darkness again.

Nicola had no issue negotiating a Sunday night at Raffles with Margaux's blessing, mentioning that even though we were opening in East, we still wanted to attract some of the West End crowd, so the "research" was important. I heard her on the phone, appealing to their egos, positioning it as a huge favor. A soft approach. In the name of our burgeoning friendship as a group.

God, Tamsin must be reeling.

When we arrive that night, Courtenay Cooper is already center stage, just as gorgeous as the other night, this time in a red midi gown, long gold tassels dripping from her ears. She looks thrilled to see us, particularly Nicola, and even makes a joke about it.

"Are you stalking me?" Courtenay asks Nicola.

"I wish I were that sneaky," Nicola replies. "But everyone knows Raffles is fabulous on a Sunday."

"Hiya, I'm Courtenay!" she says to me, positively adorable, with an accent like she's out of *Peaky Blinders*. "I'm so sorry, I didn't catch your name last night."

"Amber," I say, a little shocked that Nicola didn't tell her about me. Not even once? In their entire conversation? Well, all right then. I guess that's what I want . . .

"You should have stayed longer! We had a right laugh, didn't we?" Courtenay says.

"I heard," I say. "I just got hungry."

"Oh, I totally get it!" She nods at me, still dancing to the beat.

"Sometimes I just get to a point during a night out where I literally *need* some chips and cheese or I might bite someone's head clear off!" Courtenay lets out a laugh, like a hyena, that would sound heinous on anyone else, but it's very cute on her. "Anyway, we'll have a proper knees-up tonight, too. Should we get some drinkies?"

Margaux and Tamsin are over by the bar, watching the whole interaction with curiosity. Nicola acknowledges them with a wave.

"Yes, let's," Nicola says. "What about some French 75s?" I jerk my head back slightly as Nicola smiles at me; I don't know if she's teasing or torturing me with my favorite. Maybe a little bit of both.

Push and pull with us, always and forever.

Courtenay and I follow Nicola to the bar.

"Never had one." Courtenay shrugs before whispering in my ear. "My favorite are alcopops, the blue WKD ones, but I know that's embarrassing. And Nicola's so posh, I can tell."

"You'll like a French 75," I whisper back. "It's a champagne cocktail."

"Oh, love a bit of bubbly!"

Fantastic. Let's get those juices flowing. I want Courtenay to start spilling with some news I can use. I catch Tamsin staring at the two of us, but she looks away quickly once I pick up on her surveillance.

Back off, babe.

You made your bed.

But I'm getting out of mine.

Court's drinks go down easy, and the more she has, the more she's willing to tell all of us about her situation as we cozy up in a banquette. She grew up in a council house in Birmingham with her auntie. She doesn't mention parents. Something to push on. She got into *a lot* of trouble. She moved to London with a terrible boy-friend who promised he had music connections; she thought she might become a singer. Had a string of a few more of those types, but deadbeat guys lead to dead-end streets.

Now she lives with her current boyfriend in Camden, using the term *boyfriend* loosely since I suspect another dynamic is in play. He sounds very controlling, though she doesn't get into specifics. You can see it in her eyes. She seems afraid of him, not in love.

She's had stints as a server and a nightlife hostess at some of the seedier clubs around town. That's where she met this guy, and now she "models" sometimes. Court loves nothing more than dancing, but she never tells her boyfriend when she goes out alone, making up stories about being at a friend's house.

That's why she's not on social media.

She finally says that *of course* she wants to leave him, but she doesn't know how.

She doesn't have a lot of girlfriends in London, so she's not sure where else she can go.

She's very, *very* lost.

"I just gotta find another boyfriend, I reckon," Courtenay slurs, another French 75 gone right down the hatch. Nicola's eyes widen at that. There she goes. Nicola can't help herself when she sees a stray with potential. Not someone who's just a mess, like that other girl in Soho (RIP), but someone without a real home or family or anyone else to turn to—and they dream of something better. Then she just wants to bring them back to the Laurels and make them feel like they belong and cuddle them until they feel better about their life.

Until they suffocate.

We all notice the bright flash from a camera. My stomach flips when Courtenay looks up and darts out of the banquette with a squeal, almost losing her footing.

"Hey, mister!" She leaps into none other than Roddy Bow's arms, a warm and intimate greeting if I ever saw one. They must know each other from the clubs around town.

"Hey, Cooper!" Roddy says, setting his camera to the side, giving me a reassuring wink. Good. I need to keep his leash clipped to me. "I didn't know you were friends with Amber."

"Pretty fresh," Courtenay explains, slurring just a bit. "We met last night at 25 Paul. Do you know—"

"Nicola Claughton," Nic reaches out dramatically with a modest smile and a limp wrist, like she wants him to kiss her ring instead of shake her damn hand. I slide out of the banquette to finish the introduction.

"Nicola, this is Roddy Bow. The amazing photographer I was telling you about."

"Hey, *mister*," she says coolly, echoing Courtenay's enthusiastic greeting as he takes her hand.

"Lovely to meet you, Nicola. I'm looking forward to capturing some of the demo tomorrow night. Amber's told me all about it."

Tamsin clears her throat with a knowing wink in my direction. I don't like it. Still, I take care to introduce everyone at the table but also keep it a little chilly with Roddy.

I am playing with fire, all of us in the mix together.

Can I pull this off?

But I need to keep him close.

"Well, better get back to it. See you all tomorrow." Roddy smiles at me with a lingering stare, but I'm quick to break it, reminding him of the professional nature of our relationship.

Shortly after he leaves, Courtenay whispers in my ear that she thinks she's going to be sick.

"That's all right, let's get you home," I say loudly, getting Nicola's attention.

The three of us head to Camden in a black cab, Courtenay slung over in a window seat, just in case. When we arrive at her flat, Nicola and I both help her get out and to the door. It's an unassuming building, not large or small, that looks just like the rest on the street.

Except the lights are still on at hers.

"Oh no," she says. "David's not gonna like this. It's so late."

"Do you want us to go in with you?" Nicola asks.

Courtenay shakes her head. "No, thanks. I'll handle it."

"Are you sure?" I stabilize her by the shoulders once she releases us, but she waves us on.

"Yeah, yeah, I know his *ways*." She smiles, pulling her keys out of her bag and stumbling inside, shutting the door behind her.

Nicola and I wait silently for a moment.

We don't hear anything.

Then the shouting begins. David has a big, booming voice even when muffled. Courtenay's is high-pitched and defensive. They go back and forth for just a minute or two. Then the lights go off. Something tells me they'll pick it up in the morning. He just didn't want to wake up the whole neighborhood, but they have a routine. A rhythm. A shorthand.

This is a couple that always gets into fights.

I know that kind very well.

"Let's go," Nicola says, waving the cab off. "We'll walk from here. Get a quick bite."

"All right," I agree, but I see her take note of the house number on the flat, eyes darting to the name of the street. I do, too.

"What do you think about calling the club 'Hey Mister'?" Nic asks me as we amble down the road. "If it's good enough for Donna Summer? Toot-toot?"

"Then it's good enough for us." I grin, loving the name. Not that it matters. I'm on my way out. It's only a matter of time. "Beep-beep."

What does matter is that Courtenay will be touched by the gesture.

Bringing her closer to Nicola.

Right where I want her.

FOURTEEN

NICOLA

1840

The Winter family and the Moss family are in the parlor this evening with our family.

The Claughtons.

Mama, Papa and me.

Emily Winter, Lucy Moss and I are taking turns at the piano, wheeled out from the study for performance purposes, before we go into the dining room for a formal meal. The boys sit next to their fathers, attention minimally paid, but Mama says it's our duty as young women to entertain so we make for wonderful wives one day.

After all, it won't be long until we debut into society, and a prosperous match is key.

Emily is excellent at the piano. Her mother smiles proudly. Lucy is middling, so her mother talks over her whilst she plays. I fall somewhere in between the two of them, which appeared to be good enough for Mama and Papa. I play piano for them whenever they ask, but never for myself. If it were up to me, I would not play the piano again at all.

I prefer listening to others play.

All instruments, really.

I don't wish to be the musician.

I wish to be the dancer.

Papa speaks quietly with Mr. Winter while Thomas Winter listens to both closely, keeping an intermittent eye on me. I return these glances as my fingers move across the piano keys, and I cringe when I make small mistakes from carelessness.

The others haven't noticed, of course, but Mama has. She clears her throat in a vain effort, as if that could will me to play better. But I always wonder what the men are discussing privately. Mama would tell me that is none of my concern, but sometimes Papa will tell me the points of conversation.

He likes to remind me that I am his legacy.

But only when we're alone.

When we file into the dining room, Anna and Georgie begin to serve us the meal. A soup course to start. Vegetable. Georgie is always in uniform now, like Anna, but she still looks very pretty with her long hair pulled back off her face. She looks older than me somehow, even though we are about the same age, with more of a curve in her body than I have in mine. She appears more like an adult since she has so many responsibilities now at the Laurels. I have responsibilities, too, but Mama always reminds me that they are very different.

Georgie and I do not play together like we once did.

I tell myself it's because we are both growing up, but I miss her very much.

Despite our individual growth, Georgie shares a warm smile as she sets down the first course, giving me a squeeze on my shoulder.

I bend my arm at the elbow to pat the top of her fingers, quickly in hopes that no one will see—especially Mama.

She hasn't noticed our brief exchange of affection.

Georgie always sets Mama's dish down very carefully, waiting a moment before moving on. Mama often has a complaint or special request to follow that Georgie will need to tend to immediately, but she doesn't say a word tonight.

I imagine it's because we are hosting guests and she doesn't want to look disagreeable, particularly where the Winters and the Mosses are concerned.

They have sons.

Georgie places soup in front of Emily and then Thomas and then William Moss. When she leans over William to do so, he snickers aloud and then Thomas does as well, as if the laughter is catching. Georgie pretends not to hear them; their mirth is not harmless, it's callous, but Emily spills her glass of water all over Georgie. I know she did it purposely because she has eyes for William and he absolutely noticed Georgie's figure underneath her apron.

Anna quickly whispers to a sopping-wet Georgie, and she leaves the room, not looking at me before she goes. It is Anna who cleans up the mess that Emily has made. Afterwards, Mama mutters something to Anna that I can't make out, but Anna nods and carries on serving dinner alone, even though it takes twice as long.

Georgie doesn't return for the rest of the evening.

Mama glares at Papa, but he pays her no mind.

I am certain I will hear them argue later, when the evening is over.

I feel guilty about what's happened with Georgie, even though I don't know what I could have done to come to her aid.

I wonder if Papa feels guilty, too, but when I look over at him, he continues his chat with Mr. Winter and nibbles at his roast, as if none of the women or children are even at the table.

later that evening, when everyone has gone home, Papa asks me what I think of Thomas and William. I know what he wants to hear, so I tell him that I think they are lovely and amiable boys. He grins at me, softly gripping his gold pocket watch, passed down from his father, before retreating to bed. I wonder if he will give it to me one day.

I hope Georgie isn't lurking nearby, listening to my lies about those boys.

But she wouldn't understand why I must tell them to Papa.

She is not my father's legacy.

I am.

FIFTEEN

AMBER

suggested to Nicola that we invite Courtenay to "demo night" at Hey Mister, mentioning that she could probably use an opportunity to blow off some steam after what happened with her boyfriend the night before. Why not have her join four vampires to swing around sledgehammers and smash some walls? Seems like a perfectly normal way to get to know somebody better.

Nicola agreed, I knew she would, eager to tell Courtenay about the name inspiration.

Eager is never a word I would use to describe Nicola, but it's true when it comes to anything about the nightclub. She even puts on "Macho Man" once we all have our hard hats on, which makes me laugh and then feel ancient because Courtenay has no idea who the Village People are. Still, she leans into the fun, dancing along with us.

She's a go-with-the-flow kinda girlie.

Malleable.

Impressionable.

Young.

Everything I used to be when I met Nicola.

"We got the name from you, darling!" Nicola says to Courtenay, who puts both hands on her heart, mouth falling open with delight, well and truly touched.

Perfection.

As our little wrecking crew giggles together (minus Tamsin, of course, who is *all* business when it comes to destruction), I remember how Nicola and I used to be, the memories scratching softly in the back of my mind. She really can be so charming. I watch her bump a hip into Courtenay's, cracking jokes, looking luminous. But, no.

No.

Eye on the prize. Hands on the steering wheel. Absolute focus.

I'm not going to get sucked back into Nic's theatrics, no matter how cool this nightclub might become or how much I'm starting to like Courtenay myself.

I am getting *out*.

"Heya!" Roddy waves as he steps inside the wreckage surrounding us, camera at the ready. I catch Nicola looking him up and down like a piece of meat. Alarming. I have to be super careful. So does Roddy. God, opening night can't come soon enough. "You girls ready for your close-up?"

"Always." Courtenay smiles, posing suggestively with the sledgehammer like she's a centerfold. She really is super cute.

"Welcome, Roddy," Nicola purrs, ushering him inside with a hand on his shoulder, her red nails looking extra sharp, like claws. "Make yourself comfortable and let me know if you need any accommodations at all whilst you work. Amber briefed you on the directive, yes?"

I'm sorry, did Nicola just lick her fucking chops? Seriously, does she want to eat him or fuck him? With Nic, I can never tell, but Roddy's not her typical type at all, in either direction.

"A little secretive, sort of a blurred identity, but chic and aspirational. I got it." Roddy nods. "And I'll take a few cheeky snapshots, too. For personal use only. All images go to you for approval."

"Fabulous. Amber, may I speak with you?"

I follow Nicola to the area where the office will eventually be outfitted, not a window in sight. She looks behind me, everyone still hard at work, and then lowers her voice.

"I'm considering asking Roddy to help us out a bit during the day. Since we have him on the payroll already? Letting in the construction team for cleanup. Picking up permits. Maybe he even knows some good barmen to interview? You said he's well-versed in the industry."

Shit. I don't want her getting too close to Roddy. Gotta get her to pivot.

"But we hired him to be the photographer. Not sure he's looking to be an *assistant*."

"Oh please, would you look at him, Amber? He's a starving artist, isn't he? Probably be thrilled with some more hours for a few extra quid. We can afford it. Trust me."

"Well, what about Courtenay instead?"

A *genius* suggestion.

Nicola cocks her head to the side, considering it.

"Think about it," I say. "She's trying to get out from under that shitty boyfriend of hers. And if she does a great job, earns some trust from us, she could become more involved as we get closer to opening. We will need someone to keep an eye on things during the day, and I know we could just hire someone, but it's like you said. She's in a bad way and maybe we can help."

"Amber Wells, humanitarian." Nicola chuckles.

"I just think Roddy should focus on the art. That's what we hired him to do."

"Do you think Courtenay wants a job?"

"I think she'll do *anything* to get out of her situation. She's lucky she met you, Nic."

Nicola nods, giving me a little pet on the shoulder.

When we pitch Courtenay on the idea, she accepts right away, her enthusiasm off the charts.

"Hey Mister is going to be the *best* nightclub in Britain, babes. I'll make sure of it. I practically know them all by now, but none of them have *us*. Thank you for trusting me. You won't be sorry." She gazes at the mess around us, clocking how much work lies ahead, but I recognize the look on her face—it's hope.

She wants it.

If I get my way, it'll be all hers for an eternity.

"We're so happy to have you, Court." I smile sincerely at her and then at Nicola. I feel a tinge of guilt, little prickles on my arms, but someone like Courtenay will enjoy being Nicola's kept woman. She's in a far worse situation than I ever was. I'm practically doing her a favor.

Then Nicola drops her sledgehammer with a thud, startling the shit out of Courtenay.

"Do you *smell* that?"

Nicola is perfectly still, except for her nose inhaling deeply.

Her eyes grow wider and wider still.

I haven't seen her do this in a long time.

I never saw Pierce around the Laurels myself, but once in a while, she said she could sense him. That he liked to taunt her. As if he could threaten to take the Laurels away from her. She says he only wants to take the things she loves.

He must know about the nightclub.

Is he here?

"Do you smell *that*?" Nicola asks again, louder this time, stomping to the center of the room so all of us can hear her.

"Smell what?" Courtenay asks innocently. "The sawdust?"

"Did *you* speak to him?" Nicola accosts Margaux, moving just a touch too fast so that I wonder if Courtenay or Roddy noticed. Tamsin remains behind Margaux; both of them have their mouths clamped shut so as not to show any defensive fang.

I know Margaux wants to keep this train on the tracks, too.

Peace with Nicola.

"No," Margaux says, and nothing else.

Nicola dashes out the door, slower this time, thankfully, but she picks up the sledgehammer to take with her.

Well, it wouldn't kill him, but it wouldn't feel great, either.

"Where's she going with that?" Court asks me, dutifully following Nicola.

"She's a nutter," Tamsin mutters at me, shaking her head.

"Everything okay?" Roddy asks before I go outside myself. "Maybe I should—"

"It's fine," I chirp at him. "Just some . . . girl stuff. Be right back."

I glare at Tamsin and Margaux so they know to leave him alone. Margaux nods in understanding, but Tamsin looks thrilled by all the kerfuffle.

Outside the club, Nicola's a few paces ahead of us, marching down the street, sniffing around like a drug dog with that goddamn hammer in her hand, shoulders crouching forward, on the hunt.

"I know you're here!" she shouts, her voice reverberating through the mostly empty streets.

"Who is she talking to?" Courtenay whispers, but I just shake my head.

"And you aren't welcome! You aren't invited! You get *nothing*!" Nicola roars, tossing the handle of the hammer over her shoulder, and she goes back inside without a word to Courtenay or me.

"Is she okay?" Courtenay whispers. I nod, not altogether convincingly, and Courtenay shrugs. "I get it. Stalker boyfriend? I've had those before . . ."

"You should go talk to her about it," I urge her, taking the window of opportunity to get them closer together. "I'm sure she could use a sympathetic ear."

"You think?"

"Yeah," I say. "I mean, use a gentle touch, but I know she'll appreciate the gesture from our new girl Friday."

"Who?" Courtenay asks because she's Gen Z and makes me feel like *such* a boomer, which, technically, I suppose I am.

"Oh, that's just something my grandma used to say. Go on. I'll be right in."

After Courtenay leaves to tend to Nicola, I linger for a moment and walk farther down the road, just to see what might happen. It's been many years since we ran into Pierce together. I never forgot it. The whole night was scary, but what stuck with me most was when he whispered into my ear before we got away.

"This is a cursed life with no way out, but it will be worse if you stay with her."

I didn't want to believe him. Nicola was my friend.

But he was right.

Now I want to see him again.

"Pierce?" I call out, wondering if he's watching me.

"Oh, she didn't like that, did she?" I hear a little snicker as Pierce struts around the corner in front of me, all alone, looking sexy and suave as ever with a clean shave on his sharp face. "Wait until I bring the lads around here. We can't go in, but we can mind our own business out here. Free territory."

When he comes closer to me, I take a step back instinctively.

"I'm not going to hurt you, love. Though believe me, I considered it back then. But it's not your fault, is it? She tricks you girls. I know she does."

"You were tricked, too?"

"Not exactly," he scoffs. "But that's a long story and you don't have the time nor the toll, I'm afraid." He leans over to the side slowly, like he's floating through water, and when I turn around, I see Roddy at the end of the road, looking for me.

"What toll?"

"Amber, you and I, we're like siblings. I understand your situation completely. But I got out. Not many do . . ."

I stay quiet. I don't want to tell him anything. I'm not sure it's safe.

But why hasn't Nicola killed Pierce? Has she tried? I have so many questions, but I don't want any altercation to take place between Roddy and this wily vampire I don't trust.

"I have to go," I say firmly, taking steps away from him, maintaining eye contact.

"Very well. Should the mood strike, I reckon you know where to find me. I'd be happy to help you any way that I can. That is, if you scratch my back, I'll scratch yours."

When Pierce slithers away, I meet Roddy in the middle of the street.

Concerned, he puts his hands at my waist, giving me a gentle squeeze. I look over his shoulder to make sure Nicola's nowhere in sight. "Everything okay?" he asks, nuzzling my neck. "It's hard being around you and not being able to touch you."

"I feel the same way. But I'll make as much time for you as I can off the clock. It's just hard with Nicola around. I told you, she won't like—"

"Ah, don't worry about that." Roddy winks. "I think I'm winning her over."

"How so?" I ask, jerking back a bit at his confidence.

"Oh, no funny business! I just mean she seems happy I'm around to capture everything. She's obviously very excited about the club."

"Which is why you and I need to keep it professional around here for now, okay?" I bat his hands away from me playfully. "You go back in first."

"Whatever you say, boss." He winks and smiles at me and the gap in his teeth is just adorable and I wish I could make him understand just how careful we need to be.

Literal life and death.

I watch Nicola give Roddy careful instructions about angles and locations and specific images to capture. *Bossy.* Then she asks him politely to get her a refreshment, specifically, a sparkling water, and off he goes.

But it rubs me the wrong way.

Like she's testing him for something.

Tamsin watches me as I watch Roddy go. When we exchange a curious glance, it occurs to me that Tamsin, by Pierce's definition, is kind of like my sibling, too.

For the first time in a long time, I think of my real sister again. It hurts to imagine where she is or what she's doing now. I haven't looked her up online. Not just because I'm afraid about how much it will hurt to know the truth, but also out of fairness—she doesn't know what happened to me either.

When Roddy returns with a bottle of water for Nicola, and for all of us because he's sweet and probably trying to impress me, too, she makes a big show of opening the cap and dropping it all over, pretending the fizzy sound startled her enough to drop it. All of it an act. A test.

Because Roddy's on it.

Making sure she doesn't slip.

Cleaning it right up.

And offering to get her another one.

"She can have mine," I say, walking over and handing it right to Nicola. She takes it with a smile, just a hint of fang in the low light, and winks at me.

SIXTEEN

NICOLA

1980

Killing someone for the first time wasn't for the faint of heart, but as I tried to keep at the forefront of Amber's mind, still fresh to the ways of the vampire since her turning on New Year's Eve, we no longer *had* a beating heart, so any moral high ground she believed she possessed simply wasn't true by virtue of what we were together. Not that we needed to be nasty about it, but at the end of the day, this was how we survived. It was the food chain. The circle of life for the undead.

She was struggling with that part, a bit more than I thought she would. She hadn't *fully* embraced the vampiric lifestyle since waking, still entirely too connected to her past self, mentioning Malcolm and her sister all the time in casual conversation.

I did not care for that at all.

As for hunting? Get it together, woman. I *needed* her to take my tutelage seriously if this was going to work. I didn't know of any vampire that couldn't hunt on their own. They probably wouldn't last very long, losing strength quickly; you could only go a couple of days at the maximum without a solid feed. I allowed for *some* protestation from Amber's end, a little whining in the name of compassion, but eventually tough love had to come into play.

In those first few weeks, I had been doing most of the heavy lifting, both to show her how it was done and also so she could wrap her head around the fact that she'd have to do it herself as soon as possible.

But I hadn't seen this reluctance to hunt in a new vampire before.

Typically, they were just reborn bloodthirsty and only needed a bit of help as far as technique went. Grappling with the logistics rather than the drive. And yes, of course, Amber already adored the taste, but she was disinclined to engage with how the sausage was made, so to speak.

"Can't you just do it for me?" she whimpered as we quietly stalked a group of businessmen stumbling back to their five-star hotel off Bond Street after rollicking rounds of pints at the pub. We had watched them put *so* many away by then, I knew they'd be worth the wait.

A simple target for Amber's first solo kill.

"Not anymore," I scolded her. "Enough already. You must learn, Amber. We all had to learn." I tried to say this as delicately as I could, but I was growing frustrated.

Previously, when I turned a woman, she took to hunting like a moth to a flame. Finally, there was somewhere to put all that pent-up rage! A well-deserved excuse to behave like an absolute animal. It was liberating in so many ways. The abject violence. To be so outward with it, positively tactile, possessing the innate ability to use your bare hands to rip a man apart?

What a dream.

But Amber was different so far, which was what I wanted, after all. My hope was that she'd be more loyal to me than the rest, but that could also mean she needed more work. More pushing to embrace her new form. I had taken her when she was angry at her husband, maybe her family, too, but not terribly angry at the world yet.

That fire could do with some stoking.

"I know, I know." Amber rolled her eyes. "And I'm sure I'll pick it up eventually and then maybe my thirst will get stronger. But I don't technically *have* to do it myself, right? I just need the goods, you know, to 'stay good'?"

She winked at me, but I didn't appreciate it.

She couldn't manipulate *me*.

Amber and I walked a few yards behind the fine fellows in their suits as they drunkenly sang the chorus of a Moody Blues song aloud. It had been playing at the Iron Duke and clearly got stuck in their heads, though it was painful to hear the cacophony of their squawking. Amber was smiling so bright at me, like the oppressive lights on a lorry at night, trying to get me to bend to her will.

"What if something happens to me one day?" I asked her pointedly.

"But nothing's going to happen to you, Nic. Isn't that the entire point of being a vampire? And look how far you've come already. I mean, Jesus, you're from the 1800s. I think we're fine!"

I certainly hoped so, but if it happened to others, it could happen to us. Only a foolish vampire wouldn't consider their own demise on a daily basis, whether by a human hand or a fellow vampire's; being in the wrong place at the wrong time could be fatal if you didn't have your wits about you.

Trust no one.

Just me.

"Amber, I am quite sorry you're struggling with it, but you must learn to hunt effectively on your own. You've watched me do it so many times. It's your turn now. You must."

"If we're always going to be a team, I don't see why. I don't want to hunt alone. That's gonna be our thing, right? Dancing and dining?"

Cheeky little thing. Amber linked her arm through mine and started to skip, a misguided attempt to butter me up. Amber tripped when I didn't join in, and would have fallen down if I hadn't pulled her back up.

She thought I'd be easy.

Like a man.

Tsk, tsk.

"Come on," she teased. "You enjoy it more anyway! It's like I'm doing *you* a favor!"

I stopped at the crosswalk and put my hands on top of her shoulders, digging my nails slightly into her skin, making severe eye contact. It was long past time to get serious. Enough.

"Amber. *Everything* comes down to knowing how to hunt. To defend yourself, to sustain yourself, to stay powerful. I mean, really, if you don't know how to hunt, you could die one day because of it."

"But *you* said a starving vampire can be revived!"

Amber thought she'd caught me in a lie or a mistake, but clearly she didn't understand.

"A weak vampire could be put in a very compromising situation, hmm? You want someone to put you in harm's way and leave you there for dead? It could happen, Amber. I've heard stories. Many stories. A human could drain you of all your strength in a few days' time if they catch you and keep you, just by withholding a meal or two. Then, while you wither away, unable to fend them off much less feed from them, you could be fried up like a Sunday roast in their back garden. And I won't be able to help you then, will I?"

She nodded at me, picking up on the ferocity of my tone, not saying another word about it.

I released her, giving her a playful hip bump to lighten the mood after painting such a dark picture. Amber didn't seem to do well with anything of real weight, so bad news needed to be fast, like the snap of a rubber band. A quick pinch to receive the message before we could all move on.

"And come off it, babe, it's really not at all unpleasant," I chided her. "In fact, it's quite exhilarating with the right attitude. It's not like we're *turning* any of them. That's a real challenge. It's very difficult to contend with, just such a grave responsibility to see someone through to their new state of being. You should feel very honored that I embarked on such an endeavor with you."

Well, *that* got her attention. She stopped us in our tracks, pulling my arms towards her.

"Wait, really? Tell me everything! I only know my side of it and that was indescribably painful, Nicola. Was yours like that? Who turned you? Who else have you turned?"

I didn't plan to tell her anything about my turning or anyone else's. That was personal. Between maker and companion. As it should be.

But she was easy enough to distract with other topics of note.

"Oh, no, you don't . . . Let's focus on the task at hand. Why don't you take your pick of one of them up there and then we can pop round Annabel's or Tramp afterwards for a celebratory dance? You have to do this, Amber. You must."

Her eyebrows dipped towards her nose and she pouted at me, lips pursed, before walking forward again, accepting her reality. Good thing, too, because the gents were quickly approaching Claridge's, about to retire for the evening, hangovers awaiting them in the morning if she wasn't fast about putting them on our evening's menu.

I must have gotten through to her, because she started to move at a quicker clip, many steps ahead of me, nonsensically starting to shout the name *Bill* at the men, who of course all turned around to see the vision before them.

I clucked my tongue at this technique because now we had to engage with *all* four of them at the same time, which wasn't exactly subtle, but who was I to deny her a smorgasbord for her first independent kill? Well, *nearly* independent. She wouldn't be able to take all of them down alone, but alas, it was not the time for giving feedback.

It was time to look alive. Get the job done. I was ravenous. She must have been, too.

"Oh!" Amber exclaimed at the sight of their faces, zeroing in on the particularly oafish one in the middle who was clumsily leading the singsong. "Sir, I could have *sworn* you were my dear old dad's friend Bill! You look just like him and dress just as well."

We were steps from the side entrance to Claridge's on Davies. It wasn't entirely inconspicuous, but mostly a dead street at that hour, as it wasn't the main thoroughfare.

I wondered if going up to one of their rooms was the best course of action for the situation at hand. That wouldn't be too difficult to finagle, would it? Perhaps a whiff of danger, but who didn't love a quick nip into Claridge's? It was fabulous.

Though I could damn the genius who came up with CCTV, which had now been widely accepted as normal in our fair country. That said, they were clunky little things, relatively easy to spot should we proceed inside. It had always been simple to eat and run, plenty of unsolved murders in a city like London, and it's not like we had fingerprints or biological evidence to leave behind. But getting caught on camera could complicate matters, though solved quickly enough by a few years underground and a bit of hair dye if need be.

Anyway, I suppose we didn't *have* to eat them if it felt like the stars wouldn't align for us that night.

But I had a feeling that they would.

A switch had flipped in Amber.

Go on then, love.

Show me what you got.

"Is Bill as handsome as old Harland here?" One of the other men, donning a herringbone sport coat in a particularly putrid shade of yellow tinged with green, walloped his mate hard on the back, causing Harland to cough. They all laughed at that, drunker than shite.

"Oh, I can't say for sure." Amber smiled. "It's pretty dark out here. I'd have to get a closer look."

Get in, my girl! Was she going to tear him to shreds right out here in the middle of the street? Who knew she had it in her? I'd welcome such a turn from my progeny. I could take on the rest of them, no problem. What a rush. A dine and dash! I didn't see any of those pesky cameras out here on this side of the road. *Give in to yourself, Amber!*

She sidled up closer to Harland, emphasizing her hips in a way that these barbarians couldn't help but admire, topping off the display with a very loud and very juvenile, "*Oooooh-oooooh!*"

"Harland, you cannot be this lucky, my good man. What? Is she going to rob you?" Another one of them chuckled, this time the better-looking fellow with the tailored trousers, the one who clearly cared about his appearance, a proper well-dressed bloke and someone I'd love to dance with at Tramp if circumstances were different. He laughed even louder as Amber approached Harland, putting his forearm and head on his mate's shoulder, his whole body shaking with laughter. "We're too drunk for this!"

"Let's have a look at you, *Harland*," Amber said, putting her hands on Harland's cheeks, her breath hot on his face. "Are you married?" she asked him.

"D-d-divorced," he said, a cheeky grin on his doughy face. He could not believe his luck that this beautiful woman had her hands on him. What had he done to deserve this?

We would soon find out, because I could see what Amber's aim was with him.

She was looking for *a reason*.

Seeking justice for what was about to be a proper murder. As if she fancied herself some kind of avenger. Of course, I knew something like that would set her off. That's why we were in that part of the neighborhood. Plenty of businessmen in town with boorish attitudes about women looking for trouble. We could give them some of that.

I knew precisely what I was doing.

I was just giving Amber another little push.

"Twice!" Herringbone gave the addendum about Harland's divorces and Tailored Trousers laughed again, literally slapping his knee. God, they *were* pissed. It would almost be pathetic to prey on them in this state, but I was delighted that my plan was working. Let these cretins give Amber a reason her human self would understand . . . to create the vampiric self that would, eventually, cease to care about killing at all.

Meanwhile, the other bloke's eyes were closed; he was nodding off while standing, his hand still miraculously fidgeting with a violet pocket square popping out of his jacket. Oh, he was ready for bed, no doubt about that. He'd be the simplest one. Amber should have seen that from miles away, even if it was her first go-round.

Really, why did she pick this massive behemoth of a man instead of the obvious runt of the litter? Again, it was not the time for criticism, but we'd have to discuss her strategy after the game was over.

Amber still had Harland's head between her hands as she examined his face closely. Why did she want to examine every nook and cranny on this bloke, of which there were plenty? He had massive pores, the size and color of gnats.

"Harland. Why did you get divorced twice?" Amber asked sweetly.

All right. Enough chatter, darling. Let's get on with the show. A car drove by without a second glance in our direction. I hoped there wouldn't be another. Any more faffing about and she'd be playing with fire.

"Honestly?" Harland licked his lips. "My first wife turned into a cow after we had the girls, and my second couldn't have any, and you know what, I don't think it's wrong for a man to want a son. What do you think about that, sweetheart? You looking to have a little lad running around anytime soon?"

He said all of that as if it was a hilarious joke, but both Amber and I knew he was speaking his truth, the kind that would only make him taste so much better.

Amber wasted no time starting in on Harland, fixing her nails into his face, pushing them further and further into the skin, until he howled in pain, prompting her to snap his head to the right and clamp down on the left side of his neck.

I'd tell her later that the right side was preferable.

The veins are slightly larger, but we could get into specifics in due course.

I had to get the others before they tried to make a pathetic break for it.

Before Herringbone could make another sound, I leapt onto his shoulders and knocked his head all the way back by the hair, biting down on the front of his throat for kicks, getting two veins going at once because I knew I could handle it.

Not one of them was in any state to run after all those pints, least of all Violet Pocket Square, who finally opened his eyes, not expecting the full-on horrific scene in front of him. I didn't even need to tell Amber that he'd sprung back to life. She already was on it. Excellent. Her instincts were *finally* kicking in.

Amber wrapped the sleepy man in her arms and administered a fatal kiss to his neck like a lover saying good night. Harland continued to bleed out on the street, the sounds he emitted becoming strained and choked until there were none anymore at all.

Tailored Trousers attempted to make a run for it, and his bum looked so good in those things that I watched him go for a few seconds to indulge myself before finally zipping over, meeting him face-to-face.

"I do like your suit. You have good taste." I smiled at him, the macabre red delight from Herringbone still dripping from my painted oxblood lips, a chic contrast if you asked me, not that I was expecting a compliment from this dapper fellow before he met his demise.

"Please. I won't say anything. We all just work together. Please let me go," he begged, tears in his eyes. Oh, let 'em fall, boyo. It'll be your last time. I won't tell anyone. I had him in my clutches as I looked over my shoulder, Amber having gone back to feed aggressively on Harland once more. Tailored Trousers got the wrong girl, unfortunately. I knew Amber would have considered his plea. Foolishly so.

She'd be a sucker for a well-dressed man's tears one day, I was sure of it.

I'd have to keep an eye on that.

But I knew better, so I peeled back those sharp lapels with one hand, held him by the scruff with the other and sunk my fangs into his skin. Marvelous texture, silky-smooth blood, a kind for savoring, but we had to wrap it up now. We had gotten lucky with no witnesses, but this was a rather public performance from women like us.

"Amber!" I laughed at her, relentlessly slurping from her kill. She couldn't seem to stop, and honestly, she could get a bit sick if she kept up that pace. Harland wasn't exactly the picture of health, his cholesterol level likely not one to envy. "We have to go. *Now*."

"But we can't go to Annabel's like this," she said, practically out of breath, a fine display of exhilaration at what we do best. The beast inside her was fully igniting, my creation coming to fruition.

"No," I said, agreeing with her. "No, we can't. Bit off a bit more than we should have chewed, really. What a mess. Come on, darling. I know where we can clean ourselves up."

The two of us slithered into the hotel's side entrance, the powder room just to the left in the hallway. I'd been in that hotel a million times and I'd never seen anyone else in there before. As suspected, not a soul in sight. Only plenty of bright white flannels emblazoned with the company name and an assortment of luxury soaps at our disposal for us to quickly wash off the unsavory bits of the night's activity.

Amber made quick work of it, focused on scrubbing away the evidence as best she could, exchanging a confident look with herself in the mirror. We started to smell like rose and ylang-ylang instead of rust and metal, reapplying our lippy with care, a quick blot on some tissue.

Lovely.

Now we looked like the young wives of the old men posted up in the Fumoir down the hall.

No telltale signs were on my little black dress, but her white and pink gauzy number looked like a proper murder scene. I watched as she removed it from her body, turning it inside out and putting it back on, the blood looking like a curious embellishment through the slinky sheer fabric. Amber was resourceful *and* chic.

Best of all, she was absolutely glowing.

I *knew* she could do it, but now I thought she would *want* to do it, too.

This would only get better. Soon enough, we'd be skulking around the city together, shoulder to shoulder, like a couple of panthers seeking their prey, the world quite literally on our own silver platter. I saw it all before me. My instincts correct. She was the one.

I couldn't help but think of my sister.

This could have been us.

Amber turned her attention to me through the mirror now that she was sorted.

"I get it now, Nicola," she said. "I understand."

No smile. No laughter. All business. She was serious.

Wonderful.

Now, this was going to be *fun*.

SEVENTEEN

AMBER

Courtenay's been earning Nicola's trust these last few weeks.
Day by day.

Task by task.

All by *my* design.

I'd been egging her on with little tips and tricks about how to really impress Nicola in the lead-up to opening night, dangling the promise of growing with the club, gaining some independence—well, at least from her boyfriend—and she's starting to think the two of us are friends, too.

Hey Mister is coming together.

So's my plan.

For example, Nicola *hates* a chatty bartender, but she still likes them to be stylish and good-looking, so I asked Courtenay to get a killer lineup where the potential staff is concerned. She practically knows every barman in London, emphasis on *man*, which I also tell her is Nicola's preference: young, strapping dudes to wait on her, and others, at all times.

Then, if there are any menial tasks that Courtenay can anticipate before being asked—opening boxes of glassware and putting them away, setting up the paint sample swatches in a way Nicola can see them all at one time, or following up *yet again* about the liquor permit—she should be *on it* because Nicola will notice.

And if Courtenay can get the construction crew wrapped around her finger during the day so the opening-night schedule stays on track, she will be golden.

"Like any boss," I told Courtenay, "Nicola loves to have someone else do the dirty work for her. But if she doesn't even have to ask you first? You'll leave her no choice."

"For what?"

"To promote you! Management, baby. Hey Mister could be a big part of your future if you play your cards right. But don't tell Nicola I said that. She loves to surprise the people she cares about with good news."

By focusing on Courtenay's ambition, but also her ache to be cared for, I knew she'd jump into action, no problem. I'd have done the same in her position.

But I also need Nicola to back off with Roddy.

It's like she always finds some kind of errand or favor, outside of photography, to ask him to do. And because he's happy to be helpful and impress Nicola for my benefit—very "if you wanna be my lover, you gotta get with my friends"—he runs off and does them.

But it's driving me crazy.

Does she know something is up?

She hates men.

Why is she taking such a shine to mine?

Roddy calls me his girlfriend now. We've been going hot and heavy whenever we can steal away to his place. He's given me a key to his flat. He hardly talks about New York anymore because I know he's not going anywhere without me.

But we are *going*, buddy.

I just need to push Courtenay a bit further along . . . we're very close. Everyone at Hey Mister loves Court. I even saw her make Tamsin laugh, and she has a sense of humor like Stalin.

Sometimes it feels like Tamsin is watching me at the club. Not that I'm giving her anything to see, but I wonder if she's jealous. Nicola and I are visibly having a good time together at Hey Mister— appearances only from my end to keep up the ruse—but Margaux doesn't include Tamsin in anything, aside from barking orders. It's like Margaux wants to impress Nicola with her own iron fist. Like she's worthy of being in her company, this group effort and, in all likelihood, to show that she's Nic's equal—a fixation of Margaux's.

When I look at her relationship with Tamsin, I see the resemblance. Like Nicola, Margaux buys into the hierarchy of maker and companion, but it doesn't have to be that way, does it? Most of Nicola's recent behavior with me only proves it. Working together on Hey Mister has actually been fun. We haven't laughed like this together in years. Not that I'm changing course. I'm just observing the shift since we started. I know it's only temporary.

People don't really change.

Case in point: I see the Nicola I know when she's toying with Courtenay and me for her own entertainment. For example, she'll use Courtenay to break any ties when we disagree on an aesthetic choice for Hey Mister. With demo and reno largely complete, it's time to get into the #vibes. Colors and paint and lights and furniture and spirit selections and the music and the DJ booth are all up for debate. And I think she's being contrarian with me on purpose, testing Courtenay, too.

"What do you reckon for the DJ booth up here?" Nicola asks me, both of us sitting in the would-be area, just beneath the railing, our feet swinging back and forth where the dance floor will be built below us. Courtenay's within earshot, standing tall and surveying the space, imagining the whole club already as opening night inches closer, ready to be christened in three weeks with stilettos *and* sneakers.

"Super flashy," I say to Nicola with wide eyes and arms outstretched. "Thinking emerald green and gold accents. Tall curtains behind us, but not that trashy party-shop crunchy kind, but like a feathery, frothy light one. Like if you ran a finger across, it looks like it could turn into sand at your feet."

Nicola scrunches her face at me despite my gorgeous description of my perfect taste.

This is how I know she's toying with me.

"Hmm," she says, tracing her jawline with a finger. "I know we're eager to reprise the '70s here, but I was envisioning a more minimalist booth. Just the DJ and equipment, with a black background to blend in. The dance floor should be the centerpiece, no?"

"Of course," I scoff, knowing that honor did indeed belong to the dance floor, "but I'd argue the DJ is extremely important to the energy of the club, too. We want them to feel like a ringleader and very connected with everyone. Not just hiding in the shadows, man or woman behind the curtain."

Minimalist?

God, she really wanted to get a rise out of me.

I knew she was going to question Courtenay next, but even though Court knew it was best to impress Nicola like I said, her opinions almost always lined up with mine.

"Courtenay? Thoughts?" Nicola asks.

"Honestly, I'm with Amber. I don't think we should hold back."

Nicola nods, satisfied and amused, like we're her little pets.

When Roddy snaps a photo of us from below, Courtenay and I audibly groan.

"No low angles!" she shouts with a laugh.

"Trust me, I'm a professional! You look great." He smiles at us, maintaining a few seconds of extra eye contact with me, but I pull away before Nicola can notice.

Does she ever notice?

We're so careful.

And I have to keep going.

I'm so, so close.

We head over to 25 Paul Street for a nightcap. We've done this a few times, our camaraderie as a little group of "industry people" off the charts. We dance the rest of the wee hours away when the night's work is complete, but I always keep Roddy at a safe distance, which he understands. He dances with Nicola and Courtenay, too. Margaux's even gone for a spin, but Tamsin declines every time. She stays on the sidelines as always, observing and pouting and furious with herself that she can't get it together to change her life. Not my problem.

But my plan's been idling for a while.

Nicola hasn't mentioned the idea of turning Courtenay yet.

Not once.

So tonight, I take a few sneaky shots of Roddy and Courtenay dancing together on my phone.

Just in case.

Especially since logistics have finally picked up on my end after many, *many* conversations via burner phones. I worked out a deal with a shady group from the dark web that transfers dead bodies on the black market. He doesn't know that *I* will be the dead body in question, but nothing the quick compelling of a stranger won't handle.

He told me the timing is ideal since everyone is checked out around the holidays. They'll take care of the phony death certificate and the shipping container and make sure "the body" is on the flight of my choosing, straight to JFK.

Roddy's plane.

Once he agrees.

Once I tell him.

Once I get the courage . . .

But first to get the funds. Moving bodies isn't cheap, and I can't just take cash from Nicola. She keeps track of every pound and penny. I've hemmed and hawed over several scenarios to scrounge up some major coin.

Sadly, the fastest and simplest method won't be my finest hour.

I've been thinking about it for weeks.

And I've been watching her.

I know the security code now.

Geraldine remained in Malcolm's home in Belgravia, which surprised me. Maybe she thought she'd feel closer to him. It was in his family for years. I tried not to dwell on Malcolm, the memory of him always a painful memory of my former self, but I *knew* that house.

And everything in it.

It used to belong to me, too.

I look around the street, dead silent at this hour. I'm in all black, my hair wrapped up tight, and I wear a face mask just in case, hoping to look cautious instead of suspicious. I enter the code next to the door, open it up and step inside.

This is *wild*.

It looks untouched from the time I lived here, except for the photos of Malcolm's children and grandchildren everywhere I look.

I don't linger on them, but I briefly wonder if we would have had children together.

It doesn't matter now.

No emotion.

No regrets.

This is a material mission only.

Malcolm had plenty of bank accounts—not that I had direct access to those when we were married in the '70s, husbands often maintaining strict control of finances—but I was never worried about it because there was always plenty of cash available to me. He sprinkled it in different nooks and crannies around the house, like glass bowls full of little wrapped candies for my enjoyment.

I assume—*hope*—that his wife still maintains the old-fashioned in-house ATM, so I'm going to help myself to some of the reserves and try not to feel shitty about it.

Despite what ultimately happened between Malcolm and me, I like to think he'd be supportive of my noble pursuit of freedom from Nicola.

She took both our lives.

I'm startled by the sound of a little bell behind me in the living room. My fangs naturally pop out in defense. When I turn around, I see a little white cat watching me from the wingback chair in the corner. She hisses at me but doesn't leave her post.

I guess that's about all a cat can offer during a home invasion.

My relief is short-lived when I find Geraldine watching me with wild eyes from the staircase, her hand gripping the banister so hard I worry her frail fingers might break in two. As she takes a step, her white nightgown grazes the floor. I don't want her to trip and fall.

"Wh-who are you?" she stammers at me, eyes darting first to the cat and then to the wall near the door, as she wonders how I got in her home. I retract my fangs. She looks like she could wither away at any moment, a broken heart personified.

I can't believe Malcolm's third wife is staring at me.

She stands up straighter and squints at me now.

She recognizes me . . .

"Amber?" she says, voice firm.

I lock eyes with Geraldine again, regaining my nerve, focusing on my purpose for being here. I compel her to sit down with the cat in her arms, to be quiet and still for ten minutes. There won't be any need for senseless violence.

I'm not like Nicola.

I work quickly, gathering more than enough from the reserves I remember. Malcolm was a creature of habit. The errant cash was still in his desk, in the bottom drawer of his wardrobe, and in the study, too, tucked into some of his favorite biographies of the powerful men he idolized.

Geraldine pets her little cat, slack-jawed, running her hand through its fur mindlessly.

I tell her she will forget this ever happened, but I also tell her I'm sorry.

She'll forget that, too.

She'll never see me again.

I remind myself that Malcolm would have left her with more than enough for the time she has left, which doesn't appear to be much at all.

I think Geraldine really loved him.

wait in a quiet mews, not far from 25 Paul Street and Roddy's flat in Shoreditch. I'm going to hide any documents at his place out of fear Nicola could find them at the Laurels.

There's not a soul around.

The meeting is in five minutes.

I have an envelope of cash in hand and he's supposed to have a death certificate, dated for New Year's Eve, and all the instructions for body transport, including funeral home location, code name and number for the next point of contact, along with a confirmation of shipping container purchase and delivery date.

"Marlena?" I hear a voice not far away from me. I used my sister's name when I made the first call. I don't know what possessed me. Hearing it out loud feels like a punch to the gut.

I look up and nod slightly in the direction of the shadowy figure approaching. He wears a flat cap low over his forehead and a long gray overcoat, scarf wrapped around his neck. It's impossible to tell his age, but he is large and imposing, with broad shoulders and a heavy gait.

But something doesn't feel right. It has nothing to do with my vampiric senses, but as a woman alone in a dark alley in London with a strange man.

He starts to walk faster. I see nothing in his hand. I clutch the envelope of cash tightly.

"Do you have it?" I ask when he's in earshot. He's young. Likely spry. Fast.

And probably delicious if it comes down to it.

I stay on high alert as he wordlessly pulls a manila folder out of his coat.

When I reach for it, he yanks it back, holding out his hand for the cash.

"I need to see the documents first," I say firmly. He doesn't make eye contact with me. I can't compel him. He's perfectly still for a moment before shoving the folder into my chest and snatching the envelope from my hands and then walking away at a quick clip.

It's full of blank papers.

"*Fuck.*"

He starts to run, not expecting me to be faster.

I catch up.

He shows me a switchblade, not expecting me to be stronger.

I tackle him.

The weapon flies out of his hand and I latch firmly onto his neck, wolfing him down, reaching inside his coat to reclaim the cash.

What am I going to do now?

I feel cursed, feeding on this con artist who tried to screw me over. Regrets run through my head as his blood courses down my throat. I should have used a man's name. I should have set up multiple meetings and much earlier. Honest to God, I should have left Nicola years ago. Why did I wait so long? Why was I so afraid? Why was I so lazy? Why do I yearn for independence when it's clear I can't do anything on my own without screwing it up? Why did I think I could get away with this? Seriously, how the hell am I going to get to New York with Roddy now?

There's not much time left before opening night.

I need a Plan B.

Pierce said I could come to him.

But what will he want in return?

Before I can start concocting some kind of Hail Mary, I feel a change in the air.

Someone is watching me.

When I look up, I feel a drip of warmth fall from my chin onto my collarbone.

Courtenay's at the other end of the mews.

She drops her lit cigarette, horrified at the sight of me hovering over a dead body. God, I didn't even know she smoked, obviously stealing away to dark alleys to do so in secret.

She's frozen.

We both are.

I need to compel her immediately to forget. But she could remember down the line. Compelling is *not* for the familiar. But it's too soon for Courtenay to know the truth, and it has to be Nicola's decision to turn her.

I have no choice.

"It's okay, Court," I say, inexplicably putting my hands up like I've been caught by police. Courtenay takes a single step backward, terrified of me, and I take one gentle stride toward her before launching into a full gallop, grabbing on to her shoulders until I have her gaze locked into mine. Her body starts to feel weak in my arms, her eyelids low and hazy, as if she's lost in a dream.

She'll forget.

For now.

Courtenay heads back to 25 Paul Street, her heels softly clacking away on the cobblestones, eerie amidst the silence until they're gone entirely.

What the hell am I going to do now?

Allegedly the sound system's been successfully installed at Hey Mister after a couple of rounds of technical difficulties that got so dire and drawn-out that Tamsin decided to *eat* one of the electricians out of frustration. *Oops.* We told his boss that he never showed up to work that day. We've been assured it's firing on all cylinders now, so to celebrate, Nicola wants to host a little dance party of our own as a test run.

Glam dress, hot shoes and fire playlists encouraged to match the aesthetic at the club.

We spared no expense.

Leather, lace, velvet, silk, brocade, travertine, gold, silver, crystal.

Every fixture, every surface, every curtain, every room is a *Saturday Night Fever* dream.

Even the office turned out to be stunning, and nobody's really going to see it, except for Nicola and me. Herman Miller chairs at the desks. A chaise lounge, of course, for Nic. Top-of-the-line tech with a coded entry for admittance plus CCTV for most of the club. And she even bought some new art, nightlife photographs from disco's heyday, a project she gave to Roddy, which irritated me. But Nicola is Nicola, and she also brought in one of the old tapestries from the Laurels—scenic, pastoral, and with a beam of sunlight shining onto the grassy knoll.

She can be such a masochist.

The two of us are in the DJ booth together, awash in tones of green and gold just as I wanted, to do the honors for the first taste of sound. Tamsin and Margaux take their post on the dance floor below us, gathering just outside the glittering violet Hey Mister logo in the center. Roddy's snapping photos left and right, sneaking quite a few of me—love it, keep the adoration levels high—but also, I wish he'd be a little more subtle.

I think his chummy relationship with Nicola is making him overconfident.

Careful, boy.

For both of us.

But Nicola isn't focused on him or me.

Courtenay's late.

Twenty minutes.

Nicola doesn't like it, her thumbnail flicking at her pinky again.

"Well, that's enough waiting," Nicola snips aloud. "Why don't *you* pick then, darling?"

She puts her arm around my shoulders and I look down at the system in front of me. There are fixtures and speakers and levels and a bunch of equipment that's not exactly intuitive, but I know how to set a mood. I pick a Candi Staton remix that I love from my playlist. I've been listening to it all the time lately. It starts off too soft, and when I fumble with the soundboard to the best of my ability, which, let's be honest, is no ability at all, Nicola takes one of my fingers, placing it on one of the faders.

"I got a quick tutorial," she says, winking at me. "Not sure where you were."

I take a deep breath and we push it up together.

There it is.

The thump of the bass. The pace of the beat. Just loud enough before it starts to hurt. The perfect volume. Nicola starts to bump her hip against mine in time. Looking up at us, Margaux starts to shrug her shoulders in a red jumpsuit with a matching lip, her bob teased up high. Even Tamsin starts to bob her head, her flaxen hair bouncing on the shoulder pads of her lavender blazer. I smile at her for the hell of it, but she doesn't return the favor. Whatever.

When I feel the beat about to drop in the middle of my chest,

working its way up my throat so joyously with every repetition of
"say I'm gonna leave, a hundred times a day," I have to sing along, my
body possessed by the rhythm, my hands high above my head.

I scream the chorus.

Young hearts run free.

That'll be Roddy and me in New York.

We're going to get there.

I'm going to get there.

"A dream come true, darling," Nicola trills, lacing her fingers
through mine. "Toot-toot!"

"Beep-beep." I smile, knowing our dreams aren't the same
anymore.

Were they ever?

"Roddy, are you getting this?" Nicola calls out, but he's not in
the booth or on the dance floor. "What's he doing over there?"

Roddy's watching the hallway leading to the front entrance. He
quickly slings his camera around his shoulder, opening his arms
wide. Courtenay runs right into them, dying to be held, her body
quaking underneath his touch. I turn the music down, but Nicola
is already zipping down the spiral staircase.

"I'm so sorry I'm late," Courtenay says, wiping tears from her
face. "He won't stop calling me, but I've just shut off my phone, so
it's fine."

She doesn't look fine at all.

She looks as scared as she did last night.

"What's happened?" Nicola asks her sweetly, pulling Courtenay
from Roddy and into her chest. "You can tell me."

"It's nothing. He's just so jealous." Courtenay sniffles. "I don't
know what he thinks he saw, but it was just dancing. With Roddy!
He said a number he didn't know texted him pictures of me getting
cozy with some bloke at 25 Paul, and when I told him it was just a

friend from work, he lost it, because I've been keeping this job a se-cret because—"

"COURTENAY!"

A booming voice bellows down the hallway, echoing as it bounces off the narrow walls.

"That's him." Courtenay starts to shuffle to the door, but Nicola won't let her go.

"No, no, darling. We'll take care of it."

A behemoth of a bald man enters the main room of our club. He's much older than Courtenay, all strength and not a lick of fat on him.

"David, I told you not to come here," Courtenay cries. "This is *my* place of work and you can't just barge in here and . . ." She trails off as he starts marching toward her, ready to submit, but sweet Roddy steps between them, gallantly getting involved despite his slight frame.

We all hold our breath.

David's at least a foot taller than Roddy, with biceps double in size.

"I told you to come home!" he roars at Courtenay, ready to step around Roddy until he recognizes his face. "Oh. It's *you*."

Before Roddy can dodge his fist, David sucker punches him so he falls hard to the floor. When he grabs for Courtenay's arm, Nic-ola refuses to let go.

"Absolutely not!" Nicola shouts, smacking his massive hand away.

I feel useless.

I can't move.

I caused this . . .

"Are you the boss around here?" David asks Nicola, his fingers digging deeper into Courtenay's skin, so tight she winces. "Because she quits."

"Let go of her, mate. Now," Nicola commands him, but he's not looking her in the eye. He can't stop staring at Roddy. Like he wants to kill him. I help Roddy up carefully, pushing his hair out of his face. He's getting a juicy shiner tomorrow for sure. I'll tell him it looks hot.

"It's all right," Courtenay says to Nicola, shrugging her hand away. David, satisfied, releases Courtenay and makes for the exit, setting the expectation for her to follow him. Her face is flushed pink; she's beyond embarrassed and it's hard for me to look at her.

I know what I've done.

"You babes have fun tonight," Courtenay says with a small, forced smile. "I'll sort it out. It's okay." She mouths to Roddy that she's sorry so David doesn't hear it, then she follows him out the door.

We're all shell-shocked, rarely stuck in a position like that as vampires.

Nicola twitches, like she wants to chase after them.

But she doesn't want Courtenay to know yet either.

That's promising . . .

After I compelled Courtenay last night, I texted David the photos I took. I used a blocked number. I just wanted to move their eventual breakup along. I thought he'd kick her out. That's all. And she'd get closer to us, to Nicola; we could take care of her, accelerating everything.

I didn't know he was so big.

I didn't know he was so scary.

But maybe that's a lie I told myself so I'd go through with it.

What kind of guy did I think she was with anyway?

I knew.

Of course I knew.

But I did it anyway.

Nicola continues to stare down the empty hallway.

"At least we know the sound system works," Tamsin says, breaking the silence with an ill-timed joke, but who is surprised?

We wrap up early. Party's over. Margaux and Tamsin go home. I help Roddy clean up his face. He wants me to spend the night with him. I consider it because I know Nicola will be occupied. She's already gone without saying goodbye to anyone.

Just like I knew she would.

EIGHTEEN

NICOLA

1980

When that outrageously handsome man made his entrance into Annabel's earlier that evening, I should have known what was to come. Long locks swept back, well-kept facial hair, but not too perfect, a bit scraggly for effect, and decked out in the sort of casual dress that looked cool but not intentionally so. Rough around the edges. Jeans and a T-shirt. A jacket lent to him at the door for sake of the dress code. Very Kris Kristofferson over Andy Gibb.

So naturally, Amber had to have him.

She had taken to lusting over men who were the exact opposite of Malcolm *and* her father, leaving the more *bohemian* types, at least on the surface.

"Have you ever seen a man so dreamy before in your life?" she whispered in my ear. We were posted up in the corner, taking a little dance break and having a bit of a lookie-loo around the room. "The only problem is that I seriously doubt he's a good dancer. He has a nice gait from what I can tell, but no grace, not that I'm complaining. He's still a fox. Who do you think he knows here? I don't think this is his scene."

"Of course not," I scoffed. "He just ordered *a pint*, for God's sake." I mean really, sir. No one ordered *a pint* at Annabel's. This wasn't the corner pub. It's a fucking members-only club for the see-and-be-seen crowd. But he seemed to know that he was an anomaly there, especially when he noticed us observing him, lifting his glass to us in greeting. Cheeky prick.

"I think he's too old for you," I said to Amber, rather nonsensically, as if age mattered in the life of a vampire. I could see the appeal, even if he wasn't totally to my taste. He might have been pushing forty-some-odd years, but when you looked like that, I couldn't imagine anyone giving a fuck, least of all Amber, who was hard up for some sexual male attention in her newly embraced vampiric form.

She didn't want a meal, let's put it that way.

"Who cares how old he is?" she replied, right on cue. "You said I need to start hunting by myself on occasion. Hone the craft. Maybe he—"

"You're not going to hunt that man, Amber. You're going to fuck him."

"So what?" Amber laughed, swaying along to the Jam. She hadn't noticed, but it had been a slow burn. The demise of disco. There was more hyperbolic synth in music. More rock. Less electric strings or syncopated horns. What we loved was quickly becoming passé. "Aren't I allowed to go to bed with him if I want to?" Amber asked me sincerely.

I adored when she asked me permission about anything and wondered how much longer it would last.

Hopefully forever.

"Of course," I replied. Nobody wants an achingly horny vampire around the house unless you, too, want to lose your ever-loving mind hearing about it all fucking night long. "Just as long as you don't fall in love."

"Oh, come on, would that be *so* bad?" She cocked her head to the side like a puppy, and it made me want to give her a little kiss on the nose and a quick slap on the bum all at the same time. "Could be fun to have a man around the house."

I'd neglected to tell her yet that it's practically a statistical impossibility to successfully turn a human man into a vampire you'd want to invite into your inner circle. They became even more beastly. Not to mention that I, the lady of the manor, would never, ever allow such a thing.

Not at the Laurels.

Never again.

Absolutely not.

"Easy, darling," I said to her. "Just know that it's not that simple to hold back when you're hot for someone. Proceed with caution. You might hurt him, unable to squelch your hunger."

She pondered that idea for a moment, looking into the disco ball and then back again at the man at the bar with his pint and tight behind. Ugh, I was going to lose this battle.

"Maybe, but I haven't yet felt *so* thirsty that I kill without thinking about the person first. Besides, I only focus on jerks and jagoffs, and he doesn't seem like either."

I loved when Amber said "jagoffs." It was so foreign and charming. Did they all sound like that in Wisconsin? What a place.

"That's good of you," I said, "but I fear your barometer of justice will change the longer you're a vampire. Sometimes you just need a fix, you know? It's not about being a *vigilante* or anything. It's just survival. Our nature."

"We're different, though," she said, and I didn't disagree, at least for now, because I knew she'd come around. I had raised many young vampires to grow into their vicious nature, but I didn't want her to become *too* vicious, lest it get thrown in my direction one day.

And then I'd have to do what I'd have to do.

Amber's incessant earnestness, though, should fade with time. She was still just a baby.

Regardless, I really didn't want her getting involved with that man, or any man, in any way that was a pursuit of love. It would only end in death or heartbreak, likely both. This wasn't my first go-round with companions looking elsewhere for entertainment.

"And he looks sweet," she added, quite naively.

Sweet? A man who looked like *that?* Unlikely, my dear. Highly unlikely.

"Amber. Human men are for sex and service. That's all. Keep that mantra in your mind to avoid any sort of disappointment in the future. I only have your best interests at heart."

"I know." She nodded, appreciative of my care.

And to no one's surprise at all, the attractive man approached us with supreme confidence and a couple of cocktails in hand. He must have downed his pint, ready to mingle with the mélange, and we were his first stop.

"Right on schedule." I grimaced.

"Naturally," Amber said, flipping her hair and then twirling the ends through her fingers. Oh, here we go. I always expected the worst of people. Amber seemed to expect the best, despite nearly all evidence to the contrary. I couldn't decide if I was jealous of her for being that way or if I pitied her.

"Hi, handsome," Amber greeted him with a cross of the legs, staying seated in the banquette. Of course, I wanted to kill him instantly, but decorum prevailed in public as per usual. It was bloody Annabel's, after all.

"It's Cillian, actually," he replied, Irish brogue so fully intact that it would be damn near impossible for Amber to resist him now. She flipped for fanciful accents and thought pretty much everyone in this country had one, even the Welsh! "I'm here with one of my mates down by the bar. He's a bit shy and I'm a bit forward, so I thought I'd bring the two of you a couple of martinis and see if I could coerce you to join us."

"Absolutely," Amber said, taking the drink and then taking my hand, but I pulled away, refusing to be a sort of consolation prize for some nobody, sight unseen.

"You two go on ahead," I said. "I'm not really in the market."

"I can point him out if you like," Cillian said. "He's a stand-up fella."

Like I would believe anything this tosser had to say to us.

"Why don't you send him over here?" I grinned devilishly, toying with Amber. She knew what I might do. I could sneak him out the back and have *my* way with him . . .

"No!" Amber said, too quickly. Oh, why did she care who I ate? She didn't even know his friend. "Just come with us, Nic. Please?"

I really, *really* did not want to, but if I didn't get on board with some of her harebrained ideas at least some of the time, it wouldn't be good for long-term morale between us.

And I wanted this time with Amber to be different from the rest.

I was sure those men were harmless enough, at least in our very specific company.

We moved through the crowd, led by Cillian, Amber purposely splashing her drink over to the side a few times so that it looked nearly finished by the time we got to the bar. Cillian's friend was not nearly as handsome as he was, but pleasant-looking enough to muster up a bit of banter for Amber's sake.

"This is Benji," Cillian said to me. Benji gave me an odd little wink that looked more like a tic, and even though his mane wasn't nearly as luxurious as Cillian's, it was still lush enough to give a little tug if the situation required, sexual or otherwise.

"How'd you two get in here?" I asked, purposely combative from the start. Benji snorted with appreciation. I'd wager he was the sort of man who claimed to enjoy a spitfire of a woman, as if I was a novelty for his amusement alone. Twat.

"A friend put us on the list. We're in town for a couple of days on business," Benji explained. He didn't have the same Irish brogue as Cillian, nor the same charm, sadly.

"What sort of business?" I asked skeptically, looking them up and down. They were decidedly not dressed for conducting business.

"Haven't you heard of casual Fridays?" Benji laughed, getting closer to me. I noticed Cillian had whisked Amber away immediately to the dance floor. Now I was stuck with this bozo for the foreseeable future. But perhaps I could make it worth my while. I could eat.

"What do you do? You in school?" Benji asked me, licking his lips after sipping his drink.

"No," I said, giving him absolutely nothing in return.

"You work, then?"

"Not really." I looked over his shoulder and up and around and basically anywhere but at him, my hips teetering from side to side in time with the music, not because I particularly liked the song, but rather I wanted him to feel insulted. It was driving him crazy to be ignored, but alas, it seemed to only encourage him more.

But it was all right.

He'd come to regret it.

"You married?" he whispered now, enjoying the illicit possibility.

"Something like that." I shrugged, actively looking for Amber again, who was no longer in my line of sight. Where did they go? A sexually charged interaction with a man still required my supervision, the wily little vixen.

"What's your name, love?" Benji asked me.

"Did you see—"

"They're fine. It's just us now." He grinned at me, pulling me close by my waist.

I didn't like it.

Something felt wrong in his touch, besides the obvious disgust I had for him.

I could sense it, a nefarious motive.

I placed my untouched martini glass on the bar and started to leave Benji behind, but he grabbed me by the arm. "Relax, Nicola. I said they're fine."

I looked back at him at the sound of my name; I hadn't shared it, but maybe Amber had said it out loud moments before. Had she? Something felt amiss now. Who were they? Why did they know who we were? Did they know *what* we were?

"Of course." I smiled, getting cozier with him, bending into Benji's body ever so slightly, to suggest a familiarity but only just so. "But we look out for each other."

"Is that right?" He grinned. "You two go out a lot."

He said it as a declarative, not a question. Another misstep. Had they been watching us? I knew it. For how long? And why? I inhaled sharply, unbothered if he found it rude, trying to find Amber. I could sense that she was close by, but not in the immediate vicinity anymore.

She had left the club with Cillian.

I locked eyes with Benji. Mine were perfectly still. I would not blink, not even once, and now he wouldn't be able to help himself. He would tell me everything—if there was anything to tell.

A vacant look sailed across his face from top to bottom; his jaw went slightly slack, making his lower lip jut out a bit, revealing his bottom teeth, crooked and tinged with brown, all battered from years of tobacco; and his once confident shoulders started to roll forward, that bravado he thought he possessed completely deflated now, as I compelled him to tell me *exactly* what the fuck the two of them were doing there.

"Malcolm Wells hired us," he revealed. "He wants his wife back."

That was all I needed to hear.

Time to turn it up and take care of *my* business.

He followed me to the exit like a dog on a lead.

We stepped outside the club and tucked into Berkeley Square across the street. It was quiet and relatively deserted at that hour. I sat down on a bench and patted the space next to me. Good boy. The moment he sat, I swung my legs over and onto his lap, encouraging him to put his arm around the small of my back.

"And your job is what, exactly?" I aimed for some finer details. Were they actual police, or private detectives, or worse? What was the level of danger we were in?

Would she have to go into hiding?

"Cillian and I have been working together for years. Freelance PIs. Mr. Wells hired us after the police came up short on locating his wife. Well, they said she wasn't missing. They believed she just left him, like her Dear John letter had said, and she didn't want to be found, but he's not really accepting that as fact."

Malcolm Wells, not giving up on his lady love. It would almost be romantic if he wasn't such a prig. Besides, Amber was mine now. I'd won her, though not altogether fair and square.

"And what do you know about Amber?" I asked Benji.

"Just that she's been spending time with you these days."

"Do you know where we live?"

"No. Do you live together?"

Pfff, some private investigator he was! They knew hardly anything, but enough to do what had to be done.

I stifled Benji's screams with my hand so they sounded like moans of pleasure to any wayward passersby. I drank much faster than normal—nearly choking on him, his blood ran down my throat so fast—so death came quickly. I kept it neat and tidy, as was my usual, leaving barely any blood on my face. A professional since 1850.

I waited a few more moments for Benji's wounds to close and disappear before I left him behind. Yet another mysterious death in London Town. Still, even if these so-called PIs didn't know the full extent of Amber's and my relationship, this whole escapade could set off an unfortunate chain of events with a relentless Malcolm heading up the search.

Amber was not going to like it, not one bit, but she would have to disappear for a while, too.

didn't see her from the square, but I could sense Amber. I followed those instincts up the road until she felt closer. I saw that they'd popped into the Footman, where handsome Cillian looked right at home, with his arm around Amber and, of course, another pint in his hand.

Those blokes sure drank a lot on the job.

Probably why they were so shit at it.

Amber's glass of Cabernet was of course untouched, and for a PI, he was not very observant about the fact that she was never drinking what he was buying. Perhaps it didn't matter because they only had eyes for each other. I knew it was going to be a hard lesson for her to learn, but it was hardly the first time a girl had to learn something awful about a man she fancied from down the pub.

"Nic!" Amber looked happy to see me, then disappointed. "Did you ditch Benji already? Give a guy a chance!"

"A quick word," I said curtly, with no smile, a command rather than a request, and she could tell.

"Be right back." She smiled at Cillian and gave him a rebellious peck for my benefit. Lovely, whatever, darling. I pulled her to the far end of the small pub and whispered in her ear.

"They were hired by your husband to find you."

Her eyes widened at the thought, lips pursed together, almost turning up.

Almost as if she was . . . *flattered*?

Oh, *come the fuck on*, Amber!

"Are you sure?" she asked, a small trace of a smile on her face. How exasperating. This was not the appropriate reaction at all. How to best convey that?

"I just sucked his mate dry in the park outside and it's still early, risking being seen. So, what do you think?"

She dropped the wineglass, horrified by the revelation, and I *should* have made her do it to Cillian, but in the interest of time, I took care of Amber's dirty work.

Especially since the next bout of news was going to absolutely devastate her.

Amber sulked in her bedroom for the rest of the night after I told her that she'd have to go into hiding at the Laurels for at least a year, perhaps more, to shake Malcolm off the trail. I assured her this was very normal when newly inducted into the vampiric lifestyle because so many parts of the previous life were still fresh and alive and it was very difficult to coexist in both worlds.

I'd had to do it, too, of course, but for much longer—I hadn't wanted to risk losing the Laurels. But I wasn't going to share those details with Amber. Instead, I tried to ease her pain by talking about music. It was changing. Disco was over anyway. It would be an ideal time to reemerge when nightlife had found its footing again, hopefully with a better sound. But with Malcolm looking for her so actively and with money behind the search, it wasn't wise for her to be out at all.

"Or we could take care of him another way?" I shrugged, knowing the cavalier suggestion of killing him would get her attention.

But that's what it could lead to if he discovered anything else about her new life.

She put a hand over her mouth at the thought, looking me right in the eye, more serious than ever before.

"No," she said firmly. "I don't want that, Nicola. I do not. Malcolm is off-limits. Not now, not ever. Promise me."

"I understand, darling! I'm only looking out for you," I said, giving her a sweet kiss on the cheek, but she turned even farther away from me.

"Promise," she said again.

"Very well, I promise," I said, hoping I could keep it for the sake of our friendship. "But please trust me, this will be a blip on the radar in your life as a vampire. Don't look so cross, Amber. Our youth is eternal; so is the world. This will be the most difficult part, I promise."

"I thought you said turning was the hardest part," she said, not even looking at me anymore.

"That's different. It's just—"

"You should have told me," she murmured, heading for her room.

"Told you what?" I scoffed.

But Amber didn't say another word as she slammed the door behind her.

"Jonathan!" I called out. He was in front of me in seconds. "Amber's husband is looking for her. If you see anything, hear anything, you must tell me right away."

"Of course, madam."

"And turn it up around her, would you? Of course, you're to stay loyal to me, but we need Amber to get through this tumultuous time as smoothly as possible. Just . . . dote on her. You know what I mean? Like a brother or father would, to be clear."

"Yes, of course. Understood." Jonathan nodded. "Do *you* need anything tonight, madam?"

Oh, why not?

I deserved it.

I let the houseman take me to bed.

NINETEEN

AMBER

Nicola's been running Jonathan ragged preparing for Courtenay's arrival tonight. Her tone is overly harsh and he clearly can't stand it anymore—like an old married couple—but he does what she wants anyway. Fancy sheets. Fancy biscuits. Fancy pajamas.

Nicola's been extra short with him since we got Hey Mister going, taking her stress level out on him when I thought for sure I'd be bearing the brunt myself. I want to tell her to ease up, but I'm not ruffling any feathers with this latest win. Still, Jonathan is pushing eighty and she needs him around until she ensnares someone else to take over.

Not that I'll be around to meet her new hire.

I hate thinking about Jonathan's eventual death.

I wonder if he ever thinks about it.

When Courtenay arrives at the Laurels, she's understandably frazzled. David turned up dead last night, near a pub out in Camden. She spent much of the day with the police, but of course she was cleared of any suspicion. A lot of people wanted that guy dead, I figured.

I'm sure Nicola did, too.

She fawns over Courtenay, showing off the Laurels, keeping her close so she feels protected and welcome. I recognize the performance. I fell for it, too.

"You're always welcome here with us," Nicola says, giving Courtenay a squeeze. "Do you want to watch some telly? Are you hungry at all?"

I know Nicola will be pampering her all night, encouraging Jonathan to do the same.

"Are *you* hungry?" I ask Nic as they make their way to the study, but she shakes her head.

"I'm fine," she says, not even looking at me. "But if you want to fetch something for yourself, you should . . ."

Don't mind if I do.

The Wapping neighborhood is along the river Thames and quite the mishmash of the old and the new. Set between Tower Bridge and Canary Wharf, Wapping has plenty of old pubs and cobblestone streets plus the echoes of piracy with the aptly named Execution Dock. These days, it's a pretty chichi place to live, with stately homes, modern lofts and other waterfront property.

Including Pierce's luxury compound.

He has a whole building that spans half the street. It used to be a giant warehouse and he converted it into some kind of Playboy mansion, according to Nicola.

I'm about to find out for myself.

I push the doorbell outside the gate. I half expect a couple of well-meaning adorable bimbos to come racing downstairs to greet me, swinging open the door in bikinis and bunny tails, but Pierce shows up instead.

He slithers through the gate, closing it behind him with his foot, black shoes freshly shined. He is stunningly handsome in the moonlight, with a prominent Roman nose and dark eyebrows so full and fluffy, you'd almost want to roll around in them. He's all wrapped up in a dark gray cardigan, arms crossed, like I'm disturbing his peace.

"Yes?" he finally says.

"I'm here to scratch your back."

Pierce throws his head back, laughing warmly with his fangs at rest, but I still keep my distance. "Intriguing. What is this regarding?"

"I need to get to New York on New Year's Day," I say, straight to the point. "Do you know how I could get there safely? Any connections? I know you have quite a network in London, but something tells me your reach is broader than that."

He's still a man. Appealing to his ego should only help my case.

"Oh, Amber. Why do you want to go so far away when you could just join us here with the same result? I know you want to leave her. I don't blame you."

I'm not trying to insult Pierce, but I'm not taking up with another vampire anywhere.

I won't be under anyone's thumb ever again.

I just want to be free.

"I appreciate the invitation, but I have another plan."

Pierce leans back against the gate and smirks at me. "Doesn't sound like you do, love. You have an *idea*. You don't have a plan. Or you had one, and it wasn't very good, which is why you're here now. Am I getting warmer?"

His arrogance is so annoying. I can't believe he was Nicola's type once.

"You won't care much for New York." He grins. "You're a Londoner."

"No one's ever called me that before."

"You've been here a long time now, Amber. And it's not a simple thing to just—"

"But can it be done?" I interrupt him.

"Cheeky. As I was saying—"

"I've heard *all* of you say this already!" I shout, frustrated. "But I'm going. With or without your help. Maybe this was a mistake. You probably can't anyway . . ."

"It's not about if I *can*, love," he sneers, "but if I want to, and you'd have to make it really worth my while."

"What do you want?"

"You think I'm just going to tell you?" He laughs at me. "Where's the fun in that?"

"I don't have much time!" That only makes him laugh harder.

"Amber, please, all we have is time." He smiles cryptically—a clue? "I can help get you where you want to go, but you should know there's no guarantee you'll be safe. Different country, different vampires, but if you want my opinion, it'll probably be a lot of the same, with even more tourists. It's a cursed life, love, but it's ours. I hope you'll reconsider. You know you have an open invitation here . . . if you want to avoid the fate of *most* of her companions."

"No. Thank you," I say, treading lightly. "But I can't do that."

Pierce sighs as he opens the gate, stepping inside the courtyard.

"Then I guess you better figure out what I want and don't show up here empty-handed again. Unless of course you have a change of heart about my invitation to join us. Not to worry. I won't tell her you were here . . ."

He closes the door, disappearing behind the hedges.

I think I know what he's talking about.

If I have the guts to take it.

When I get back to the Laurels, Nicola ushers me quietly toward the study.

"Let's have a chat," she says, winding a finger through my hair. "About our future."

I'm on edge immediately. Her tone is gentle but her words ominous. Does she know I went to see Pierce? She couldn't, right? Impossible. They weren't on speaking terms, were they? If she knew, she'd probably lock me away to starve and kill me without a second thought. Congregating with an ex is the ultimate betrayal.

I follow her into the study, staying close to the door.

She leaves it open.

Nicola stretches out on the chaise, taking an audible breath, a happy little sigh.

I sink into the leather chair closest to the exit.

What is going on? Should I be worried? Can she *smell* Pierce on me?

"It's been good having Court around, hasn't it?" Nicola finally asks, crossing one leg over the other.

Oh, thank God. My shoulders relax. This is about Courtenay. Exactly what I want.

"Absolutely," I say. "She's great. A kindred spirit. And good for the club, too."

"She is, isn't she?" Nicola chuckles to herself. "She has certainly proven herself worthy of employment *and* our friendship, I'd say. An intriguing addition to our dynamic, really mixing it up, just as we wanted."

I nod, not saying too much.

Lead the way, Lady Claughton.

"It's like she's one of us, hmm?"

"Definitely," I say. "Aside from, well, our situation."

"Our situation . . ." Nicola's voice has slowed considerably, like honey dripping into a cup of Earl Grey. "What if Courtenay *was* one of us?"

Bingo.

Piping-hot tea!

Nicola waits for my reaction, sitting up straight on the chaise again, leaning in toward me to get a closer look at my face. I'm not sure if she wants a positive response or something more hesitant. If the former, she might take it that I fully trust her judgment, which she loves. But the flip side could make for a better emotional response from her, like I'm jealous of Courtenay. She also loves feeling valuable and wanted.

I'm not sure what's best, so I answer her question with one of my own.

"When would she turn?" I ask, keeping a neutral tone, even though I'm sure of her answer already.

"She has to accept first, of course."

"When?" I ask again, now with a small smile. I know she'll love it. She has it all planned out.

"Opening night. New Year's Eve."

"Wow," I say.

Nic laughs aloud with a small clap. "Birthday twins!"

"That's coming up fast."

I have to tell Roddy soon, too, but I'm so afraid of what he'll say or do.

Or what *I'll* do if he says no . . .

"Are you upset, Amber?" Nicola asks, confirming my poker face has improved. "She's become your very good friend. And, like we've all been saying, it's wise to get our numbers up, especially now that we're getting comfortable with Margaux and Tamsin. The five of us will have Hey Mister, and you'll have everything you wanted, right?"

Her voice has the slightest hint of desperation.

I haven't heard it before.

There's a heavy pause between us.

Does Nicola know I want to leave?

Is that what Hey Mister is all about?

"Not to mention the poor dear doesn't have anywhere else to go," she finishes her thought, regaining her normal tone of authority.

"So she won't say no."

"What do you mean? Of course Courtenay could decline," Nicola says with a scoff, as if she's reminding me that I, too, had a choice. But I don't believe her. How many others, like Pierce, did she turn against their will? How many of us had she tricked, found at a low point, like Tamsin and me? Like Courtenay. Did her sister say no? Did Nicola say no to her sister? "I won't do this without your blessing, Amber."

"My blessing?"

"Yes. It's always been the two of us. This is unprecedented."

I'm stunned she's asking for my approval at all. Since when?

"Yes," I say. "Let's do it."

Nicola immediately looks to the door and flaps her fingers at Jonathan, waiting nearby.

"Jonathan!" she shouts at him, shriller than ever. "Bring her in!"

"Now?" I ask, incredulous. "Isn't she asleep?"

"She'll sleep when she's dead." Nicola laughs.

A few moments later, Jonathan returns with Courtenay, any life behind his eyes all but gone now. I think he feels sorry for her. Did he feel sorry for me? Courtenay shuffles into the study, tired and disoriented, away from home, but did she ever feel like she had one?

She's in silky red pajamas, matching sleep mask on her head.

"What's going on?" Courtenay asks, her voice groggy. "You're both up so early. Is everything okay? Are the police here?"

"No, darling. That's all over now. Come sit down next to me."

Courtenay joins Nicola on the chaise. I don't say anything.

"How are you feeling?" Nicola asks.

"I don't know, really," Courtenay says. "I'm not sure if I'm grieving or feeling relieved or maybe a bit of both. But I am so appreciative you're letting me stay with you until I get on my feet somehow."

"You will, darling. Don't fret about that. You've been through so much, but we'll always be here for you. Right, Amber?"

"Absolutely," I say, starting to feel remorseful that the time is here. I know the part I've played in this seduction, and even though it was necessary, I'm not proud of it.

I avoid eye contact with Courtenay.

I don't want her to remember that night she saw me kill a man in Shoreditch.

"Have you . . . ever noticed anything different about us, Court?" Nicola asks.

"How do you mean?" Courtenay asks, looking at me for a clue, but I keep my eyes on the floor.

This should be between the two of them.

Nicola will be the one to turn Courtenay.

Leave me out of it.

"You've spent a lot of time with us and never wondered why we haven't done a brunch or a fitness class or gone for a mani-pedi with you on a Sunday afternoon?"

"I suppose it's a bit weird, but you told me you're busy during the day with other things, which is why you needed my help. And you've been nothing but kind and generous to me, so it's not really any of my business, is it? We all have our . . . stuff, you know? I mean, fuck, you just witnessed some of mine."

Courtenay is so sweet. Was I ever that sweet? I don't feel like it anymore.

"What if we had a big secret to tell you?" Nicola allows just the tips of her fangs to emerge, but Courtenay doesn't notice. She's watching me, an unease creeping into her bright spirit.

Is she remembering what I did?

"What's she talking about?" Courtenay asks me, like Nicola isn't in the room, her least favorite feeling.

"I'll let Nicola explain," I say softly. Of course, Nicola nods in agreement. She has to be the one in charge.

"Courtenay," Nicola continues. "I want you to listen carefully to what I say next and know I'm telling you the absolute truth, all right? Amber and I, well, Tamsin and Margaux, too . . ."

Nicola is nervous, having a hard time finding her words, tapping her fingers on her knee.

Was she this nervous when she told me?

I barely remember the specifics, just that I was stunned and ran away like a bat out of hell, even though one of my favorite songs was on and I knew I'd never hear it again without thinking of Nicola.

I should have kept running.

But I won't say that to Courtenay.

"We're all . . . vampires," Nicola says definitively.

One of Courtenay's slippers drops to the floor, making the only sound in the room. She slowly extends her toes to slip it back on again. Silence fills the air again. She shifts uncomfortably in her seat, moving a few inches away from Nicola, who breathes heavily, her fangs on full display.

"I'm sorry, *what?*" Court starts in with her adorable hyena laugh, laced with fear, much faster and louder than normal. I don't blame her. How can anyone think straight when life feels messy or awful or hopeless? You just want someone to take care of business for you because you don't have the strength.

Nicola loves to take care of other people's business.

For a price.

"We're not going to hurt you," Nicola reassures Courtenay. "Right, Amber?" She motions for me to show my fangs as well, but it's hard to look friendly when the sharpies are out.

Courtenay stands up.

She wants to run.

We can all feel it.

And Courtenay keeps looking at me.

Why does she keep looking at me?

"Amber. Show her," Nicola commands.

If I compel Courtenay again, she'll remember I've done it before, for sure.

But if I don't, Nicola will suspect something is wrong.

I'm not quick enough.

Nicola takes over, but I know she's disappointed in me.

Looking into Courtenay's eyes, she tells her not to move, tells her to listen.

"We don't want to hurt you, Courtenay. We want you to join us. To be a vampire *with* us. Forever. We'll have Hey Mister. And when that gets tired, we can open another club. And another one. We can do whatever we want to do. Together. As a family."

"Would I live—"

"Here, of course! At the Laurels. It'll be like a slumber party every night. Tell her, Amber!"

I clear my throat and add my two-faced two cents to the pitch. "I've been with Nicola for almost fifty years," I say. "What does that tell you?"

Nicola jerks her head back. Disappointed in me again. This is not good.

I could try to find another replacement.

Start from square one again.

An exhausting thought.

But I *cannot* have Nicola knowing I want to leave her.

So I take Courtenay's hands in mine and lie straight to her face.

"Courtenay, it's the best decision I ever made. It'll be yours, too. We're the same, you and I."

Nicola nods nearby, exhilarated, with a maniacal grin on her face that she should really think about toning down if she wants to close this deal with Courtenay. I keep Courtenay's attention on me.

"Do you have any questions?"

"You're all vampires. So that means . . . you kill people?"

I swear I see judgment in her eyes, directed at me, like she knows what I've done. Is she going to bring it up? Nicola will want to know why I compelled her before. Why she saw me feed. Who was it? When was it? Why wasn't I being more careful?

But instead she just says, "David?"

"We only hunt the ones that deserve it," Nicola says.

She's a liar, too.

Courtenay laughs again, more intensely, the cadence of a machine gun. She's going totally off the rails; her eyes look like they're vibrating in their sockets.

She's going to get out of here as fast as she can.

She keeps looking at me.

Then the door.

Then at me again.

"Don't," Nicola says, her voice calm and steady. "It's nearly sunrise and we must rest. We can discuss further, in more detail, tomorrow evening. Will you be at Hey Mister? You're still welcome to be a part of it. Our friendship isn't contingent on your decision if you were to decline."

"It's not?" Courtenay's voice is soft and childlike.

"Of course not! But we adore you and we selfishly want you to be around all the time. Forever. Just like us. Courtenay, Amber and I think you're a true kindred spirit."

Courtenay stands up slowly.

Eyes on Nicola.

Then on me.

She smiles, laughing softly.

Then Courtenay looks at the door again before making a mad dash for it, off like a bullet, her bare feet running right out of the slippers.

"I think that went as well as could be expected," Nicola says to me, reclining into the chaise, satisfied with herself. "You took a little time, too."

"What if she doesn't come back?" I ask.

"She will," Nicola replies confidently. "Because you'll find her. Give her the push she needs."

"But what if she doesn't want to—"

"Amber, come on!" Nicola shouts, rolling her eyes at me as she stands back up again. "Where *else* is a girl like that going to go? This isn't a hard sell, you know."

"And if she's not buying?"

"She knows too much," Nicola says, without a hint of remorse, confirming my worst suspicion about my so-called best friend.

If I had said no to her back in 1979, I'd be dead.

TWENTY

NICOLA

1983

We had been lying low for almost no time at all, in the grand scheme of *forever*, and yet Amber groused daily, nay, hourly, as if she were a miserable prisoner and I was her menacing captor. She missed being around other people, apparently.

Imagine that.

She claimed to be bored at the Laurels even though we watched dozens of films, played cards and board games, not to mention I kept her plenty well-fed, bringing back a bevy of boys for her dining pleasure, the benevolent leader that I was, putting on records and letting her play with them a bit first whether via a dance or a dalliance, if she so chose.

It was not like I had her bound and gagged in an attic for years, like she was behaving. She simply could not pop around the city for a short while, not with Malcolm on the prowl for his wayward wife. I was being perfectly reasonable; she just couldn't understand it yet, not fully grasping the concept of endless time for creatures like us.

Not to mention that I bought Amber everything she asked for

to ease this alleged pain. I purchased very expensive materials for learning French and Spanish, including a tutor once a week with an odor so delicious it was a miracle I didn't have him for myself. Any and all music purchases were instantly approved. Fashion, too. I even let her redecorate her entire bedroom to her liking, and I'd never let anyone touch the Laurels like that before.

I mean, truly, what more could I have given her?

She had been confiding in Jonathan from time to time. They had become quite friendly, but not *too* friendly, and he always briefed me on what they discussed, which wasn't anything of note, just lodging more complaints about feeling trapped. But keep an animal in a cage long enough and they'll be ready to run wild upon release.

That's what I wanted her to do *with me*.

Not *away* from me, which I'm sure she might have considered.

I'd have to head her off at the pass.

We still entertained one another at home, despite her misgivings about the current arrangement. She wanted to be furious with me—and I knew she was some of the time, thanks to Jonathan—but Amber was the type of person who could always manage to make merry, especially with me. It was one of the reasons I cared for her so much. Everyone loves the life of the party, no matter how small the guest list.

Still, she'd always end the night with her standard question.

"Nicola, how much longer?"

My answer was always the same.

"When we know for certain that Malcolm has completely moved on."

I knew that he had already remarried last year, but she didn't need to be privy to that information just yet. More time away from one's human past was never a bad thing for a vampire.

I was always looking out for her own good.

She had to know to rely on *me*, not Malcolm any longer.

Her old life was over.

Still, a sulking Amber wasn't great for overall morale, so eventually I made the executive decision to have her official re-coming out party on New Year's Eve in Trafalgar Square. A bit of a birthday celebration, too. Of course she was delighted by the news, practically screaming my ear off when I tossed a brand-new sparkly red frock with an excessive fringe in her direction for the occasion.

"Keep calm." I laughed at her. "You're out of practice in crowded public spaces, so I need you to adhere to my plans. New Year's Eve in Trafalgar Square is a veritable smorgasbord, and as a result, some other London vampires may make an appearance."

"*Other* vampires?" she asked, too curious for my comfort.

"Yes. Stay close to me for that reason. They cannot be trusted, but of course I will briefly introduce you should we cross paths."

I did not divulge my motive to Amber, but I wanted to run into Pierce and the little gang he'd been collecting over the years. Look at *my* pretty new plaything, you fool. She is not for you and neither am I. *Jealous?*

They were a devious bunch, so I'd have to keep a careful eye on the situation, though Pierce initially presented as charming. Amber wouldn't be able to resist him. A run-in with those rabble-rousers would be perfect for the purpose of the evening. She needed to learn not to stray, no matter how tough she perceived the times at hand.

I never planned on telling Amber about my history with Pierce. It's not a time I reveled in revisiting, though I couldn't seem to shake his firm grasp on any tenderness that still remained inside me.

Ridiculous, but there would always be a fire between us, a flame flickering between love and hate. When we met, I thought I had found the man I would be with for the rest of my life. I had so much to offer him. And Pierce? He made me laugh, he made me feel sexy and even though I knew he was a bit of a cad, I believed I could change him.

We could belong to each other.

Forever.

I was so young.

I still believed in love.

And even more foolishly, I thought he did, too.

After he left, I learned to prioritize loyalty in friendship, seeking sisterhood, and so far, I believed in Amber. So yes, I ran a tight ship, purely for her benefit as my companion, but at least she would never be at the mercy of five men with a Peter Pan complex of the vampiric variety.

Now, that would be a treacherous outcome indeed.

This is *wild*!" Amber yanked on my arm excitedly, taking it all in. It was just after nine, still early, and Trafalgar Square already teemed with revelers of all ages, shapes and sizes, the majority less than desirable. Sure, we could be out dancing with the glamorous and beguiling patrons of the members-only clubs, but she said she wanted to be around people again, so let's give her the people! Miraculously, she looked charmed by all the miscreants who surrounded us.

"Is it true someone was trampled here last year?" she asked me as we linked arms through the horde.

"That's what they say, but it could have been a great number of things." I winked at her before a group of girls shoved into us, apologies slurring out of their hot-pink and neon-purple mouths. Goodness—the concept of taste had really taken a dive in this decade!

"Let's get the hell out of here and keep moving," I hissed at Amber, annoyed by the common folk, but she didn't seem to mind them at all.

"Oh, it's fine!" she shouted back at the lot of them. "Happy new year!"

"Happy new year!" they crowed back at her, tossing one of their gold-foiled paper tiaras in her direction. Of course she put the tacky thing right atop her head. Amber could not stop smiling, lighting up with every step we took. After all, she was finally somewhere bustling and exciting again, and as far as she knew, the night was brimming with possibility. She'd been waiting on this for years. I suppose I couldn't fault her for enthusiastically rubbing shoulders with the plebeians.

"Watch it," I mouthed at her, motioning to her lips, her fangs already flickering out of her control. She needed more practice, sweet girl.

"Ope," she said, a funny little colloquialism of hers that I treasured, and popped them back into place. But when she caught her first glance of the Nelson monument in the square, coupled with the giant Christmas tree still lit for the hols, she was completely swept away again, fangs out, eyes lit up and ready for a party.

I could sense Pierce, of course, and his company in our general midst, but I hadn't pinpointed their exact location considering the throng of partygoers surrounding us. Everyone was dolled up and dressed to the nines, with hats and headbands and noisemakers and an assortment of all that festive shite that I hated.

The people who were already sozzled beyond measure were easy enough to weed out, but then again, I did want to keep an eye on them for feasting purposes later should we care for a quick bite. "*1984*. It just sounds so futuristic!" Amber yelped excitedly as we bustled about in the crowd, going with the flow of it, even though I'd have rather just compelled all of them out of our way. But we hadn't been out together in ages. Why not get the full experience for Amber now that we were? I was hoping she'd experience more of a sensory overload, looking to me for leadership, but she was constantly jumping ahead of me like an unruly toddler.

But then the mass in front of us began to part with an ease that was not my doing.

Each one of them locked in his gaze, moving out of the way.

Ah, there he was.

Right on schedule.

Five hulking men approached us with a devil-may-care strut, almost as if rehearsed. All tall. All fit. All striking. The smell was intoxicating and menacing, top notes of oud and sandalwood with a base of venom and aftershave. I didn't have to tell Amber what they were.

She *knew*.

And she'd never seen this many vampires before, much less any of the opposite sex.

"Men always stick together," I whispered to her, knowing what she was thinking before she could say it.

There was a clear hierarchy as they marched towards us, like a flock of ducks soaring in the sky together in a V shape. They were all dressed head to toe in black Burberry that night, a chic little gang. Pierce had always lusted after the finer things, which of course I would have bestowed upon him, had he stayed. Freshly shined shoes. Tailored vests. Nearly all of them had some sort of manicured facial hair. Thin mustaches or full beards with sharp edges. They were wildly handsome, but also pretty for men, George Michael adjacent, which Amber immediately noticed, brushing a hand through her hair. A tell of hers that was meant to suggest "come hither."

I could not have planned it any better. I knew I looked phenomenal, too, when Pierce swallowed me whole with his eyes. Miss me, you wanker?

"Good evening, Pierce," I said. "You all right?"

"*Lady Claughton.*" Pierce laughed mirthlessly. "Fancy seeing you out tonight—a rarity per our agreement, hmm?" He made no effort to conceal his fangs as he picked at them with the long fingernail on his pinky. A snarl more than a smile. He winked at Amber. "And who is this? She's taken a new companion again? A very pretty bird, I see. The other one flew—"

"That's none of your business," I interrupted him quickly.

Amber needn't know about my previous companions.

Pierce latched on to her with his long fingers on her collarbone, getting close to her ears and her neck. She shrugged him off instinctively, but I could tell she was titillated by his touch. I buried any jealous feelings that started to rise within me. This was what I wanted, wasn't it?

Amber exuded confidence, introducing herself to the lads, and Pierce raised an eyebrow at me, uncertain about my endgame with this planned interaction, but why would I confide in him ever again after he left me behind? He made his bed and undoubtedly had hordes of women in and out of it for many years now.

"Amber Wells," he purred at my companion. "Are you planning to stay out here with the commoners all night? Or do you want to go to a proper fête with us?"

She looked to me for approval first, which pleased me no end. Yes, dear girl, this was exactly how a maker and companion should operate. I nodded at Pierce, acknowledging the potential danger but confident about the outcome despite the risk.

Amber *had* to learn.

And I could handle them, especially Pierce.

He was only alive because I allowed it.

Stupid, really, but I *could* go through with it.

If I really had to.

If he pushed me enough.

"Sounds great," Amber said, taking Pierce's hand, reaching behind for mine. We all linked up as he led the way. The other men followed us without any formal introductions. I never bothered to get to know them. I didn't want to know about their debaucheries around London. That was the life Pierce chose.

Amber looked like a lamb to the slaughter, but I didn't worry.

For I was her shepherd.

Pierce took us down an unassuming lane away from all the hoi polloi and into the back room of a dark bar hosting a goth rock night. Oh God. Everyone in black, bumping into one another forcefully, listening to music that could only be described as the deranged love child of banshees and Barry Manilow. Could this have been any more cliché for a group of vampires? For heaven's sake, the song playing was about Bela Lugosi himself.

Pierce could tell I was less than impressed when he shouted into my ear, "Not good enough for Lady Claughton?" His breath smelled metallic. He was freshly fed.

"A bit on the nose, don't you think?" I shouted back, and he chuckled mightily, turning his attention to Amber.

"And how do you find it, Amber?" Pierce asked, tracing the HAPPY in the HAPPY NEW YEAR on her little tiara with his finger.

"It's different." She smiled, gently smacking his hand away, knowing she looked especially out of place. "But I'm game for *anything* these days."

Ouch, like a dagger to my heart.

"When did you shack up with that one?" Pierce asked Amber, nodding in my direction.

"A few years ago," she said. "To the day."

"Ah, happy new year *and* happy birthday, then. Are you enjoying it?"

I hung on her every word, every response.

"Still learning," Amber admitted. "Anything you'd like to teach me?"

What a saucy little minx—I needed to be on high alert. I kept close watch on the two of them, but I lost track of Pierce's remaining crew, which didn't sit right with me. Where had they run off to? Pierce and Amber continued to get chummy on the dance floor, so I joined them, never leaving her side in the seedy place.

Pierce kept his hands all over her and she seemed to enjoy it, despite the atrocious music, managing to sway with the *unique* sound, putting it mildly. I had hoped she'd be more outwardly frightened by this whole endeavor, but it seemed keeping her inside for so long had wrought a rather audacious Amber.

She wanted a bad boy.

That was Pierce, all right.

I could feel it flowing from her, an unharnessed energy, as she writhed against Pierce, her back creating friction on his front. When she caught me watching them, she made pointed eye contact with me and *smirked*. Not a smile from my girl, no. She wanted to make me angry or jealous or feel something close to how she had felt, all cooped up at the Laurels.

I could see right through her.

So why was it working?

I no longer yearned for Pierce as I once had. For what? He would still run around town on me like a wild animal. He was no longer my concern. This rendezvous was purely to scare Amber straight, but all was not going to plan.

Then Pierce leaned closer to her, whispering once again.

I couldn't hear him.

But she stopped dancing immediately, as if turned to stone by his words. Whatever he had said, she was petrified, potentially making the perfect time for our exit.

But what did he tell her?

He followed the furtive message with a flick of his tongue in and around her ear, and when she jerked away from him, he raised one arm above his head, curling his hand into a solid fist, one finger at a time.

Then his crew descended on Amber.

They took hold of all her limbs, flailing along with the crowd, carrying her away from me and into the wilds of this depraved dance floor. Not one person appeared alarmed, as the movements everywhere were just as peculiar and manic and violent.

Amber cried out for me immediately, but the music was so deafening, I could hardly hear her screams.

"All right, that's enough." I grabbed Pierce by the arm with all my might, but he shoved me off so forcefully that I fell to the floor. His strength had only grown over the years. "Give her back! You don't get to do this to me. Not after what you've done."

"Wha-ha-haaat?" He howled with laughter, looking down at me with disgust. "More like what *you* did to *me*? I can do whatever I damn well please, *Nicola Claughton*, and I like Amber. She'll fit right in with us over in Wapping. I'm certain. After all, she's like my sister, no?"

I rose from the floor, enraged, getting close to his face, missing and hating him in equal measure. "Absolutely not. Come on, now, or I'll—"

"Or you'll what?" he spat. "What are you doing here? This is sad. Even for you. Showing off your new pet as if I give a proper fuck? Let me tell you something. *I don't.*"

"She's my companion and I am her maker. Not that *you* would understand such a concept, but she belongs to me."

He belonged to me, too, no matter what he thought he'd gotten away with . . .

"You don't know how to have a companion, Nicola. You should be alone for what you do to other people. Especially your sis—"

"Fuck right off, Pierce!" I seethed. My fangs felt like they could fly right out of my mouth. "Return my companion to me now or else."

"What are you going to give me?" He grinned, not fazed at all by my threats since he incorrectly thought they were empty. I hated that I still found him so attractive, even in these infuriating moments. "You know what I *really* want."

"You could have had it!" I shouted. "You could have had everything, Pierce."

"I didn't want *this*," he hissed, waving his hand dramatically. "But I've certainly made the best of it, haven't I?"

"If you hurt her, I will kill you, *finally*, and that's a promise."

I meant every word. I would not stop until it was done. Yes, he left me and I had come to terms with it the best I could, but taking another vampire's companion? That should be punishable by death.

"Sure, Nicola." He chuckled. "But funnily enough, I'm certain *we* could take you on by now. Did you count five? More to come, I'm sure. There's plenty of men who want in on a life this depraved.

Maybe you should be watching out for us now. Who knows? Maybe Amber will invite us back into—"

Before I could lunge for his throat, he held up his fist again as a signal.

His mob returned safely with Amber in tow, placing her down gently in front of me.

I'd never seen a more frightened woman in my life, and I had seen so many.

"The neutral territory, Nicola? It's over," Pierce barked. "This is a massive city; we should be able to stay out of each other's business. If not, well, we'll start to bite back. Understood? Stay away from us. Stay away from *me*."

I took a weeping Amber in my arms, waving one hand at him in acknowledgment, holding back tears of my own. How could I have loved a man like that? Shaking off the night, I escorted a shivering Amber out of that hellhole and back to our home.

It had hurt, but it was worth it. Amber would be afraid of other vampires now, most certainly. And Pierce could be as beastly as he liked, but nobody gets a bee in their bonnet like that unless they still harbored feelings. Hate and love are so often the same thing.

"What did he whisper to you?" I asked Amber as we headed for home.

"I don't remember," she whimpered, lying straight to my face.

TWENTY-ONE

AMBER

The second the sun goes down, I'm on a mission to track down Courtenay.

She's the only thing that counts right now.

I have to start taking everything on one step at a time before anything else goes out of whack. I've been so overwhelmed. My focus has been pulled in multiple directions, making me feel like I've been running in circles. New York. Being afraid to tell Roddy. Getting the money. Getting the documents. Getting tricked. Wondering if Roddy will accept me. Wondering if Pierce can actually help me. Wondering if Courtenay's run off to tell Roddy what happened last night.

But if I don't bring Courtenay back to Nicola, none of this will matter.

Getting Courtenay on board will keep Nicola at bay.

Why would Nicola ever come looking for me, go through all this trouble, when she has a new companion to control to her heart's content?

And if I don't convince Courtenay, she's dead.

Then I'll be back at square one or worse . . .

I think about where Courtenay could be at this hour. Early evening. She's definitely not in Camden; I doubt she'd go back to David's. Possibly Hey Mister, but doubtful since she's likely just as scared of Margaux and Tamsin, too. Even though everyone is scared of Tamsin.

If I text her, will she respond? If I call her, will she answer? She's Gen Z, so probably not, but maybe it'll be so surprising, she'll pick up out of curiosity.

The phone rings and rings and rings.

No voicemail set up.

Figures.

I'm about to hang up when I hear a voice on the line.

A man's voice.

Fuck, it's Roddy.

"Hey," he says, in his standard tone.

What did Courtenay tell him?

"Hi!" I say brightly, like everything's completely normal. "I called Courtenay, right?"

"Yeah." Roddy chuckles. "She's asleep on the couch now, but I saw your name flash on the screen, so I took the liberty. She's having a rough go of it, isn't she? But why isn't she with you two?"

What should I say?

Is he testing me?

"Maybe she's in love with you!" I joke, but he doesn't laugh. "She's known you longer, hasn't she? I don't know. She could be more comfortable there. A lot just happened . . ."

"Yeah. Maybe."

He sounds weird.

Did she tell him?

"What if I came over?" I invite myself.

A long pause.

It's killing me.

"You're always welcome over here, babe."

"Is everything okay?" I ask him, desperate for validation.

"We should tell Nicola soon. About us. What do you reckon?"

"You're right. We'll talk about it."

"Right. See you soon."

I ask Jonathan to take me to Shoreditch, just in case things get messy. Nicola doesn't protest. She waves at me from the study, endlessly amused by this madcap adventure she's sent me on.

Since we're alone for once, I sit in the front seat, next to Jonathan, but it feels silly to crack jokes or talk about the weather like we always do. Not when so much is on the line. And even though I know he cares about me in his own way, I need to watch what I say around him.

Still.

I want to push where I can.

Keep up the big swings.

It's all I can do.

"What do you think of Courtenay?" I ask him, careful to wait until he's finished navigating an extra-horrendous roundabout. I never did learn to drive here.

"She's a lovely girl," he says, keeping his eyes on the road and the speed high. He's impressive behind the wheel, considering his age, but I think he knows what could happen to him if he were to slow down with any of his duties. "I do hope you can get through to her."

"Me, too. I know she's very important to Nicola."

"You have no idea," he says, with a tone of caution in his voice.

I've never heard anything like it from him before. "I know you may feel a certain way, Miss Amber, but please try your very best with Miss Courtenay. I fear what madam may do if you fail."

"Me, too," I say gravely.

"Just remind yourself that it's better than the alternative, hey?"

I nod.

But is it?

When Roddy buzzes me up to his flat, Courtenay's still there, awake, but he obviously didn't tell her I was coming. When I walk in the door, receiving his kiss, I hear a gasp just behind him at the sight of me.

"Oh, like you didn't know." Roddy laughs. "Doesn't everyone?"

"No!" I say, pinching his arm.

"Can you keep it between us, then?" he asks Courtenay, who won't stop staring, still barefoot in Nicola's silk pajamas. "Please? We're going to tell Nicola soon enough."

She doesn't give a shit about the kiss.

She's afraid I'm going to rip her throat out.

"Courtenay," I say, staying behind Roddy. I want to look as non-threatening as possible. "I'm sorry about what happened yesterday, but I want to talk to you more about it. Just us. Can I take you out to dinner? Anywhere you want. Are you starving? I know Roddy, and all he has is, like, beer in the fridge and those weird old crackers in the cupboard."

"You never want to eat anything!" He laughs at me. "And Weet-abix is a cereal, I'll have you know."

"If you say so." I roll my eyes, keeping it light for Courtenay. "What do you think, Court? I brought you some clothes."

"Anywhere I want?"

The first sign of a smile.

Keep it up, Amber.

C ourtenay decides on Dishoom, which is kind of a shit show with no reservations and long wait times. Perfect. I use the situation to my advantage, showing her exactly what we can accomplish—not that scarfing down Indian food will be on her mind after she turns.

I compel the hostess to seat us right away.

Courtenay scoffs, very impressed, as we shuffle through to our table.

She orders pretty much everything, even though I'm not joining in. The scent of the spices paired with the heat of the room is pleasant enough, but it's still wild to me that every time I'm around food that I know is absolutely delicious, my body doesn't seem to care at all.

I don't have a human hunger anymore.

But I miss it *so* much in my mind.

Not the flavor per se.

But the enjoyment.

I watch the noisy diners around us. Families. Date nights. Girlfriends. Some of them close their eyes at an extra-juicy bite, audibly moaning because it's *so* good. Others slurp up sauces left behind on their plates, using a fork to get just one more tiny taste before it's all gone. A woman takes a nibble of a fresh dish set down on the table and then shares it with her lover immediately, eyes wide with joy, so they can experience the same feeling at the same time.

That's when the jealousy creeps in.

Imagine that.

Eating!

A simple, sensual pleasure I used to not only take for granted, but even scolded myself about. All the time. What the hell was I thinking?

"So . . . no food, obviously?" Courtenay asks, sipping on her glass of white wine.

"No. But you won't miss it." I'm trying to sound like Nicola, lying through my teeth.

"Did you tell your family? Did you have a family?"

"Yes." I gulp at the thought of them, guilt-ridden as always when it comes up. It hasn't come up in so long. "They didn't know what I chose, but we weren't close. I was newly married, too, but it wasn't a good situation."

"Did he hurt you?" Courtenay asks me so sincerely that it almost makes me want to cry. I'm thankful for the server returning with the food. Courtenay indulges in everything, every bowl, every plate, like it's her last meal.

Does she think it's her last meal?

I need to close the deal.

I go on and on about "the lifestyle" as she eats. The money, the power, the possibilities. Everything that I thought was true at the beginning but came to learn would only be true for Nicola. I rattle off the clubs we go to, the men we indulge in, showing off our highlight reel of hedonism. Courtenay's eyes light up with every single story and every single lie as I do the devil's work in the middle of Dishoom.

"You did that thing to me. That you just did with the hostess. Didn't you?"

I nod. There's no use in lying when I know she remembers. I know how I can spin this.

"Who was that man? The one you—"

"He wanted to hurt me," I lie to her once again. "He obviously didn't know what I could do to him. But I'm glad it was me, because now he can't do it to some other girl."

"Oh . . ." Courtenay sighs, understanding.

"And it wasn't time to tell you yet. So please don't tell Nicola. Promise?"

Courtenay nods. "Why did you go through with it?" she asks.

I think about how to best answer the question.

This one?

I can tell her the truth.

"I wanted a really big life. I didn't think I'd get one if I went back home. Simple as that."

"Do you ever regret it?"

I answer that one fast.

"*No.*"

I'm almost short of breath as I lie to her, like the word tried to choke me on its way out.

When Courtenay excuses herself to use the restroom, I start to relax, sinking into my chair, taking in the sights and sounds.

That wasn't so bad.

I think I got her.

A few minutes go by.

Too many minutes.

Did she leave?

She's out.

She doesn't want to do it.

I start to panic.

What will I tell Nicola?

Just as I really start to sweat it, Courtenay sits back down with a big smile.

"Sorry," she says. "Nicola rang me."

"What did she say?" I ask, surprised, and wondering if she thought I couldn't finish the job.

"She asked how it was going."

"And?"

"I said it was going well. I'm interested."

"Good."

"She has a surprise for me."

"What kind of surprise?"

"She said since you took care of the dining, she'll take care of the dancing."

Courtenay reaches for my hand.

We're going back to the Laurels.

Nicola is waiting for us, all dolled up in a slinky black gown, hair blown out to perfection, absolutely sparkling, complete with diamonds on the decolletage. She pulls us into her boudoir, wardrobe doors wide open, showing off every gown, dress, jumpsuit and jewel on offer.

"Take your pick, Court!"

And as if we're in a movie makeover montage, we dress up Courtenay like she's a living doll: Disco Barbie. She never did this with me.

"Well done," Nicola whispers in my ear. "We're going to Tramp tonight. Let's give her a taste of the good life with us!"

Nic and I haven't been to Tramp together in a while and Courtenay has never been—it's a couple ticks above her usual stomping grounds—and the three of us waltz to the center of the dance floor like we own the place, all of us in sequins, shimmering in the light with every step we take, Pat Benatar's "Shadows of the Night" blasting through the speakers.

Throwback.

Nicola and I still know every single word.

1982.

God, I wish my hair was bigger right now.

We danced to this song a million times in the Laurels, when I was still inside.

Nicola would play it to make me feel better.

To make me believe that my dreams would come true soon enough.

Not long now, darling.

I can still hear her.

Courtenay doesn't know the song, of course, but she *feels* it.

Our little midnight angel herself.

We turn and spin and shimmy and shake and join hands and laugh and smile, and I haven't seen Nicola look this happy in my life.

More than that, though?

I think she's relieved in a way I don't recognize.

Shoulders loose, smiling freely, like she's finally getting everything she ever wanted.

Like this was always meant to happen.

The two of them will be just fine together, won't they?

God.

Will I miss this when I leave?

Is this the new Nicola?

Or the old Nicola finally coming back to me?

The sting of holding back my tears is too much to take.

I gotta get out of here.

I need to clear my head.

I whisper in Nicola's ear. "You should have some time alone, too. You'll be the one to turn her. It's a good idea."

"You're leaving us?" she asks, looking genuinely concerned. She pulls me over to the side of the dance floor. "What's wrong?"

"Nothing. I'm fine."

As I turn to go, Nic grabs my arm again, firm but gentle, eyes locking with mine, like she wants to compel me, if only she could.

"Amber." I swear her voice almost breaks as she smiles at me. "Don't worry. No one can ever replace you."

I don't know what to say.

I gotta get out of here.

I want to think about literally *anything* else.

I need a fix.

Roddy rolls up in front of Tramp on his vintage black Triumph, no bells and whistles, just loud and proud with clean lines and questionable emissions. It feels like we're flying through London, sailing through every stoplight, no need to stop or slow down, wind whipping through my hair peeking out under the helmet. I wrap my arms around Roddy's waist and nuzzle my cheek into the back of his neck.

We don't have to say anything tonight.

He knows what I want.

When we get to the Laurels, I grab his hand as we shuffle through the pebbles along the path to the side entrance, our feet crunching on top of them.

It feels so illicit to bring a man back here.

I've never done it before.

One of her rules.

Are the rules changing?

Once we're through the gate, he can't keep his hands off me, his mouth on my neck, arms wrapped around me, hands linked just under my chest, his thumbs taking welcome liberties as I open the door for him.

The lights are dim in the hallway as we make our way into the parlor, his fingers caressing the inside of my palm as he follows my lead. I pull away, just for a moment, to turn on the table lamps instead of the overhead lights, to really set the mood.

The only time Roddy stops staring at me is when he takes in the beauty of the Laurels. The parlor is stunning and recently refreshed with red roses from the garden, thanks to Jonathan, looking like the set of a steamy music video from a bygone era, blurry lens and all.

"Fuck me." Roddy gasps. "You and Nicola live *here*?"

"Did you bring your camera?" I ask him, a seductive growl in my voice. I don't want to hear her name right now. I start to light a few of my favorite candles, especially the ones that smell like rosewood, a scent that all but demands nudity once it floats up your nostrils. Then I go over to the turntable, knowing he'll appreciate the vintage touch, and select a Rod Stewart album with a knowing wink.

"Very funny." He laughs, giving me a once-over with his eyes before pulling out the camera from his bag.

He always has his camera.

"Where do you want me?" I ask him, running a hand through my hair. He nods at the sofa and I trot on over, more than ready for the Jack and Rose of it all. Heaven. I lean back into the soft cushions, one arm overhead, the other moving down my decolletage, my dress creeping up my thighs just enough to tease him. I look up, down, right at Roddy, through the lens and under and over it. I feel like a natural. Like a real woman. He's treating me like one.

Click.

Click.

Click.

I motion for him to follow me into the study, sliding over the top of the piano on my stomach, playing a few high notes with my fingertips, placing another finger in my mouth, grinning devilishly. I sit up, toss my hair back, and cross my legs one way and then the other. I start to take my heels off, and the strap of my dress falls to my shoulder. When I go to fix it, Roddy only says, "Don't," and snaps another picture.

I just stare at him with my bare shoulder out, hair tousled, trying to channel Evelyn Avedon and the heat of our first date. All I want to do is jump on his hips, wrap my legs around him and have him carry me to bed already.

Forget the pictures.

Make love to me, Roddy.

No.

No.

It's just sex, Amber.

He was supposed to be a way to escape.

But you know he's going to leave without you.

How are you going to pull this off?

Do you want to pull it off anymore?

Can you?

You can't love him.

You can't love anyone.

Click.

Click.

Click.

He stops again, popping his head up from behind the lens.

"How old is this house?" he asks me. "It's—"

"Who cares?" I reply with a shrug, which makes him laugh out loud, that adorable gap in his teeth on full display. "Ask me something else. And make it good."

He licks his lips and then bites the bottom one, slinging the camera over his shoulder.

"Where's your bedroom?"

Attaboy. That's the one. I pick up my loose heels and hang them on my fingertips over my shoulder, accentuating my hips as I stroll out of the study.

I don't have to look back.

I know he's following me.

Click.

Click.

Click.

I want to forget everything.

Just for the night.

When Roddy holds me in his arms, my bare chest close to his, I know this is the moment I should tell him. He's in a vulnerable space. So am I. We're naked, for God's sake. It could be perfect, but can I really pull it off? So much of this plan is contingent on trusting other people. Roddy. Courtenay. Pierce.

How can I—

"I have something to tell you," Roddy says, interrupting my train of thought.

"What?" I ask breathlessly, but I know what he's about to say.

"I'm falling in love with you, Amber. And Hey Mister. This life we're all building together as a weird little fucked-up family. How can I leave now?"

"But New York is your dream!" I feel so guilty that I've pulled him off course, away from what he wants for his life.

"Dreams change, Amber. Did you hear me? I love you."

This is what I wanted. Why do I feel so awful? There's so much about Roddy to love. He's loyal and sweet and talented and *hot as fire.*

But he shouldn't stay.

Not for me.

Courtenay is one thing.

But Roddy?

Nicola would never allow it.

Would she?

"Roddy," I whisper, taking a deep breath. "Why don't you sleep on it?"

I needed to sleep on it myself. What if things could be different around here? Would I still want to leave? I think about Hey Mister and Courtenay and Roddy and Nicola.

What if it could all work out somehow?

"What are you on about?" Roddy laughs. "Did you hear me, you crazy bird? I love you!"

I wish I could love him back.

But I'm not sure I can.

I say it anyway.

It's what you do.

watch Roddy leave from the side window, ambling away, love drunk, and I don't know what's going to come next, but I'm startled by the sound of Jonathan clearing his throat behind me.

"Oh, apologies! I didn't mean to frighten you, miss."

"I didn't know you were here," I say, feeling slightly violated. "Were you . . . listening to us?"

"Not exactly, but—"

"Please don't tell Nicola. She doesn't know and I'm not sure how she'll take it and—"

"I wouldn't dream of it," he says, looking down at his feet. "But I do feel, um, almost a duty, or rather, an obligation to, I—"

Jonathan appears to be short-circuiting, clearing his throat over and over again, like he wants to tell me something, but then he takes a few steps backward, away from me.

"What is it, Jonathan?" I put a hand on his shoulder. "You keep my secret. I'll keep yours. I promise."

He clears his throat *again*, twice in a row, fast and short. "Did you mean what you said to the boy? That you love him?"

"Why? You said you won't tell her—"

"I won't. Never . . ."

Jonathan takes a deep, slow breath and closes his eyes. I remember when we first met. He was young and handsome and polite, with kind eyes and nice hands. His hands are knobby and spotted now, but his eyes are still kind, just smaller, slightly hidden amidst the large folds of his lids.

"She'll kill the ones you love," he finally says.

I look down and think of Malcolm. Jonathan knows the truth. He knows everything, doesn't he? It's sweet of him to look out for me, dangerous even, so I try to ease his heart.

"I know what she did to Malcolm, but—"

Jonathan interrupts with another loud, deep breath, the heaviest sigh, almost laced with gravel, like a man who's not long for this earth.

A man with sins to confess before dying.

"Oh, miss." Jonathan wipes away the tiny beads of sweat forming on his brow. "I'm not talking about him."

TWENTY-TWO

NICOLA

1990

The moment I stepped out of my bedroom for the night ahead, Jonathan was waiting for me to emerge, on edge, with a twitch of his nose and a frog in his throat. "Might we have a chat in the garden, madam?" he croaked.

This was *very* alarming. Jonathan never requested a chat.

It was also the first time I noticed how much he had aged since he started his service. I didn't even remember the last time we made love. He was admittedly growing older, closer to fifty now than forty, and even though I technically had more years on him, my sexual attraction to Jonathan had been waning. Still, we had plenty of time left together as mistress and servant, but I knew he wouldn't be here forever. He had been my favorite, though. I didn't even want to think about replacing him one day. Not that I'd admit to *missing* him, but he had been the best suited to me so far. Even Amber enjoyed having him around the house. He was amiable and competent and loyal. He took our agreement seriously. Everyone has a price, and he had been willing to come to the dark side for that delectable promise of safety and security for life.

Jonathan and I took a seat on the garden bench near the flower beds where the daffodils had begun to bloom. "Someone came to the door today, madam. I happened to be up and about to receive her," he told me, no beating around the bush due to the urgent matter at hand.

"Here?" I gasped in disbelief. Yes, this was most distressing news. We never had an uninvited visitor. The Laurels was like a fortress. We didn't have a doorbell reachable by the public. It was purely for show. How did this person even enter the premises?

"Yes, madam," he continued. "She was shouting so loud at the gate, shaking it, that I heard her from my quarters. And she was calling for Miss Amber."

"Who was it?" I asked, and he hesitated. "*Jonathan.* Who was it?"

"I don't want you to get upset with her," he admitted, speaking well out of turn, his not-so-secret soft spot for Amber on full display. "I don't reckon she meant any harm by it. I don't reckon she thought this would happen at all."

"Who. Was. It?"

Jonathan bowed his head.

"Miss Marlena Borkenhagen. Miss Amber's younger sister."

I froze upon hearing the news. How in God's name did *Miss Marlena Borkenhagen* know to come to the Laurels? Amber knew my rules. She wasn't to make contact with anyone from her past or tell them where she would be. She said she hadn't. She *promised* me.

Were we breaking promises to one another already?

"She only wrote a letter, madam," Jonathan said. "And it was dated from years ago, during the early time inside. Miss Marlena showed it to me. Said she held on to it all this time. Didn't show it to anybody, though she did show it to me. But it didn't say very much. It referenced the Laurels, in name only, not a full address or a neighborhood or a city. And Miss Amber went on in the letter that she just missed her sister and that she was all right and that she shouldn't tell anyone she had made contact. And Miss Marlena said she did not tell anyone, following her sister's wishes."

"What did you do with it?"

"I gave it back to her with my apologies but nobody by that name has ever resided here."

"And she said?" I could feel my shoulders rising closer to my neck with each question, tension gripping my whole body.

"That she was sorry to bother, had herself a little cry and saw herself out down the street. It was heartbreaking, truth be told."

"*Out* of turn, Jonathan," I scolded him openly, tired of his compassion for others, when it was explicitly reserved for me by our ironclad agreement. "You mustn't tell Amber about any of this. Understand me?"

"Of course I do, madam." Jonathan bowed his head in reverence again. I was sure he wouldn't dare. I *would* kill him. He knew that. "I only wanted to tell you so you knew about the potential situation at hand. That Miss Amber's sister is in London as of a couple of hours ago."

"Did she mention how long she'd be in town?"

"Madam, I didn't think it prudent to make conversation, in order to keep up appearances that I didn't know anything about her sister." The judgment dripped from his voice, but I'm not sure what he was expecting with that tone. A family reunion was simply not going to occur.

"Very good. Thank you, Jonathan. Not another word about any of this ever again. Understood?"

He nodded and I hustled out the front gate faster than perhaps I ever had, taking in every scent imaginable, aiming to catch one that was similar to Amber's. I stood still in the middle of the avenue, waiting for some clarity to come.

Yes, I could still sense Amber, as I always did when she was nearby, but I was trying to sense a similar essence to see if that could lead me down a promising path to Marlena.

I took a few steps in one direction.

No. That wasn't it. It was fading away.

But when I moved in the other direction, just a few more steps, *bang*—it hit me again full force. That innate sweetness, like a ripe summer strawberry, mixed with verve and nerve, plus glorious human flesh and blood.

It went in and out, this essence I knew so intimately now with Amber and that was also within her sister. It grew faint especially when I was around other humans on the high street in Hampstead that night. But the fact that it kept wafting here and there reassured me that I was on the right track to find Marlena.

As I proceeded farther into the residential part of the village, her destination became quite obvious. She had popped into the Holly Bush for tea. An inviting pub indeed, with warm lighting, a cozy fireplace and plenty of tourists relaxing after a day of sightseeing.

Marlena Borkenhagen sat at the bar with a pint, and it struck me as funny how similar she was to Amber in how she carried herself. Shoulders back and confident. Legs crossed elegantly. But they were sisters, not twins. Marlena wasn't as pretty as Amber, her nose more upturned, rather swinelike, and her eyebrows massively overgrown, but she was certainly as gregarious and friendly, chatting up the couple sitting next to her.

And she was very obviously already a bit drunk.

I snagged a spot at the end of the bar, one seat away, so I could listen in and decide the appropriate course of action.

"I go back on Wednesday," Marlena slurred, her Wisconsin accent even thicker than Amber's.

The couple nodded at her, friendly enough, but they'd settled their bill, ready to leave. "Good luck to you." The wife smiled at Marlena as the husband took her hand. "You have a safe place to go tonight, love?"

"Yes, yes!" Marlena waved them off, placing a piece of Yorkshire pudding in her mouth. "Good night, you guys! Great meeting you!"

Leaving an opening for me. She was clearly dying to talk to somebody. *Anybody.*

When I switched seats, it was more than apparent she was an open book.

"Hi! I'm Marlena!" She smiled.

Oh, tell me everything, darling.

But the letter is all I have to go on. And the Laurels thing was a dead lead." Marlena sighed before taking another gulp of her pint, having fully unloaded the whole story on me. "I've even thought about going to see her ex-husband, but . . ."

"But?"

"I didn't want to upset him. He was sick over her leaving him, on the phone with my parents daily with an update. I doubt he'd have any clue anyway. He tried to find her, but when the people he hired ended up dead, he gave up pretty quickly after that. He's remarried. He has a bunch of kids. He probably doesn't think about Amber at all anymore. Nobody does but me."

"What about your parents?" I knew I wanted everyone to forget about her, but it was hard to believe they actually had—she was their daughter, for God's sake.

"My dad won't speak about Amber," Marlena said. "And I can't mention her to my mom. It makes her too sad. That's why I was hoping I'd find her and be able to convince her to come home. Or at least visit us. I really do think she's alive, but maybe that's stupid. I just don't get it, but I guess I never knew her that well. How well does a twelve-year-old know anybody? It's not like adults are honest with kids. But it must have been pretty bad if she never came back, right?"

"So where will you go from here?" I asked her, finding her charming despite myself. She reminded me a lot of Amber. Easy to talk to. Easy to love.

Marlena shrugged, nearly throwing herself off-balance enough to fall off the stool. "I can't give up on her, but I also can't let this define my life anymore. I have a job; I finished nursing school. I wanna be my own person, but it's weird living in her shadow. It's just that she sounded so full of regret in the letter. Like she made a mistake or needed help but didn't want to ask for it because how would I have gotten here? But I'm here now."

Marlena looked down at her trainers and pointed her toes, stretching out. Was she a dancer, too? She had a small backpack and not much else with her. "Where are you staying?" I asked. "Just want to make sure you get home safe."

"Some crappy hostel in Soho." She laughed. "Couldn't swing the Ritz this time. It took everything I had to get here. I really saved up over the years. My mom thinks I'm crazy. She says Amber doesn't want to be found. And we didn't tell my dad."

I picked up the tab for Marlena's dinner.

It was the least I could do.

Marlena was tipsy as she made her way back to her hostel. She used the bus with no issues to get back to Soho, exuding the confidence of a local instead of a tourist, though she sat on the upper deck, which was rather charming.

I stayed a few yards behind her for the journey and she didn't seem to notice, never looking back, gaze remaining forward to keep her eye on the prize: a warm-enough bed in a room with other young tourists who would hopefully keep it down so she could get some sleep.

I picked up the pace behind her, walking with purpose, slightly faster than the average human. Brisk, but nothing untoward, nothing unseemly. I mean, really, what were the odds she was staying in Soho? It was our territory, after all.

When she went inside, I listened to her conversation with the receptionist.

"I'm *knackered*," she said, in a bad impression of a Londoner. "Do I sound like a Brit?"

"Not really, but looks like you drank like one tonight." The receptionist laughed and Marlena joined in, stumbling up the steps to her room, missing a couple, finding her footing slowly but surely.

So I waited.

When I entered the hostel and started upstairs, nobody questioned me. I appeared just as they did. Young and eager to take on the world, traveling on a shoestring, living my life before I would ultimately have to settle down one day. Meeting Marlena felt a bit like meeting Amber's potential future, not only if she hadn't met me, but also if she hadn't met Malcolm. Staying in Wisconsin, near her parents, near her sister, searching for something, bored to tears, staying bravely bright and cheery through it all. How depressing.

Thank God we found each other.

It would make the news. Young American woman found dead in a London hostel. Was she drugged? Was she suffocated? Her wound would be gone, the autopsy would be unable to reveal anything concrete, aside from an inexplicable blood shortage. They would probably display her photo, too, but only for a few days or so.

I could keep Amber busy enough to stay off the television and avoid the papers.

The story would be gone in a few days.

Amber would never have to find out.

How would she?

I watched Marlena sleep soundly, clutching her backpack for safety even though the other two beds were empty, roommates probably still out for a party. I gently peeled the bag away from Marlena and quietly rifled through it. A few tops, socks, passport, her ticket home in three days' time, and the letter from Amber.

I opened it.

She was vague but very upset.

> *I wish you could help me.*
> *The Laurels is beautiful, you'd like it.*
> *But I might have made a mistake.*
> *I'm not sure yet.*
> *I miss you and I love you.*
> *I loved being your big sister.*
> *I wish I still could be.*

I would have to destroy the letter, not only because it was difficult to read, but also because no roads of any kind could lead back to the Laurels.

I leaned in close to Marlena, fast asleep, taking long and slow breaths. I grazed her neck with my nose before whispering in her ear.

"Wake up."

Marlena's eyes popped open.

I clicked mine with hers instantly.

She didn't say a word.

She couldn't move.

She looked just like her sister, but there was no need to be gentle this time.

I pierced Marlena's neck with my fangs and drank from her slowly.

She was so delicious.

Amber Lite.

I muffled her screams with the pillow until she was gone.

TWENTY-THREE

AMBER

I wrote a letter to my little sister. Only one time. When I was inside during the early years with Nicola. I think it was more for myself than for her. A way to get down some of the thoughts in my head about what happened to me. What I chose. I hoped something lyrical and profound would come out of me. But all I could get out were these short sentences.

It probably sounded like a hostage note.

Did it scare her?

I never really thought about how it might have affected my sister, being so young, asking her to keep a secret like that. Did she show it to our parents? I don't know. I purposely didn't put a return address. I wasn't calling out for her to find me. It wasn't her responsibility.

I just wanted *someone* to hear my voice who already knew it. And I wanted her to know that I was thinking about her, too. She was still a teenage girl. I remember being a teenage girl, and it felt like no one was ever thinking about me. I could at least give her that. I couldn't give her anything else. I should have been there. An older sister to call, someone to run to when things went bad with a boy, or really, really good with one. Someone who understood where we came from. But I left her all alone with my miserable parents. I wasn't a good big sister at all.

After I sent her the letter, I planned to put them all to bed in my mind. I needed that relief. I was spending so much time alone back then, and even though I was keeping busy the best I could, it was hard not to think about them all the time. Mostly, I thought about my sister.

But I had to stop thinking about her or I was going to go insane.

I made my decision. I had to live with it. I decided to trust Nicola. So I wrote that letter, sealed it up and sent it off. I promised myself that I'd try not to think about any of them again. It got easier over time.

For God's sake, I can't tell you the last time I thought about that letter.

Once the internet came around, of course I considered looking up my family. Especially my sister. I knew she'd be on there. All of them, right? MySpace, then Facebook, then Instagram, and so on. It was so tempting to look into her life, but I never did.

Sometimes I'd get so depressed just seeing Malcolm out with one of his wives.

Why would I torture myself even more?

I left my family behind. I didn't think I deserved to know what happened to them.

They never got to know what happened to me.

Living in the unknown is often worse than the truth.

But not today.

She was my first thought when Jonathan spoke.

I can't even say her name out loud.

I type it out.

Come on, Amber. How would she have even gotten here? How would she know where to look? How would Nicola find her? How could Nicola go through with it?

She had a sister, too, didn't she?!

I press enter.

It's brief, archived, but it's there in black and white.

Marlena Borkenhagen, age 23, of Wauwatosa, Wisconsin, passed away suddenly on Saturday, July 28, 1990, while traveling in London. She was a registered nurse at Children's Wisconsin in Milwaukee. She was the beloved daughter of Donna and Robert Borkenhagen and dear sister to the late Amber (Malcolm) Wells.

While traveling in London.

1990.

Eleven years after I left.

She looked for me.

She didn't give up on me.

My hands shake as they hover above the keyboard. I retch, putting a hand over my mouth even though nothing will come up. I want to shut it down, but I can't stop looking at her face. It's a graduation photo. From nursing school. A broad smile. The little white hat. I can see she's so proud of herself. She was a nurse? What did she say she wanted to be when she grew up? Did we ever talk about it? She was so little, we were so far apart, I don't remember. Was she in love? Did she have a boyfriend or a girlfriend? Did she live by herself or with roommates? Did she still live with my parents?

Twenty-three years old.

She was so young.

She had a whole life with so much more to go.

Twenty-three years old.

Just like me.

Did my parents survive this?

They thought I was dead, too.

The late Amber Wells.

Gone at twenty-three years old.

I dry-heave again, sick to think that Nicola took not only my life, but my sweet sister's. An innocent. I have nothing to give, nothing to expel from my body, but how can that be? I feel like I need an exorcism, like there's a demon inside me, but I'm the demon, aren't I?

No.

No.

Nicola is the demon.

I start laughing through tears, like a crazy person, remembering how she almost tricked me again earlier at Tramp. With all of her *darling*s and dancing and diamonds. All I want to do is fly at her in a psychotic rage the second she walks in the door, brutally tear her apart with my bare hands, bite into her flesh, but there would be no point.

There's only one way.

I imagine her body sizzling in the stark sunlight of midday, crackling loudly until she bursts into flames, the ashes to be swept away by the wind, unable to hurt anyone or anything ever again. But even death feels too kind.

She deserves something even worse.

What would be the worst thing imaginable for Nicola?

She cares about the Laurels, her sister, and me.

But I'm the only part of that triumvirate that I can control.

I'm not staying here.

I'm getting out even if it kills me.

Either way, she'll be in pain, which is exactly what she deserves.

When Courtenay and Nicola return to the Laurels, I'm already in my room. I listen closely to their whispers. They sound like we used to, but I can't go out there. I can barely stand to hear Nicola, much less look at her. No. I don't trust myself and what I might do in the heat of that moment. I need to stay focused because this isn't about escaping her anymore.

This is about revenge.

Careful revenge.

When she knocks at my door, I stay silent.

She's listening.

I give her nothing.

Finally I hear her voice, muffled behind the closed door.

"She's in."

Good.

I know exactly what I need to do.

Dole out my punishment to Nicola.

Piece by piece.

Before opening night.

And then.

I'm gone.

All of us are due at Hey Mister at eleven as usual. Opening night is in forty-eight hours. Everything is just about finished—the club sparkles and shines from top to bottom—but Nicola wants us to go over the game plan, *yet again*, and do a first listen to some of the DJ sets for Hey Mister's first weekend.

But Courtenay and I are not going.

She's hanging out in the parlor, playing cards with Jonathan, apparently waiting for Nicola and me to rise.

"Who's winning?" I ask.

"Me." She smiles.

"Do you want to see a show with me tonight? I thought we could go to the West End to celebrate. Nicola told me the news."

"What about the club?"

"We won't be late. I promise. We can see anything you like."

"*Mamma Mia!?*" she asks excitedly. "I know it's cliché, but I've always wanted to go. I love the movies."

"Sure." I laugh. "Great choice."

"What's a great choice?" Nicola peers around the corner, slinking into the room. Her mere presence sets fire to my veins, and it takes everything I have not to grab the nearest hideous tchotchke of hers and whip it right at her face.

I want to draw blood, maim her, disfigure her, but I can't.

Just wait.

Patience, Amber.

"Good morning, sunshine." I greet her with more bite than I should, but I change my tone quickly. "Courtenay and I are going to the *thea-tah* tonight! Wanna come?"

Jonathan watches and waits for Nicola's response.

She's going to say no, isn't she?

"For what?" Nicola scoffs.

"We're going to see *Mamma Mia!*. It starts at half seven," Courtenay says, scrolling through her phone to look up the tickets.

"I don't think so . . ." Nicola trails off.

"Are you sure? It'll be a right laugh."

"A right laugh," I echo Courtenay, keeping eye contact with Nicola.

She grimaces at me because we both know she'll decline.

"No, thanks. You two go on ahead," Nicola says with a wave of her hand. "But don't be late tonight. The DJs start right at eleven."

She curls one of her long fingers at me. It kills me as I join Nicola on the other side of the room, but I keep up appearances.

"What's this all about?" she asks.

"Nothing! Something to do before we clock in for the night. I wanted to celebrate her decision. Are you sure you don't want to join us?"

A long pause.

"I'm sure."

"It'll be good for Courtenay and me to bond a little bit more, don't you think? The birthday twins? Like you said."

"Mmm." She nods, smiling at the thought. "Enjoy."

Courtenay and I bound out of the Novello Theatre singing "Waterloo" at the top of our lungs, skipping and holding hands down Aldwych like a couple of freaks. I bought her a few glasses of bubbly, before the show *and* during the intermission, and I was honestly jealous that we couldn't clink glasses together. In another life, I'd have loved to tie one on with Courtenay.

But Court's not my friend.

She's my replacement.

It's time.

Courtenay raises her hand to get a taxi, but I pull it back down gently. She cocks her head to the side, a quizzical look on her face so sweet that it almost makes me feel sorry for her.

But I've snapped and I need her and I won't back down.

No mercy.

Nicola didn't have any for my sister.

"So it seems like you're feeling good about your decision?"

"Definitely." Courtenay nods. "You're so sweet to worry, and I get it, but honestly, I know it's the right thing. My days have nothing for me, Amber. Do you know what I mean? The nightlife is what I've always loved, even when I was small! I've always been a child of the moon. It's the only time I feel free and like myself. Why wouldn't I want that forever?"

She sounds a little nuts, but I remember feeling the exact same way about turning.

Like it was meant to be.

"My mom used to say that when I wouldn't go to sleep." Courtenay smiles. "That I was her moonchild, born under a full one. She was into that stuff. I guess I am, too."

"What stuff?"

"Destiny." She sighs.

I know this is the part where a normal person would ask more about her mother and listen attentively and then break the news that she wouldn't want this life for her daughter, moonchild or not. I almost want to say that I know she'll crave the sun on her skin again and feel crazy for being wistful about a gnarly burn after a day at the beach, remembering the sweet relief of a cold shower. I want to tell her that she'll miss scarfing down chips and cheese from a shitty kebab shop after a night out with a bunch of other drunk people and that she'll only lust for blood moving forward; nothing else for the rest of time will satisfy her the same way. And I want to tell her that she will actually ache for her past, her family, even if they were bad or boring or never around, because at least they knew you were a human being who existed on this planet just like everyone else. All of it, a proof of life. All of it, gone forever. All of it, leaving a hole that will stay empty, the dull pain emanating every night, even when you convince yourself you don't feel anything at all anymore.

Because of course you do.

But I don't tell Courtenay any of that because I *need* her to turn.

I push down any nerves that start to bubble up.

No, I haven't done it before.

But I'm going to be the one to make Courtenay a vampire.

Tonight.

Nicola won't be able to *stand* that I'll be Courtenay's maker, but she won't say a word. She wants to keep me. She wants to keep Courtenay. And she wants to keep us at the Laurels.

Part of me wonders if she might even get a twisted little kick out of my coup. How would it feel for her to watch me take something of my own for once? She might even be proud.

I know it's a sick game she's been playing with me, but I know the full score now.

I'm going to win.

"Moonchild." I grin at Courtenay. "Nicola will love that. Perfect for our surprise."

"What surprise?"

I call Nicola once we're back at the Laurels, close to eleven. The Rolls is gone from the driveway. Jonathan took her to Hey Mister. Perfect.

"Courtenay isn't feeling well," I tell her on the phone. "She overdid it a little at the theater, kind of a last-hurrah moment, and I don't think she should be alone right now. Someone's gotta hold her hair back. Think you and the girls can hold down the fort? I trust you."

"You trust me?" I hear Nicola smirk through the phone. "Is Courtenay all right?"

"She'll be fine. It all just needs to come out, you know?"

Nicola is silent for what feels like a full minute.

"You used to love a bender, too."

"Party girls like to party."

"Well, do take good care of her."

"I will. Don't worry about that."

"Roddy's been wondering where you are. He'll be disappointed you're out tonight. He's leaving so soon," Nicola says. "But I'm sure we'll be able to lift his spirits even in your absence."

Did Jonathan tell her about Roddy and me?

She's never alluded to knowing about our relationship before.

I'm not sure what to say.

"You're going to miss him, aren't you?" Nicola asks. "Me, too."

"Roddy's great," I say, keeping a cool head. "But we've always known he was going on his merry way after opening night."

Another bout of lingering silence between us.

"Merry, indeed." She laughs before hanging up the phone.

I text Roddy that I miss him and love him and I'll see him tomorrow.

And that I have something *very* important to ask him.

No matter how nervous I am about his reaction.

watch Courtenay freshen her makeup in the mirror, sitting at my vanity, taking it very seriously. "You can still change it up afterward," I remind her.

"I know," she says, not looking away from the mirror as she applies her lashes. "But I want to look hot."

"I did the same thing." I smile at her, remembering all the effort I put in for my turning on New Year's Eve, and then I didn't even get to enjoy any of the festivities.

Nicola told me nothing.

"Does it hurt?" Courtenay asks me, biting her lip. Well, for starters, she won't be able to do *that* anymore.

"You'll be fine," I say, needing her to go through with it. I watch her apply a sparkly red lip gloss to her pillowy pout, smacking her lips together. The final touch. "You look super hot, Court. Ready?" I pat the spot on the bed next to me.

She sits down and nods.

I watch her chest rise and fall, up and down, faster and faster.

Let's lighten the mood a bit.

"What do you wanna listen to?" I ask. "No wrong answers."

"Don't laugh." She smiles, already giggling herself. "But I need the Spice Girls and I need them now."

"An unexpected choice!" I exclaim, prancing over to my laptop. "I thought you'd be all about, like, Charli XCX or Dua Lipa."

"My mum loved the Spice Girls," she says, smiling, a tear falling down her cheek. "It's one of the only things I remember about her. Calling me her moonchild and that she was absolutely mad for the Spice Girls, especially Geri. She had red hair, too."

I don't say anything.

If I do, I might cry, too.

I press play and hear the familiar laugh from the track. Courtenay lies back on my bed, head on the pillow, eyes to the ceiling. I feel a fiery energy buzzing inside me. I can't tell if it's good or bad, but I'm terrified I might screw this up. It's my first time.

But just as Nicola said I would, I remember *every* second from my turning.

All it took was a few drops from Nic's wrist into my mouth.

She looked like she was doing the most natural thing in the world.

I pull Courtenay up and into my arms, her limbs shaking, her teeth chattering, the fear all-consuming. Her eyes are shut so tight that little bunny lines form on her freckled nose. I move closer and closer to her neck, releasing a quick hot breath when I'm nearly there, so she knows what's coming.

I don't want her to be afraid, but that's impossible.

It was the single most terrifying moment of my life.

But also, I can admit, the most exciting one.

The extreme push and pull of emotions was so intoxicating, I never once considered it would grow into such regret.

You don't think you'll ever regret anything when you're twenty-three years old.

I whisper along to the lyrics so she'll laugh, keeping spirits bright as best I can.

When I release my fangs, Courtenay opens her eyes, and I instantly recognize the terror and thrill inside them, coexisting at once, accepting the finality of her choice without fully understanding it.

Zig-a-zig-ah.

TWENTY-FOUR

NICOLA

2006

I came upon Amber's MySpace profile, her latest obsession, and pored over it from top to bottom at least a hundred times. Reluctantly, of course; I wanted nothing to do with the computer. The amount of photos she took of herself with that digital camera I bought for her was obscene. The vanity of it all. But now I completely understood why she wanted to spend so much time on that bloody website. She got *constant* male attention. She also got to talk about her favorite thing, aside from music.

Herself.

What she likes to listen to, what she likes to read, how she speaks French and Spanish, how she's a trained dancer. Just on and on and on. I wanted to read her private conversations with these men, the ones who posted public messages on her page, but I haven't been able to access them. I couldn't seem to crack her passwords—all this technology sadly felt beyond me—but she willingly told me about a lot of it, almost as if she was bragging about being so in demand.

"It's just for fun, Nic. Takes any pressure off telling them the truth, like when I meet a guy in person and have to come up with all these excuses. Online, we're just talking. No harm, no foul."

"But you have me to talk to, darling." I smiled at her, but she didn't respond to that. So I asked her where all these blokes live, and she said pretty much everywhere. UK. America. Someone in Athens with great hair. She wouldn't stop raving about his luscious Grecian locks.

It *was* all online, like she said, so I wasn't wildly concerned, but what if it escalated?

I did like to leave Amber alone on her solo nights, the best I could, but curiosity sometimes got the best of me. I didn't see the harm if she didn't know about it. To be fair, once I followed her around enough times, it all seemed relatively innocent. Dancing, chitchatting at pubs to source prey, popping into museums and galleries in our territory, things of that nature.

I noticed that she checked in with Malcolm on occasion, but I knew it was just to scratch a pesky itch left over from her old life. She didn't speak to him or touch him or anything of the sort, so I haven't brought it up to her directly.

If she did, I'd have to break my promise to her.

A bridge too far, though I suppose she'd say the same about me. She'd be furious to know that I ever spied on her, but she never knew I was there, lurking in the shadows. I kept my distance for fear of her sensing me. At any rate, it would be better to "innocently" come across her making a mistake rather than have her find out that I could track her so easily, my radius so much larger than hers.

The advent of the internet truly displeased me. Surely it was only going to get worse from here on out. I could scarcely believe that the future had arrived like this and in such an obtrusive fashion. So much information at our fingertips could not be good for any of us.

You wouldn't necessarily know it by looking at her, but Amber had always been somewhat of a little sponge, thirsty for more knowledge about the world around her. She learned foreign languages. She read widely. And she adapted to the computer right away, and while I tried to stave it off for as long as I could, I started to look unreasonable or, worse, like a proper dolt.

So we got the dial-up, the modems, the Wi-Fi, upgrade after upgrade. She liked staying busy, all of it, and I rationalized that it kept her home more, right where I wanted her—that is, when she wasn't out with me—even if I didn't fully want to understand it.

Of course, she still loved to dance and strut around our fabulous London haunts, but I could see her interest in nightlife was waning at times. Stuck in our territory—her words, not mine— she'd have loved to go broader across London, maybe the country, but I could never risk someone taking her from me. Or what if she got the urge to run? She wasn't available. She was mine.

I told her all about the potential dangers of leaving our designated territories. That Margaux, and of course Tamsin the traitor, could not be trusted. She already knew that Pierce and company were a slick bunch not to be trifled with. As for traveling? Who knew what other vampires lurked out there in the wild? Not to mention the variables with leaving home at all. Where can you rest safely? What if there's a delay? What if something goes awry at a crucial time?

I wanted Amber to constantly worry about what would happen to her if something went wrong—that would keep her close to me forever.

But she was on the damned computer all the time, so much so that sometimes she forgot we needed to *actually* eat. Once she got on MySpace, our next few feasts had been so ho-hum because she just wanted to run back home to get back on the bloody machine to see if she had any messages or new contacts. It was like an addiction.

But when she stopped speaking to me in jest about her online boyfriends, that's when I knew something was seriously amiss.

I worried one of them had turned into a real boyfriend.

"Should *I* get a MySpace?" I asked Amber as I lingered in the study doorway, watching her at the desk giving the computer all her attention and none of it to me.

"Definitely," she replied without looking up. "It's fun! I'll put you in my Top 8."

"I don't know," I mused, not knowing what the fuck she was talking about. I got a bit closer to see for myself. "Couldn't I just poke around a bit using yours?" I put my head lightly on her shoulder and she shrugged me off instantly.

"No!" She moved her head in front of the screen, changing it up somehow with a click of the little rat or whatever. "It's private. You should personalize your own. It's an experience. I could help you set it up. You'll like it. Maybe you could use it for hunting."

"Do *you* use it for hunting?"

"Not yet." She grinned. "Want to try it?"

"I don't much care for shooting fish in a barrel."

She snorted at me, but I didn't know what she meant by that.

"Where are you off to later?" I asked Amber, flopping onto the nearby chaise, raising my voice an octave in the hopes she'd actually look up at me. "I heard there will be a great DJ at Tramp if you want to swing by tonight. We haven't been in a while. Prince Harry's been spotted recently. What do you reckon?"

"I'm not in the mood." She sighed, still looking at the screen, typing every so often, even giggling a bit. Who was she speaking with now? Someone more interesting than Prince fucking Harry? "I'm going to a show tonight. It's not far."

"To see who?"

"A band." She grinned, a bit snarky really, like a teenager aiming to get a row going with a domineering parent. "You wouldn't know them. You don't like going to gigs anyway."

Listen to her. *Gigs!*

Meanwhile, Amber loved going to concerts, *gigs* and shows of all kinds, and luckily for her, a great deal of the venues happened to be in our territory. Safe and sound. I knew she found them all entertaining, but sometimes I wondered if the real allure was to relish time spent away from me because I wouldn't attend any with her.

She *never* knew that sometimes I waited outside regardless, just to watch her come and go.

"You're going alone?" I asked.

"Yep!"

Oh, for fuck's sake, I knew she wasn't going alone.

What kind of fool did she take me for?

"Have a wonderful time," I said, slipping out the door of the study, waiting for her to leave so I could follow.

Then I knocked like a madwoman on Jonathan's door, demanding his service yet again.

We followed a few cars behind Amber's taxi, and she was going much farther afield, which she had failed to mention. We were all the way in Brixton. At Carling Academy.

Not our territory.

"Is she out of her mind?" I exclaimed, opening the door.

"You *sure* you want to go inside, madam?" Jonathan asked me. "I know it upsets you."

Of course I didn't want to go inside, but I rolled my eyes at him anyway and got out of the car. I could do this. For Amber. For us.

I knew something was different tonight.

I could feel it.

I needed to be involved.

She might need my help.

"Don't worry," I said to Jonathan. "I'll be fine."

Staying far enough away that she wouldn't sense me, taking full advantage of the maker's larger radius, I watched Amber standing outside the venue, dressed like a blonde Amy Winehouse, nervously scratching at her arms.

She was looking for someone. And she was *very* anxious about it.

A few moments later, she waved at a strange man approaching. *Oh God.*

She *was* meeting someone from the internet.

It didn't look like he would cause much worry, by the state of him. Not just because Amber was a vampire, but because he looked like you could crack him right in half, clocking in at only about ten stone, and that was being generous. He was short and thin with long hair and sad eyes.

Was this *really* her new type?

Everyone shuffling into Carling Academy looked the same, and it was distinctly not my crowd. Skinny jeans. Swooping fringe. Man or woman, it didn't matter. They all looked like they wanted to get into an emotional verbal altercation with someone and then go cry about it in a dark corner alone later.

Amber was dipping her toe into the look with that new fringe of hers and the black leggings under her dress, but you could pry the pink out of her cold, dead hands. She looked electric. Heads above the rest, but oh, didn't she know it?

The slight chap held out his hand and Amber laughed, pulling it in, and then snogged him full on! He kissed her back, of course; he wasn't blind. And straightaway, they looked like a proper couple, not two idiots from the internet who'd just met for the first time.

What false intimacy hath the World Wide Web wrought? They held hands and went inside.

Oh, I was absolutely going inside, too.

I held my breath because I knew it would hurt.

But Amber was worth it, wasn't she?

There were enough bodies around; I didn't think she'd know I was there unless she was specifically thinking about me.

And clearly, she was not.

watched Amber and her paramour dance and snog and laugh and look like they'd been together a hundred years. They shared lingering stares into one another's eyes. Furtive lovers, swapping whispers, swapping spit, too. All in the front row. They didn't care who was watching. They didn't think anyone was. Least of all me.

Then I noticed her taking deep breaths, as if she was bracing herself for something insurmountable.

Oh God.

Amber.

No.

She whispered into his ear again.

And then she showed him her teeth.

His face fell, mouth agape in horror.

I knew immediately what she had done.

And it was not going well.

He started to run away from her.

I almost felt sorry for Amber, but what on earth was she thinking? Telling a man she's a vampire at a bloody Arctic Monkeys concert? A seduction like that required careful planning, but she hadn't consulted with me, knowing I would not be best pleased.

Now she was seeing red after his rejection, following him

closely, compelling everyone around her to get out of her way. The band even exchanged a concerned look, because they were playing their biggest hit now, and everyone was moving out and away from them instead of dancing their arses off as close to the stage as possible. It was only a brief moment, but they noticed.

God, she was being lazy.

Finally, Amber got the boy to turn around and face her, and I saw it all happen.

His vacant stare. The slack jaw.

Bloody hell, was she going to turn a man against his will?

That wouldn't end well.

I would know.

I couldn't let it happen, so I hurried outside after them, a bit thrilled, honestly, about what was to come.

A mber had him in her clutches behind the venue, holding the poor sod up by his tiny little T-shirt at the sleeves. We could still hear the music from inside, muffled, but setting the right tone regardless. Anger and sex and heat and all the emotions Amber was experiencing, feeling duped by this man she wrongfully thought she could trust. Now she was ready for all that hurt to pour out of her so she could pour his blood down her throat in mere moments.

But she didn't need moments.

She didn't even look around first.

Oh, she wasn't going to *turn* him.

She was going to *kill* him.

Luckily it was just the empty tour bus and nothing else nearby as she launched into a violent rage, tearing him from the jawbone to the collarbone, a total fucking mess, a fountain of blood erupting from the gullet, and we were going to have to hightail it out of there soon because there was no cleaning this up without a proper bio-hazard team.

Good thing Jonathan was close by waiting for us. I knew Amber would be cross that I'd followed her. But also perhaps present a modicum of gratitude? This was a cut-and-run situation and she knew it, but she must have been craving it subconsciously, because even though I'd seen her get sloppy, I'd never seen her eat like *this* before in my whole life.

It was a marvel to witness.

She was finally the monster I'd always hoped she'd become.

Amber finished fast. I didn't help myself to the scraps. It wasn't my place. He was all hers.

"Darling . . ." I approached softly, revealing my presence. She whipped around to look at me, still breathing heavily, but her eyes grew large and wild, like she wanted to pounce on me next.

"Come here." I spoke to her softly. "It's all right, Amber. I forgive you."

I held out my arms for her, but she sneered at me, distrusting.

"What are you doing here?" she asked, an accusatory tone I didn't much appreciate. How dare she ask me that? After all my care and keeping of her over the years. After she left our territory without telling me. Who knows what would have happened if I wasn't here to take care of her?

"I'm here to help you!" I hissed.

But the look on her face suggested she didn't believe that.

Not for a second.

Jonathan fetched us in the Rolls from an appropriate hiding place near the venue. A mobile phone was a modern convenience that I'd grown to appreciate in times like these, including the delightful shock of pink on its exterior. It certainly beat having Jonathan run circles around our perimeter, hoping to cross paths with us without being spotted, a couple of bloody birds bobbing around the streets looking rather suspicious indeed.

We clambered inside the vehicle.

He had already prepared the plastic covering in the back seat just in case.

Jonathan knew us well.

Amber was quiet for most of the drive. I wanted her to open up to me without having to ask, but she left me no choice but to push her, yet again. "Why did you keep him a secret?" I asked her. "You always tell me when you fancy someone, no matter how ill-advised."

"I thought he was different." She sighed, looking morosely out the window. "The conversations we had were incredible. Hours and hours of them. I just don't understand. I thought for sure he'd want to be with me. I really did. I feel like such a dumbass."

She wasn't a *dumbass*, she was a romantic, but same difference depending on who you asked.

"You should have told me," I said, taking her hand, but she pulled away from me. "I could have saved you the heartache."

"I didn't want to involve you," she said plainly.

Ouch. But I had to stay calm. She was a loose cannon.

"Why? I always tell you the truth."

"When it's convenient," she scoffed at me. "You don't tell me everything."

"Well, you clearly don't tell me everything either!" I barked back, but then I reined it in, softening my approach. "Come on, darling. We're best friends. So yes, I could have helped you through this. You wanted to *turn* him and that's something you should have discussed with me first. I don't want men at the Laurels and I am your—"

"Maker. I know," she said, sulky little beast.

"You're in denial," I said. "But falling in love is a fool's errand. I've told you this before. A human will age, and even if you manage to turn one, it will change everything. It's as simple as that."

"How do *you* know? You've never even been in a real relationship with a vampire, have you?"

"It's hard enough being in a platonic relationship with one, don't you think?" I started to spar back with her, unable to help myself; she was being such an evil tart.

"Maybe that's just how you operate," she sassed me right back.

I did not want to get further into this conversation with Amber—there would be no victor—so I thought it best to shut it down and focus on the positive instead. Her monstrous side was blooming. She had killed him herself. A first where someone she cared for was concerned. That was an excellent development.

"Just tell me next time, all right?" I asked, even though I meant it as a command. "Instead of going rogue on us?" I smiled at Jonathan in the mirror, but he looked away from me.

When Amber didn't say anything in return, I thought I'd twist the knife to put her in her place again.

"What was his name?" I asked.

"Michael," she replied, looking me straight in the eye now. "He was from Margate. He said that I'd like living by the seaside with him one day." Amber let out a dour laugh, one I hadn't heard from her before, laced with a casual cruelty in my direction.

Then she turned her focus back out the window, sucking the dried blood of Michael from Margate off her fingers.

TWENTY-FIVE

AMBER

I stayed up all day long with Courtenay as she finished turning, pulling the vampire version of an all-nighter. I'm *exhausted*. I kept her quiet when Nicola came home, just before dawn, popping out quickly to say good night instead of waiting for her to come to us.

"How did it go?" I asked her, whispering as I shut my door behind me.

"You were both missed, but tomorrow night will be just as important. The full run-through and *another* fun surprise for you."

"For me?"

"Obviously." She winked before disappearing into her bedroom.

I don't think she suspected anything. Courtenay wasn't fully cooked yet, so to speak, so Nicola wouldn't sense a new vampire in the mix, but I can't stop thinking about what she said.

I need to look *alive*.

A surprise for me?

What the hell does that mean?

I watch Courtenay on my bed. God, she still looks like roadkill.

She hasn't woken up yet. Why hasn't she woken up yet? I think it went well. The worst is over. The burning, the chills, the nausea, the cold, not to mention the swollen gum and tooth pain, so sharp you wish for death.

I talked softly to her through all of it. I stroked her hair. I held her hand. I told her it was almost over, even when it wasn't. I gave her all the care that Nicola gave to me when I turned.

I crawl into bed next to Courtenay.

Face-to-face.

Willing her to open her eyes.

"Wake up," I whisper. "Wake *up*!"

But she still looks . . . dead.

Is she dead?

Oh my God.

Did I do it wrong?

Did I fuck this up?

Did I *kill* her?

I lean in closer to Courtenay, nearly nose to nose, checking for any sign of life at all, and just when I'm about to really start spiraling, her bright eyes pop open like a doll's.

They look warmer and brighter than before, the colors of cinnamon buns swirling in a soft glow. When she smiles at me, I see her fangs have sprouted for the first time. They're adorable!

"I think I'm hungry."

I laugh, but it sounds like a cough, the shock of relief.

"Of course you are. Come with me."

Courtenay is light on her feet as she bounces out of my bed. She's even cuter in her vampiric form, curls overflowing and extra shiny. Her skin is so clear, like a thin sheet of glass. I offer one of my party dresses for the big reveal. It's the only thing about her that's no longer perfect. Her pale yellow dress is soaked in red.

She admires herself in the mirror as I hand her the dress. Vintage by now. Pink sequins. Nicola bought it for me years ago, right after Christmas. I know she'll remember.

I'm presenting Courtenay's surprise turning as sentimental.

Something we did *for* Nicola, not something I did *to* her.

"What have we here?" Nicola practically floats into my room, draped in her silky robe, makeup half-complete. Her voice is low and biting, but she manages to smile, surely for Courtenay's benefit.

She's absolutely *stunned*.

"Are you *so* surprised?" Courtenay asks Nicola, complete with her wild laugh, full hyena, and I join in myself, clapping along with her, trying to look innocent. Like a couple of little girls who just wanted to do something nice for Mommy.

"That's one word for it." Nicola chuckles, but I can hear the underlying darkness when she lets her laugh trail on longer than she should.

Time to start talking.

"I know you wanted to wait until opening night, but I just thought Courtenay should be a part of the fun as one of us already. We all know just how much it hurts, and the worst is over now, so tomorrow night will be a real party for everyone! And in the end, it's about the three of us here at the Laurels. So what difference does it make?"

I know exactly the difference it makes.

I keep going.

"You have so much on your plate right now, Nic. We thought this could be one less thing for you to worry about on opening night. Especially when you've already given us so much."

Nicola nods, lips pursed, with her eyes on the floor, taking it all in.

After a moment, her gaze rolls up to meet mine.

She inhales sharply and holds out her hands toward Courtenay and me.

We form our trio for the very first time.

And one of the last.

"Well done, Amber," Nicola lies through her teeth. "We'll have to tell the others, but first, baby needs to eat, hmm? And fast. Shall we?" Nicola glares at me expectantly.

"Let's go!" I reply with enthusiasm.

Courtenay is eager to join us, but Nicola tells her to stay home.

"All in good time, darling. We'll pick up the tab for now."

Jonathan keeps an eye on Courtenay while Nicola and I go for a quick hunt in Hampstead, something we've never done before. It's way too close to home, but Nicola says we're in an emergency situation with a new vampire at home.

"I would have told you to have someone ready. She must be starving," Nicola hisses as we linger outside the Holly Bush in the village. "But there will be a lone tourist or two here this evening. Lucky for you."

Her anger is set on simmer. Like she doesn't want me to know she's *too* upset. Focusing on the logistical missteps only.

"Not sure if you remember your first feed," she continues, "but I lured the doorman from Tramp to come home with us that night you turned. I kept him in the study until you woke up and prepared him for you like a little bowl of soup. Do you recall?"

I forgot.

My first few days as a vampire were a blur.

I remember feeling tired all the time and very hungry and uncertain of my new body.

It was a fucking trip.

But once I'm gone, Nicola will teach Courtenay just like she taught me.

"She'll do, no?" Nicola gestures at a gorgeous young Scandinavian woman leaving the pub with a large backpack. She's all alone. I hate this, but before I can protest, Nicola clucks her tongue. "Beggars can't be choosers, especially with a newborn at home and a nightclub to launch. Go on, darling. I'll help you bring her back to the Laurels."

I do not want to kill this woman, but I don't have a choice. She's the only one to come out of the pub by herself in an hour. God damn Hampstead for being so charming and safe and festive for solo female travelers, even at night.

"Come on, Amber! Don't waste any time. For all we know, Courtenay could be nibbling on Jonathan as we speak!" Nicola barks. "Do it. *Now.*"

I can't ask Nicola to do it for me. She'd just laugh in my face. Even though she hasn't said it out loud yet—maybe she's still too shocked—I know what she's thinking.

You made her, you feed her.

I ladle the woman's fresh blood into a bright white ceramic bowl for Courtenay. I didn't even know we had bowls in the kitchen. Nicola left in a huff for Hey Mister, muttering about how "some of us have a business to run." Jonathan will take care of the woman's body. As usual. I never know what he does with the bodies. I don't really want to know.

"You were right. I do like it." Courtenay smiles at me, red all over her lips, new fangs sharp like a puppy's. Is this what I looked like all those years ago? Fresh and eager and feeling like I just made the best decision a girl could ever make? I push the guilt out of my mind.

Focus, Amber.

It's the night before the opening.

I run through the remaining steps of my plan in my head.

I repeat them like a mantra.

Roddy's up next.

Can't wait to see you, I text him. He responds with a million x's.

But there are so many variables.

So many things can go wrong.

Still.

Courtenay turned, so I can check her off the list.

One step closer to freedom.

Margaux and Tamsin smell Courtenay before they see her, fangs at the ready, as if an intruder could just sneak their way inside Hey Mister without an invitation. They should be more careful. Plenty of humans will be here soon. All the new staff. Bartenders. DJs. Doormen. Go-go dancers. Every star that Courtenay aligned for us before she turned, and all of them know they need to impress the hell out of Nicola before opening night.

Tamsin has an inscrutable look on her face upon seeing Courtenay as a vampire for the first time. She won't stop staring.

"What do you think?" Courtenay asks, giving them a little twirl.

"Congratulations," Margaux says sincerely. "Nicola's never done *this* before." She's impressed, peering at Courtenay with curiosity.

Tamsin's eyes dart from Courtenay to me and back to Courtenay.

"No, she certainly hasn't. You must be really special," she says, but her focus is on me.

"You know something? I believe Nicola is seeing the path forward, just as she said when we had our meeting," Margaux muses, taking in the glamour of the club. "Look at everything that's come to fruition. Opening night's upon us, our newly formed girl gang still intact—and growing! Between us, I always wondered if she had some ulterior motive, never fully comfortable in the moment, but now I see."

"See what?" I ask her.

"She might actually be a changed woman." Margaux smiles. "And, Amber, I think it's all for you."

Tamsin glowers at me again, picking at her nails. "People don't change," she scoffs. "Nor do monsters."

"What are they talking about?" Courtenay whispers, clueless about vampire dynamics, but Nicola will have to fill her in on that once I'm gone. I won't get sidetracked with Margaux seeing the light. Especially since they don't know *I'm* the one who turned Courtenay.

"Nothing," I whisper back, before looking at Tamsin and Margaux. "Have you guys seen Roddy yet?"

"Oh, he's in the office." Tamsin grins at me, a little too pleased with herself for my liking. "With Nicola."

race down the hallway to the office. The lights are on behind the shut door. She wouldn't dare, would she? Yes, I expected some retaliation for turning Courtenay. Making me kill the woman when I didn't want to. Leaving me alone to feed her. And of course, a life of passive-aggressive remarks about it, since she believes I'm staying in the trio when I most certainly am not.

But screwing around with Roddy?

She doesn't even know about us.

Does she?

None of them do.

Except for Courtenay.

Did she slip up?

When?

After I left Tramp?

I open the office door with the code. Nicola hovers above Roddy on the chaise, legs straddling him as he writhes and moans. His arms are wrapped around her, pulling at her back, almost violently, and I see his legs jerk underneath her, not in pleasure, but in pain.

When she turns around to see me, the blood from his neck is running down to his chest.

His eyes meet mine. The fear. The helplessness. The life about to leave them.

I open my mouth to scream. Nothing comes out, but still, I act fast. I take a running leap and soar right onto Nicola's back, yanking her waist with one arm and her neck with the other, pulling her as hard as I can so she'll let go of Roddy.

I push away from the chaise with my feet, launching the two of us across the room, attached as one wild being, flailing and fighting. We land on the ground with a heavy thud, her body on top of mine, my arms still wrapped around her waist, my hands clutching my wrists tightly.

I cannot let go.

She'll finish him off.

And I think there's still time to help him.

"Stop it, Amber!" she shouts, elbowing me in the stomach, the force temporarily knocking the wind out of me, stunned by the physical sensation, no matter how temporary. We've never fought like this before.

Nicola looms over me now, eyes wild and vengeful.

"What are you doing?" she bellows.

"What are *you* doing?" I scream back at her. "Roddy!" I crawl back toward him as fast as I can. He grasps at his gaping wound, hands shaking as blood runs down through his fingers, all of it seeping out at the jugular on his right side. Without a second thought, I release my fangs and bite into my own wrist, reaching out for him. His face goes white as a sheet as his eyes meet mine, in disbelief that I'm really a monster, too.

But I have to turn him.

It's the only way I can save him.

More blood.

It will always take more blood, won't it?

But Nicola seizes me from behind, landing on my back with all fours like a feral cat, pulling me away by my shoulders. After she steps in front of me and pushes me flat on my ass, she stomps right on over me, marching back to Roddy, hanging on by a thread, to finish him off.

"Nicola! *Please!*" I sound like a little girl, my voice high and distressed, unable to wake up from a nightmare. "Stop!"

Roddy doesn't deserve a death like this—he doesn't deserve to die at all; he just wanted to make art and make love and make his mark in the world. He was going to do it. I believed in him. I never believed we could really be together, certainly not for forever, but I believed that he could do everything he set his mind on doing. And I believed that he loved me and that when I asked him, he would take me to New York with him. We would have found a way together.

"Nicola, I'm begging you!" I cry out, but she doesn't even acknowledge me before sinking into Roddy's throat again, the left side this time. His feet jerk out again, and more blood rushes down his arms as he tries to put pressure on the previous wound, while Nicola digs in on the fresh one.

Finally, his hands fall to his sides, at rest.

His fingers tremble outward from his knuckles.

The rest of his body goes still.

He's giving up.

"Why are you doing this?" I scream at her, but Nicola stays crouched over him, slurping ravenously and with so much cruelty, making eye contact with me, her eyes dancing with dark delight as I come closer.

"Why aren't you joining me?" she growls.

That's when I see Pierce's watch hanging out of Roddy's pocket.

What is he doing with that?

Did Nicola give it to him?

When?

I shove Nicola off Roddy again, hoping for a miracle I don't deserve, and hold my bleeding wrist to his mouth. She doesn't try to stop me. She just laughs, standing up to watch me. She tosses her hair over her shoulder with a casual haughtiness that makes me feel ill, the red from Roddy smudged all over her face.

"It's already done," she growls at me again, but I don't want to listen. I don't want to believe it. I use my fingers to pull Roddy's bottom lip open. I don't deserve a miracle, but doesn't Roddy?

He won't swallow. His chest rises and falls and rises once more, slower with each breath, and when he looks at me for the last time, it's a shock to my system, an emotional pain that might lodge in the void I carry forever. It's no look of love.

Just pure terror.

His lips feel bitter cold under my thumb.

He's dying.

"Come on, Roddy, please. *Please*," I sob, but I can't coax him into swallowing. The brightness in his eyes is long gone; my blood coats his teeth, dripping through the little gap; and his neck goes still, the puncture wounds on either side pooling red all over his shirt.

"Amber. Stop it. You're embarrassing yourself," Nicola snarls at me. "You can't turn a dead man. You don't even know what happened."

Roddy stops breathing.

It's too late.

I can't move.

I can't speak.

How can I do this without him?

But that's not the right question.

How could I do this *to* him?

"I'm sorry, Amber, but I had no choice," Nicola says, sitting down next to me, all of us drowning in red. "I misjudged him, but I don't want you to think this was your fault."

I shake my head in disbelief, not trusting a word she says.

Does she know I wanted to leave with him?

Does she know everything?

"My fault?" I finally lock eyes with her. "How would it be *my* fault?"

"Shh, Amber. You were right about Roddy," she says gently, stroking the side of my face, pushing a piece of hair behind my ear. "He was a lovely man, very talented and so accommodating, but a bit rough around the edges. Perfect for us and for the club." She takes the gold watch out of Roddy's pocket and gets up to set it on the desk. "And so I thought he'd be perfect for the Laurels, which is why I thought he'd be more eager about the offer I presented to him. That was my surprise for you. Sadly, he was not interested and even made some threats, so I couldn't—"

"Threats about what? What kind of offer?" I ask through my tears. It's like they won't stop coming.

"I offered him Jonathan's position. We're both aware he's in decline and needs replacing. Roddy would have been perfect, but he was so shortsighted about the opportunity, even threatening to tell the press what we really are, as if I'd ever let him go after that. He had just told me the other night he was rethinking New York because he loves the club so much. Loves *us*." She raises her eyebrow at me. "He could have had everything he ever wanted."

"What did he say? When you told him?"

"He laughed, but when I showed him? He did what all men do, Amber. He tried to run away and then he threatened me and then what else could I reasonably do? I know you cared for Roddy, Tamsin suggested as much, but I also know you're aware of the rules. Sex and service, with the emphasis on the latter."

"Tamsin said *what*?"

"She didn't need to say anything, Amber. I *know* you. I'll always know you. It's my role as your maker. We are connected forever, but you'll see, won't you?"

I can't even look at her.

"With Courtenay?"

Every emotion conflicts in my head and I consider letting it all out on the table right now, every fucking thing I want to say to her, but I'm pulled back down to earth when I watch her heave Roddy over her shoulder.

"Where are you going with him?" I ask.

I know it's impossible, but he would want to be with his nan up in Newcastle.

"You sure you don't want a little taste first? Satisfy the curiosity?" Nicola grunts at me as she tosses the tapestry off the wall. "He can't have gone too far off yet."

She reveals an incinerator of our very own at Hey Mister and puts Roddy's body inside it, slams the door shut and fires it up, laughing at me when she sees I'm completely mortified by the sight.

"Where do you think Margaux got the idea? Where do you

think all the bodies go at the Laurels? You never ask the right questions, Amber, even though you're always looking for answers."

The flames consume Roddy, his future and mine.

"I'll give you a minute to pull yourself together, darling," Nicola says. "I need to do the same before the others arrive. Meet me in the ladies' for a freshening? And be discreet. Let's not mention this to Courtenay just yet. She won't understand. *You'll* have to protect her."

When Nicola opens the door, she nearly bumps right into Tamsin, waiting in the hall with a sinister smile on her face. She heard the whole thing. That miserable bitch wants me to fail. If she can't get away, why should I?

But it's not just about getting away anymore.

It's about getting even.

For me.

For Malcolm.

For Marlena.

And now for Roddy, too.

I grab that gold watch from the desk and brace myself, holding on to the sides, my nails scratching at the mahogany. When I know Nicola's gone, when I hear the DJ begin his set, the music growing louder and louder, the bass vibrating through the walls, I finally let out the feral scream that's been clawing to get out of my throat all this time.

Let's.

Fucking.

Go.

TWENTY-SIX

NICOLA

1843

Last week Papa surprised Georgie and me with some wonderful news. He is going to bring the both of us to the opera for her sixteenth birthday. It's as if we've turned back into little girls since he told us. Georgie was permitted to buy a dress and gloves with the allowance Papa gave her for the occasion. Anna took her to the shops. I was not allowed to join them. Mama said they would not be going shopping anywhere of interest to a young woman like me.

Georgie knocks lightly at my bedroom door once she is dressed for the evening. Her cornflower-blue dress is modest but tasteful, and the white gloves give it a refined touch.

"Oh, Georgie! You look marvelous!"

She opens her hand to show me a small gold tin and twists off the top, placing her finger inside the silky dew of a bright pink hue.

"I bought this when Anna wasn't looking. What if we use just the tiniest bit for tonight?"

I knew Mama would notice. She always said makeup was for

actresses and tarts and unsavory women, but it was irresistible to me all the same.

"How can something so pretty be so bad?" Georgie shrugs, dabbing just the slightest touch of pink on my lips, then onto her own. Our mouths glow as we look into my mirror at each other. Georgie puts the tin in my dresser drawer, concealing it underneath a skirt, and closes it back up.

A forbidden gift for me.

When we go downstairs, Mama says nothing at all to Georgie, but she rarely does unless she's barking an order of some kind in her direction. Mama doesn't say a word about our lips, but she holds me back as we head out the door, taking her handkerchief to my face, gruffly removing the makeup.

She will not be joining us tonight.

It's just Papa, Georgie and me.

Papa checks his pocket watch and says we must be going.

When we finally arrive at Drury Lane, Georgie gives me a big peck on the lips, sharing what's left on hers. She makes a big smacking sound to get a laugh from me, which she always could. Knowing even just a hint of color is there, even if nobody else notices, makes me feel like we have a sweet secret together again.

Like when we were little girls.

The opera is magnificent. *The Bohemian Girl* isn't the first I've ever seen, but it is my first with Georgie, and watching her admire the performers is a different sort of entertainment all its own. Her applause is so robust. Even through her gloves, I can hear the fervor with which she's showing her appreciation for the music. I witness the tears that fall from her face; she's so moved.

And I see the way she gently embraces Papa's hand, crossing my body, whispering, "Thank you for bringing me here, Mr. Claughton."

His face is so tender towards her, I'm almost jealous, but I know I'm the legacy and Georgie has so little in comparison. So I decide to be happy for her tonight. All she's ever wanted is to be a real part of our family. Mama would never allow it, but Papa and I are her family, as much as we can be. We would always be her family.

"Happy birthday, Georgiana," Papa says.

When we return to the Laurels after the opera, Mama has already put herself to bed, but in her stead, there is a small trunk of clothes at the entrance. It's been left open and full of Georgie's belongings, except for one of Mama's lovely green scarves laid over the top.

Papa sighs heavily and looks down at his feet.

"Come, girls," he says, motioning for us to join him in the parlor. Georgie picks up the scarf before she follows me, running it through her fingers. They're shaking.

The three of us sit down and Papa looks at me for the entirety of his speech, which I find strange since it's all about Georgie.

Why won't he look at her?

"I wanted to have this discussion tomorrow morning, but I've arranged work for Georgiana in Leeds. There's a textile mill and the boardinghouse is nearby. She'll meet other women in the same, *ahem*, position. And I'm sure she will meet a nice young man as well. And she'll have a very pleasant life. I promise you that, Nicola."

Georgie has no expression at all on her face, her muted pink lips now a thin line.

I can't seem to find any words of my own.

Georgie is leaving us in the morning?

How can this be?

"I see your mother has attended to Georgiana's trunk," Papa continues. "I've also allotted some funds for her to get sorted. And please know I am very sorry that this isn't the news you both wanted to hear, but it was always going to be this way, my darlings. I promised to care for Georgiana in her childhood, but now she must make her own way as a young woman."

"What about Nicola?" Georgie asks Papa, her face devoid of any expression. "We are the same age."

"Papa, she cannot—" I begin to protest, but he interrupts me, raising his voice.

"One day, Nicola will marry one of her suitors," Papa says, looking at Georgie this time. "I wish I could do the same for you, Georgiana, but the circumstances do not allow for that."

"Am I to assume Mrs. Claughton selected Leeds for my departure?" Georgie scoffs as she looks out the window. I'm surprised by her tone in Papa's direction, but also understanding of it. What had she done so wrong that she had to leave? "Leeds! That puts me just about as far away as—"

"No, Georgie," Papa explains, using her pet name, softening his tone. "I simply thought you might want a fresh start elsewhere. That it might be too painful to stay in London."

I cannot believe this is happening to our family. I don't want Georgie to be *banished* from the Laurels! Yes, we are different, but this is her home. Why can't she stay? I want her here with me. I like knowing that she's here, even when we can't be together.

"I'll be on my way now," Georgie declares, standing up from her seat, pressing her hands down the front of her dress in a show of dignity and pride.

She stares Papa in the eye once more.

He looks away first.

"But the Laurels is your home!" I cry out to Georgie, tears starting to stream down my face. "Papa, she must stay. She must!"

"I will not stay where I am not welcome," Georgie says pointedly at Papa. "But *I* know that I am your kin, Mr. Claughton. Still, I do not mistake your obligation to me over the years for kindness or affection. I should have known the opera tonight was not for me, but rather for you. Something for your conscience, perhaps? Well, thank you very much. I won't soon forget your efforts as my father."

"Georgiana," Papa says in a hushed tone, but nothing else.

What can he say?

Georgie is right.

He knows it.

I know it, too.

"I will make my own way now," Georgie says, wrapping Mama's scarf around her neck as she closes the trunk of her belongings, pushing the latch in tight. I can't seem to stop crying, pleading for Papa to change his mind, when Georgie finally addresses me.

"Nicola, would you like to come with me?"

I'm stunned by her query.

Did I want to go with Georgie?

Would Papa ever allow it?

Could I decide for myself?

"She's not going to go with you, Georgiana. That's preposterous," Papa says gravely.

"Let her speak for herself!" Georgie roars at Papa.

We are both stunned by her volume, the impudence in Papa's presence.

I hope I can be as bold as her one day.

But I'm not like Georgie.

I'm not sure what I can reasonably say or do. I love her very much, but I know we're different. She knows it, too. She's much stronger than I am. Even though I don't want her to go, I know she will do well. She always knows what to say, what to do, how to do it. Even when it's not proper or ladylike. I always admired those qualities in her. The qualities I don't have.

But I am my father's daughter.

His legacy.

I am a true Claughton.

Before I can respond, she picks up her trunk and opens the door to leave.

"I shall write to you, Nicola," Georgie says.

And I watch her leave.

TWENTY-SEVEN

AMBER

clutch the gold pocket watch outside Pierce's gate in Wapping, my other hand shaking as I ring the bell. I feel rabid and out of control, like anything could happen, like I could *do* anything, because I have no fear at all anymore, making me dangerous and powerful, willing to risk everything.

I couldn't even look at Nicola when I left Hey Mister. She didn't follow me. Tamsin watched me go, satisfied, but everyone's wrapped up in opening night tomorrow, Courtenay included.

No one knows where I am right now.

When Pierce appears at the gate, his lips curl into a slow smile; he's enjoying the sight of my pain.

"She has returned!" He laughs.

I shove the watch into his chest.

"I brought you what you wanted. Now help me."

He looks at the watch curiously, opening it once, closing it up again, dangling it by the chain from his fingers before handing it back to me.

"Not familiar," he says with a shrug. "You can't hold what I want in your hand."

"Stop speaking to me in these fucking riddles, Pierce!" I shout at him, waving the watch around. "Whatever you want, I'll give it to you, I swear to God! This isn't about leaving Nicola anymore. I want to make her feel what I feel. She's taken everything from me, Pierce. Everything! Don't you understand that, or are you just completely full of shit?!"

Pierce crosses his arms at his chest, looking at me from top to bottom and then straight into my eyes. He stares so deeply, I feel exposed, but maybe now he understands.

"Would you like to come inside, Amber?"

I look behind him, but all I see is an empty foyer across the courtyard with white walls and a gold elevator door.

"I can tell you're up for a bit of bargaining, love." He grins. "And since we seem to desire the same result, perhaps you won't have to do much haggling."

I follow him inside.

Being brave's all I've got left.

Going up.

Before the elevator doors open at the top floor, I hear the penthouse party going already. Pitbull is blaring through the speakers and women's voices whoop and holler and giggle. And despite the sophistication a guy like Pierce oozes, once the doors open to the inside, I learn his place looks like a roadside strip club in Middle America, complete with neon beer signs, gleaming silver poles and platinum blondes.

Colorful lights pop around the room, different fixtures twirling on the ground and installed in corners of the vaulted ceilings.

Alcohol, among other things probably, is freely flowing amongst all the gorgeous human girls wearing bikinis or lingerie or nothing at all. All of them wave or smile at me, welcoming me to this soiree of sin, maybe thinking I'm about to join in myself. Oh, just another night at home!

Meanwhile, Pierce's bros are all cozied up in cashmere sweaters or plush bathrobes, watching the girls as they go about their business, but they don't really touch them, much less kill them. It's like the girls are behind glass, models in an aquarium, for observation and admiration only. Even though I doubt it's always this way.

Pierce picks up on my judgment, nodding at one of the girls, who comes over for a squeeze like he's Hugh freakin' Hefner. "Don't worry about them, Amber. They're happy."

"Are they?" I ask skeptically, but I agree that no one looks under duress or in danger. Everyone's audibly having a great time together. Expectations and boundaries must be clear enough. Otherwise, why would they stay? Or does he not let them leave?

"Of course they're happy in old Wapping," Pierce scoffs. "Some of 'em stay for months. A few even years. No complaints. Everyone's free to go whenever they want. Ask 'em if you like."

"Do you ever turn them?" I ask. Then, lowering my voice: "Or hunt them?"

"No," Pierce says firmly. "That is not part of the arrangement. I'm a very senior vampire, Amber, and as you can imagine, much like Nicola, a man of means. These girls have everything they want as my guests and I'm more than happy to oblige. It's a right laugh, watching them enjoy some of the things we can no longer indulge in, although we do join in on the one thing we still can, if invited. All under one condition."

"What's that?" I ask, eyebrow raised.

"They will never ask me, or any of the lads, to become a vampire themselves. Strictly forbidden. Once they've had their fill of the high life, they can take off, just say the word. We compel them before they go. Only once. Then we almost never see them again except out and about, once or twice, but that's rare, and in passing, they won't remember. When they decide to leave, they cannot return, and I make sure they understand the provision. Everyone understands. All aboveboard."

Pierce watches with amusement as the girls form a conga line to "Fireball" and they all start laughing hysterically. I mean, it does look fun, at least for a couple of weeks.

"What if one of them asks to turn?"

Pierce winces, eyes closed, as if he's trying to forget.

"Then, sadly, they get what they deserve. The girls understand the rules. Most of the time. I believe no one should covet this cursed life. If so, a punishment is appropriate."

"So you'll turn men, but not women?" I scoff.

"I turn sad young men with nowhere else to go, but just to improve my ranks, Amber. It works. She's fearful of us, you know. What if we took it upon ourselves to take her on one day?"

"Will you?"

"I just want Nicola to get her due, to feel what I feel, like you said. She's a taker. Someone should take from her for once. Margaux had the right idea with Tamsin, but she's certainly changed her tune . . ."

"But didn't *you* ask for this life?"

Pierce looks around the penthouse, taking in his sordid little kingdom, the culmination of his life's work as a vampire.

"Why don't we go somewhere a little quieter?" Pierce offers his hand and I take it, darting together through the party. At least twenty or so girls are here tonight, living out some kind of sorority girl fantasy, all young and beautiful, and while I'm sure he thinks he's being generous with them, he's still behaving like a dirty old man, not to mention his penchant for punishing the women and not the men.

Appreciation for Pitbull aside, I could never live here.

Is he just going to invite me to stay again?

Or make me stay?

Pierce opens the door to a room with giant floor-to-ceiling windows, a beautiful conservatory, complete with a big balcony overlooking the Thames, the lights of the city hitting the water below us, Tower Bridge shining in the distance. I could survive the deep drop, if it came to that.

He motions for me to take a seat in one of the swiveling club chairs and joins me in the one opposite. "Does she know you're here?" He grins. "God, I hope so!"

"I don't know. I don't care. I hope she bursts into flames."

"You want to kill her?" He gasps with excitement, like this is his favorite type of dirty talk.

"Not before she feels the pain that I do. She killed everyone I love, Pierce. My husband, Malcolm. My boyfriend, Roddy. She even—" My voice breaks. I almost can't say it. "She even killed my sister. Marlena."

I have no business showing weakness in front of this vampire, but when I start to cry, he offers a silk handkerchief from his pocket; a reflection of his time, maybe?

"And she basically killed me, you know? So I want to take away what she loves, too. And the only thing I can think of—aside from me, and maybe her own sister—is the Laurels."

He nods in understanding as I blow my nose.

"The Laurels is exactly what I want," he says with an evil grin. "It was supposed to be mine. Well, ours, together. But when she finally invited me there, I didn't yet know what she had become."

"What are you talking about?" I ask, feeling the bass hum through the walls, the girls outside taking it up a notch.

"I knew her before," he says simply. "And after."

Oh my God.

Of course.

That's why she lets Pierce live.

He's the only one left who knew her before.

Like Malcolm was for me.

"I didn't want to join her, Amber," Pierce explains. "When she told me what she turned into, what she agreed to, what she *asked* for?! I couldn't believe it and I didn't understand. Yes, I loved her, but she was changed. Forever. She grew even more unhinged when I denied her proposition, but she wanted to keep me, force me into becoming her companion. She compelled me and took me for her own."

"Pierce," I say, a hand over my mouth. "I'm so sorry."

"She didn't think I'd run away."

"How did you do it?"

"I suspect she believed I'd falter somehow. Come crawling back. That I would need her to show me the ways of the vampire, but she didn't consider the fact that I'm a man. Perhaps this isn't as pertinent today, but I was able to make my way in the world without her, just as before and maybe with even more ease. Look at all that I've built through investments and time and a bit of negotiation over the years . . ."

What did he mean by that?

"Which brings us back to the Laurels—"

"But I don't think that's the only thing Nicola loves," I interrupt him, keeping this new information about Pierce close to my chest. He is still very important to her. Much more than I thought. So now he's important to me, too. "I want to find her *sister.*"

Pierce erupts into enormous laughter, heaving with his whole chest, cackling like a supervillain, and I have no idea what could be so funny, until it hits me. Did he negotiate something with Georgie? Could Nicola's sister be *here*? All this time?

The girls are allowed to leave, but they all want to stay.

Some of them have been here for years?

How *many* years?

Is this why Nicola can't talk about her sister?

Is this how she was betrayed?

I dash out of the conservatory and run back into the party, screaming for her at the top of my lungs. "GEORGIE?!" Looking each woman in the face. "GEORGIE?!" Hoping one of them reminds me of Nicola. "GEORGIE?!"

The music comes to an abrupt stop, everyone looking at me, stunned by my behavior.

"I'm looking for Georgie! Is she here? Georgie?!" I ask desperately.

No one has a clue what I'm talking about.

In fact, they all look annoyed that I'm being such a party pooper.

Pierce appears behind me, his gentle hand on my shoulder.

"Come," he says.

Out of breath, I follow him back to the conservatory.

"Sit," he says, motioning back to the chair. Finally, he drops a giant tome into my lap. "I nicked this before I ran away, knowing it was all she had left of her. She always talked about her sister."

"She still does . . ." I trail off as I open an old Victorian photo album, leather-bound and ornate with its gold clasp and the letter *C* emblazoned on the front. As I start to carefully leaf through it, I recognize the couple from the portrait hanging in the Laurels. I always suspected they were Nicola's parents.

These are the oldest photos I've ever seen, captioned in beautiful calligraphy, maybe by Nicola's mother. Large, swooping letters that are so decorative, they're almost difficult to interpret. I stop at one of the photos with the couple in question, plus a child I've never seen before.

There are no portraits of children at the Laurels.

The names are scrawled beneath the photo.

Albert Claughton.

Louisa Claughton.

Nicola Claughton.

I delicately flip through more of the pages, examining the photos of the family, watching as the little girl grows into a young woman.

But she doesn't look like Nicola at all.

Not the Nicola I know.

It can't be . . .

"You see," Pierce says, "I met Nicola in East London, out on her arse after the family sent her away, ashamed. Back when she was still—"

"Georgie," I finish for him.

Nicola Claughton isn't Nicola Claughton at all.

She's the sister I've been looking for.

The real Nicola Claughton?

Oh my God.

I understand now.

I understand everything.

TWENTY-EIGHT

NICOLA

1850

Anna is preparing Georgie's favorite meal for her visit tonight, even though it isn't Christmas Eve. Georgie always dined with us on Christmas Eve. Papa insisted, no matter what Mama said. Roast chicken and vegetables with a delicious pudding.

She's going to be so happy.

I hope so.

There has never been any animosity in her letters, though she never provided her return address, until the most recent one, ending the correspondence with a wish that we could pick up where we left off.

As friends.

As sisters.

I hope so as well.

So much has changed, but of course my affection for her remains.

I wonder if she knows that I am engaged to Thomas Winter. Papa more than approved of the match, and he is quite particular, especially since I am his legacy, but he believes Thomas will be good for the family, for me and for the Laurels one day, when Papa is gone. I know he believes this because he gave Thomas his gold pocket watch. A union between the Claughtons and the Winters will be a prosperous one, and of course, I do care for Thomas. I am happy to marry him for my family and for myself.

It will be a blessing.

It is the right thing to do.

I am the legacy, but alas, I am also a woman.

Papa has invited Thomas to tonight's dinner with Georgie as well, but he is late. I'll have to express my disappointment about his tardiness when he finally arrives. I do want Georgie to feel welcome here. He can assist with that, an amiable man. She will remember him, I'm certain. He had been to the Laurels several times when she lived here as well.

I cannot imagine how she must feel returning home after all this time.

Papa was hesitant about extending the invitation, but it was my turn to insist.

For myself and for Georgie.

He knows it's the right thing to do.

"Where is Mama?" I ask Papa as we await Georgie's arrival in the parlor.

"My darling, please do not give your mother any grief about her absence tonight. I've given her enough of it for one lifetime," Papa says softly.

"But it's not *Georgie's* fault that you—"

"It is entirely my own, I know," Papa laments. He is wearing his finest suit, perhaps feeling sentimental about Georgie, or guilty. It's my favorite suit that he owns, in the darkest blue hue.

Thomas dresses well, too.

I prefer a well-dressed man.

"Perhaps if I spoke with Mama she would change her mind," I say, standing up to call on Mama in the study, where she surely is. *Sulking.* I love her very much, but I don't want to grow up to be a woman who sulks in the study, or anywhere, for that matter.

"Nicola, please," my father scolds me. "Leave your mother be. If she wishes to join us, she will."

I do as he says.

I have already pushed so much with Georgie's dinner invitation.

It is very quiet as we wait for her to arrive. Thomas is still not here. The silence makes me regretful that we didn't arrange for a musician, like Papa suggested, but I thought Georgie would find it crass. He gives me a gentle squeeze on the knee.

"You shouldn't feel guilty about Georgiana, my love. We treated her well and with respect and she has made her own way, just as we knew she would. I'm looking forward to hearing about her life and I'm sure she'll be eager to hear about yours. This is a happy occasion."

I hope he's right.

We hear the brass knocker bang on the door three times, each louder than the one before. She doesn't use the bell. I find it ominous and charming at the same time, kind of like Georgie.

"I'll fetch her!" I exclaim, and Papa doesn't stop me.

I catch my breath, pushing my ringlets to the front of my face carefully. I wonder what she will think of me after all these years. I'm nervous and thrilled and anxious, but after everything and all those letters, she has finally returned to me.

My best friend.

My sister.

When I open the door, I gasp at the sight of Georgiana standing before me. I never called her that, I always referred to her as Georgie, but she looks so different. Very grown-up and, my goodness, she is stunningly beautiful in a way that I don't remember from our youth.

Her eyes still possess that forceful nature, her posture is still that of a confident, if not altogether uncouth, woman, but her smile feels effervescent in a way I haven't seen before. Almost like she has a secret she wants to share with me and she's about to burst at the thought that the time to divulge it is nigh.

She wordlessly embraces me and gives me a big smack on the lips, taking me by surprise as she mimics our kiss before the opera.

The last night we saw each other.

"It's wonderful to see you, darling!" She grins at me before looking quickly behind her. "It smells delicious in here! Forgive me for the short notice, but I have brought a guest to dine with us. This is my dear friend Victoria."

Behind Georgiana is an even more striking woman, very tall and slim, donning a hat with feathers, a long coat with large buttons and diamond jewelry. She nods at me politely but does not smile or speak a single word.

I want to ask Georgie who she is, but it feels rude to do so.

"It's no trouble at all!" I say. "Come in, dear. Come in!"

I put my arm around Georgie's waist and whisper in her ear. "You look wonderful. What's changed? How are you so different? Are you . . ."

"In love?" she whispers back. I raise my eyebrows, waiting for more. "*Yes.*"

I squeeze her tighter and lead both women into the parlor, where Papa stands stiffly in the center of the room.

"Georgiana," he says, clearing his throat. "Welcome."

Georgie giggles, lightening the mood instantly, as she introduces Victoria to Papa. Victoria is still eerily silent, but Georgie's essence is so light, so carefree. She seems very happy, and I'm overjoyed to see her coming into her own after all this time apart. I cannot wait to hear more about her paramour and tell her about Thomas as well.

She wraps Papa in her arms very tightly for a full moment.

It's as if they breathe as one.

"Lovely to see you, Mr. Claughton," Georgie says, finally pulling away from him. "The Laurels is just as I remember it. Where is Mrs. Claughton?"

"I'm afraid she's resting in the study with tea and toast and the fire. She's been feeling under the weather," Papa says, looking at me in a way that suggests I should agree.

"You know Mama," I say to Georgie, but she clucks her tongue.

"Pity. I was so looking forward to seeing her. She practically raised me. Perhaps I can greet her briefly—"

"I don't think so," Papa interrupts, shaking his head. "Come. To the dining room. Anna's prepared a special feast for your triumphant return."

"Triumphant, indeed." Georgie smiles, linking her arm through mine, Victoria silently following us. "It's high time we've seen one another again, sweet Nicola."

She pushes a ringlet away from my face, tucking it behind my ear.

We all sit around the table quietly, waiting for our meal, but Georgie has no problem leading the charge with conversation. She tells us all about living in East London for all this time. Shoreditch, to be precise.

She never went to Leeds as Papa arranged.

She says that she's been working as a governess, which impresses me no end. How in the world did she come into a job like that with no formal education? I don't ask questions, but I can tell Papa is charmed, too. She is a far cry from a factory girl. Look at her. She is glowing.

Well, I suppose she is a Claughton, too.

In her own way.

Victoria whispers into Georgie's ear, to which she replies, "Yes, of course."

The two of them stand up at the same time.

"I'm going to show Victoria to the toilet. Shall I check on Anna?" Georgie asks.

"Oh, I can inquire with Anna about dinner," I say, starting to rise from my chair.

"Nonsense!" Georgie waves two hands at me. "I know my way around the kitchen here, after all." She winks at Papa and the two of them leave. Both of us are flummoxed by her presence. Georgie seems to be doing well.

Very well indeed.

"See," Papa says to me with a knowing smile. "We did the right thing. She needed to stand on her own two feet, and just look at her now."

"Mr. Claughton!" Georgie calls out from the kitchen. "May I have your assistance, please?"

Papa grimaces at a woman raising her voice in his home, but he stands up from the table anyway. "Excuse me," he says to me before going to the kitchen. "She's simply full of surprises."

A few moments pass, then Georgie returns with the chicken and vegetables on a silver platter. She looks radiant as she takes Papa's seat at the head of the table, placing the platter down in front of her.

"Anna wasn't in the kitchen. I caught the chicken right before it burned!" Georgie laughs, setting it down in front of her. "Shall I serve you?"

"Oh, you don't have to do that."

"Please, Nicola." Georgie laughs. "It's my pleasure. And it wouldn't be the first time, hmm?"

Georgiana slices the dark meat from the chicken with a large knife and then places it on a dish. She knows the dark is my favorite. She brings the plate over to me, carrying it with one hand, and holds out a finger from the other hand, the one with the juice dripping down, for me to lick.

"Go on. No one's looking," she says, putting her finger in my mouth. "*Madam.*"

Then she puts the plate down and gives me a kiss on the cheek, leaving more lipstick on my face.

But it's not soft pink this time.

It's red.

Georgie proceeds to watch me intently from above, as if she's waiting for me to eat.

"Aren't you going to have any?" I finally ask her. "Roast chicken is your favorite. I requested it especially for you. Also, we should wait for Papa. Did Victoria find the toilet all right?"

"Don't worry about her." Georgie grins. "And you're right. This was my favorite meal."

"No longer?"

I jump in my seat when I hear a banging sound.

I don't know where it's coming from.

But it's growing louder.

And faster.

Georgie bends to look me in the eye.

"No, Nicola. Roast chicken is no longer my favorite meal." When she smiles again, an unsettling feeling washes over me. It's a grim smile. Menacing. I've never seen anything like it from her. "My tastes have changed," Georgie says.

"Oh?" I say, my mouth growing dry. Why is Thomas so late? Where has Papa gone? And what on earth is that infernal banging sound?

"Do you hear that?" I ask Georgie.

"Nicola, my darling. I have a proposition for you. The proposition of a lifetime. You were just a girl when I left. We both were. I know you couldn't do anything to help me. I have forgiven you, over time, through our correspondence. I can't blame you for your silence back then, but now is the time for restitution. I want you to join me. We're best friends, aren't we? Sisters?"

"Oh, Georgie. I'm engaged. I can't go with you anywhere. I'm sorry. And where is—"

"Papa?" Georgie starts to laugh, booming with amusement.

"You're frightening me, Georgie. What is that sound?" The banging is relentless now, so much so that I want to find the source, but Georgie holds my wrists tightly. I could not pull away from her if I tried.

"Sit down, Nicola. And listen closely to me."

The horrors she describes are monstrous and deviant and nothing at all that I wish to be a part of, but of course I consider it. Because I do love her. Because she makes it all sound so wonderful.

She was a good girl.

But she is no longer good.

Whatever she is.

Of course, Papa was wrong to send her away, but to *kill* him?

She tells me Thomas is gone as well.

He didn't deserve this.

Victoria is a vampire.

Georgie, too.

Georgie met her months ago and changed her life forever.

When she told Victoria about the Laurels, she was intrigued, wanting it for her own.

"But I would never allow that," Georgie purred. "I saved the Laurels for us. It's our home. For Claughtons only. And one special man, but I'll introduce you in due time. And we'll find someone new for you, Nicola. Thomas Winter? He was a dreadful boy and they only grow into dreadful men. You will find someone more suitable soon enough."

Georgie has Victoria locked in the study.

The latch is still strong and unyielding if one is not careful.

How many times had Georgie been locked in the study?

"The banging will stop come sunrise," Georgie says.

Mama was in the study.

"I'm the only one you have left, Nicola."

My sister says all these wild things as if possessed by the devil himself. The Laurels belongs to the Claughtons, not the Winters. It's for us and it can belong to us forever and everything that comes with it. She has Papa's gold watch now. It belongs to us. All of this belongs to us.

I don't know what to do or what to say, and I can't seem to move at all as she stares into my eyes. And when I see her smile morph into something so demonic, I want to scream, but nothing comes out, until I feel the shock of pain when her body is on top of mine, enveloping me, with her mouth on my throat, her teeth deep inside it, carving each one into my skin and extracting my blood like she's inhaling it as fuel.

"Say yes," she says to me, coming up for air, her fangs shining bright as they hover over her wrist. Before I can fall to the ground, she catches me with her other arm, holding me close.

The room feels darker.

Everything feels faint, especially my breath.

Is this a dream?

Am I dying?

"Say you'll join me!" Georgie roars at me.

But this is not my sister.

This is a monster.

"No," I manage to whisper. "I can't."

I want to tell her that I'm sorry, for everything, but nothing more will come from me.

Georgie doesn't cry. Her face reminds me of the day she left the Laurels. Emotionless.

"I didn't want to believe you'd betray me *again*," she says, letting me go.

As I fall to the floor, she walks away from me.

I hear her footsteps retreating, but I cannot call out to her.

I try again to say her name, but only a hoarse sigh comes out.

And soon enough?

Nothing at all.

I cannot even try.

I'm perfectly still.

I can no longer see a thing.

All of it has gone black.

I hear only a soft ringing in my ears.

And an even softer voice.

Posh. Put-on. Airy.

It sounds as if . . . as if someone is mimicking *my* voice.

"Pleased to meet you," I hear. "I'm Nicola Claughton."

It's Georgie. *Georgiana.* She says *my* name.

Over and over and over again.

"Nicola Claughton. Miss Nicola Claughton. I'm Nicola. Nicola. Miss Claughton. *Lady* Claughton."

A laugh, that soft little laugh, just like mine, and once again before I go:

"My name is Nicola Claughton."

TWENTY-NINE

AMBER

I thought for sure Nicola would be perched on the chaise in the study, waiting for me and a full report of where I've been all night, prepared with some half-baked apology about Roddy and what she *had* to do.

But when I get back to the Laurels, her bedroom door is shut.

Courtenay is waiting for me in mine, surely a message from Nicola. Courtenay is my responsibility now, but she's the least of my worries. She's not for me. She's for Nicola. I'm still getting out of here tomorrow night.

Even if it kills me.

Courtenay sits up in the bed, her legs outstretched, arms crossed. "Where did you go?" Her voice is soft, almost crackling, extreme vocal fry. "You left me all alone."

"Nicola and the girls were there," I scoff. "I had somewhere to go. Sorry. How was the run-through?"

"But I needed you, Amber," Courtenay whines, not letting me off the hook. "You're my maker. That's what Nicola said."

But I'm hardly listening to her bellyaching.

I can't stop thinking about tomorrow night.

I'm running away, but not before I see Nicola's face on opening night.

Not before she's seen what I've done.

And not before I say to her face that I know exactly who she really is.

Then I'll use the Underground for safety from the sun. I can pull an all-nighter again. I'll people watch as all of London goes about their day, zipping around the city, keeping my appetite under control. I'll wait for the first evening train to Paris, going out of St. Pancras.

Maybe Paris isn't far enough, just like Tamsin said.

Nicola might be out for blood after what I've done.

But I don't give a fuck anymore.

I'm not staying here with her.

Not another year.

Not another month.

Not another night.

I'd rather die first.

You can chase me forever if that's what you really want to do.

I'll always be watching and waiting for you if I must.

Looking over my shoulder.

I'll keep moving from place to place.

Fine.

Come and get me, bitch.

"Just rest now," I say to Courtenay, crawling into bed next to her. "We have a big night tomorrow."

"Am I going to get my own room?" she asks hopefully. "I liked the guest room from before, but Nicola said you have to get it prepared for me. Keep the sun out . . ."

"You'll get your own room, Court." I smile. "Don't worry about that."

I close my eyes, hoping Chatty Cathy takes the hint and pipes down.

"Where did Roddy go?" she asks, sucking all the air out of the room. "Nicola said I should ask you about him."

I flash back to the terror Roddy must have felt in his last moments.

He was afraid of me, too.

I can't think about him.

"He had to pack tonight," I say. "Going to New York tomorrow."

"But I thought—"

"Courtenay. *Enough.*" I don't mean to be so harsh, but if we don't stop talking about him, I may start crying, and I can't get distracted. Not now. Not tomorrow.

"Are you mad at me?" Courtenay sounds timid and small, making me feel guiltier than ever, but that's the kind of vampire I have to be for now.

Focused. Ruthless. Cold.

Like Nicola.

"No," I say. "Good night."

Nicola makes the first move when we wake, knocking softly on my door. I don't say anything, but she opens it wide with excitement, like it's Christmas morning and we're her little girls. "Look at you two lovelies, all snuggled up together. Amber, you should start thinking about the guest room renovations for Courtenay. Don't worry about the budget," Nicola says with a wink. She has a dry-cleaning bag folded over her arm, clutching something tightly in her other hand. "Court, would you excuse us a moment?"

Courtenay looks to me for approval, and when I nod, Nicola scoffs. I can't tell if she's pleased or perturbed. She closes the door, eager to chat, but I remain sitting up in bed, looking at her blankly.

I want to put her on edge.

Just a touch.

For now.

"What's the matter?" she asks me. "Did the baby keep you up last night?"

"Knock it off, Nicola," I snarl at her.

"Oh, come now, Amber, I *loathe* when we quarrel. It's opening night! I know you're upset about Roddy, but he wasn't who we thought he could be."

"Who *you* thought he could be," I correct her, and immediately wish I hadn't. Even though I'm fuming on the inside, I need to remain calm. I don't want her to suspect anything else is up tonight.

Nicola glides toward me, already dressed for the evening, a vision in an emerald Halston gown that I instantly recognize. She was wearing it when we met.

"I brought this for you," she says, hanging up the bag on my wardrobe and revealing what's inside: my ivory jumpsuit from the same fateful night at Tramp.

"I just had it pressed," she says. "Go on. Put it on."

She watches me with admiration in the mirror as I dress, motioning for me to come closer so she can zip up the back. "Let's tease your hair a bit, too." She takes a comb to the crown of my head, giving it gentle but quick strokes, lifting up the strands from the root.

We look great together, of course.

We always did.

There's no trace of time on our skin or our souls.

Like it's 1979 again.

"Are you ready for this, darling?" Nicola asks, wrapping her long fingers around my neck, giving my earlobes a quick, unexpected squeeze. I roll my shoulders at the sensation, practically vibrating over what's about to happen on opening night.

"I'm always ready," I say coolly, turning around to face her. "You look amazing, Nic."

She really does. She's always been striking. God, there's always been something about Nicola, hasn't there? And I can see the world where everything would have worked out between us. If I was different. If she was different. Seeing us like this, together again, the way we once were, almost makes me want to cry, but I keep my mouth shut, afraid of saying something sentimental—something *stupid*—because despite every fucking terrible thing she's done, there is a part of me that still loves her.

She was my best friend.

She's the only family I have left.

How could it end up like this?

"Here," Nicola says, pulling me toward her.

She has my wedding ring from Malcolm in her hand, plucked from her jewelry box, and slips it on my finger, smiling so big that can I hear the smack of her lips, the saliva against her teeth. "There now. That's exactly how I remember you."

Nicola looks near tears, too, and we can't have that, so I pop my hands under her breasts to give them a quick lift, making her laugh out loud. Emotional tension broken. But then she pushes me back, way harder than I expect, so much so that I almost tip over from the force.

Nicola steadies me by my shoulders, looking me square in the eye.

"I hope you know I did this all for you."

By the time Nicola, Courtenay and I arrive at Hey Mister, there's already a huge line forming in front. Nicola was right: everyone stepped it up with the fashion. Sequins and feathers and silks on the women. Slick jackets, tight pants and slick shoes on the men. They all understood the assignment, eager to step back in time, to a place where only the music matters until the sun comes up.

"Let's go in the back." Nicola redirects us to the rear of the club. Courtenay trips on some loose, thick chains strewn along the ground in the alleyway. "Oh! Mind where you're going, Courtenay! There's always so much shite back here. Awful neighbors."

Tamsin and Margaux are already inside, running around like headless chickens, checking that the staff are all at their appropriate stations. The disco ball glitters above us while the DJ does the sound check—Lulu Lynn, a total It girl, her long dark hair parted down the middle, wearing a midriff-baring dress, looking as glamorous as Norma Kamali or Bianca Jagger. The outrageously good-looking barmen are clanking around bottles and glassware, prepping for the swarm outside, slicing up limes and lemons. We've all agreed to let the line trickle in—and only if they look the part. The doormen know the drill. Courtenay poached the best ones.

"I'll go make sure they have the most recent version of the guest list," I say to Nicola.

"Take Courtenay with you!" she commands with a sassy grin. Of course Courtenay follows me, stuck to me like Velcro.

"Are we . . . eating soon?" she asks, on our way to the front entrance. *Shit.* I forgot how hungry I was at the start myself.

"Can you make it until tomorrow?" I know I sound unreasonably annoyed, but I can't babysit Courtenay tonight, no matter how much I like her.

"I'm not sure." She shrugs. "What are the rules?"

God damn it, she has zero clue how to be a vampire. I'm not interested in teaching her.

"Nicola knows all about rules," I sneer.

"But yesterday she said I should come to you with any questions."

"Courtenay!" I turn around, a little shocked at how shrill I can be when I'm annoyed. "I cannot deal with this right now. It's opening night!"

When she cowers away from me, I instantly feel like an asshole. Who am I—my *dad*?

"I'm sorry, Court." I sigh. "Really. I'm just a little anxious."

"I understand," she says, giving me a sweet hug. God, now I feel like even more of a jerk. We would have been good friends in another life, I know it. "I'll be fine. I forget everything when I'm dancing anyway. And that's what tonight's all about."

Something like that . . .

Before I check in with the doormen out front, Courtenay's eyes grow wide.

"Who are *they*?"

I look up and smile.

It's time.

Pierce and his crew plus a whole herd of hotties strut down the street toward Hey Mister, the sight of them like something out of a music video, ready to party and raise some hell, dressed to the nines, chicer than shit.

"That's Nicola's ex. Probably coming to wish her well . . ."

Pierce approaches us with a girl on each arm, releasing both of them with some major drama, holding out his hand for mine.

I take it.

Because we're walking in together.

"Right this way." I nod at the doorman as he opens the velvet rope for Pierce and me. Courtenay trails behind, and the rest of them, too, like little rats after the Posh Pied Piper. I hear the line of people waiting outside, bitching and crowing about the wait time, and God, it feels good. See ya, suckers. Not the point, *I know*, but it feels damn good to own the place.

For now.

'm positive Nicola could smell Pierce before we stepped inside Hey Mister, because when I see her glaring at us from up in the VIP section, flashes of red and purple lighting up her face, she already looks completely psycho.

Her nostrils alone look like they've grown three sizes, not to mention her wild eyes, more alert than I've ever seen, darting from Pierce to me and then to Pierce once more, and her hands are shaking in anger, hanging out just at her belly, each knuckle bending like she's grasping in front of her, but at absolutely nothing at all.

Probably envisioning my throat.

But most unnerving of all is her deranged smile.

Like this is exactly what she wants.

Maybe it is.

You know what?

Maybe it's what I want, too.

Let's get it all out, Nic.

Right now.

With a brief nod, Pierce's boys spread out around the club right away, staking a claim in all corners. He waves at Nicola, moving his fingers one at a time, but she doesn't even blink. She's not looking at him anymore.

She's looking at me.

I watch Nicola descend the steps at an exaggerated pace, like slow motion. Her hand traces along the curved banister; the sparkles on her emerald dress catch the light; the slit at her leg opens and closes as she moves.

I match her pace, aiming to meet her at the center of the dance floor, waiting while everyone else grooves around me, soaking in the music, the crowd and the incredible atmosphere that we created.

She gets closer.

Closer.

And closer still.

She's inches from my face, her grotesque grin growing with every step, her white teeth practically glowing in the darkness. She opens her mouth to speak.

"Have you *lost* your mind?"

I give her a crazy girl smile of my very own.

"How could you do this to me? After everything I've done for you? Look around, Amber! All of this is for you! And you're just going to give it all up? Over what? *Roddy?*"

"This place isn't for me," I say calmly, knowing that will only rile her up more. "Nothing has ever been for *me*, Nicola. Or for Pierce. Or for Tamsin. Or for any of the others whose lives you took from them. It's *always* all about you, every goddamn day, and I'm fucking sick of it."

Courtenay sidles up next to me while Tamsin and Margaux watch by the bar. Pierce gets closer, too, because everyone wants a front-row seat to the fight of the century.

"Amber, please, you can't be serious. Pierce? Tamsin? As if they can be trusted to tell—"

"YOU can't be trusted, Nicola!" I screech at her, losing my shit, but it feels *so* good. "And you want to stand here and say that Hey Mister is for *me*? When all you want to do is trap me here with you forever because that's the only way you can get anyone to stay with you. But they've all left you, one way or another, right? Well, I'm not staying either. You're going to have to ki—"

"Hey Mister was supposed to be for us!" Nicola screams in my face, throwing up her hands madly, gesturing at Courtenay. "The *three* of us, but now you've gone and cocked it all up and—"

"The THREE of us?!" I scream even louder. "Courtenay was never supposed to be the *third*! She was supposed to *replace* me, Nicola! That's why I brought her into the fold in the fucking first place! I found her! I was looking for someone just like her! Just like how I used to be. Someone who wouldn't say no to you and your propositions because you find us when we're at our lowest so you take advantage and—"

Nicola starts laughing.

It's infuriating.

"Wait, wait, *wait*. You think *you* brought Courtenay to me?" She throws her head back, really cackling now. "*I* brought Courtenay to you! Oh my God. Amber. You really believe that *you* could manipulate *me*? Come off it. I was searching for the past few years to find the perfect pretty little plaything for you. I had a short list going and Courtenay was at the top."

Courtenay looks down at her feet, embarrassed to be a pawn in our perverse game.

I reach out to give her hand a squeeze, but she pulls away from me.

"I didn't expect you'd go so far as to turn her yourself." Nicola laughs again, wiping tears from her eyes. "But I admit I enjoyed seeing something of myself in you for the first time. Don't you realize you'd be so much happier if you embraced what we are? Who *you* are now, whether you like it or not?"

Her revelation almost knocks me to the ground.

But now I want to dredge everything up.

All of it.

Every. Goddamn. Thing.

"Nicola, I have been trying to leave you since you killed Malcolm!" I shriek, getting more attention from everyone in the club now, human or otherwise. "And I can admit that I've wanted to leave *for years*. Which is exactly what I'm going to do now."

"You're not going anywhere," she hisses. "How dare you."

"How can you say that after everything you've done to me? How can you say that after what you did to *my sister*?!"

"That's not— You don't— There's more—" Nicola chokes on her words, stunned that I know the grisly truth.

"Why would I believe *anything* you say ever again?!" I can't stop screaming in response; my throat feels like it's on fire.

"Because I *made* you, you ungrateful little cunt!" Nicola roars at me.

I swear her eyes go black.

A predator closing in.

"I've given you everything," she growls. "And I can take it all away if I want to, though you already took care of that, didn't you?" She looks daggers at Pierce, who raises his eyebrows, completely unapologetic.

I know they're going to ravage the place tonight.

This will be Hey Mister for one night only.

"Inviting Pierce? That's really low, Amber. Might as well let everyone in now, this place will be destroyed, but I will take everything—"

"*You* deserve to have everything taken from you, Nicola!" I know she can feel the heat from my mouth all over her face. "You only take from others. But nothing belongs to you, does it? You've earned nothing. You were born to nothing. And I'm sorry about what happened to you, Nicola, I really am, but what you did? To your own sister? It's unforgivable. Do you hear me, *Georgie*? Unforgivable! Everything you've done is unforgivable!"

Nicola backhands me across the face so hard that I fall in a heap to the ground; the cracking sound echoes through the club. The DJ turns the music off. Everyone watches us. No one knows what will happen next or what the hell we are talking about.

Nicola quickly bends down to my ear, under the guise of helping me, whispering as she takes my hand, yanking me up.

"If you *ever* try to leave me, Amber, I will find you and I will kill you."

Wow.

Well.

She really said it.

I knew it, but still, I'm stunned.

Courtenay is completely terrified, seeking comfort *from Tamsin* of all people, who looks extra thrilled by the night's events. After all, this is what she wanted. For Nicola to keep me or kill me, or for me to end up in Chelsea with them, running to Margaux for escape.

Tamsin always wanted me to stay trapped, just like her.

"DJ!" Nicola shouts, pointing at Lulu Lynn, locking eyes, compelling her to keep the party going. Then she hisses into her walkie at the doormen. "Let them all in. Every last one."

The hordes of people outside begin to flood into Hey Mister, taking it to fire-hazard levels quickly, not to mention all the hungry, wild vampires running around.

Pierce couldn't be happier. They're not keeping the club. They're going to tear it to pieces.

Tamsin was right about one thing.

This *is* going to be a fucking bloodbath.

I gotta get out now.

"Georgiana!" I shout at Nicola, knowing *that* will get her attention.

She turns around slowly on the tips of her toes.

"*What* did you just say to me?"

"Let. Me. Go," I demand simply.

"Why would I ever do that?" she sneers, fangs out.

"Because the Laurels means more to you than anything."

Nicola cocks her head to the side, her tongue on the roof of her mouth, confused.

"If you don't let me go, I'll invite him in. All of them. You'll be outnumbered. And I can't imagine Pierce would let you stay."

Her face contorts into something monstrous, full of fury and anger and fire as she creeps closer, her hand outstretched toward me. Instinctively I pull my head back, but she strikes fast, like a cobra, wrapping her fingers around my neck tightly, lifting me up off the ground, but I fight back with everything I have, digging my nails into her hands, aiming to pull them apart, and then I thrust my knee into her stomach as hard as I can.

She lets go, huffing and puffing.

So do I.

This is a pointless exercise.

The pain fleeting.

The physical doesn't exist for us.

We stare at each other in silence for a moment, our breath quick and short.

"How do you know about her?" she finally whispers.

"I found your letters to Nicola. She kept them in the dresser. And when Pierce showed me the photos of your family—"

"Nicola wanted me in those photos, but her mother wouldn't allow it," she says softly. "My father had no spine whatsoever, but Nicola tried. She always did. That's why I believed she would want to be with me when I came back for her. After I turned."

"So you took everything from her instead?"

"But I was a Claughton as well!" Nicola roars again, standing up. "I am a Claughton! The Laurels and the money and all of it was rightfully mine to take, especially after how they treated me! I didn't want to hurt my sister, but she gave me no choice!"

"You always have a choice." I shake my head as I get back up, too.

Nicola closes her eyes and sighs.

Her dream of Hey Mister is falling apart once she reopens them.

Everything is falling apart for Nicola.

I begin to put more distance between us, taking steps to the entrance.

Slowly.

Carefully.

If I run, will she chase me?

Would she catch me?

Kill me?

Courtenay watches the two of us in horror, not knowing what to do.

It's all over, but I don't know exactly how it will end yet.

Nicola believed she could control others into loving her, and if they failed to do so, she made them pay the ultimate price. I understand why, even though it's evil. But that eternal hurt she felt inside—still feels—from her family's rejection only propelled her forward to meet her fate as a vampire.

Someone found her, just like she found me.

She's only become worse because of it.

Have I?

I still hope I can turn the ship around somehow.

But Nicola?

She's beyond saving.

She's been beyond saving for a very long time.

"Let me go," I say to her again. "The way you should have let your sister go."

Courtenay watches as we go back and forth, not knowing where to go or whom to trust. I can't look at her because it reminds me . . . I've done something unforgivable, too, haven't I?

"I'm not leaving you alone," I remind Nicola. "You have someone new." I look down at my feet, away from Courtenay, as I use her for the last time. My final chip for all the money on the table. "We're done, Nicola. I hope you do better with her . . ."

I turn away from them.

I'm leaving.

"Amber." Nicola's voice breaks. "Don't go, or I'll come and—"

"Pierce!" I turn around and call out to him, always at the ready.

Nicola shuts her mouth tight.

Hey Mister is teeming with all sorts of people now, the environment getting increasingly wild. Pierce's guys have every corner on lock, pacing and waiting for the right moment to set it all off; his girls are taking center stage in the middle of the dance floor, enjoying the freedom of the music; and then there's Nicola, rabid and probably ravenous, licking her chops anxiously and flicking her pinky finger to her thumb. The nervous tic returns.

Scenes from our life together screen in my head.

The good, the bad and the very, very ugly.

Is she doing the same thing?

"Go on then, Amber," she snarls at me. "Leave."

I hesitate, almost tripping over myself.

Is she serious?

Then she darts back over to me again, faster than I've ever seen her move before, her nose practically touching my own, close enough to bite it right off if she really wanted to.

"You want to leave? LEAVE!" she shouts, and I wince at the volume, which makes her smile. "Now you can *really* be alone."

I hold her gaze for just a second longer and then push my way out of the crowded club.

I won't look back, not even when Courtenay cries out for me, her voice shaking me to my core because I made her.

But I'm leaving her behind.

The street outside Hey Mister is dark and empty. No one is outside or in line anymore. It's an eerie, unsettling energy, the bass growing softer as I drift away.

But what disturbs me most of all is thinking about Nicola's twisted smile when she delivered her parting words to me.

Am I *really* alone?

Has she truly let me go?

THIRTY

NICOLA

2021

A mber was getting bolder with every passing day, so this was perfect timing in many ways, and not just because there were some bargains to be had where real estate was concerned. It had been a gradual change with her, happening over many years, but she would keep pushing our boundaries, the ones I put in place for a reason.

To protect myself.

I knew she'd never stop until she burst right through them.

With Amber, it had started small, like anything.

The request for solo jaunts, following Malcolm around, feeling maudlin about her old life. She was desperate to connect with him again on a real level. A human one, despite the impossibility. I'd have to make it a point to be there when she did. I didn't care how old he was.

These thoughts of Malcolm brought her back to the past, made her feel some type of regret, and we couldn't have that anymore.

What was done was done. This was her reality now. Why didn't she see that yet? After all this time?

Connecting with Malcolm, even briefly, could push her in the wrong direction.

Away from me.

I could feel her emotions bubbling over at every turn. The way she'd snap at me in regular conversation. I knew she didn't believe in a proper love connection any longer—Michael from Margate had really pushed her over that particular edge—but stranger things had happened.

The way she carried on with men from the internet and the apps was still concerning to me. She might have been telling herself—and me, for that matter—one thing about falling in love, making promises that it was just for hunting or casual sex, but that didn't mean the unthinkable couldn't reasonably happen.

And then where would we be?

It's like I had to cut her off at the legs, again and again.

n 2012 it was a man called James, who was married, unbeknownst to Amber. Knowing how she would feel about that information being left out of their relationship, I texted Amber, under the guise of being the bastard's wife, and she took care of business right away.

He was dead within hours.

n 2015 she took a shine to some grad student at LSE, *also* named James because this is England, who was very handsome and intriguing, and I totally understood the appeal, because even though he was studying business, he had a fabulous sense of humor. I'd have to stop myself from laughing sometimes when I was observing their dates from afar. I liked him, too. But when I compelled him to arrange his next two semesters in Singapore and America, respectively, you know, to get the broader global perspective—it was for the sake of his career!—she ripped him to shreds the night after she found out.

See, no one likes to be left behind.

At first, I wondered if she considered going with him somehow, but seeing how it turned out, she must have been too afraid to push that far. What if she couldn't find a place secure enough or fast enough? A very real worry when it came to any sort of travel for a vampire. And what if James II did not accept her as she was, reminding her about what happened with Michael? The frustration of it all must have been driving her mad, but still, she wouldn't take the leap out of fear, or perhaps laziness, which was exactly what I wanted.

And in 2017, perhaps not my finest hour, Amber started taking an early evening dance class for recreational purposes. I didn't see the harm in that until she started staying late afterwards to chat with one of her classmates, Deborah, some lady she had hit it off with, this "woman of the world" vibe, and they were becoming fast friends in their little tap shoes and pale pink shoulder shrugs that tied under their rib cages. Adults pretending to be children again, but I could read between the lines.

Amber never told me about her, wisely, but I couldn't have my companion having any sort of confidant who wasn't me, even one of a platonic nature. I don't like to kill women, emergencies only or to make a point if I must, so I simply compelled the instructor to move the class up an hour.

Unfortunately, it was no longer good timing for Amber, what with the sunset hour and all.

Eventually, she and Deborah lost touch.

Adult friendships are always the most difficult to maintain, particularly when everyone else continues to grow and you must stay the same.

But of course, Deborah got hers in the end.

Much like Amber's sister, it was a necessary evil.

What if Deborah called?

didn't want to keep playing defense, though, so I started to think in reverse. A bit more like Amber. What could I do that would keep her around of her own accord? How could I be proactive about it? Because I couldn't have another runner on my hands and I could sense she was getting ready to lace up her trainers. I did not want to kill Amber, or worse, drive her into Margaux's arms or those of someone else who didn't deserve her the way I did.

The thought first entered my mind when the Italians started singing to one another on the television. Such theatrics! But of course, I knew, too. This was not good. It was going to get ugly. Terrible, really. Something like no one on earth had seen before or will again, except for the few of us ancient creatures who had seen it all.

Normally I wouldn't be so concerned. Of course, it'd be an inconvenience, not to mention a massive change in tastes for us vampires, akin to going from banquets to bread lines, but I knew how to make my way in a world that came to a standstill.

We always found a way to keep the chins up. Keep the mouths fed. All of us did.

It was in our ice-cold blood.

But where Amber was concerned, this time spent in dire straits could decimate the two of us for good. When it all blew over, and it would blow over—slowly, perhaps very slowly, but surely, it would, it always did—she might be at her final breaking point.

There was almost no question about it.

Unless . . . I got ahead of it somehow.

I had to do it differently with her.

Take a new approach.

Something ambitious.

Amber looked positively grief-stricken over the news of everyone falling ill. She was biting her fingernails, a dangerous practice for us, her mouth in a distressed little pout. I didn't blame her. It was upsetting to see what was going on in the world and what would soon be coming for us.

Good-time girls loathe to see the party come crumbling down.

Reality? No, thank you. We lived to escape it. At every chance we got. It was depressing to watch her take it all in, so I determined that we were going to *go out* that night—I wouldn't take no for an answer. I didn't care if she wasn't in the mood. Donna Summer would flip that frown of hers into felicity.

The second the needle dropped, I could have sworn she was about to tell me to turn the music down so she could listen to the news ad nauseam, but then the beat infected her, despite her initial resistance.

Glorious. All of it. Soon enough, we were dancing together in the Laurels, like we always did, like we used to do, like no time had passed at all. It had been so long and it felt like we *needed* to go out because no matter our differences these days, we both love the nightlife.

Soon enough, we wouldn't be able to enjoy it for a good long while.

I knew it.

Not for a very long time indeed.

Well, to Amber, anyway.

That night, I thought long and hard about Amber and me, our happiest times together. It pained me to admit that it was the weeks before I turned her and perhaps the first few weeks after, until we caught wind of Malcolm searching for her.

But oh, those last lovely weeks of 1979 were essentially the last weeks of our beloved disco. And that's what brought us together, wasn't it? If I were capable of feeling guilt or regret anymore, I'd also admit that this lifestyle squashed so much of what I loved about Amber. An unfortunate byproduct of vampirism.

She was the polar opposite of myself in so many ways, attracted to lightness and merriment and, above all, having a good time. I suppose we both had that in common, but the difference was that people liked her. Instantly. They were drawn to her, like everyone was drawn to my sister, too.

She had the world on a string, didn't she?

I never had that.

We all want what we can't have.

I think that's why I sought out the sunnier and lighter companions, despite all evidence to the contrary that it would work long-term. And I always wanted those few girls who miraculously seem to have acquired the taste for my special brand of darkness with no effort at all. Like Amber did at Tramp that night. Like Tamsin did at the dance hall. They both just *took* to me immediately, because they were drawn to the danger, I suppose, and it was like I wanted to ruin them for their curiosity, punish them for their misjudgment, but somehow keep them exactly the same.

Because I adored them, too.

It was an impossible balance to strike, wasn't it? Try as I might, and I've tried with many in vain. So how could I make it work with Amber? She still had so much light in her. She wouldn't merely be running *away* from me like Tamsin did, like the others tried to do, I *knew* that, but she would be running *towards* something, eternally hopeful there was something waiting for her on the other side.

I saw that light in Amber and felt it every day. The optimism that everything was going to work out somehow, despite the cold hard fact that she was a monstrous killer. That's why she'd ultimately want to leave the Laurels, and me, if she could ever muster up the courage to do so.

She didn't believe she had become such a beast.

But I knew she had.

And in difficult times such as these, the times that were clearly coming around the bend, it could really change people. So how could I get her to stay once they were through? I had to think less about fear, less about punishment, and more about what she loved.

What we both loved.

And what did we love more than anything?

Dancing. Disco. And being the center of goddamn attention.

Now I was on to something.

had looked at so many spaces, but none of them were right for the mission at hand. I needed something specific. I needed a space with *options*. Plan A for Amber, but also for the others. Since it would be such a massive undertaking, it wasn't a bad idea to get the other two involved, once the party really got started. I had even targeted a few young women, flirting with the idea of having someone new join us at the Laurels. A potential third. Amber would do well with a little sister. Some fresh blood in the house.

But she had to be perfect.

I was getting closer with the search, one in particular.

Amber wouldn't be able to resist her.

They were so alike.

And women working together? What a concept. Amber would eat it up.

But then, of course, we could settle old scores, show some semblance of strength against the horrible men who were always lurking about, and if everything went my way, Amber and I would be happy again, hearkening back to our earliest days together, the ones I knew we must have both been pining for all this time.

But there was also Plan B to consider.

If she didn't want to stay.

If she still decided to run.

I needed a space where I could pull the trigger on all of them, and on everything, and be done with everybody, because what would be the point anymore? I didn't want to find another companion, not if it always ended the same way, leaving me feeling worse off, reminding me of exactly what I'd done to end up this way in the first place.

Amber was *it* for me.

This was our last shot.

I knew it.

I wanted it to be different with her.

So I'd go all in for Amber.

I'd have to make a change.

My most ambitious plan since reclaiming what was rightfully mine all those years ago.

And wasn't Amber rightfully mine as well?

I *made* her.

I always took what was mine.

Amber was mine, too.

And now so was this dump in Hackney.

But with all this space?

And a chimney that just needs a bit of a rewire?

And the best part, with that beautiful glass-domed ceiling?

All I had were options.

So when the time was just right, we could make it the nightclub of our dreams.

I'd just have to hold on dearly to the blind hope that it wouldn't all crumble into a nightmare.

One where I'd be left all alone again.

THIRTY-ONE

AMBER

I meander around East alone for what feels like hours, struck by how long I've lived in this big, beautiful city and how little I've seen of it. Stunned by the concept of freedom. Floored that Nicola seemingly granted my wish. That's what just happened, right?

Still, I can't stop thinking about our last moments at Hey Mister. Our life together.

Everything she's done, everything I've done, her threats, my threats, all of it.

I know I should get on the Underground before dawn, wait out the day and get out of London, so why do I still feel stuck?

I can't get it out of my head.

Nicola said she knew about Courtenay before I did.

Was that true? Were we both using her as a prop to get what we wanted, but our goals were in total conflict? She thought Courtenay would be a reason for me to stay. That she would make things better between us. That's what Nicola hoped Hey Mister would be, too. The alliance with the Chelsea vampires, too.

She really thought she had changed.

For me?

Maybe she had.

But what she had done was unforgivable.

To me, to Malcolm, to my sister, to Roddy.

The toxicity between us eternally intertwined.

I flash to Nicola's face when I left Hey Mister. She had that horrible, sinister smile on her face, like she knew something that I didn't. Why was she smiling? She was about to lose the club to Pierce. She had lost me.

Her last words echo in my head.

"Now you can *really* be alone."

Really.

She emphasized the *really*.

Why was she smiling?

Really be alone.

What did she mean?

Really.

Alone.

Oh my God.

By the time I have eyes on Hey Mister again, I hear the screaming from across the street. Horrible, bloodcurdling, ear-piercing screams. They sound like death disguised as a party, amidst the heart-thumping music.

There's not a soul out there / No one to hear my prayer

It's after four. No one is leaving? The street is still empty. Still quiet. *Why* isn't anyone leaving? The shrieks grow louder as I approach the doors, the reason becoming clearer when I see the chains and padlocks wrapped around the handles.

I hear banging and thumping and desperate pleas for someone to open the door.

Please God, open the door!

Oh no.

Is anyone out there?

Was that Courtenay's voice?

Open the doors!

Nicola said this location was perfect. The glass-domed ceiling. That wasn't for the aesthetic. That wasn't about the Laurels. Her sick and sad smile makes total sense now. A backup plan, and Pierce was the cherry on top.

She let me go, but she's going to take everyone else out.

All the vampires in London.

Maybe herself?

Except for me.

Then I'll be *really* alone.

But all I can think about is Courtenay, her magical essence surrounding me, filling me back up again, pulling me toward her because the fact of the matter is that I am her maker.

Like I can't leave her behind.

I won't.

The thought of sweet Courtenay Cooper being left to burn alive at the first rays of the sun beating down into Hey Mister is too much for my conscience to bear. I try my best with the padlocks on the chains, plucking a bobby pin from the crown of my head, as if I have the wherewithal to be that resourceful. Of course it doesn't work. These chains look ancient, from another time, made to last, made to work.

Nicola had a plan.

But every plan has holes.

There's almost no time to find them, but I have to try. The

screams of terror are dying down inside, everyone beginning to accept their dark fate.

It's just the music now. Nothing else.

I run at full speed to the rear of the club, where there's a similar setup on the back door.

How can she do this?

I know Nicola has done dark things, things I'd never do myself, but this is beyond comprehension.

Nicola said the end of a vampire's life is the most painful event we can ever experience.

Would she really do it to herself?

I have a hard time believing that . . .

Is she out here somewhere?

Waiting for me?

Or is she waiting safely for next nightfall in the office?

When I turn around in a panic, the surprising sight of Jonathan briefly calms me down. He's snoozing on the steering wheel, the Rolls parked just nearby. I bang on the window as hard as I can, jerking the poor guy awake, but this is an emergency! He looks horrified to see me as he fumbles out of the car, but before he can say anything, I demand the keys to the locks.

I *know* he has them.

He did this for Nicola.

He did everything for Nicola.

"I'm sorry, but I cannot give them to you, miss. She made me—"

"But you have to let me back in there, Jonathan. Please! You know what she's doing to all of them? Is she—"

"I can't," he says, interrupting me, tears in his eyes. "I promised madam, and my duty is to her. You don't want to go back inside, Miss Amber. It'll be over soon enough, but you should go."

"Is she . . . staying?"

"I don't know, miss. But once you left, I got the call and the orders."

I release my fangs in frustration, but we both know I'm not going to hurt him.

I love Jonathan.

"Did you know she was trying to replace you?" I scream at him. "Did you? With Roddy! But she killed him when he turned her down!"

Jonathan's chin falls to his chest.

He didn't.

"I'm sorry, miss. But I can't . . ."

"God damn it!" I exclaim, racking my brain for how to get inside and back out again, escaping safely with Courtenay, not attracting any attention. It's not like I can crash through the ceiling undetected, and even if I could, how the hell would I even get up there? But wait a minute . . .

Oh my God.

This is fucking crazy.

"You're not going to let me back in," I say to Jonathan, holding his face in my hands. "But you'll let me out. Because you don't want me to end up like the rest of them."

Jonathan looks down but doesn't say another word.

"Stay right here."

"Miss Amber!" Jonathan calls after me desperately, but I'm already jetting around to the side of the club, banking on his affection for me and summoning every ounce of bravery I have left in my body.

If Jonathan doesn't let me out, I could be dead, too.

jump in place, hopping from one foot to the other, psyching myself up before racing up the fire escape on the building next door. Of course, I'm second-guessing this whole stunt, but if I run away without trying to save Courtenay, I'll never be able to forgive myself.

Jonathan will be there on the flip side.

I'm sure of it.

I'm betting our lives on it.

I scurry on up the neighboring fire escape, looking out to the gorgeous city when I reach the top, taking a quick moment for myself before I risk it all.

I don't want to live with regret anymore.

I'm a vampire, but that will never change.

Everything that has happened made me who I am, *what* I am, and London is my home now.

Maybe Courtenay and I could have a new life together, with a totally different rhythm from the one I had with Nicola. Different from all of them. Tamsin and Margaux. Pierce and his crew.

Courtenay and I could be true friends, our relationship based on equality over hierarchy.

A real partnership.

I can do this.

We can do this.

Okay, Amber.

All you gotta do is get in, get Court and get out.

I ditch my heels and, like a regular Dick Van Dyke, I leap across to the roof of Hey Mister and hop up to the chimney. Looking down the chute, I try to put the thought out of my mind that I'm about to jump into a fully operational incinerator.

But it's the only way in.

I shimmy down the chimney, using my hands and feet along the sides to maneuver my body until I feel some ground beneath my feet. I crouch down and put my feet out toward the tunnel with the metal door until I can feel it with my toes. I kick at the door as hard as I can with my feet. Once. Twice. And then finally I tuck both of my knees into my chest and send my legs out again, pushing harder from my heels, and the door finally swings open.

The thud of the metal catching at the hinge is so loud, I worry Nicola might hear me.

Is she here?

The lights are off.

When I slide all the way through the tunnel and jump down inside the room, I notice the cameras are off, too. I take a quick sweep of the perimeter, but I don't sense her close by. When I open the door to the club and close it behind me, I hear it lock.

Shit.

I should have checked the code first.

This is a safe space.

I cross my fingers with one hand and put the code in with the other.

She didn't change it: 311279.

Nicola made it my "birthday."

The code was just for us two.

Before I go farther into the club, I change it to my *real* birthday, the one she never bothered to ask me about, the one I never celebrated again.

And I put it in the American way, just for good measure.

She doesn't get a backup plan.

Not anymore.

step lightly toward the main room, the dance floor still glowing, the music still coursing through the sound system, at an ear-piercing decibel now, as the disco ball turns and the fog machine smokes, but most of the screaming and fighting for life has come to an end.

From the vampires.

And from the humans who've been trapped alongside them.

Collateral damage.

Now I only hear smacking and spurting and slurping, the sounds of torture and violence and decadence, Tamsin's bloodbath prophecy in process. I can smell it everywhere as I huddle my body lower to the ground, seeking out Courtenay amongst the carnage. I try not to get distracted by my own hunger, the sensational lure creeping in through my nose and down my throat, lighting a fire in my belly, a bloodlust that can only be satiated by one thing.

But no.

No.

Courtenay and I are getting out of here alive.

The vampires are going full throttle, enjoying what they know are their last hours on earth; it's a devilish party on the dance floor, like a celebration thrown by Satan himself, and they're painting the club *red*. It's a full-on melee of frolicking and fucking and, of course, feasting. These kills tonight have been very drawn out, savored by the vampires, many of the victims still miraculously alive as the monsters feed slowly to luxuriate in the suffering.

Some of them try to hang on for dear life, believing in a world where they actually survive the night. Most of the others just want to give in and give up already, but their bodies still fight to stay alive, betraying their minds, which keep hoping for sweet death after each labored breath. Maybe the next one. Or the one after that. Their screams have turned into cries now, soft whimpers, silent prayers that will go unanswered.

There is no God here.

Just blood.

It's absolutely everywhere, dripping along the walls, pooling on the floors, covering the glittering Hey Mister logo in the center, all of it tempting me no end as I lurk in the shadows, but I stay focused on why I came back to this hellhole in the first place.

Where is Courtenay?

Pierce and his crew are all scattered around the club, feeding on men and women with reckless abandon, nothing left to lose, their girls from the Wapping compound all dead or dying now. The party is *over*.

Tamsin's at the foot of the VIP section, affixed to DJ Lulu Lynn's thigh at the femoral artery like a goddamn animal, while Margaux has just come up for air from some poor soul in a tank top and tennis shoes who never should have gotten in, in the first place, with that outfit. Margaux wipes the blood from her face with an arm full of body glitter, the two making a shimmery paste.

I don't see Nicola anywhere, even though I've started to sense her, the little hairs on my arms stick straight, the tuberose wafting into my consciousness.

And then finally I see her.

Courtenay Cooper.

She's up at the DJ booth all alone, without a drop of blood on or near her, leaning over the computer, perusing it with curiosity, clutching none other than a blue alcopop, just for the hell of it.

Then I see a half smile creep up the side of her face, growing into a full-blown grin. When she starts nodding at the first beat of the song, I almost laugh out loud. She's drumming on the railing now and it's so ridiculous and stupid and sweet.

In a last-ditch attempt to amuse herself before dying, Courtenay plays the ultimate party-ending song, which has sunk its catchy hooks into the UK since its release in the mid-aughts. It's absolutely an upbeat pop-rock banger, even though it's about some guy discovering his girlfriend is cheating, but the way people sang it at closing time in this country, completely off their faces, you'd think it was the national anthem. God Save the Killers.

And Courtenay must think "Mr. Brightside" might be a nice song to die to.

Not on my watch.

She sits with her legs crossed, quiet and contemplative, bopping her ankle along to the music, knocking her head from side to side, looking up at the glass ceiling, going somewhere else in her mind. Somewhere far, far away from Hey Mister.

It's almost beautiful to watch her wait, silently and privately and with dignity, for her death to come, while the other vampires kill and maim and lurch right toward it, ripping into any sign of human life without a second thought, hedonists until the end.

Courtenay was different, too.

Like me.

We weren't like Nicola.

We weren't like any of them.

How can I get her to see me without anyone else clocking it?

Because I'm not letting the real monsters out of here with us.

Let them all burn.

I stare at Courtenay intensely, hoping *something* will kick in between maker and companion and she'll look back at me, but no dice. I can't wave at her without blowing my cover, but I have one trick left to try . . .

I crawl over to the back bar and duck below it, coming around the side, and use the diamond from my wedding ring, along with the disco ball up top, to shine a light right into her eyes.

Once.

Twice.

Three times and *fuuuuuck*, it's not working.

But then, by some miracle, she finally squints at the flash and looks for the origin. When we make eye contact, her mouth falls open, stunned, but I put one finger up to mine and then curl it toward me.

She understands.

Right.

On it.

Get. Over. Here. Now.

Courtenay sneaks a look around the room to keep her eyes on the other vampires. She knows we have to go unnoticed, too. She slips by Margaux and Tamsin, who are sharing a snack *and* a dance, against all odds, before they burn alive in the most painful of fashions. I guess no one can resist the allure of Brandon Flowers, not even Tamsin.

Pierce and the other guys are in a full-on fight club on the dance floor, now that most of the living are dead, getting decades-long resentments off their chests, dueling each other for the pain alone, no other payoff to be had, because what else is there to do when the end is hurtling toward you and you're powerless to stop it?

I can't believe that *all* the vampires have given up on escape entirely.

Why aren't they trying anymore?

I wonder if they see it as Nicola doing them a favor. Something they could never do for themselves. But living each night just like the one before it, forever in the dark, forever in the shadows? I think they've had enough, happy to throw in the towel.

But Court and me?

We have the will to live.

Because it'll be on our own terms, as equals.

I snake along the wall behind me and soon enough I feel Court at my heels. I reach for her to take my hand as we make our way to the hallway on the other side of the room, hoping Jonathan is wait-ing with the keys at the ready at the rear entrance.

Once we're off the main floor, we sprint down to the door as fast as we can.

I try pushing it, softly, but it's still locked from the outside.

"Jonathan," I whisper. "Please. Are you there?"

Nothing.

"Jonathan."

I hear him breathing.

Thinking it over.

"How do you think she'll get rid of you once she does find your replacement?"

I'm starting to wonder if Court and I should head to the office, my own backup plan, but then I hear the clanking of the keys on the other side of the door.

Oh, thank God.

He's letting us out.

But that's when I sense her more than ever before.

All of it.

The tuberose, the copper, the spice, the blood.

"AMBER!" Nicola cries out at the end of the hallway as Jonathan opens the door. She moves as fast as she can, almost as if she's about to take flight, but Courtenay and I rush out the door together, ready to slam it behind us. Nicola pushing mightily on the other side. Her strength rivals both of ours combined, showing off the innate power that's grown over endless seasons, going on two hundred years, now fully charged with rage.

"Rope the chains back on the handles!" I tell Courtenay. "I'll hold her off."

We push and pull, back and forth, but I can't do this for much longer.

Jonathan stands idly by, out of duty, but when Nicola hisses at him to help her, her command laced with obscenities, he joins me instead, pushing the door shut as much as he can with his bony fingers and feeble arms.

Sweet man.

Courtenay wraps the chains once around the handles, then twice, as quickly as she can, clicking the padlock tight, leaving just a small crack in between the doors.

Nicola continues to push in vain, laughing maniacally, fangs out.

"It *should* be the three of us!" Nicola shouts, completely unhinged. "Amber, please. Let's all go home to the Laurels. We must make amends. Just the three of us now. It'll be different, once this is all over. I got him. I got them. Now it's just us."

But I shake my head at her.

There's no way in hell.

"But I am so sorry, Amber! I really am. I'm sorry about everything. I love you, Amber. You know I do. And you love me, too. I don't know when it got so dark between us, but I know we can get back to how we were. We were so close! Didn't you see how I was trying? Look how much I tried! *Look* at this place! I've never done anything like this for anyone before! You've changed me, Amber! You changed me!"

But I don't say anything.

Not a word.

Enraged, she pushes on the door again.

There's not much time left.

"What else do you want to hear?" she cries, tears falling down her face. "I don't want to lose you! I didn't want to lose anyone! How can you not see that? You know the truth now about my family.

How can you blame me? I'll be better, Amber. I swear it. I'll be better. For you."

Our eyes meet.

I shake my head again.

I don't know what to say.

"Did you hear me? I said that I'm sorry! I'm so sorry, Amber."

The tears continue to fall, smearing her mascara. Her red lipstick is smudged. There's no blood. She hasn't fed on anyone inside?

So it wasn't going to be her last night after all.

What if I hadn't come back for Courtenay?

She was going to kill them all and then come for me.

I keep quiet.

"Come the fuck on, Amber! Open the door! How can you do this to me?" she shrieks, a pitch I've never heard, an unprecedented anger. She's shaking the door harder and harder, like she wants to rip it off its hinges. "After everything I've given you? You were meant to be a vampire, Amber. You said it yourself back then. And you were meant to be a vampire *with me*. You know that. You always knew it. You just needed a push."

"A push?! I didn't need anything!" I finally shout. "I didn't need you."

"You don't remember how you were crying about Malcolm? Not having anywhere else to go? Not knowing what to do with your life? Not knowing why you married him? You were a lost little girl without me, Amber. You would have just gone back home and had an ordinary life, the exact thing you didn't want. I gave this extraordinary life to you. *Me*. I mean, my God, Malcolm didn't have *an affair*!" She laughs.

I freeze.

It's like I can't breathe.

"But I think you knew that, Amber. Come the fuck on. You just wanted a reason to jump, so I gave it to you. I gave you everything you said you wanted!"

"*What?*" My voice is low and sharp.

Nicola manipulated me worse than I could have ever imagined.

She targeted me.

From night one at Tramp.

And I fell for it.

I fell for it all.

Nicola cackles louder and louder, no longer on the apology tour. Her minutes are numbered and she knows it. She can't seem to stop herself. She keeps going and going . . .

"I did you a favor, darling. And if you don't do me a favor right now and let me out of here, I will make you fucking regret it. All of you," she growls, especially at Jonathan. "You won't be able to run from me forever."

Courtenay takes a step back. Jonathan puts his arm around her.

"And how are you going to do that?" I ask, daring her to challenge me. "Wait out the day? In *our* office? Go ahead."

Nicola's face falls; her bottom lip quivers.

"Amber. What have you done? Did you—"

I shrug at her.

"What? The code is still my birthday."

"You didn't . . ."

Nicola hits the door even harder, screaming my name over and over again, demanding I free her, but I won't.

I can't.

I grab Courtenay's hand and we follow Jonathan to the car.

It's over.

We all know it.

Nicola does, too.

The banging stops, and when I look over to see her one last time, a sliver of her face through the crack of the door, she starts to laugh again. Not the sinister or deranged one this time, but the fun one, the sassy one, the one I loved so many years ago when all we had was each other and the nightlife and nothing else mattered.

"Toot-toot," she says to me softly, but I hear it so loud around me, almost as if it echoes through the night sky, enveloping my body, surrounding the entire club, this magical place she wished to create for us, the dreamland that would save our friendship.

I know that's what she wanted, not this nightmare, but it's too late.

All of it is just too late.

"Beep-beep," I mouth back at her.

And Nicola Claughton retreats backward into the darkness, for as long as it will have her.

Not much longer at all.

"Madam?" Jonathan says to me, holding the back door of the Rolls open. "I'll hurry."

Courtenay's already inside, still shaking, waiting for me to comfort her.

I take my post next to her.

Jonathan drives us home.

Back to the Laurels.

It's almost sunrise when we get back. I take a moment to give Jonathan the gold pocket watch, thinking it must belong to him, something Nicola stole when she bargained for his servitude.

He looks at it curiously, taking it out of my hand.

"I thought I lost it. God, she made me feel terrible about that. She gave this beauty to me, not long after we met. She said it was a token of her appreciation for our agreement and that I would be a part of the Claughton legacy, too. It belonged to her father. She made it sound so . . . so—"

"Wonderful," I finish for him. He nods. "I know. I understand."

After he puts the watch back in my hand, I return it to Nicola's room, back to her jewelry box with the rest of her treasures.

Now they all belong to me.

Everything in the Laurels belongs to me.

"Courtenay!" I call out, asking her to join me in the study. I lie out on the chaise, crossing one foot over the other. She lingers in the doorway.

"You can have my bedroom, Court." I grin. "Feel free to make it your own."

She smiles, too, joining me on the chaise. "Thank you."

"But I'll take care of everything else. You have no idea how long I've wanted to redecorate around here. We have to rest now, but we'll go out tomorrow night for a bite. You must be starving. Did you get any of the . . ."

Courtenay shakes her head.

"I didn't know how. I was bloody scared back there, but you'll teach me, right?" she asks, tilting her head, resting it on my shoulder. I put mine on top of hers.

God, was there anything more irresistible than a brand-new gal pal?

We must look like an absolutely adorable mess together.

Like two wild girls who stayed out all night until dawn.

The kind of girlfriends who would do it all over again the following weekend.

Every night if we want to.

"I'll teach you everything I know," I say.

I won't make the same mistakes as Nicola with my companion.

She couldn't break the cycle, but I think I will.

Because I'm not like Nicola Claughton, am I?

"Happy new year," Courtenay says with a giant grin, her fangs out and proud.

I do the same.

That's right, darling.

New year, new us.

ACKNOWLEDGMENTS

Thank you to my incredible editor, Jen Monroe, at Berkley and my amazing agent, Hillary Jacobson, at CAA. Not only are they absolutely wonderful at their respective jobs, but the way the three of us worked together on this novel was truly life-changing for me. The twists and turns this story took were surprising, sometimes grueling, and even though I felt challenged and pushed by my team to make the book as stellar as possible, I also felt supported beyond measure. They were rooting for me each step of the way. I'm very grateful to you both.

And of course, a big thank-you to Austin Denesuk at CAA, Ryan Goodell at Yorn Levine, and the entire team at Berkley, including Candice Coote, Cat Barra, Jessica Mangicaro, Lauren Burnstein, Chelsea Pascoe, Loren Jaggers, Craig Burke, Jeanne-Marie Hudson, Claire Zion and everyone who had a hand in making this book a reality. Also, Vi-An Nguyen once again created the cover of my dreams—thank you for making my vampires so sexy and chic!

Since *Stone Cold Fox*'s release last year, I have met so, *so* many incredible writers and readers, all of whom have been beyond supportive and lovely as I embarked on a career as a full-fledged novelist. It's impossible to name every single one, but special thanks to Julie Clark, Samantha Downing, Laura Hankin, Eliza Jane Brazier, Liv Stratman, Liz Fenton & Lisa Steinke, Katy Hays, Nina Simon,

May Cobb, Vanessa Lillie, Lauren Nossett *and* to my new Booksta-gram besties Dennis @scaredstraightreads, Jordy @jordys.book.club, Kayla @kayreadwhat, Emily @emilybookedup and Hannah @booksandbitesroc. You are all such a joy! I'd also like to thank all of the booksellers far and wide who recommend my novels to their loyal customers, especially Mary Pluto at Diesel, Erin Neary at Book Club Bar, Mary Mollman at Madison Street Books and Barbara Peters at The Poisoned Pen.

Thank you to all of the sweet people in my life who seem to be constantly duking it out to be my number one fan. I'm so lucky to have such great pals who know when to cheer me on *and* when to keep me humble: Michael Marino, Jenny & James Gaiser, Sheila & Joe McCrink, Liz & Ryan Mansholt, Lisa Balzo, Claire Burgart, Brad Milison, Maria Dirolf, Rachel Crouch, Ryan & Eric Wineinger-Schattl, Becky Flaum DelGuercio, Kristin Martini, Caroline Hayes, Katie Wadsworth, Nick Kilgore, Nina Steffel & David Frey, Rachel Scanlon & Nazara Ali, Whitnee & Jordan Ferrer, Spencer Berry, Da-jana & Darren Buonaguidi, Michael Calabrese, Carli Haney, An-thony Raimondi & Theo Lencicki, Ashley Andrews, Abbey O'Brien, Karina Rahardja, Emily Cummins, Shelby Petta, Julie Plec, Rachel Kim, Eli Edelson & Coral Dabarera, Laverne McKinnon, Leslie Belz-berg & Nancy Dewey.

Please know I'm already sick at the thought of forgetting some-one, so by all means please don't ever tell me and let the resentment stew between us just enough that I remember you for the next book.

My friends in England get a special spot in the acknowledg-ments for a host of reasons. London is obviously an important place to me—truly my favorite city in the world, sorry LA—and the peo-ple in and around it are always close to my heart: Alannah Ferguson and Ella Berman, thank you for being the loveliest girls and taking a closer look at Nicola's voice for me. Meghan Wilson and Ricky

Hinds, my expat darlings, I am working on living there part-time with Charles soon, but my extended residencies will have to do for now. I know I can count on you both for encouragement in that arena! Deborah Britz, Lulu Williams and Lynn Francis, I could not be more thrilled we stumbled upon one another over oysters and champagne that afternoon in Marylebone. Adore all three of you— thanks for letting me crash your parties! Stu and Romy Spindler, I am so very happy we got to spend all that quality time together. And finally, to my UEA girlies whose influence is *aaaaall* over some of these chapters—Alannah Ferguson (two mentions, petal!), Gels Anderson, Emily Dundon, Courtenay Sebastian and Leanne Liddell— I had the time of my life with all of you back then. It feels so weird to use your married lady names now because in my mind's eye all I can see is us running wild on the streets of Norwich, on the hunt for chips and cheese, singing Girls Aloud off-key after a night out at Mercy, where we had multiple vodka lemon limes in Topshop or Primark dresses over black leggings with ballet flats. God, there is just nothing better than being a party girl in one's prime, and we did it to perfection! I hope to see you all again very soon.

Speaking of party girls, I wrote this book for all of you. I hope you love it. I was a party girl, I remain a party girl, and I truly love all party girls forever because we prioritize having fun!

Thank you to Alexis and David Tate, who take the most extra-special care of Juniper when my husband and I are traveling. It's always hard for me to leave her, but I never worry because I know she lives large with you guys in the Hollywood Hills. We love you!

Obviously I listened to *a lot* of fabulous music while writing this novel. Peep the Spotify playlist. Extra thanks to Rod Stewart, ELO and Donna Summer for the inspiration—and of course Pitbull, who I managed to sneak into this disco story against all odds. I love you all. And this feels like the right place to thank my personal heroes,

Michael Jordan and Judy Blume. I thought of you both a lot while drafting, for different reasons, but you guys really kept me going!

Thank you to my family. We are very fun and funny and that has informed my writing in tons of creative ways. Despite any fractures, I always say that on both sides of the family, the one thing we can all agree on is that we like to party! So, thanks to my brother Kit, Auntie Carole, Uncle Will, Uncle Rob, Robin, Erik, Jen, Olivia and Evan. Tyler, Jonathan, Jenica and Jason, too! Thanks for hyping me up and for the constant laughs—it's always a good time when we get together and reminisce about all who have wronged us! I am (mostly) kidding about that last part.

And I have so much appreciation for my mom, Christine Koller, (and Merle Tomasello!) and my dad, Don Koller, (and Dormie Koller!). My mom told me that funny story in the dedication off-handedly a long time ago when Alicia Bridges's "I Love the Nightlife" came on the radio, and I just thought it was the most hilarious thing. I never forgot it. And you should know that when I showed my dad the dedication—before telling him the title—he knew exactly what song she meant. Dad, indeed, still likes to boogie, too. Don't we all?

Thank you to my sweet family on my husband's side, who welcomed me into the group with open arms from the start: Phyllis, Mace, Rozy, Julian, Ami, Jill, Dave, John, Jennifer, Romy, Stu, James, William and David. Special thanks to my mother-in-law, Amy Croft, and my father-in-law, Gary Croft—Gaz, it was so special to go back to UEA with you. It's one of my favorite fun facts that we both went to the same uni. What are the odds? I'm so happy to have you all in my corner.

Thank you to my sweet grannies, Dolores and Gloria, who are not with us any longer, but I feel them around me all the time. They would *love* this book. So would Uncle Mike, who I also miss very much. Lots of love to Dorinda and Marley.

And to the great loves of my life: Junie, you're the world's greatest pup and pal. Charles, you're the world's greatest husband and my best friend. We have so much fun, literally all the time, that it almost feels illegal. I hope you're as proud of me as I am of you. You're the best and I love you more than anything. Schmees for schmees.

Author photo © Kinsey Wilder

Rachel Koller Croft is the author of *Stone Cold Fox* and *We Love the Nightlife*. She's also a WGA award–nominated screenwriter. Rachel lives in Los Angeles with her husband, Charles, and their rescue pit bull, Juniper.

VISIT RACHEL KOLLER CROFT ONLINE

RachelKollerCroft.com
RachKollerCroft

Ready to find
your next great read?

Let us help.

Visit prh.com/nextread

Penguin
Random
House